HERE
ARE SAYING ABOUT
KEITH A. ROBINSON'S
ORIGINS TRILOGY:

Logic's End is a great read, and I highly recommend it. It explores the question of what life would be like on a planet where evolution really did happen. The surprising result helps the reader to see why life on Earth must be the result of special creation. For those interested in science fiction but who are tired of all the evolutionary nonsense, *Logic's End* is a refreshing alternative.

—Jason Lisle, PhD, Astrophysicist
Institute for Creation Research

In this book, Robinson has discovered a 'novel' way to communicate vital information to young adults and readers of all ages. Mainstream indoctrination on the origin of species and the age of the earth are regularly encountered and have long needed combating. Through this unique story, truth is conveyed.

—Dr. John D. Morris President
Institute for Creation Research

Pyramid of the Ancients will challenge you to reconsider the conventional wisdom concerning the history of our world.

—Tim Chaffey, Writer/Speaker
Answers in Genesis, Co-author of
Old-Earth Creationism on Trial

Escaping the Cataclysm is an edge-of-your-seat thrill ride back through time. It brilliantly explains the plausibility of the biblical account of history, especially Noah's Flood. It also explores details of the feasibility of the Ark itself and the Flood's impact on the earth. A great read!

—Julie Cave
Author of *The Dinah Harris Mysteries series*

Picking up where *Pyramid of the Ancients* leaves off, *Escaping the Cataclysm* hits the ground with both feet running. I found my faith renewed again and again as I was reminded of the many arguments that demonstrate why evolution cannot be the explanation for our origins.

—Joe Westbrook
Co-author of *The
Truth Chronicles*

PRELUDE AND ABDUCTION

Getter family,

Play your part with excellence!

Keith A. Robinson

MASTER SYMPHONY TRILOGY
Mvt. I

PRELUDE and ABDUCTION

IN A MINOR

KEITH A. ROBINSON

Cover design by Amalia Chitulescu
Interior design by Melody Christian

Published in the United States of America ISBN: 9781092618588
1. Fiction / Christian / General
2. Fiction / Dystopian

Unless otherwise noted, Scripture quoted is taken
from the New International Version.

OTHER NOVELS BY KEITH A. ROBINSON

THE ORIGINS TRILOGY

Book 1: *Logic's End*
Book 2: *Pyramid of the Ancients*
Book 3: *Escaping the Cataclysm*

THE TARTARUS CHRONICLES

Book 1: *Elysium*
Book 2: *Dehali*
Book 3: *Bab al-Jihad*
Book 4: *Labyrinth*

To all my students.

I hope you find yourself getting lost in this universe. May you be inspired to achieve more and reach for higher goals. Don't miss the message of this book.

ACKNOWLEDGMENTS

First and foremost, I want to thank the Great Composer of our universe. Father, thank you for the gifts and talents you've given me. May I always bring you pleasure by using them for your glory.

Next, I want to thank my family for their amazing support, especially my wonderful wife, Stephanie, who is so patient when I ramble about my story and universe, and who pretends to like science-fiction when I read each new chapter to her. Also, a huge thank you to my mother. She is always the first to read every chapter and offer feedback. I want to thank my children: Marissa, Tyler, Alejandro, Sebastian and Joshua, as well as those who are like children to me: Caleb, Donald, Angela, Liliy, Anastasia, and all the rest. Thanks for putting up with your "old man's" goofiness. I love you all!

I need to thank my brother, Kevin, who is like my own version of C.S. Lewis. He is one of the few who truly understands sci-fi/fantasy, writing, and all things in geekdom. I always dreaded and loved his input. I dreaded it because it meant many hours of rewrites, but I loved it because I knew it was making the story and characters SO much better. Bro, thanks for helping make this story shine. We really need to just write a book together sometime soon!

I also want to give thanks to my editor and sister-in-law, Aimée Robinson. Thanks for working with me to make this project as clean and error-free as possible and for teaching me new ways to take my writing to the next level. You're awesome!

I want to give a special shout out to the man who made the images in my head come alive with his sketches. Michael Lynch did an outstanding job of working with me to get the look of each character just right. Thanks for your patience, brother!

In the early stages of this project, God connected me with Andy Dunn, who worked with me to create the CD accompaniment to the novel. It was a dream of mine to include music with this book, and he made it happen.

Amalia Chitulescu made my vision come alive with a phenomenal, gorgeous cover. Your colorful artwork is top-notch! So thankful for your talents.

I want to thank Melody Christian for her excellent work on the layout of this book, and the 2nd editions of my other books. I'm thankful to God for connecting me with you, Melody. You're amazing! And I still think it's no coincidence your name is a musical term!

Thanks to Wayne Thomas Batson for his friendship and insight. You are a master wordsmith, my friend!

Finally, a big thank you to my beta readers: Cindy Johnson, Robert Pucillo, Victor Muller, Danielle Robinson, and especially Sophia Hanson. Thanks, Sophia, for all your suggestions and corrections. I owe you one!

Contents

LIST OF RACES AND GOVERNMENTS

Interval	Solfège	Pitch	Name
Perfect Unison	Do	C	Dominuus (DOH-mee-noose) – Creator/Great Composer

The Major and Perfect Races & Governments

Interval	Solfège	Pitch	Name
Major 2nd	Re	D	Rey-Qani (Ray-KAH-nee) Enclave
Major 3rd	Mi	E	Mih'schen (ME-shen) Expanse
Perfect 4th	Fa	F	Faluvinal (Fa-LOO-vin-al) Commonwealth
Perfect 5th	Sol	G	Solemsiel (So-LEM-see-el) Communion
Major 6th	La	A	Lah'grex (LA-grex) Sovereignty
Major 7th	Ti	B	Ti-Koona (Tee-KOO-na) Federation

Minor and Diminished Cultures & Governments

Interval	Solfège	Pitch	Name
Minor 2nd	Ra	Db	Ra-Nuuk (Ra-NOOK) Regency
Minor 3rd	Me	Eb	Meh'ishto (Meh-HEESH-tow) Supremacy
Augmented 4th	Fi	F#	Fiihkren (FEE-kren)/Tritonus Ascendancy
Diminished 5th	Se	Gb	Seyvreen (Say-VREEN)/Tritonus Ascendancy
Minor 6th	Le	Ab	Ley'cryst (LAY-crist) Empire
Minor 7th	Te	Bb	Tey-Rakil (Tay-ra-KEEL) Dominion

To view a map of the Twin Galaxies, visit www.apologeticsfiction.com

MAJOR 2ND – REY-QANI

Mariska and Teg-lakis

MAJOR 3RD – MIH'SCHEN

Khalen Daedark & Drallmari

MAJOR 3RD – MIH'SCHEN

Belenger Roth

PERFECT 4TH – FALUVINAL

Riveruun

PERFECT 5ᵀᴴ – SOLEMSIEL

Roakel Balikye

PERFECT 5TH – SOLEMSIEL

Saryn Balikye

MAJOR 6TH – LAH'GREX

Raena and Brin'tac eth Galithar

MAJOR 6TH – LAH'GREX

Inspector Mak'sim and Vel'vikis

MAJOR 7TH – TII-KOONA

Jov and Nara

MINOR 2ND – RA-NUUK

Slag

NARA'S REMOTE
Roadblock

DODEKAPH

1

URGENT MESSAGE

Third Phrase – 5640 A.E.

City: Saroth Kang
Planet: Mih'schrell'aka
System: Vespilles
Region: Mih'schen Expanse

"**TRUST ME.** When we save their lives, they'll overlook these minor transgressions. Now get your bindara out and be ready. That attack force is gonna be here within the hour!"

Khalen Daedark stepped back and squared his shoulders, drawing himself to his full height. He could not exactly stare down his mentor, but few races could see eye to eye with the Faluvinal whose heights typically neared eight feet. Right now Khalen needed Riveruun to act and not debate. Riveruun's hair, which resembled blades of grass, was standing taller than usual, a sure sign he was worried. Despite his misgivings, Khalen was at least thankful the Faluvinal was heeding the instructions. Riveruun removed the bindara case from his shoulder and cradled it with his lower pair of arms while his upper hands began opening the latches.

"Yet, I remain deeply concerned," Riveruun stated as Khalen finally succeeded in opening the protective housing around the portal inhibitor device. "We abused the special security clearance I was afforded as an Arranger, and we clearly broke several laws by entering a restricted area. I am not convinced this is a wise course of action."

Khalen growled under his breath at his companion's strict code of ethics and conduct. While he admired his friend's convictions and even believed in them, at least in theory, he struggled to apply them to his own life. Fighting back a stream of curses, he spun around to face the Arranger.

"If we have any hope of stopping this attack, we have to see Governor Gabrimon," Khalen stated through gritted teeth. "We already tried the polite approach and got the door slammed in our faces for our troubles. Now we try it my way. Just get ready to open the portal."

Khalen reached into the compartment and placed his hand on the manual power switch of the portal inhibitor. A second later, the slight bending of pitch told him Riveruun was tuning the six primary strings of the musical instrument. Khalen knew the tuning was essential but still cast an impatient glance at Riveruun. As the Faluvinal's hands deftly turned the pegs while plucking the strings, Khalen saw the thin, twisted strands of vines growing from Riveruun's arms quiver with sympathetic vibrations beneath the cuff of his shirt.

Once the task was completed, Riveruun nodded, his expression fixed in a mask of uncertainty. Praying for the best, Khalen flicked the switch on the portal inhibitor, shutting it off.

He cursed under his breath as an alarm blared throughout the building. Fortunately, the grating noise did little to break Riveruun's concentration. The first strains of music from his bindara filled the air as he played the instrument with his lower hands. Ribbons of colored light accompanied the sound and flitted around the instrument as the strings produced the tones. After only a few moments, the Faluvinal music master used his upper arms to conduct the triple meter of the song as he began to sing.

Using the talent inherent in all beings in the Twin Galaxies, Riveruun split his voice into three distinct pitches. One

of the pitches sang the melody, while the other two sang harmony and blended with the tones of the bindara. The solfege syllables sung by Riveruun shaped the light and energy created by the song. As Khalen watched, the Faluvinal used his upper arms to cause the energy to swirl until a circle eight feet in diameter formed in the air in front of them.

Although it only took fifteen seconds for the song to become established enough for the portal to be stabilized, it seemed like an eternity to Khalen. A heavy pounding from the door behind them heightened his anxiety and added to the bizarre concert of peaceful song and blaring alarm.

Khalen noted the expression of concern on Riveruun's face, but to the maestro's credit, he continued the song without interruption. Crossing over to the portal, Khalen looked through it to the other side.

The elegant meeting room was dominated by an oval table with a dozen plush chairs set around it. Standing behind or beside those chairs were ten figures, all with shock and alarm etched on their faces as they stared back through the portal.

Khalen hated corrupt, bureaucratic, political leaders. And in his experience, all political leaders were corrupt. Yet if there was one thing he could count on them to do, it was to save their own hides and fight to preserve their power. Right now, he was counting on Regional Governor Tabreth Gabrimon and his cabinet to do precisely that.

Khalen raised his hands in a posture of non-aggression and strode through the portal. As expected, the security guards grabbed his arms roughly from behind and shoved him to the ground the moment he entered the room.

"We have an urgent message for Governor Gabrimon!" Khalen cried out as the guards pinned him and bound his wrists. "There's an attack coming!"

Although he was unable to see what was happening behind him, he guessed by the scuffling, grunting and muffled cries, and by the sudden ceasing of Riveruun's song his companion had also passed through the portal and was similarly staring at the luxurious carpet.

"Krast, let them up," a commanding voice said from somewhere to Khalen's left. A moment later, the pressure eased from his back and the guards lifted him to his feet.

"Master Riveruun?"

Khalen turned toward the speaker and was surprised to see a Solemsiel couple staring in shock at Riveruun, whom the guards had now moved into position to stand on Khalen's right. The Faluvinal offered an expression to the pair which was half-smile and half-grimace. "Masters Roakel and Saryn. Khalen, the Great Composer smiles upon us indeed."

The Solemsiel couple were easily as tall as Riveruun, and, like the Faluvinal, they each had four arms. But the similarities ended there. Both Solemsiels wore beautiful robes of silver with purple trim, which contrasted with the bluish tones of their skin. Saryn's slender arms had tiny musical notes and symbols painted on her skin in a glittering gold dye. Her light green eyes sparkled with wisdom and intelligence as they shifted from Riveruun to examine Khalen. Many of the thin strands of her dark blue hair were wound together into smaller braids streaked with splashes of light pink. Like all beings of her race, her hair seemed to flow as if blown by a soft breeze, although none was present. Khalen knew the effect was due to some peculiar trait which caused the hair follicles to repel each other, yet he still found the motion hypnotizing and somewhat distracting.

In contrast, Roakel's blue skin had swirls of green throughout, which was most prominent on his neck and the backs of his hands. Although his left hands were empty and hung at his side, his right pair held a staff that was just a foot shorter than him. Khalen recognized it as a windstaff — a musical instrument used by some maestros. It was comprised of numerous long, thin wooden tubes rolled into a cylindrical shape. Complex mechanisms made of metallic keys covered dozens of holes spaced throughout the staff.

"Who are these intruders, Master Roakel? What's the meaning of this intrusion?"

Khalen turned to see Governor Gabrimon leaning forward with both hands on the table, his face filled with a curious mixture of outrage and fear. The sight of the pudgy, richly-clad politician made Khalen's ire spike.

Roakel turned to address the governor. "Your excellency, while my wife and I have no knowledge of the reason for Master Riveruun's presence, we can vouch wholeheartedly for his character. He is an Arranger from the Faluvinal people and servant of the Great Composer. If he felt it necessary to interrupt our meeting, I am positive his actions are not accomplished needlessly. I implore you to hear him out immediately."

As if to punctuate his words, the blaring alarms ceased, leaving behind a heavy silence.

"Very well," the governor said as he leaned back. "Explain yourselves."

Riveruun placed his four hands together in front of him and bowed toward the governor while Khalen simply crossed his arms in front of his muscular chest.

"Governor Gabrimon, the esteemed Arranger Roakel is correct," Riveruun stated. "We beg your pardon for this unseemly and unorthodox incursion. We attempted to follow the normal channels of protocol, but we were turned away by your staff — whom, I must say, were most discourteous. But owing to the critical timeliness and urgency of our message, we were forced to find other means to reach you."

Khalen scanned the faces of the governor and his advisory council as Riveruun spoke. To his utter lack of surprise, they appeared disgruntled and impatient. Yet he knew what was coming, so he pushed past his own desire to wipe the expressions from their faces with a few swift kicks. Instead, he relished the moment Riveruun dropped the "bomb" on them.

"We bring word that the secret forces from the neighboring city of Corcoran have been launched! They will reach the East border of Saroth Kang in less than one hour!"

Khalen was not disappointed. Reactions ranged from paralyzing shock, to outrage, to incredulity. Had the situation not been so serious, he would have relished the moment. He knew from experience how those in power felt invulnerable. It felt good to see them squirm.

"How absurd!" one of the advisors blurted out, interrupting Khalen's musings. "Our agents in Corcoran would have notified us."

Most of the remaining advisors nodded in agreement. Khalen guessed they wanted desperately to believe anything but the truth. Frustration at their idiocy welled within him. He could remain silent no longer.

"I told you they'd be too stupid to believe it," Khalen said to Riveruun. He stifled the lopsided grin that fought to make its way onto his face at the sounds of gasping from the council. Turning his attention to the governor, he pulled out a data stick he had stored in his pocket and held it up. "Maestro Riveruun and I have spent the past year working in the slums of Corcoran helping the poor. Without boring you with the details," he said sarcastically, "we saved the life of a soldier who told us of the attack. Of course, we—"

Khalen was forced to stop as laughter from the same advisor interrupted him. "This is your proof? The word of a soldier from the slum? Really?"

Khalen flicked his wrist and the data stick bounced off the man's chest, silencing him and causing him to stumble back as surely as if it had been a knife. Immediately, Khalen felt his arms pinned to his sides once more as the guards restrained him. "There's your proof! And if you'd shut up long enough for me to finish, you might just have enough time to save your precious city!"

Governor Gabrimon glanced first at the Solemsiel couple, then at Riveruun, a questioning look on his face. "Master Riveruun, it is only because I respect our distinguished Solemsiel Arrangers and their judgment that I am even willing to hear what you have to say. But I will not tolerate the impudent agitation of your associate and find myself forced to question the counsel of an Arranger who travels with such rabble."

Khalen gritted his teeth and was about to respond when a warning look from Riveruun silenced him. Biting his tongue, Khalen closed his eyes and forced himself to release his anger.

"Governor, please forgive the outburst from my colleague," Riveruun said. "His anger stems from his passionate desire to stop the coming assault. I assure you, the data disc contains video proof showing Mayor Derler ordering the attack. Our soldier friend managed to smuggle the video to us but paid the ultimate price in doing so. We barely evaded the forces of Corcoran ourselves. I implore you to overlook our desperation and manner at this moment and soberly consider this imminent threat. According to our sources, they are set to strike the eastern section of the city and have been planning this attack for several months."

The advisor with Khalen's data stick pressed the button on the device, sending the information streaming into a nearby computer. A moment later, a holographic projection appeared over the table. For the next several moments, those in the room fell silent as they watched the recorded scene play out in front of them.

When it had finished, one of the aides closest to the governor turned to him, her voice filled with both fear and outrage. "This vid has to be a forgery! Mayor Derler wouldn't *dare* attack us! There has been peace between Saroth Kang and Corcoran for nearly thirty years! The entire *region* has known peace for twenty years, since the signing of the Kirmani Peace Accords. The Assembly would never allow such a blatant violation of the treaty. Derler would be removed from office immediately."

Riveruun interjected. "I cannot speak to Derler's motivations in this attack. I can only assure you of its certainty. You will find the data stick contains further forms of corroboration. Many of the files hold the personal seal of Mayor Derler. However, I advise you to peruse the documents rapidly. Time is of the essence. The 'why' of the attack can be sorted out later. It is imperative you raise the defenses at once. Due to the enhanced strength and speed afforded to the Corcoran Augmented soldiers by their armored suits, your regular soldiers will be no match for them. You will need to meet them with equal force. I would suggest sending in your own Elite Augmented troops."

As one, the governor and his aides began sifting through the files on individual screens embedded in the surface of the table. Silence reigned in the room for several tense minutes.

Finally, to Khalen's relief, Regional Governor Gabrimon looked up, then reached out and pressed the comm button in front of him. "Get me an open channel to General Skeans!" Once the channel was connected, he continued, his tone forceful. "General, move all available troops to the eastern border of the city immediately. Prepare all units to engage Augmented troops within the hour!"

A stoic voice crackled through the open channel in response, "Copy, sir. To clarify: you said Augmented troops?"

"That's correct. This is not a drill. I repeat. This is not a drill!"

2

LOST RELICS AND
WINGED BEASTS

"YOU SEE, RIVERUUN? I told you my plan would
work," Khalen stated, a smirk spreading across his handsome
features. "Those in power always fight to preserve their power.
All we had to do was convince them the threat was real."

His companion looked away from the governor and his
advisors, who were scurrying about to make preparations
for the defense of the city, and glanced down at him. Khalen had traveled with Riveruun long enough to recognize
that although his friend was glad their message had been
delivered successfully, he was still concerned about the outcome of the coming battle. "Yes. You were indeed correct.
However, beware of generalizing the actions of all people. I
have known many politicians who sincerely seek the welfare
of those under their administration. And it speaks well of
Regional Governor Gabrimon's character that he has chosen
to overlook our intrusion into his meeting."

"He had *better* overlook our 'intrusion'! We're saving his city! But, at the same time, let's not push our luck," Khalen added dryly. "If things turn south, political types are wonderful at keeping fools in their back pocket to take the fall. I'd rather it not be us. And, by the way, I noticed you didn't mention I happened to be undercover and involved in aiding Kryton in discovering the attack."

Riveruun nodded. "I reasoned that, based on your rude behavior, mentioning your involvement might have given the governor and his aides more reason to doubt our story. If you had controlled your emotions more efficiently, I would have been forthright with giving you credit."

Before Khalen could say anything more, the conversation was interrupted when the Solemsiels crossed the room toward him and Riveruun. As they approached, they offered the typical Faluvinal greeting by steepling the fingers of their lower hands together while spreading wide their upper hands. Riveruun returned the greeting, then wrapped first Roakel and then Saryn in a warm embrace.

Never having been one to show physical affection, Khalen was thankful the couple did not extend their hugs to him. After several moments, Riveruun stepped back from the couple and gestured toward his companion.

"Masters Roakel and Saryn, please allow me to officially introduce my companion, Khalen Daedark."

The Solemsiels inclined their heads toward Khalen in greeting. Saryn gazed at the hooded jacket buttoned asymmetrically on his left breast and nodded. "You wear the attire of a maestro. It is always a pleasure to meet a fellow musician, particularly one who travels in the company of one of our Faluvinal associates and is willing to place his own life in jeopardy to save the lives of others."

"Yes," Roakel said, his tenor voice colored by the seriousness of the situation. "You do honor to the Mih'schen race."

Khalen winced at the comment. Collectively, the Faluvinals and Solemsiels were known as the Perfect races. Unlike the other four Major races, they never rebelled against the Creator according to the teachings contained in the Sacred Songbook.

Although Khalen had lived in the company of Riveruun and numerous others from the Perfect races for the past several years, he still found some of their ways, beliefs, and customs to be foreign. While he appreciated Roakel's words, he wondered if the Solemsiel would change his opinion if he knew the dark secrets Khalen kept.

"Thank you for defending my character," Riveruun offered, steering the conversation back to the matter at hand. "It was indeed providence the two of you were present. I do not believe the governor would have believed us so readily had it not been for your intervention."

Saryn nodded. "The Great Composer once more conducts our paths."

"Yes, and the harmonies in his symphony draw us together," Roakel said. "This time, we are the ones in need of assistance."

Riveruun raised his eyebrows questioningly. "Indeed? How so?"

"After you delivered your message, I approached Governor Gabrimon and asked that you be allowed to accompany Saryn and I on an errand of cultural and religious significance here in the city."

Although Khalen was relieved the governor was allowing him and Riveruun to leave, his burning desire for self-preservation made him want to get away from the city as soon as possible. The last thing he wanted was to get dragged into another mission, especially considering the streets of Saroth Kang were about to become a battle zone.

Saryn took over. "While it is true we came to Mih'schrell'aka and to Saroth Kang in order to serve as peacekeepers and to aid in negotiations between several of the cities involved in the current conflict, we were also driven by another purpose. Over the past three years we have tracked the location of a collection of rare and priceless artifacts, several of which could be of historical importance to followers of the Great Composer."

Saryn paused and took a deep breath before continuing. "However, before we could procure the necessary clearance to inspect the collection, we discovered that the government's Council of Antiquities decided to move the relics to the Great Star Song Cathedral, located in the eastern quadrant of the city!"

Khalen felt his stomach twist as he finally realized where the story was heading. "You want us to waltz into a war zone to retrieve some relics for *historical* purposes?" Khalen asked incredulously. "With all due respect, Riveruun and I have risked enough already."

Roakel turned his full attention to Khalen. "Master Daedark, if they were merely trinkets or baubles, I would never disgrace myself by asking such a thing of anyone. But if the research Saryn and I have conducted is correct, and we are certain it is, then there are items or instruments of great power within this collection — instruments which could be used by evil beings to sow discordant harmonies and chaos throughout the galaxy. They must not fall into the wrong hands. In fact, we are both experiencing a growing sense this sudden attack may be related. The timing of the assault is disturbingly coincidental and seems overly aggressive, don't you agree?"

Riveruun looked down at Khalen, then back to the Solemsiel couple. "While I cannot speak for Khalen, you may rest assured I will join you."

Khalen raised one eyebrow. "Really? You can't speak for me? You've been getting me into messes ever since you saved my sorry hide twelve years ago. And I've been repaying the favor ever since! You're welcome, by the way."

Riveruun smiled at Khalen's bravado. However, the Solemsiels failed to pick up on the humor between the two friends.

"It is by the will of the Great Composer that you both live," Saryn said. "Without his protection, even our most sincere efforts—"

"Maestra Saryn," Riveruun interrupted with a knowing sigh, "you misunderstand Maestro Khalen's poor sense of humor."

Khalen laughed. "*My* poor sense of humor? Yours was drier than a borta tree in the middle of the Kolimaga Desert the first time we met. It took five years just to get you to understand sarcasm!"

"Ah yes. Sarcasm," Saryn stated with a smile of her own. "Although I now recognize the jest, we should return our focus to the trial at hand."

Khalen barely suppressed a groan as he gave the ever-serious Arranger the sober response she sought. "Yeah. Well, I'll need to get my weapons. I didn't bring anything with me on this trip. I thought it might be just a *little* harder to convince Governor Gabrimon we were friendly if I was armed."

The Solemsiel couple frowned at the obvious statement before a slow grin spread across Saryn's face. "You were making an exaggeration, am I correct?"

Khalen gave her a lopsided grin. "Of course I was. See that, Riveruun? She picks up *way* quicker than you ever did. My guns are only ever a portal jump away. Let me grab them and we can meet at the cathedral."

Roakel's expression became apologetic. "Unfortunately, portal travel will not be possible at this time. Governor Gabrimon has activated the city-wide portal inhibitor."

Khalen winced. "Of course. I should have seen that coming. Well, I'm certainly not running headlong into a war zone without some kind of weapon. Maybe you can talk to your governor pal and see if he has an extra one lying around somewhere."

"I will speak to one of the governor's men about procuring a weapon for you," Roakel said.

"Good. Then let's get moving. The sooner we get those relics, the sooner we get out of here," Khalen said, resigning himself to the situation.

"Very well," Roakel said. He turned and spoke with one of the governor's private guards. After several moments of intense negotiation involving the governor and three guards, Roakel returned to the group and handed Khalen a large rapid-fire laser rifle.

Khalen hefted the weapon in satisfaction. Although he preferred hand-held pistols, he appreciated the weight and power of the device. He continued to inspect the rifle as he followed the others out of the conference room and into the hallway.

Roakel started leading the group down a passage to the left when a sudden disturbing thought struck Khalen. "Wait a second. With the portal inhibitor in place, how do you intend to get to this cathedral?"

"By Wind Song, of course."

Khalen shook his head emphatically. "No thank you."

Roakel looked down at him curiously. "What is the matter? We Solemsiels use it all the time."

"Khalen has a fear of flying," Riveruun interjected.

"No, I don't. I've got no problem flying in a machine or on the back of an animal," Khalen corrected. "I just don't like floating through the air with nothing under me but a long drop to a quick death."

Roakel smiled at Khalen reassuringly, yet the tightness in his face revealed his impatience at another delay. "I understand your concern. Could you perhaps make an exception in this instance? Every moment we delay could mean the difference between success and failure."

Khalen scowled. "I'm *not* flying by Wind Song. You go on ahead. I'll just have to find my own way to meet you there."

"Khalen, please reconsider," Riveruun said.

The conversation was brought to a momentary halt as several guards came around a corner and shoved their way past the small group. Khalen's expression shifted as the men headed down the hallway. "Wait a second. This is a Mih'schen city. There's gotta be a ruuq kennel nearby. They're used all the time because of their ability to evade radar. Knowing Gabrimon, he's probably got a full kennel in the building somewhere near the hangar with his military craft. You three get out of here. I'll catch up. Ruuqs can fly faster than your Wind Song anyway. You're going to need all the head start you can get."

His mind made up, Khalen left Riveruun and the Solemsiels standing in the hallway and sprinted after the guards. Although he was thrilled by the prospect of being able to ride one of the magnificent ruuq steeds, he found himself frustrated by his current predicament. He made his way to the nearest stairwell and nearly collided with a pair of passing aides.

"Is there a ruuq kennel in this building?" Khalen asked. When the two aides exchanged glances with each other in shock, Khalen tried once again. "In case you hadn't heard, there's an attack coming! Now don't waste my time. Is there a kennel?"

"Yes. On the floor below us. Take the stairs over there. When you get to the next floor, go left."

"Got it." Khalen ran in the direction of the stairs and fought once more against his rising frustration.

Why do I allow Riveruun to get me into these messes? Khalen asked himself irritably. *I never should've let him drag me to Corcoran in the first place. He seems to have a knack for sniffing out trouble. If I didn't owe him...*

Several minutes and a few brief wrong turns later, he reached the security area just outside the kennel. He was forced to wait for Roakel's request to be approved, but at last, he was through.

The kennel and launching pad looked similar to a small hangar bay with more than a dozen cages—each containing a large beast—lining the three inner walls. The ruuq's were winged canines whose muscular, feathered backs stood five feet from the ground, and whose thick necks supported proud heads another foot above that.

Khalen entered the room and strode over to one of the beasts with a deep blue and black pattern in its feathers. As he reached its side, he called out to the nearest worker. "I need you to get this one saddled immediately."

"Hey, get away from that animal! It hasn't been tamed yet. Who do you think you are, a maestro?"

His irritation spilling forth, Khalen let out a brief curse. "As a matter of fact, I am. Now get it saddled for me!"

The woman glanced at his hooded maestro's jacket and nodded. "Right. But you're going nowhere without some sort of clearance."

"My name is Khalen Daedark. I've been cleared by Regional Governor Gabrimon to take one of the ruuqs for an important mission. Check the log!"

Khalen felt the press of time as the woman pulled out her scroll and studied the screen. Moments later, she offered him a brief nod and rushed to saddle the animal. Several minutes later, she opened the kennel door and led it by its bridle toward Khalen. As the beast drew near, he set his laser rifle on the floor in front of him and began to sing and conduct. The solfege syllables combined with the three notes produced by his vocal chords to create a stream of light and energy that he directed toward the animal.

The animal's pointy ears perked up as the vibrations from the music reached it. The ruuq strode forward and bowed its head in obedience to Khalen. He kept the song going for a few moments longer as he placed his hand to the canine's long snout to allow it to take in his scent. When he was confident the bond had been established, Khalen brought the song to an end.

"Thank you," he said, taking the reins from the worker. "What's his name?"

"Stermer," she replied as she handed him a pair of flight goggles.

Khalen offered a nod of thanks as he took the goggles and placed them over his eyes. He was impressed by their quality the moment he activated them. In addition to complete night vision, they also contained a digital display and military message feed.

Khalen grabbed his weapon, then slid his right foot into the stirrup and lifted himself into the saddle with ease. One of the workers activated the pulleys to raise the hangar door and Khalen felt his insides clench at the sight before him. The launching pad was at the top of one of the tallest buildings in Saroth Kang. From his vantage point near the opening, he could see the entire northern portion of the city.

The night sky was filled with lights from the numerous military craft and other ruuq riders already on their way to the eastern side of the city. Far below, convoys of military transports and combat vehicles flooded the streets, some working to evacuate the citizens from that section of the city and others continuing on to join the coming battle.

Khalen activated the safety lights on the animal's reins, saddle, and feather attachments, took a deep breath, and urged the ruuq forward.

Although he had ridden numerous animals through the skies across a dozen worlds or more in his lifetime, it had been years since his last flight. The exhilaration of it was overwhelming. Lost in the rush of wind and focusing on controlling the animal beneath him, he found his thoughts wandering back to the past. In his mind he could hear the

KEITH A. ROBINSON

voice of his maestro tutor, Kunath Pressel instructing him on the finer points of musical communication with animals. Then there was the last time he had ridden a ruuq. The memory brought forth pain that had been long buried.

"These creatures are magnificent, Khalen. We need to do this more often."

Khalen heard his friend's voice through the headset and glanced over at him. Belenger Roth rode beside him through the evening skies of Oclion. Although Belenger was a member of the Mih'schen Augmented Elite Corps, he had traded his armor for standard clothing for this particular job.

"I'm heading back to the ship to check on the rest of the shipment. Teg-lakis and Mariska should just about have everything loaded. You and Skaret finish up at the refinery and head back."

"Got it, boss," Khalen replied. "See you soon."

As Belenger steered his steed to the left, Khalen turned his focus to the refinery below. He was anxious for this job to be finished. The Renegades had made quite a few enemies during the sixteen years Khalen had been part of the group. The longer they remained on the planet, the greater likelihood one of those enemies would find them.

Khalen arrived at the refinery and dismounted. He could see lights on in the main offices of the building complex not far from where he landed. If all was still going according to plan, Skaret would be there wrapping up the final details with the owners.

| 49 |

"Skaret, I'm on my way in. Everything still on schedule?" Khalen asked into his commlink.

"Oh yeah. Everything's going exactly as planned."

Something in Skaret's voice felt odd to Khalen. The fighter had joined the Renegades a couple years after Khalen, and although they were never close friends, they had a mutual respect for each other and shared a bond forged from surviving many dangerous and sticky situations together. Yet lately he had been acting different.

It took Khalen a matter of minutes to make his way through the outer factory and into the office space. The instant he opened the door, he knew something was wrong. But his instincts were too late. A stun blast struck him, setting his nerves on fire. His body hit the floor and he almost blacked out from the impact.

"Yes. This one will make a fine addition to our crew of slaves."

"Just be careful. According to my source, he's quite a proficient maestro. You may want to keep a mute on him."

Khalen came to his senses and looked up at his captors. He felt bile rise in his throat at the sight of the Tey-Rakil male standing over him. *"Imoleth..."* Khalen said hoarsely.

"So my reputation precedes me. Belenger must have shown you a picture or two of me. That means he likely also told you all about how I framed him and his dear Jindara. It was nothing personal. Just business."

"Like selling me into slavery is 'just business'?" Khalen spat back.

"Oh, you misunderstand," Imoleth said, his voice mocking. *"I wasn't the one that arranged this transaction. It was my new associate."*

The truth of the situation struck Khalen like a physical blow. *"Skaret!"*

A voice from nearby confirmed his guess. He had been betrayed.

"Thank you, Khalen. I've been looking for a way to regain my rightful land and title for many years now. This transaction and partnership with Imoleth will go a long way in making that a reality."

"Don't get comfortable. Once Belenger frees me, I'll come after you."

"I wouldn't count on it. I'm sure Belenger and the others will be grieved to hear how you and I were ambushed here at the factory. While you fought valiantly, you were knocked into one of the vats and your body was never recovered."

"Skaret, you dirty—"

"Goodbye, Khalen. I hope you enjoy slavery!"

The hopelessness he experienced while a slave on Oclion turned his mind toward Riveruun and the hope his mentor had brought. The Faluvinal prophet had given him life and purpose.

Face it, Daedark. Riveruun may have a knack for sniffing out trouble, but if you stopped traveling with him, where would you go? You've got no home, your family hates you, and the only friends you had haven't seen you in more than two decades. Riveruun is all you've got.

The thought of Riveruun brought his mind back to the present. Giving the reins a tug to the right, Khalen turned the ruuq toward the east.

3

PREPARATIONS

ALTHOUGH THE JOURNEY to the Great Star Song Cathedral took longer than traveling via portal jumps, Khalen was thankful he did not have to constantly look over his shoulder to make sure an enemy combatant had not suddenly appeared through a musical wormhole behind him. He had been in enough battles where that had been a real problem.

But it also meant he and his friends did not make it to the cathedral before the battle started. As they drew within a mile of the enormous building, explosions erupted from the edge of the city several miles further to the northeast.

Khalen scanned the entire area surrounding the cathedral, his senses heightened by the proximity of the conflict. From the high vantage point afforded by the ruuq's flight path, he saw numerous military craft moving toward the explosions as well as a swarm of pedestrians heading toward the cathedral itself, no doubt hoping to ride out the battle inside the walls of the religious structure.

The more Khalen studied the giant building, the more he understood their decision. The Great Star Song Cathedral was massive, easily able to hold fifty thousand worshipers. Besides the central worship center, the entire campus consisted of multiple buildings, many of them interconnected. It was as good a place as one could hope to find when trying to escape a combat zone.

When he and Riveruun arrived on the Mih'schen homeworld of Mih'schrell'aka two years ago, the Faluvinal had made a point of relating the history of the building to Khalen. He had explained that the building and the surrounding complex had been constructed nearly two thousand years ago at the end of the Synth Uprising. Once the merciless overlord Araklial had been defeated by the alliance of the Major and Perfect races, worship of Dominuus—the Great Composer—was at an all-time high. The cathedral was built as the primary worship center of the city. However, in subsequent years, belief in the Creator had waned. Now, several of the buildings were in disrepair and served as office spaces for various corporations and businesses. The only reason the cathedral itself still stood was that it was an exquisite architectural marvel. If the stories Khalen had heard were true, some pilgrims traveled from the farthest edges of the Twin Galaxies to experience the beauty of the cathedral: a beauty that now served only to make the opulent building a giant target. Of course, the citizens below could not know that as they scrambled for cover within its walls.

Ahead of him, Khalen could tell the Solemsiel couple was finishing their song. As the notes of the melody began to lower in both pitch and dynamic, the winds began to die down, allowing the trio to descend to the ground.

Khalen prepared to guide his steed in that direction; however, flecks of movement in the southeast sprang into view as another explosion illuminated the dark sky. As the light faded away, he turned on the night vision on his goggles. His pulse quickened at the sight before him. Instead of urging his ruuq toward the ground, he pulled back on the reins and directed the beast to the right, then flicked on his commlink.

"Riveruun, your Solemsiel friends were right after all. It looks like the attack to the northeast is a diversion. There's a flight of twenty or more ruuqs headed toward us from the southeast. At their current speed, they'll be here in a couple of minutes."

"They must be using the ruuq's to avoid detection from electronic sensors," Riveruun responded. "Roakel and I will do what we can to slow them down. We need you to escort Lady Saryn into the cathedral to retrieve the relics."

"What? You need me out here. She can get the relics."

"No. There are too many cases for her to carry alone. Besides, even with all three of us, it is likely some will make it into the cathedral. We need you to aid Saryn in searching the facility."

Although he recognized the logic in Riveruun's words, a small part of him still felt like he was running from the battle. "Fine. I'm circling back to your location now."

Khalen guided Stermer in a tight circle until the cathedral was once more in front of them. As they approached, Khalen saw that Riveruun already had his bindara out and had begun to play, conducting the music into ribbons of energy that fell to the ground like rhythmic raindrops all around him. The process was not only powerful and effective, but magnificent to behold.

Khalen was proficient in the musical sciences, but his abilities paled in comparison to those who have had thousands of years to hone their skills. None of the Major races performed their art with the outstanding beauty of the Perfect races.

In response to the Faluvinal's composition, all the plants within two hundred feet began to grow at a rapid pace. Grass, hedges and vines from the surrounding landscape began to overflow planters and parkways to form a living barrier surrounding the complex. The canopy of trees in the immediate area thickened and extended over the walkways below.

As Riveruun sang, the two metallic discs resting in their magnetic holsters against his thighs glowed brilliant green. Khalen had seen Riveruun use the Twin Discs of Arrguin several times and knew how effective they could be in a fight. Created from the special metal known as resonite, the eight-inch diameter discs could change shape in response to specific cymatic frequencies and were able to store enough musical energy to shock most beings into unconsciousness if they were struck with a direct hit. To guide them to their target, a proficient musician could control them by singing. One disc responded to the higher frequencies, the other to the lower.

Roakel sprinted over to greet Khalen as the feathered canine's paws touched the ground just outside the range of Riveruun's song. "Master Daedark, may I borrow the ruuq?"

Khalen slid out of the saddle, removed the goggles, and handed them to the Solemsiel. "Yeah. Give me a moment to transfer command to you." Reaching into the holster in front of the saddle, Khalen withdrew his laser rifle, tossed it on the ground in front of him and began to sing. Stermer nuzzled him with his wet nose several times, then turned to face Roakel. The maestro added his voice to Khalen's song and the two sang in unison until Khalen finally dropped out, allowing the Solemsiel to take over control of the animal.

Khalen retrieved his weapon and sprinted toward the cathedral as Roakel climbed into the saddle. Just before entering its doors, Khalen glanced one last time toward Riveruun to see he had begun walking around the outside of the building, his song continuing to forge the plant life into formidable defenses.

Saryn was waiting for him when he arrived. Standing next to her was a dark-haired Mih'schen woman dressed in the finely crafted blouse and suitcoat of a Conductor—a religious leader and follower of the Great Composer.

The moment Khalen was within earshot, Saryn addressed him. "Master Khalen, this is Conductor Jora. She has agreed to guide us to where the relics are being housed."

Khalen nodded toward the woman in greeting. "Let's move. We don't have much time."

"I understand. This way!" Jora ran through the foyer in which they stood and headed down the hallway to their left. Saryn followed close on her heels, leaving Khalen to guard the back. The further they moved into the building, the more they became aware of just how many citizens had taken refuge inside.

Groups of panicked and frightened people pushed and shoved their way through the hallways as employees of the cathedral struggled desperately to create some semblance of order. Small skirmishes broke out on occasion as the more aggressive pushed passed the weak, elderly, or infirm.

"The people are clogging the hallways! We have to find another way," Jora stated as she pulled the three of them into an alcove.

"Isn't the main sanctuary to our right?" Khalen asked, pointing toward where a steady flow of citizens was making its way through a pair of doors. "Couldn't we cut across the center of the building by going in there?"

Jora looked hesitant. "Normally, yes. But the other conductors are attempting to calm the people by holding a service. It's probably our best bet, but it's still going to be difficult."

"Perhaps," Saryn said. "Come. Allow me to lead the way for the moment."

Using her full eight-foot height to her advantage, Saryn headed for the doors. The sight of the tall Solemsiel heading toward them caused many to move aside in order to let her and her companions into the sanctuary.

When they entered the massive worship center, Khalen understood why so many came from vast distances to view its beauty. The sprawling ceiling displayed a map of the Twin Galaxies. Farthest from the stage near the back wall of the auditorium was the representation of the center of the Dominuus Segundus galaxy. Spreading out from there, the domains of each of the six races, each with their representative colors in dazzling displays of moving light and textures, were arranged in reverse order leading to the galactic center of the first of the Twin Galaxies called Dominuus Prime, which was said to be the representation of the Great Composer Dominuus himself.

In this case, the galactic center was the stage. Flowing streams of nature were held in place by the gentle strains of music being continuously played by the automated robotic instruments attached to strategic points in the ceiling. Fire swirled, light floated, plants twisted and turned, wind blew, earth moved and shifted, and water flowed from the outer edges of the sanctuary toward the stage, confined only by the musical craftsmen who built the living artwork.

Unfortunately, the sight of the mass of frightened people filling the magnificent chamber prevented Khalen from being able to truly appreciate its grandiose splendor. Several of the conductors had formed a group on the stage and were currently singing a worship song. In sharp contrast to the rest of the crowd, pockets of the faithful joined in, their arms lifted in reverent praise. The swirling, multi-colored light from the song further enhanced the beauty of the auditorium.

Khalen felt his spirit lift. He was once more reminded of the power of belief. Here, in the midst of chaos, was a peace that defied comprehension.

The sound of Saryn's voice snapped Khalen back to the moment. He immediately recognized her song and opened his mouth to protest. However, before his lips could form the words, he felt himself being lifted off the ground by a strong gust of wind.

His stomach twisted into knots as the floor of the sanctuary receded below him. Yet, despite his own misgivings about traveling by Wind Song, he realized the wisdom of Saryn's solution. While the mass of citizens pushed and shoved each other below, Khalen and his companions were able to cross the room unimpeded.

However, as they drew within a hundred feet of their destination, an explosion ripped a huge hole through the center of the sanctuary roof, raining fiery debris upon the refugees still trapped within.

4

THE AUGMENTED

THE FIRST THING KHALEN FELT in the wake of the explosion above was that the cushion of air supporting him was weakening. He, Saryn and Jora were now dropping rapidly into the sea of terrified civilians. To her credit, Saryn managed to maintain some semblance of control in her voice after the shock. Yet despite her best efforts, the three of them landed hard. Khalen dropped between two rows of chairs and struck his left arm, dropping his rifle.

Fortunately, the people who had been there when the blast hit were already scrambling for the aisles in both directions, allowing Khalen a moment to catch his breath without being trampled. His arm was numb from the impact and his ears were ringing from the shockwave.

Khalen caught sight of several dark shapes moving along the rim of the gaping hole in the ceiling. He tried to contact Roakel several times on his commlink to call for assistance, but the Solemsiel Arranger failed to respond. Khalen put his comm away, stood and retrieved his weapon.

Chaos reigned in the cathedral. The singing had stopped and been replaced by screams. The crowd pushed and shoved in a mad rush for the exits. Cries of pain rang out from those being trampled or crushed against walls.

"They're coming for the relics!"

Jora's cry drew Khalen's attention. He glanced back to where she and Saryn stood and saw the Conductor's eyes fixed on the hole in the ceiling. Khalen picked up his rifle and made his way toward his companions. As he approached, he saw that while Saryn appeared to be uninjured, Jora was clearly in pain and clutching at her right leg.

"Master Khalen, you have to—"

Before Jora could finish, a fresh wave of screams filled the air from those still trying to exit the sanctuary. Five ruuqs flew through the opening in the roof in single file, each bearing two armored and armed soldiers. Once inside the spacious cathedral, the beasts turned and headed toward the stage.

Khalen ducked between the seats and lifted his weapon. He took aim and unleashed a volley of laser blasts at the two riders the moment the lead animal was within range.

The front rider took several hits to the chest and head. Despite his armor and helmet, he was knocked out of the saddle by the attack. The remaining figure shifted his weight forward and managed to retrieve the reins.

Khalen prepared to fire once more when the riders on the other ruuqs sent a hailstorm of laser blasts in his direction. He dove to the ground between the seats just as the bolts of energy mercilessly tore through his previous position.

Suddenly, the sound of several songs of different styles, keys, and meters fought its way through the laser fire to reach Khalen's ears. The attacks instantly shifted away from

Khalen to focus elsewhere. Khalen climbed to his knees and peered over the edge of the nearest seat to make sense of what was happening.

Spurred on by Khalen's strike, the music masters in the crowd flung melodic countermeasures against the intruders. Streams of fire came from one direction while hailstorms of ice and rock were hurled at them from another. Saryn stood nearby, her own Wind Song causing the ruuq whose riders had attacked Khalen to fly erratically as it was buffeted by strong gusts. The other maestros, most of which were Mih'schen, used their natural inclinations toward communicating with animals to disrupt the riders' control over their steeds. As the ruuqs became unruly, the armored soldiers leapt off the animals. Despite many of them falling twenty feet or more to the carpeted aisles, nearly all landed on their feet and were unharmed.

Khalen swore under his breath as his fears were confirmed. These were not typical soldiers. These were the Augmented.

Once on the ground, the black clad troopers fired into the crowd at anyone offering resistance. Khalen knew that Saryn's height and the Solemsiel reputation for being powerful maestros would make her a primary target. He sprinted toward her and tackled her to the ground just before the barrage of laser fire could cut her down.

A scream from nearby drew Khalen's attention. He glanced up just in time to see Jora's body topple onto the backs of two of the chairs. Based on the angle at which the body rested, Khalen knew what he would find. He crawled over as quickly as possible and pulled Jora down into the space between the seats. Beside him, Khalen heard Saryn gasp in horror and grief.

Jora was dead.

As Saryn wept, Khalen felt his rage intensify at the deaths of so many innocents. Now that the attack on Saryn had ceased, he crawled forward until he reached the end of the aisle of seats. He peeked around the edge, hoping his movements had gone unnoticed by the Augmented soldiers.

Although his line of sight was limited, he was able to see enough to confirm his suspicions. "They're after the relics all right," he said, once Saryn had joined him. "They just ran through the door by the stage. My guess is it leads to the private offices designated for the Conductors."

"We must find a way to stop them," Saryn replied, her eyes still moist from tears. Then, after a short pause, she added, "Thank you for saving my life. I am forever in your debt, Master Daedark."

Khalen offered her a slight grin. "You're welcome. And please, call me Khalen. Master Daedark is way too formal. And, just for the record, situations like this are *exactly* why I don't like to travel by Wind Song!"

Saryn offered him a forced grin in reply.

Turning serious, he continued. "I haven't been able to reach Riveruun on his commlink. Have you heard from your husband?"

"I have. He and Riveruun are struggling to keep the remainder of the invasion force from getting near the cathedral. In fact, he asked me to relay to you his sincerest apologies for failing with the first wave."

Khalen shook his head. *Leave it to a Solemsiel to apologize in the middle of a battle,* he thought wryly. Aloud he said, "We can sort it out later. C'mon, the attackers have left the sanctuary."

Khalen stood and helped Saryn to her feet, then the two of them sprinted after the enemy soldiers. Once they arrived at the door, Khalen hit the control on the wall. The door slid open with a hiss and he peered into the hallway beyond. He moved cautiously through the opening with his rifle leading the way.

After several twists and turns but no sign of the intruders, Khalen began opening some of the doors in the labyrinth of offices and meeting rooms. Upon opening the fifth door, he was greeted by wails of terror.

At the sight of the people cowering in the room, Khalen pointed his weapon toward the floor and entered. Saryn stepped in behind him and moved compassionately toward the dozen men, women and children who had taken refuge in this room. The presence of the Solemsiel female had an instant calming effect. After a moment, one of the men detached himself from his family and stepped toward the newcomers. Based on the yellow-gold jacket the man wore, Khalen guessed him to be one of the cathedral musicians

"Thank the Composer! We believed you were the attackers. We heard them running down the hall."

Saryn smiled at the man. "We are here to offer our assistance. We believe the intruders are after the relics that recently came to be housed in the cathedral. Do you know where they are?"

"Yes," the man said quickly. "There're in a heavily locked room below us. If that's what the soldiers are after, they would have either taken the lift or the stairway. Come. I'll show you."

Saryn expressed her thanks and followed the man as he began heading toward the door. Before they reached it,

Khalen moved up to stand beside them protectively.

The musician led them past several more doors and around two more corners until they arrived at the stairwell. "Stand back," Khalen said to his companions. He reached up and hit the switch on the wall to open the door, then leveled his laser rifle at the stairwell. Despite his readiness, the Augmented soldier waiting on the other side of the door was able to knock the weapon aside before Khalen could squeeze the trigger.

Khalen's combat instincts kicked in, allowing him to dodge the follow up strike from the attacker's other fist. He had worked with Augmented soldiers numerous times in the past and even faced them in combat. As such, was well aware of their strengths and weaknesses. While the armor made them stronger and quicker, it also caused the wearer to overcompensate. Khalen used his martial arts training to launch a series of blocks in order to gauge the competence of this particular opponent.

He quickly realized his mistake. This soldier was no simple grunt in a fancy suit of armor. He was every bit as well trained as Khalen himself.

Within seconds a side kick from his attacker broke through his defenses and struck him hard in the chest. The blow knocked the wind out of him and sent him crashing backward into the wall. As he struggled to catch his breath, he was shocked to see Saryn leap forward. But instead of trying to fight the soldier, she used her much larger frame to drive him to the ground.

The trooper's enhanced strength allowed him to use Saryn's momentum against her. As they fell backward, he kicked his leg up and sent her somersaulting over him to land hard on her back.

However, the momentary distraction was all Khalen needed.

Fighting against the pain in his chest and the injury to his left arm from his fall in the sanctuary, Khalen raised the laser rifle and fired. A second later, the Augmented soldier lay unmoving, his armor scorched by half a dozen blaster holes.

Khalen leaned back against the wall to recover as Saryn stood, walked over to him, and reached out a helping hand. Brushing aside his pride, Khalen took her offer of aid and allowed her to help him to his feet. "Thanks," he stated, his chest still aching from the power of the soldier's kick.

Their guide, who had been cowering in the hallway, finally stood and approached. As Saryn spoke with the man, Khalen walked over to the downed soldier. He crouched next to him, reached under the man's chin and hit the release button, allowing him to remove the helmet. What he saw confirmed his fears. The soldier's face and neck were covered with tattoos and his shoulder-length hair was twisted into dreadlocks.

Saryn gasped in surprise. "He is a Meh'ishto! But...I do not understand. Why would a Mih'schen mayor bring Meh'ishto warriors into his army?"

Although the Meh'ishto were biologically the same race as the Mih'schen, their cultures were vastly different. While the Mih'schen strove to have an ordered society based on liberty and freedom, the Meh'ishto were ruled by violent tribal leaders who sought only to gain power and to do the will of their powerful Overlords. The Meh'ishto ruled a region of space bordering the Mih'schen Expanse. As a result, the two groups had been at war for thousands of years.

"How did you know?" Saryn asked.

"See this insignia on the helmet? It is the crest of the Ugarte tribe. They are a particularly nasty group of Meh'ishto."

"Dominuus protect us!" their guide stated, his voice laced with fear. "Augmented Meh'ishto soldiers! I must return to my family. May the spirit of the Great Composer guide your path and protect you against these vile spawn of Araklial."

Khalen bristled at the obvious prejudice. The fact it came from a servant of the church only sickened him further. Turning his back on him, Khalen headed cautiously into the stairwell, his senses alert for signs of other attackers. Saryn joined him a moment later and the two of them descended into the lower level.

They were greeted by silence as they reached the bottom. After positioning themselves on either side of the door, Khalen activated the switch. His muscles were tensed and his finger nearly pulled the trigger of his laser rifle from sheer anticipation. However, when the door opened, he was shocked to find the room empty.

Not only were the soldiers gone, but several of the other doors stood wide open, including one blasted off its hinges.

"We are too late," Saryn said, her head lowered in defeat.

"They must have found another exit," Khalen said, his eyes darting around the area. "They probably guessed we'd follow them and decided it would be quicker to take a different route rather than fight us." Letting out a howl of rage, he kicked a nearby chair and sent it careening into the wall.

Khalen turned back to face Saryn once more. "I knew this was a waste of time. We've gotta get up there. Contact your husband and tell him and Riveruun to watch their flank!"

5

BATTLE AT THE CATHEDRAL

SPURRED ON BY THE KNOWLEDGE that his friend and mentor was in danger, Khalen led Saryn up the stairs and out of the basement of the cathedral. He knew now that the Meh'ishto soldiers had what they came for they would no longer bother to post rear guards. Their only concern would be a quick exit, and their Augmented armor gave them a significant advantage over Khalen. He only hoped that Roakel had gotten the message Saryn sent.

Khalen and Saryn burst through the final doors and came to a halt at the sight of the battle raging before them. Their quarry stood directly ahead surrounded by half a dozen cases of varying shapes and sizes housing the stolen relics. Khalen smiled at their poor tactical position. They had obviously underestimated the power of two music maestros from the Perfect races. Based on the scorch marks from explosions and the shredded remains of several heavy tree branches, as well as a renewed wall of foliage around the immediate area, Khalen knew Riveruun had not only gotten the warning but had used the time it bought him to quite literally hedge in the enemy, pinning them against the building.

All but two of the invading Augmented soldiers had taken up position behind a pair of trees surrounded by a three-foot high wall just outside the doors. They were firing their weapons into the overgrown hedge in all directions, not even sure where their opponent was concealed. The remaining two were working their way left and right of the others. The pair darted from bush to bench, from bench to waste container, or whatever else was available. Their path zigzagged in opposite directions as they worked their way across the plaza in an attempt to flank the Faluvinal.

Unfortunately, their progress was hampered by two glowing objects that pierced the hedge like angry emerald glowing insects with deadly stingers. Khalen recognized them as the Twin Discs of Arrguin, his master's only weapons. Guided now by Riveruun's song, the discs spun, dipped, and shifted trajectory at seemingly impossible angles until they reached their targets. Their unpredictable dancing motion and flat shape made them nearly impossible targets to hit, though the soldiers gave it their best efforts. But at last, the discs struck home, releasing their payload of energy and dropping the flanking soldiers to the ground.

Khalen took advantage of the distraction caused by Riveruun's attack and opened fire on the remaining soldiers. Caught by surprise by the unexpected attack, two of the Augmented were hit by numerous laser blasts and dropped into the long grass.

"Get back!" Khalen called out as he pushed Saryn into the cathedral doorway. As expected, his attack drew immediate return fire from their comrades. Hidden behind the protective wall, Khalen saw the slightest hint of thin green streaks flying back through the hedge wall toward their master.

Khalen risked another glance outside from his cover in the doorway and saw flashes of light and shadowy movement in the sky above. Four ruuq riders were driving a fifth to ground. A howl of pain rent the air as the creature was hit by laser fire. Khalen winced as the rider leapt from the wounded beast to land awkwardly on the ground.

"Roakel!" Saryn shouted from behind him.

When the downed Solemsiel failed to get up or move, Khalen feared the worst.

"We must help him!"

"I'll try to keep the soldiers occupied." Khalen exhaled in frustration. The two of them were pinned down within the building and enemy soldiers stood between them and Saryn's husband. All he could do was keep them too busy to bother with Roakel. He leveled his rifle once again at the soldiers and peppered their position with laser fire. Another fell under his attack, but before Khalen had regained cover, he heard Saryn begin to sing the Wind Song again. Only this time, it contained a stronger rhythmic drive and thicker harmonic texture.

She was not trying to lift something with the wind: she was pushing it.

Khalen spun around to face her in confusion. At the sight of her expression, he felt a sinking feeling in his stomach. Her face was a mixture of concern for her husband and determination to stop the thieves. With the power and energy

Saryn was gathering from the song, Khalen knew she was underestimating the damage it would do.

"Saryn, wait!" Khalen called to her in warning as she came up and positioned herself in the doorway. "You need to—"

With one arm extended, she directed the energy of her song toward her husband's attackers with the force of a hurricane. The glass in the ornate doors on both sides of Khalen exploded outward, and one door was blasted from its hinges by the gale force. The unexpected explosion caused Khalen to reflexively drop to the ground and protect his head.

Still crouching, he turned his gaze outward to see the effects of Saryn's song. The resulting powerful rush of wind struck the ruuqs that had attacked Roakel and launched them hundreds of feet into the air. All but two of the riders flew from their mounts and fell into the streets of the city. Although the main focus of the energy was directed toward the sky, the blast was strong enough to knock the remaining four Augmented soldiers on the ground from their feet.

It also uprooted large portions of the hedge that had been protecting Riveruun, leaving him exposed.

Khalen felt his blood turn to ice in his veins. Reaching out, he snatched up his rifle and leapt to his feet. Shoving Saryn roughly with his shoulder to get her out of his way, he raised his weapon toward the soldiers.

But he was too late.

The strong green glow of the charged Discs of Arrguin lit the area surrounding Riveruun. In that light, Khalen saw his mentor through the demolished hedge. The Faluvinal was down on one knee half covered in bracken from the devastated hedge around him. He shook his head, clearly stunned, and to Khalen's horror, Riveruun stood up in the center of the gap in the hedge.

Khalen began to shout for him to get down, but once again, the Augmented soldiers were quicker. Though still lying on the ground, they raised their laser rifles and opened fire. Riveruun's body convulsed as the blasts tore into his torso.

Fueled by anguish and rage, Khalen let out a wordless cry as he fired at the soldiers. Behind him, he heard Saryn attempt to rekindle her Wind Song. However, due to grief and worry, her voice kept faltering, causing the song to waver.

Several laser blasts lashed out from the darkness of the sky to the left, indicating the arrival of several more ruuqs. The blasts struck near Khalen's location, forcing him and Saryn to take cover further inside the building. The steady barrage of blasts continued for nearly a full minute, forcing the two companions to remain hidden. Then, as suddenly as it started, the attack ceased.

Peering cautiously around the corner, Khalen discovered why. The remaining soldiers had loaded the relics onto the ruuqs, climbed behind the riders, and were launching into the sky. It was over. The relics were now in the hands of the enemy.

Fearing the worst, Khalen and Saryn ran out of the cathedral. Saryn veered off toward her husband as Khalen sprinted toward Riveruun. The sight of his mentor's mangled body sent a rare wave of raw emotion to wash over him. He dropped to his knees, hoping beyond hope there was still life in his friend. The laser fire had ripped several deep gashes in Riveruun's chest and legs.

Khalen was startled when he felt Riveruun's upper hand grasp his arm weakly. Knowing time was of the essence, Khalen prepared to do what he could to save him. However, he paused as Riveruun's faint voice reached him.

"Keep….the code. Do not….doubt….He is still….in….control."

His message delivered, Maestro Riveruun Pineraya, Faluvinal Arranger, music master and prophet of the Great Composer, passed into eternity.

Overwhelmed by grief, Khalen leaned back, took in a deep breath, and let out a feral cry of mourning.

His grief gave way to a fiery rage and hatred that scorched his soul. "WHY?" he shouted to the sky. "Why would you take him? He was your servant! He was making a difference in this twisted, sick universe. What kind of God are you?"

He tore his gaze from the heavens to look once more upon his friend and mentor. Although the age of sixty-two was still considered young for his race, it was still long enough to experience an abundance of pain. Yet in all that time, he had only cried once—at the death of his father. He had always seen tears as a sign of weakness, but now his eyes brimmed with moisture. For the first time since his childhood, Khalen realized he had allowed himself to care.

He heard a brief rustle behind him, followed by the gentle voice of Saryn. "I am…I am so sorry." Khalen turned and saw both Saryn and Roakel, the latter leaning heavily on his windstaff, were walking toward him with their heads bowed.

Khalen stood, his anger rekindled. "You did this! You let your emotions cloud your judgment, and now Riveruun's dead!"

Saryn bowed her head in shame. "I was only seeking to protect my husband."

Roakel drew his wife closer. "Khalen, you must understand that Saryn did not realize the blast would compromise Riveruun's position. And if she had not released the downburst, Riveruun may still have died, and I as well. We cannot know what might have been."

"Save your explanations," Khalen spat back. "We may not know what might have been, but we certainly know what *did* happen: Riveruun died. Tell me this, 'oh wise ones,' why Dominuus would allow this to happen to his own prophet? Is it because the Great Composer isn't quite as good as you say he is, or is it because he lacks the power to stop it? Why do evil men prosper while those who do good, like Riveruun, are murdered?"

Roakel looked down at Khalen, his countenance replete with compassion. "I, too, feel the anguish of Riveruun's passing. I have known him for over a millennium and have many, many fond memories of our shared journeys. Yet it has been years since we have spent significant time together. For that, your loss is the greater."

Khalen stared at the Solemsiel for a moment, the other's words catching him off guard. However, his anger pushed all possibility of empathy from his soul. When he remained silent, Roakel continued.

"The questions you have are valid, and they deserve an answer. And there are indeed reasonable answers to those questions. But now is not the moment for such discussions. Now is the time for mourning. Yet we must not grieve as those without hope. We must find solace in the truth. When the moment is right, I vow to present you with the answers you seek. But for now, you must not doubt the One who holds the universe in his hands."

Khalen was about to shoot back with a snide remark but checked himself when he realized how Roakel's words reflected Riveruun's dying command. *"Don't...doubt."*"

Pushing away the thought, Khalen let his frustration take control. "There are no answers...especially none I'll accept from either of you!" With that, he turned and walked into the darkness of night.

The next day dawned to find the city in disarray. Due to the advanced warning, the city's defenses were successful in thwarting the attack. At least, that was how the city officials explained it. All Khalen knew was that the battle had been a costly one. And now that it was over, he was left feeling hollow.

He kept to himself for the better part of the day, lost with his own thoughts and wondering what to do next. River-uun had been the one with the mission. Khalen had simply tagged along.

Adrift in the maze of his own mind and emotions, he was startled by a sudden knock on the door of his hotel room. He leapt to his feet, grabbed the laser rifle and held it at the ready. However, when Saryn's voice came through the door, he relaxed his guard. He lowered his weapon and turned away from the door in disgust.

"Master Khalen, if it is not inconvenient, Roakel and I would be most appreciative if we could have a moment of your time."

Not really in the mood for visitors, Khalen almost rejected the request. Yet, after all that had happened the day before, he felt he at least owed them this much. He strode over to the door, opened it, and invited the Solemsiel couple inside.

Khalen offered them the room's only couch, then moved to the window overlooking the ravaged city, his back to them. "What do you want?"

"I wanted to begin by asking for your forgiveness," Saryn said softly. "I erred in my calculations. If I had shifted the focus of the Wind Wall a little more, Riveruun's protection would not have been destroyed. While I did not directly kill him, my actions opened the opportunity for the enemy to do so. Please...please forgive me."

Although the death of his mentor was still raw, Khalen recognized the sorrow in Saryn's voice and knew Riveruun would not want him to heap further condemnation upon her. Yet he also knew he was not ready to absolve her. Turning around, he looked into Saryn's tear-filled eyes.

"You did what you thought best at the time," he said. "Let's leave it at that for now."

Although he had not noticed it when they had first entered, Khalen now saw that Saryn carried Riveruun's bindara case while Roakel had a wrapped bundle in his lower pair of hands.

"What's that?"

Roakel lifted the bundle and held it out toward Khalen.

"We thought it would be appropriate for you to become their new owner."

Confused, Khalen grabbed the gift and unwrapped it. As his eyes recognized the familiar writing along the edges of the circular, metallic shapes, he felt his grief threaten to return. "Riveruun's discs. I...I don't...Thank you." Not knowing what else to say, Khalen ran his hand along the edges of the Twin Discs of Arrguin, his mind drifting to the memory of when Riveruun had explained how he controlled them.

Pulling himself out of his reverie, he looked up at the Solemsiel couple to see Saryn offering him the bindara case. He accepted it reverently and set it beside him on the floor. "Thank you for these gifts. When I use them, it will be to honor Riveruun's memory. Did he...did he ever tell you how we met?

When both of his guests shook their heads, he continued. "I was a slave, beaten by my captors and left for dead. Riveruun rescued me and nursed me back to health. He helped me discover purpose in life."

Saryn smiled compassionately at Khalen. "Yet if Riveruun were here, there is no doubt in my mind he would tell you to look to Dominuus for your continuing purpose. And it is to that end that we have come here today."

Khalen frowned. "What's that supposed to mean?"

"Master Da—, I mean, Khalen," Roakel said awkwardly, "we have taken time to examine the list of relics that were stolen. As we surmised, one of them was indeed a powerful ancient instrument. There are others like it, and if certain forces in the Twin Galaxies get hold of them, it could unleash a great evil upon the universe. Saryn and I plan to continue to track down the others to prevent them from being stolen as well. We would like to offer you the opportunity to join us."

Surprised by the request, Khalen remained silent. In his mind, he heard Riveruun's weak voice. *"Keep....the code. He is still....in....control."* Immediately, the beginning of the Symphonian Code came to the forefront of his mind. *"We serve Dominuus, the Great Composer, as his instruments. We must be content to play the notes assigned to us. And as we play our part with excellence, it weaves together with all others to become his Master Symphony."*

Closing his eyes, Khalen honored the memory of his master. *Now I understand what you were trying to tell me. Goodbye, old friend. Thank you for showing me the way.* As he opened his eyes, he felt a sense of purpose fill him as he looked at his new companions.

"I accept. But first, tell me what's so important about these ancient instruments."

6

SUMMONS

Third Phrase – 5641 A.E.

City: Bel'veth
Planet: Mitrik B3
System: Jusufi
Region: Leh'cryst Empire

"BRIN'TAC ETH GALITHAR, Lady Crisenth has summoned you."

Brin'tac felt his stomach turn. He had heard rumors and wild tales about the Thirteen Overlords, but he had never met one in person. Popular legend said they belonged to a race of godlike beings called the Tritonus and imbued with strange powers of the mind. Others claimed they were powerful aliens from beyond the known universe sent to rule over the Twin Galaxies. Still others said they were simply highly-evolved beings. Many in the religious community held the belief the Tritonus were Faluvinal and Solemsiel who abandoned belief in the Great Composer and delved into secret musical powers.

What all the tales agreed upon is that the Thirteen Overlords were very ancient, powerful, and cunning, and were once the servants of the legendary tyrant Araklial. They ruled the planets belonging to the Minor cultures and often waged war against the rest of the Twin Galaxies.

And for some reason, one of them had brought Brin'tac, the Lah'grex governor of the Katloum Province on the planet Gal'grea, deep into the heart of the Leh'cryst Empire for a face-to-face meeting.

Brin'tac studied his reflection in the large mirror of the holding room in which he waited. He had no idea why his ship had been intercepted, or why his presence had been forcefully "requested", but he knew it was never wise to appear before a Tritonus, especially one of the Overlords, without an impeccable appearance.

He examined his long, gold-lined overcoat for any hint of spot or wrinkle and found none. Reaching up, he probed the edges of his headcrest in search of any imperfections. While other races took pride in modeling their hair or its equivalent, Lah'grex, who are hairless, took pride in their crests. Over the millennia, the configuration of one's crest became a sign of status in Lah'grex society—the wealthy with elaborate family crests, and the serfs and craftsmen with simple patterns.

Brin'tac was thankful he had just visited his crestsculptor four days ago for his regular checkup. The artist had worked for an hour under the specialized heat and humidity of his salon to shape the excess, clay-like skin atop Brin'tac's scalp into the form of the Galithar family emblem. How he missed the days when his crest would retain its shape for months at a time. Middle age and the increased burden of governing his people were taking their toll.

He frowned at the new stress lines that were creasing his spotted, indigo-colored complexion. *Great. I'll need to have the skin-smoothers fix those when I get back...if I get back,* he thought. Brin'tac turned his gaze from his face to his ever-thickening waist that was a reflection of both his age and privileged status. If the stories about the Tritonus were to be believed, they valued strength and despised weakness. Brin'tac now wished he had not skipped so many of his physical training sessions.

Yet the Tritonus also valued cunning. And in that area, Brin'tac excelled. If he was to make it out of this alive, he would have to rely on his wit.

He stepped away from the mirror and moved into the hallway. Four imposing Leh'cryst guards surrounded Brin'tac as he fell into step behind the servant who had summoned him. The servant led the small group down the hallway of the magnificent palace in which Lady Crisenth resided. The exquisite architecture of the building was highlighted by furnishings and artwork from some of the greatest artists in the known universe. Automated instruments hung from the high ceilings, the soft strains of their music echoing down the long corridors.

Armored guards stood vigilant as various groups of dignitaries, servants, and officials of the powerful Overlord made
their way through the hallways of the palace. Before long,
Brin'tac's guide led him away from the main traffic and
through two security checkpoints until at last they arrived
at the massive double doors that led to the private suite of
Lady Crisenth.

The doors opened of their own accord to reveal a spacious
room with marble floors and walls speckled with golden
veins. Sitting in a throne on a raised dais at the far end of the
room was the female Overlord.

The sight of Lady Crisenth took Brin'tac's breath away.
Never before had he seen a being of such beauty and grace
in person. Her tall, eight-foot frame was clothed in a flowing
sapphire dress made of the finest of materials. A magnificent headcrest studded with priceless jewels rose out of a
full head of bright orange hair that fell across her shoulders
and framed her delicate features. The base tones of her skin
were lavender but were highlighted by intricately designed
patterns of silver swirls, stars, and crescents.

But the feature that captured Brin'tac and held him captive were her shimmering violet eyes. A dark desire burned
in those deep radiant pools; a desire that could consume and
devour those who failed to please.

For the first time, Brin'tac understood why she was called
Crisenth, Lady of Pleasure.

"Ah, yes, Brin'tac eth Galithar. How nice of you to accept
my invitation."

Mesmerized, Brin'tac crossed the floor to stand at the foot
of the dais. He offered a deep bow of respect, then struggled
to find his voice. "My...my Lady Crisenth. You are...the tales

I have heard of your flawless beauty have fallen far short of the truth. Never before have my eyes beheld such splendor."

A smile creased the corners of her full lips. "Flattery is a good start, but predictable. I certainly hope you have more to offer than the typical abject deference. Perhaps I was mistaken in my choice."

Brin'tac's heart quickened. "I assure you, my lady. I am more than capable of accomplishing whatever task you have for me. My only desire is to see the will of the gods fulfilled."

Crisenth raised an eyebrow. "Gods? That is much better. Before we proceed, it is imperative you have a correct understanding of whom you are addressing. You would do well to remember that you, a mere mortal, stand in the presence of one who has been alive since the dawn of time. Furthermore, I hold the power of life and death over you. No matter how important you may think you are in the eyes of your people, a mere word from me will bring about your destruction."

"Yes...yes, my lady," Brin'tac stammered. "I am...I am fully aware of my position. Again, it is my honor to serve you."

Crisenth frowned. "I must say, so far I am unimpressed."

Brin'tac fought against a rising panic. *What does she want from me?* he wondered. *What game is she playing? I'm treating her with the respect she deserves...*

Taking a deep breath, he called upon his training and put a commanding edge to his voice. "Very well, your *eminence*," he said sarcastically. "I'm certain a person of such extreme importance as yourself has more important things to do than exchange banter with a mere Lah'grex governor. So if you don't object, I suggest we dispense with the obligatory groveling and move on to more pressing matters."

Crisenth's eyes flashed and she sat up straighter in her throne. "Or perhaps I should have my guards take you to the Island."

Brin'tac had seen firsthand some of the holovids of the "games" that took place on the small continent. Lady Crisenth designed the games herself. The holovids of the inhabitants of the Island on Mitrik B3 fighting against each other for survival were the main source of entertainment for the Minor cultures. Only a handful of those unfortunate enough to be sent there ever made it out alive.

Years of political maneuvering allowed Brin'tac to keep his expression emotionless in the face of threat. Trusting his gut, he continued with his chosen course of action and laughed. "With all due respect, my lady, you are terrible at bluffing. You are far too intelligent to go through all the trouble of kidnapping me and bringing me out here just to fuel your twisted games. Besides, a nearly one-hundred-year old Lah'grex governor would make for very poor sport and probably bring down your ratings. Now, if you had threatened to ransom me or kidnap my family, it would've been much more believable."

Brin'tac held his breath as Crisenth continued to glare at him. After several intense moments of silence, the tension eased as a genuine smile spread across Crisenth's face. "Yes. That is more like it. Perhaps Lord Dakath was right after all. You do have some potential."

Crisenth stood and descended the steps until she stood directly in front of her guest. Uncomfortable at her proximity, Brin'tac forced himself to once again remain calm and assertive. He was caught off guard a moment later when she opened her mouth and began to sing.

The power of her song infiltrated his mind like a parasite. Summoning all his strength, he fought against the invasive nature of the musical threads. He could feel her mind probing his through the song. The force of her will pried into his memories and sought to unravel his most private thoughts and secrets. Brin'tac lost all sense of time as he struggled to push her out. At last the song ended.

Brin'tac swooned and nearly collapsed from the mental exertion. As he strove to recover his senses, he saw the Overlord turn and climb the steps back to her throne. Crisenth sat down once more, a satisfied expression on her face. "Well, Lord Shatterstrom. It appears we have found our agent."

To Brin'tac's shock and horror, the area to the right of the dais shimmered and rippled. Seconds later, another of the Thirteen Overlords stepped through the apparent rift in reality.

Lord Shatterstrom's physical presence and stature filled the room with a sense of power and intimidation. The sleeveless shirt he wore allowed his broad chest and the massive muscles of his four arms to be prominently displayed. Although he had a headcrest and his skin tones were similar to those of the Lah'grex, the skin itself was hardened and had sizable plates covering large sections of his body like natural armor.

Brin'tac shrank back as the towering figure drew closer to him. Lord Shatterstrom stopped at the foot of the dais and studied the Lah'grex politician with his three eyes that seemed to move independently of each other. The shifting movement of the eyes combined with the haphazard arrangement of the Overlord's headcrest to give him a wild, erratic look.

"Seems soft, cowardly, and weak does this one," Shatterstrom said, his words coming out slightly slurred and disjointed.

"Yes, but he has the qualities and training necessary to serve our purposes," Crisenth replied. "Lord Dakath has given me leave to select our agent, and I have made my choice."

Brin'tac battled against the urge to flee for his life. He wanted nothing to do with being an agent for these mighty beings. Yet he knew if he showed weakness now, he would never make it out of the palace alive.

"I will use every means at my disposal to be of service to the Tritonus cause," Brin'tac lied.

"Yes, will you," Shatterstrom stated with a sneer. "For family suffer will, otherwise should do you."

The mention of his family brought a new fear into Brin'tac's heart. "What task do you wish me to accomplish?" he managed.

Crisenth's eyes bored into him. The room seemed to grow darker as she spoke. "There is a certain pair of Solemsiel Arrangers who are seeking out some ancient relics that are of interest to us. Our forces managed to reclaim one of these relics from Mih'schrell'aka a year ago. We want you to befriend these Arrangers and earn their trust. At the appropriate time, you will receive further instructions."

Brin'tac had made many shady deals in his past, but in those instances, he always held some leverage or means of power over the other party. Never had he felt so helpless and trapped. Putting more bravado in his voice than he felt, he said, "Provide me the names of these Solemsiels, and I will set events in motion immediately."

"Oh, no need to worry about the details," Crisenth said, her voice laced with venom. "Lord Shatterstrom and I have taken the liberty of baiting the trap for you. All you need to do is play your part and follow the script we provide. And if you deviate from that script in any way, you will come to an extremely painful death, but only after first watching your wife, son, and daughter suffer!"

Despite his best efforts, the threat against his family succeeded in breaking through the stoic mask he had in place to hide his emotions. "I...I give you my word. I will do what you ask. There is no need to involve my family."

Lord Shatterstrom let out a throaty laugh. "That for too late."

The blood drained from Brin'tac's face at the pronouncement. "What...what do you mean?"

Crisenth, Lady of Pleasure smiled broadly at his discomfort. "Dearest Galithar, don't you see? Your family is the bait!"

7

GALITHAR MANSION

Third Phrase – 5641 A.E.

City: Stron'zek
Planet: Gal'grea
System: Ru'ricka
Region: Lah'grex Sovereignty

RAENA GALITHAR sat in front of her vanity mirror and admired for the fourth time that day the work the professional crestsculptor had done. The Lah'grex artist was one of the most talented in the city—the kind only the wealthiest landowners could afford.

Fortunately, Raena fit that description.

As the wife of the ruler of the entire province of Katloum, money was no object. Her wardrobe contained only the finest outfits, made of the finest materials. It was, therefore,

natural she would have the most elegant crest as a sign of her station. Raena's crest, with jewels and diamonds worked into the Galithar family design, gave the appearance of a crown resting atop her head. Her flowing blue gown brought out the slight bluish tint of her indigo-colored skin.

She stood, satisfied her appearance was suitable to the occasion. Walking out of her dressing room, she headed down the hallway to the primary living space. The large area was nearly the size of the average Lah'grex home. It was richly furnished and contained a set of full windows that spanned the entire wall, offering a magnificent view of the countryside below which was bathed in the orange glow of the setting sun.

The Galithar Mansion rested near the apex of the city of Stron'zek. Like most Lah'grex cities, it was built inside a mountain. Using their natural proclivity for shaping rock, the Lah'grex musicians carved out the inside of Mount Stron'zek, fashioning multiple levels of homes, businesses, arenas, governments buildings, a starport and, at the peak, the Galithar Mansion.

But Raena was not interested in the view. Instead, she focused on smoothing out the wrinkles in her dress by studying her reflection in the glass. Once more satisfied, she turned from the window and spoke to the home's computer system. "Enris, call Rav'ok and Shea."

"They are currently in their bedrooms," the pleasant female voice stated. "Would you like me to place a three-way call to both rooms?"

"Yes."

After a brief pause, the computer's voice returned. "Neither are answering. Would you like me to have one of the servants visit their rooms and relay a message?"

Raena frowned. "Never mind. I'll just do it myself." Sighing in frustration, she descended the stairs and headed toward her daughter's room first, knowing she would be the one that would take the longest to get ready.

Upon entering, she immediately discovered why her daughter had not answered the call. She was standing in the middle of her bedroom practicing her conducting. Her back was to the door, and it was apparent she was listening to a recording of a song on the microspeakers in her ears. She continued to practice her conducting gestures, oblivious to her mother's presence.

A music maestra herself, Raena decided not to interrupt Shea for the moment, but rather to watch her practice. Although her daughter had been studying the science of music seriously for only a few years, Raena was proud of her progress. Shea had learned the basics of the clarichord and six-stringed situur, and how to create light and energy from simple chords and specific harmonies years ago, before she reached her first decade birth celebration. At age twelve, she began to learn to use the solfege syllables necessary to shape the music, and how to split her voice into three separate pitches in order to sing triads. Now, at sixteen, the focus of her private lessons was on the art of conducting. She long ago demonstrated a natural talent for music. If she continued at her current rate, she might even achieve the rank of maestra, or master, before her second decade birth celebration. Raena smiled at the thought. She had not achieved that rank until the age of twenty-two.

Shea suddenly let out a growl of frustration and dropped her arms to her side with a huff. She reached over to pause the recording and was startled as she noticed her mother standing in the doorway. "*Matri*, you scared me. How long have you been standing there?"

Raena stepped closer to her daughter and smiled broadly, admiring the teen's beautiful light-gray skin. Although Shea had her mother's knack for music, she had her father's skin and complexion. "What piece was that?" she asked, ignoring her daughter's question.

"Elin'ton's *Caravania*," she replied. "I keep missing the extra six-eight measure at the end of the transition going back to the recap."

"Keep practicing. You'll get it. Your form looks good. Just remember to keep your wrist relaxed so the pattern flows smoother. But for now," Raena said, glancing at the chronometer on the nearby desk, "I need you to finish getting ready. We're leaving in a few minutes."

"Did you remind Rav'ok yet?"

"I'm heading to his room next."

Shea raised her eyebrows and gave her mother a playful expression. "Good luck with that one. If he's in the middle of a race with one of his friends, you're gonna have a hard time convincing him to quit early."

"Well, it'll be his fault for forgetting about the symphony concert. I reminded him an hour ago. Anyway, be in the foyer in ten minutes," Raena finished, then turned and left the room. A few moments later, she gave a quick knock of warning on her son's door before pressing the button to open it.

As expected, he was sitting in his favorite seat in the house: his Remote Command Chair. The state-of-the-art system filled the entire back quarter of the spacious room. Surrounding the finely-upholstered chair were numerous buttons, knobs, levers, and two joysticks, which Rav'ok had gripped in each of his hands. A sleek red and gold helmet lacking a visor covered his head. In fact, the design of the helmet was to remove all outside stimuli so the wearer could become completely immersed in piloting the remote.

Raena fought against the frustration rising within her as she strode over to a display screen connected to the Command Chair in order to determine how much time her son had left in his current race. Although only two minutes remained, she nevertheless felt her irritation flare as she studied the display.

The Galithar family owned numerous remotes ranging from walking droids, to small vehicles, to flying machines—all of various sizes. Some remotes were here within the mansion, while others were housed in buildings on the other side of the city.

But the ones in the arena, like the one Rav'ok was currently piloting, belonged solely to his father and were explicitly off limits to him.

With an average lifespan of three hundred years, it was not uncommon for Lah'grex youth to live at home until their third decade. However, the heightened tension she had been experiencing recently in her relationship with her twenty-two-year-old reckless and apathetic son was pushing things toward a breaking point.

Lost in her thoughts about her son's future, she did not realize the two minutes had expired until Rav'ok's sudden cry of victory brought her back to the moment. She watched impatiently as he extricated himself from the Command

Chair and removed his helmet. The asymmetrical crest atop his head seemed a mockery of the family design.

"Ha! That's what you get you sorry sacks of...oh, hi, *matri*," he said, filtering his curse at the last second as he caught sight of her. "What're you doing in here?"

"How did you get access to the command codes for your father's racing remotes?" she asked sternly, her voice barely controlled.

Rav'ok shrugged. "It's not that hard to get around 'em. My friends showed me how to do it years ago. I race 'em all the time without *patra* knowing. Don't worry so much. I'm always careful."

"This kind of blatant disobedience has to stop, Rav'ok! Your father—"

"*Patra* doesn't care about me!" he shot back in anger. "Between his duties as regent, his late-night meetings, and his gambling, he simply doesn't have time for his children. Or his wife."

Raena bit her lip as her son's words cut into her soul. After a moment, she regained her composure and stood. "Get yourself dressed appropriately," she said, choosing not to engage in the previous discussion any further. "We're leaving in five minutes. This is an important concert, and you're expected to be in attendance." Without waiting for his reply, she turned and strode out of the room.

Rav'ok's words had stung her more than she cared to admit. They stung because they were true. Her husband had not been around much over the years, and now their children were paying the price. Shea struggled with perfectionism to earn her father's approval, while Rav'ok failed to care about anything.

An alarm suddenly rang out loudly through the mansion, snapping her out of her reverie. Seconds later, Rav'ok appeared at her side, his eyes wide.

"What's going on? Is that...is that the security system?"

Not wasting time to respond, Raena called out to the mansion's computer. "Enris, why is the alarm sounding?"

Raena felt her body go cold as the computer responded in its calm, emotionless voice. "The portal inhibitor has been disabled. A musical portal just opened on the second floor allowing twelve armed intruders to enter the building."

8

INTRUDERS

"INTRUDERS? How did they...how *could* they shut down the inhibitor without the proper codes?" Rav'ok asked, on the edge of panic. "I thought our security system was unbreakable!"

"I don't know how they did it," Raena said, her voice trembling as she struggled to retain her composure. "Enris, notify the authorities."

"Authorities notified."

"*Matri*, what's going on?" Shea asked as she ran toward her mother. "Why is the—" She never finished her sentence. Instead, Raena saw her eyes grow wide, a blood-curdling scream erupting from her lips.

Spinning around, Raena watched in horror as a figure emerged from the utility room at the end of the hallway and began walking toward them. In a panic, she raised her arms and searched her memory for a song of attack.

She drew in a breath to begin singing when a voice came from the intruder. "Raena Galithar, my name is Urith'an

Tral from Liakrana Home Security Services. Our computers detected an unauthorized portal activation in your home. Please come with me for your own safety."

As the figure drew nearer, Raena exhaled in relief. "It's okay," she assured her children. "This is one of the four security remotes your father purchased several years ago."

Although she had not paid much attention to it at the time, Raena vaguely remembered some workers bringing the Lah'grex-sized robots into the mansion and tucking them away in hidden closets on each floor. Like the racer Rav'ok had been using moments before, these remotes could be virtually piloted by personnel located across the city at the Liakrana Security headquarters.

The heavily armed remote stood over six feet tall. The largest source of Raena's initial confusion was a feature of the remote which was designed to make it appear friendlier to those under its care. The entire head of the machine projected a perfect holographic representation of the pilot's own face and headcrest. The overall effect was such that it seemed as if the pilot himself were standing in front of them wearing a robotic suit.

"So...you can stop them, right?" Rav'ok asked hopefully.

The percussive sounds of numerous laser blasts suddenly filled the air before the pilot could reply. From her position, Raena could tell they were coming from the level below.

"Come!" Urith'an said. "We have to get you to safety. Whoever these people are, they came prepared. The other three security remotes are moving into position to engage the intruders, but they're heavily outgunned. They'll only be able to slow them down. We have to get you to one of your ships."

"Wait!" Rav'ok called out. "Can't we…I mean, *matri,* can't you create a portal to get us to safety?"

Urith'an shook his head, answering for Raena. "Whoever shut down your portal inhibitor reactivated it again the moment they were inside—no doubt to keep you from escaping and the police from entering. Now hurry!"

The small group bolted up the nearby stairs. Urith'an's remote paused for a moment upon entering the primary living space on the next floor. "Our sensors indicate the intruders have split up. Three went downstairs, but the rest are still coming toward—"

Urith'an suddenly stopped speaking and spun to the right with his weapons at the ready. He lowered them at the sight of two of the servants cowering together in a corner.

"Come with us," Raena commanded before turning her attention to assess the situation. "We need to slow them down," she said, more to herself than to any of the others.

She closed her eyes and began to sing. Her right hand kept time, flowing through the four-point pattern: down, left, right, and up. With the harmonic progression of the changing musical chords established, she switched one of the three pitches to shape the melody. Bursts of indigo-colored light surrounded her as her lips formed the necessary solfege syllables, allowing her to shape the energy produced by the music.

Opening her eyes, Raena used her left hand to direct the pulsating electricity. A stream of light flew from her outstretched fingertips and struck the landing at the top of the stairs. The swirling radiance coalesced into the shape of a wide circle of reddish-colored rock. Within moments, a giant mound of stone covered the entire top of the stairs.

"Well done, my lady," Urith'an said as Raena finished her song and turned back to face him. "That should buy us some more time. Now let's get you to safety." The remote he was piloting pivoted and began heading toward another set of stairs at the end of a long hallway. As the rest of the group followed behind him, they heard laser blasts striking the rock Raena had just created.

"They're hitting the rock barrier!" Shea stated. Raena could tell by the expression on her face that fear was threatening to paralyze her. "*Matri,* do you think…will it hold?"

Before anyone could answer, the laser blasts coming from the floor below them stopped unexpectedly. Seconds later, an explosion broke the silence and shook the building, nearly knocking everyone off their feet. Regaining her balance, Raena continued running.

"They broke through!"

Rav'ok's panicked voice caused her to stop and look back at her son. However, Urith'an urged her forward. "It'll still take them time to remove the debris. It served its purpose. Keep looking ahead. Concentrate on getting to the hangar. We're almost there."

Casting one last glance backward, Raena felt a fresh wave of angst wash over her as she glimpsed two of the intruders working to clear some of the rubble. Apparently stunned at the sight, Rav'ok remained where he was for a second too long, allowing one of the intruders to spot him. "Rav'ok! C'mon!" Raena shouted, her words snapping him out of his stupor. Turning toward her, he sprinted forward and followed her down the hallway to where Urith'an stood at the bottom of a stairway leading to the hangar.

The small group reached the steps and began to climb while the remote stood guard, its laser pointing down the hallway. Raena was halfway up the stairs when laserfire erupted behind her. She scrambled up the remaining steps, then turned long enough to see Urith'an's remote open fire on the intruders.

They had made it to the top floor, which housed a small fleet of flying vehicles and space cruisers. Raena glanced to the left and noted with dismay that the giant door which led outside was still closed.

"*Matri*, the remote won't last long. We're not going to make it!" Rav'ok exclaimed as he, too, recognized their predicament. Ahead of him, his sister and the two servants were racing toward one of the larger family vehicles.

"Get in the *Windrunner* and start the engine, then open the hangar door," Raena commanded. "I'm going to hold them off a little longer. Once the engine is primed, you can pick me up."

She could tell by his expression he did not want to leave her. However, after a moment's hesitation, he did as commanded. For a brief moment, Raena's eyes lingered on her children, wondering if it would be the last time she would ever see them. Rav'ok's longer legs allowed him to quickly gain on the others, who had nearly reached the vehicle. Her eyes moist with tears, she tore her gaze away. She knew if her children had any chance of escaping, she had to bury her feelings and focus on the task at hand. Facing the stairs, she took a deep breath to steady her nerves and began to sing. However, the song she produced this time contained a completely different melody.

This was a song of attack.

Raena reached back into her training from decades past to remember the chords, rhythms, and melody. Within moments, dozens of sharp, rocky shards about four inches long flew from the outstretched fingers of her left hand toward the top of the stairs. She had timed the attack perfectly. The stone fragments struck just as the front two intruders reached the top of the stairs.

The rocks embedded themselves into the helmets of the mercenaries, who toppled limply onto the hangar floor. Undaunted, the remaining intruders laid on the last couple of steps and fired their weapons over the edge toward her.

Anticipating their attack, Raena changed the key of her music once more the instant the shards were released. The new song she performed was nearly identical to the one she had used to create the boulder over the stairway below. Only this time, she used it to form a vertical shield of rock in front of her. The first laser blasts struck as the six-foot wall was still solidifying.

However, the stress of the attacks threatened to break her concentration. Willing herself to remain calm, Raena kept her thoughts focused on her performance. She huddled behind her rock shield and continued to sing and conduct. Color and energy flowed around her gown as she sent another volley of shards over the shield and toward her attackers. Muffled cries of pain told her at least some of her projectiles found their marks. Sudden movement in her peripheral vision demanded her attention. She leaned into the rock wall just as a volley of laser blasts flew past her. Several of the intruders had worked their way around the edges of the hangar, flanking her. Shifting her song once again, she redirected her energies to curve her shield in order to protect herself from both sides as well.

The sound of moving gears and pulleys echoed through the hangar as the heavy outside door began sliding open. Risking a glance behind her, she saw that Shea and the servants were already inside the *Windrunner*. However, Raena's anxiety spiked at the sight of Rav'ok leaning against the door of the vehicle with his left leg clearly injured.

Raena suddenly heard another voice singing over the din of the battle. Recognizing the song, Raena desperately attempted to reinforce her own. Yet the sight of her injured son had distracted her just enough for her enemy to gain the upper hand.

The rock wall in front of her shattered as if struck by an enormous hammer. The force of the explosion hurled her backward. Stunned, she fought to remain conscious.

"NOOO!"

Rav'ok's cry reached her ears, the anguish in his voice fueling her resolve. Pushing herself from the ground, she shifted into a kneeling position and prepared to sing once more.

An electric jolt sliced through her body, sending her tumbling to the ground once more. As she lay on the hangar floor, she realized the terrible truth of her situation. The bolt that struck her had merely stunned her. The intruders were not trying to kill her and her children. They were trying to abduct them.

Unable to move, Raena was forced to become a spectator for the remainder of the battle. She could just see the *Windrunner* and her children from where she lay. Despite her frustration with her son, she knew that when necessary, he rose to meet challenges head-on, as he was doing now. He risked his own safety to make sure his sister and the two servants were safe. The slightest smile played at the corner of her mouth. Her son was acting like the leader she always knew he could be.

A solitary tear slid down her cheek as she wondered in despair whether she would be around to witness future moments of pride, or any moments at all with her son...or daughter.

Helpless, Raena watched Rav'ok open the driver's door of the vehicle and prepare to jump inside. Before he could do so, the intruders managed to get close enough to get a clear shot at him.

A stun blast hit him in his back and dropped him to the hangar floor. Raena wanted to scream, but her muscles refused to comply. The cries of her daughter and the two servants echoed through the hangar as the intruders reached the car and roughly pulled them out of it.

Raena watched in horror as one of the mercenaries threw Shea to the ground. In defiance, she managed to kick him in the shin. Letting out a growl of pain and anger, the intruder reached down, picked her up, and smacked her hard across her face.

Suddenly, the sound of a laser discharging rang out in the hangar. The Lah'grex male assaulting Shea howled in pain. Releasing his grip on her, he fell backward and clutched at the large hole that had been blasted through his left thigh.

A moment later, a voice spoke, its coldness sending a shiver down Raena's spine. Although the speaker's tone appeared calm, the menace in his voice commanded immediate respect.

"I told you *not* to harm our prize. I don't care what you do with the servants, but the Galithar girl is to be well cared for. Did I not make myself clear?"

Raena saw the Lah'grex male's eyes turn pale in color, an indication of his stark terror. Following his gaze, Raena craned her neck backward to see what kind of apparition could afford such fear.

She understood the moment her own eyes caught sight of the black-robed figure.

Although Raena had never met one in person, she knew immediately by the black, red, and orange coloring of the long ribbonmane this being was one of the Ra-Nuuk. The thin strands extended out through the criss-cross pattern of cloth holding the pieces of the robe together across his back. The ribbons ran from the crown of his head to the tip of his snake-like tail. The presence of the unmistakable heartvein pulsating hot red between the cracks of his deep gray skin further confirmed her assessment. Unlike most of their Rey-Qani "cousins," the Ra-Nuuk were cruel, harsh, and evil. But as frightening as that knowledge was, what inspired so much terror was the hideous mask worn by the dark attacker.

The metallic, silver mask covered his entire face. Sculpted with high cheekbones, it had the outline of a nose, but no mouth. Streaks of white paint slithered down from the forehead to just above the eyebrows. Although they might have once been clear and prominent, the lines were now obscured by numerous cuts, scratches, and gouge marks from former battles. However, the most prominent feature was the severe damage along the entire bottom left side of the mask. The marred surface left Raena with the impression that the silvery outer "skin" had been eroded to reveal a gruesome skeletal sneer beneath.

Raena's perusal of the hideous visage was interrupted as Shea, who had been lying facedown on the floor, finally turned to look at the Ra-Nuuk leader. Raena's heart constricted in sorrow as her daughter's scream pierced the air. Reacting to Shea's fear, the masked figure turned toward her. He began to sing as he conducted a lilting pattern of three with his gloved right hand while waving his left hand hypnotically in the air in her direction. Within moments, her head drooped to the ground as she drifted off to sleep.

Raena tried to move, but even the slightest motion caused an intense throbbing in her skull. She closed her eyes and groaned in pain until it subsided. The soft but deliberate steps of the Ra-Nuuk's booted feet grew louder as they moved in her direction. She pushed back the pain in her head and opened her eyes to glare at her captor.

To her surprise, the Ra-Nuuk was crouching, his head mere inches from Raena's own. The fathomless eyes stared back at her through the metal holes of the mask. "Lady Galithar," the mercenary leader said, his voice icy. "I compliment you on your valiant effort. But unfortunately, it was wasted. Don't worry. We won't harm you or your precious children. This isn't even about you at all. Your capture is but the catalyst that will start a chain reaction; a chain reaction that will change the future of the galaxy."

As she began to lose her grip on consciousness, Raena watched through a haze as the Ra-Nuuk male stood and began calling out commands to the others. "The portal inhibitor is deactivated. Grab the son and daughter and bring them here. We leave immediately."

Seconds later, the masked figure began singing. Raena managed to roll her head to the side one last time just enough to see the forming portal. A moment later, unconsciousness claimed her.

9

THE ARRANGERS

"ETH GALITHAR, the Arrangers you summoned have arrived. They are waiting in the foyer."

Brin'tac looked up from the report he was reading and responded to the message from his home's computer. "Thank you, Enris. Tell them I'll be down in a moment."

He turned off the handheld device and glanced over at the mirror on his wife's dresser. His heart ached as he imagined her sitting there, fussing about her appearance. Instead, he saw only his own weary reflection staring back at him. He looked away from the mirror and took one more wistful glance around the bedroom as if desperately hoping to bring his family back by sheer force of will. The emptiness he felt pressed upon him, making it difficult to breathe. Setting his resolve, he took several deep breaths and corralled his wayward emotions.

No matter what, I will *rescue my family,* he promised himself. *But how do I save them from the Tritonus? They left me with no options. I have to play the role they assigned to me.*

Anything less will mean the death of everyone I hold dear. I have to see this through.

Brin'tac pushed aside his conflicted emotions, exited the room, and headed toward the foyer. He reached the top of the stairway that led down to the entrance and took a moment to study the Solemsiel couple that awaited him.

The pair stood examining the flowing rock sculpture which rested on a short pedestal in the center of the expansive foyer. Although the work of art was over six feet in height, it still only reached to the chest of the eight-foot-tall aliens.

Their exquisitely crafted clothing was typical of Solemsiel culture. The female wore a simple, but beautifully woven dress that reached to just above her ankles. The flowing garment was made primarily of yellow fabric highlighted with streaks of silver across the shoulders and around the waist. The bright colors of her dress complemented the teal tones of her skin.

Her companion wore a white shirt with a crisscross pattern over the chest, a simple pair of gray pants with gold embroidery around the cuffs, and an elegant black overcoat that came to the backs of his knees. He leaned on the windstaff held in his right pair of hands as he examined the sculpture with intensity.

Brin'tac mentally prepared himself for what lay ahead, took one last deep breath and descended the stairs toward his guests. "Master Arrangers, thank you for coming," he said as he reached the final few steps.

At his greeting, the two visitors turned away from the sculpture and offered polite bows to their host. "It is a distinct pleasure to meet you," the Solemsiel male said. His tenor voice, which was light and soothing, rose and fell as he spoke with an almost singing quality to it. As he addressed his host, he adjusted his hold on the windstaff so it rested solely in his lower right hand. Free of the staff, he and his partner simultaneously lifted their upper hands to touch the back of their heads, circled them around to the center of their foreheads, lowered them, then extended them toward Brin'tac, completing the traditional Lah'grex greeting. "My name is Roakel Balikye, and this is my bride, Saryn."

Brin'tac mirrored the greeting before responding. "And I am Brin'tac eth Galithar. Again, thank you for coming so quickly."

"And how should we address your companion? The servant who welcomed us to your home did not divulge that information."

Brin'tac followed Roakel's gaze to see a burly Lah'grex male standing in the shadows of the foyer near the hallway dressed in a black jacket and pants. Although his skin was indigo in color, it was spotted with large patches of dark gray. An exceptionally large patch stretched from the back of his head over his right eye and across a portion of his mouth before extending down his neck. His Lah'grex headcrest consisted of two rows of ridges in a "V" shape and several two-inch spikes that stuck out of the back of his head.

"Ah, my apologies. This is my chief of security and personal bodyguard, Vel'vikis Kor'nyt. I didn't realize he had joined us, or I would have introduced him sooner."

"It is our pleasure to make your acquaintance, Vel'vikis," Roakel said, once again offering the traditional greeting.

The bodyguard merely nodded in acknowledgement of the gesture.

"I hope you find the humidity acceptable," Brin'tac said cordially. "I had my home's computer lower it to more comfortable levels for your visit."

Roakel inclined his head. "That was most kind of you, but unnecessary. We have been in many Lah'grex cities recently in our efforts to bring aid to those affected by the current civil war. As such, we are quite accustomed to the increased humidity. We understand it acts as a balm to keep your skin from drying out. Our preference is that you and your staff be comfortable."

"That's most generous. Perhaps we'll split the difference."

Roakel smiled at the suggestion. "Your home is very beautiful, Noble Galithar," he said, his eyes roaming once more around the room in appreciation of the architecture. "We are particularly fascinated by this magnificent sculpture," he stated as his eyes came to rest upon the work of art that filled much of the center of the room. "If I am not mistaken, this is one of the eight *Living Spires of Ennorin* by the renowned Lah'grex musical sculptor, Gir'an Rodintel."

The sculpture consisted of three jagged spires of rock that twisted, grew, intertwined, shrank and rotated to form various shapes and patterns, as if trapped in a never-ending dance. A circular instrument consisting of numerous metal bars of incremental lengths rested beneath the moving sculpture and was built into the pedestal on which it rested. Above each bar was a mallet attached to a rod which ran around the diameter of the instrument. As the mallets struck the specific bars, they created a pleasant song that repeated every couple of minutes. The light produced by the tones of the automated instrument swirled around the sculpture, enhancing its aesthetic impact as the energy it created powered the artwork.

"You have a keen eye," Brin'tac confirmed.

"The artistry is exquisite," Saryn stated as she bent to study the pedestal in more detail. "It is interesting that Rodintel selected the metallophone as the auto. I would have surmised the belafon to be better suited to this piece. Do you not agree?"

"Perhaps," Roakel replied. "But considering he elected to use metal tips on the mallets, I imagine he wanted the specific brightness the metallic bars provide. This is but one of a series of sculptures he created. If memory serves, he used the belafon as the auto for several of the others."

"You're right," Brin'tac stated, impressed by the Solemsiel's knowledge. "There were eight sculptures in the original set, four of which used the belafon. Unfortunately, two of those were lost during the War for Lah'gre in 3615."

Saryn's expression fell. "That is indeed a shame. It is always a tragedy when magnificent art and culture are lost."

"Yes, but we beg your indulgence," Roakel said apologetically. "You no doubt invited us here to discuss more than artwork. Your message stated it was a matter of utmost importance. How may we be of service?"

"Please, I...come into the sitting room where we may be more comfortable," Brin'tac said, fighting against the lump forming in his throat. Holding out his left hand, he gestured for the two Solemsiel to enter into the house proper.

As Brin'tac led his guests down the hallway, he noticed them frowning at the sight of recent scorch marks along the walls. Their expressions darkened further once they entered the sitting room, which bore the unmistakable evidence of conflict and violence.

"Noble Galithar, what transpired here?" Roakel asked, the tone of his voice subdued.

Brin'tac motioned for his guests to sit on one of the sofas as Vel'vikis, who had followed them into the room, stood stoically to Brin'tac's left. Roakel leaned his staff against a nearby wall, then, once his wife was seated, he sat beside her. Accustomed to having visitors of various races, the Galithar's had purchased furniture that adjusted to the height and weight of its occupants.

Brin'tac, who chose to remain standing, waited until his guests were comfortable before speaking. When he did so, his voice was filled with emotion. "Two nights ago, while I was attending an important meeting, a group of mercenary scum hired by the Dumah Dynasty managed to break into my home and…and…"—his throat constricted as if the words themselves were attacking his vocal cords—"and took my wife and children!"

Saryn let out a slight gasp at the revelation and covered her mouth with her hand. Disturbed by the news, neither Solemsiel spoke for several moments. Roakel finally broke the silence. "Based on your family lineage and wealth, I would venture to guess they are seeking some sort of ransom, yes?"

Brin'tac shook his head, his eyes moist with heartache. "It's more complicated than that." *Way more complicated*, he added silently. "How much do you know about the history of the Dumah Dynasty and the Dhun'drok Rebellion?"

"We are quite familiar with Lah'grex history," Saryn replied. "After all, you must remember that we Solemsiel do not age. My husband and I have both been alive for over fourteen hundred years. We have experienced a majority of that which you call 'history'."

"Yes, of course," Brin'tac stated. "I only meant that..." He paused, unsure how to continue without offending his guests.

"You only meant that perhaps we might be unfamiliar with the specific history of the Lah'grex, since the vast majority of Solemsiel do not venture into the rest of the galaxy," Roakel finished for him.

"I apologize. I meant no offense," Brin'tac said in embarrassment.

Roakel held up a hand to assure him. "No offense taken. It is true our people can be somewhat...reclusive. But Saryn and I are Arrangers. As such, it is our calling to bring aid, comfort, and hope to those outside the Solemsiel Communion. We have lived among the Major races of the galaxies for many centuries. Be at ease and continue your tale."

Nodding, Brin'tac continued. "As you no doubt are aware, Dhun'drok is a large moon that orbits the fifth planet of the Thrar'sig System—the gas giant Dhun. It's rich in resonite and was founded by the Dumah Dynasty in the year 2422.

"However, as the number of citizens increased, they grew frustrated at being ruled from afar. The people rebelled against the queen—or reksani, as we Lah'grex call her—of the Dumah Dynasty in 5002. With the aid of several other dynasties seeking to weaken Dumah, they were eventually successful. Wanting to do away with rulership by a reks or reksani, their new leader set up a republic. As you can imagine, that didn't sit well with any of the rulers of the four dynasties."

Brin'tac picked up a small crystalline decoration from a nearby table, and absentmindedly stroked its smooth surfaces as he related the history. "Weakened, the Dumah Dynasty lacked the resources to retake the moon. Although that was over six hundred years ago, the current reksani, Srisu Dumah, attempted to retake it last year. The current president of Dhun'drok called for aid from the other planets. Despite the fact they disliked the rebellious citizens of the large moon, they also didn't want Dumah to regain those resources. Hes'groc therefore decided to send some of their forces, causing the Dumah Dynasty to retaliate."

Setting the decoration back on the table, Brin'tac turned toward the Solemsiel couple. "Hoping to remain neutral, Reks Tronsen of the Jorlinari Dynasty sent medical aid to both sides. However, whether through deliberate means or misinformation, both Dumah and Hes'groc accused Jorlinari of siding with their enemies and attacked his workers. There were other...political reasons for attacking him, of course. They were still angry at him for founding the colony on the newly discovered planet of Nur'adula over a hundred years earlier. They felt it upset the balance of power and had been looking for an excuse to attack him ever since.

"And now my tale comes full circle," Brin'tac said with a sigh. "The kidnapping of my family by the Dumah Dynasty is directly connected to the current civil war that rages within the Lah'grex Sovereignty. For as it happens, I am the cousin of Tronsen reks Jorlinari."

10

THE CALLING

ACCUSTOMED TO the fawning gazes he usually received from others when the extent of his political power and connections were revealed, Brin'tac found himself mildly unnerved at the lack of response from his guests at his statement. *Just like Lady Crisenth. I guess when you're practically immortal, you aren't as easily impressed*, he thought.

"I see now," Roakel stated, interrupting his thoughts. "The Dumah Dynasty seeks to use your family as political leverage against Jorlinari."

"Yes," Brin'tac said matter-of-factly.

"If I may ask, how did the mercenaries manage to circumvent your security system?" Saryn asked, her delicate features creased by a slight frown.

Brin'tac was about to respond but turned toward his silent bodyguard instead. "Vel'vikis, please ask Inspector Mak'sim to join us." The burly Lah'grex male withdrew a communicator from his jacket and stepped out of the room to place his call. Returning his attention to the Solemsiel couple,

Brin'tac answered her question. "According to the report from Liakrana Security Services, it appears they somehow acquired the access codes for the system and shut it down. How they received those codes is still a mystery. An investigation has already been launched. Once the system was off, it was easy enough for them to remotely disable the portal inhibitor and enter through a music portal. The security footage shows that although the rest of the scum were Lah'grex, they were led by a Ra-Nuuk music maestro wearing a silver mask who goes by the name Slag."

Roakel and Saryn both raised their eyebrows in surprise. Roakel glanced at his wife before responding. "A masked Ra-Nuuk leading a contingent of Lah'grex mercenaries? That is indeed a mystery. Noble Galithar, I know I speak on behalf of my wife when I express that you have our deepest condolences. But I must ask: why have you invited us here? Surely you know we Solemsiel are peacekeepers. We do not get involved in political conflicts, nor do we choose sides. We remain neutral so we can offer our services freely to all."

"Yes, I'm aware of the philosophical and religious beliefs of the Solemsiel culture, Master Arranger," Brin'tac replied. "And I would never ask you to go against those guiding principles."

"That is encouraging," Saryn stated with a warm smile. "But then, how may we assist you? Would it not be better to simply alert the Jorlinari military and have them find your family?"

Before Brin'tac could respond, Vel'vikis returned, followed by another Lah'grex male. The newcomer was dressed in a dark red jacket with a high collar. Several insignia and

official-looking patches adorned the military-type uniform. Though lacking the sophistication and complexity of Brin'tac's headcrest, the one adorning the inspector's head showed both strength and resolve in its design. The ridges of skin were molded into the shape of a circle within a circle.

Several other ridges with the appearance of flames spread outward from the second ring. These "flames", or spikes, extended down the back of his head and neck. In addition, portions of the skin on his chin were molded into a kind of beard two inches in length.

Vel'vikis stepped aside and took his post near the hallway, allowing the newcomer to pass him.

"We *have* contacted the Jorlinari military. However, they're stretched too thin with the current conflict and sent me to negotiate on their behalf," the Lah'grex said, picking up the thread of the conversation.

"Maestros, this is Inspector Mak'sim Zilik," Brin'tac stated. "Inspector Mak'sim, may I introduce you to Maestros Roakel and Saryn Balikye."

Mak'sim offered a slight bow of respect to the two ancient beings. "On behalf of the Jorlinari Dynasty, thank you for coming. We trust that, as is the custom of your people, you'll keep all that's discussed here in utmost confidence."

"You have our solemn promise as servants of the Great Composer," Roakel replied as he and his wife once again performed the Lah'grex greeting. "We do not bear the title of Arrangers lightly. It is a matter of honor for us that we have earned the reputation among the Major races as beings that can be trusted to speak the truth and be worthy of your confidence."

"Yes. Which is precisely why you're here," Mak'sim continued. "Just over four hours ago we received an encrypted communication from one of Reksani Srisu's advisors and using her personal transmission codes. The message stated that the Dumah Dynasty demands that eth Galithar and I meet with their representative to negotiate for the release of the Galithar family. They also demand the presence of a pair of Solemsiel Arrangers to serve as witnesses and mediators of the agreement."

"I see," Roakel said softly. "We are to be present to ensure fairness and civility."

"Precisely," Brin'tac said. "In addition, two of the music masters who pilot my ship through Stream travel were injured in the attack and are unavailable. I was also hoping that, since Solemsiel are legendary in their piloting skills, you would allow my ship to link with yours and bring us through the Stream travel together. I promise you'll be handsomely recompensed, and you'll forever have an ally and friend with the Galithar and Jorlinari families. Will you help us?" Brin'tac asked, his voice filled with emotion. "The lives of my wife and children are at stake."

As Roakel turned toward Saryn, Brin'tac studied the Solemsiel female's expression. He could see his plea was having a forceful impact on her compassionate personality. After a moment, Roakel turned his gaze back to Brin'tac. "Noble Galithar, I am sure you are aware we Solemsiel believe strongly in the Great Composer. As such, it is our custom to always seek his wisdom and advice before making important decisions. Furthermore, I have learned over the centuries that a wise husband always consults his wife before making meaningful decisions if he wants a jubilant marriage! Therefore, I must ask: do you have a private room we could utilize momentarily?"

Having expected the request, Brin'tac nodded and pointed toward a nearby doorway. "There's a study just down the hall on your right. It should serve your needs."

"Thank you," Roakel said. "We will provide you our answer shortly."

With that, the two Solemsiel rose from the sofa. Brin'tac watched as Roakel retrieved his staff before escorting his wife over to the indicated doorway and stepped into the study. Once the door was closed, Brin'tac glanced over at Mak'sim, who gave him a sideways nod.

"Well, there's nothing left to be done now but wait."

Once the door had closed behind them, Roakel faced Saryn and, together, they closed their eyes and sought the presence of their maker.

Roakel activated the windstaff, causing the pump hidden within the instrument to begin moving air into the various tubes. Placing his four hands on the numerous metallic keys, Roakel began using them to open and close the dozens of holes placed at strategic locations on the tubes. A gentle melody accompanied by simple chords emanated from the instrument.

Softly, the two Solemsiel began to sing. Having been married for over one hundred years, their voices immediately harmonized and became as one, joining the harmonic progression produced by the windstaff. Color and energy swirled around them as the musical notes permeated the still air of the study. Once the two were engulfed in a cocoon of multi-colored light, they felt the presence of another. Their pulses quickened; for here was the One who was the source of all life. In him was true harmony.

They lost all sense of time as they communed with the Great Composer. At last, as his presence dissipated, they ceased their song and once more rediscovered their surroundings. As with every other time they dwelt in his presence, Roakel and Saryn found tears running freely down their cheeks, joy flooding through their hearts, and an ache for more of him burning in their chests.

They remained in the peace and stillness of the lingering communion for several more seconds, as if drinking in the very last drops of the most refreshing drink. At last, Roakel looked intently into Saryn's eyes and sang to her using their telepathic bond. When alone, the Solemsiel couple reverted to the custom of their people by singing instead of speaking. Since other races found it irritating or annoying, they only continued the practice when others were not present.

Reservations still remain in my heart
Yet I feel we must aid this Lah'grex.
For the will of the Conductor is manifest,
His path for us flows clear.

Yes, Saryn replied, *I agree.*
Yet a sense of warning weighs on me.
Caution must be our accomplice.

Roakel nodded.
Expressions overwhelm me.
Discretions shout, "beware"
However simple the moment may appear.
Hidden currents flow beneath the surface.

Though traps may lie ahead
And snares seek to capture,
Yet still we must proceed.
For of utmost importance and
Placed before us is this need.

I feel unworthy of the calling.
May another take my place.
Yet not my will but his be done
E'r we look upon his face.

Again, I am agreed, Saryn sang, lowering her eyes briefly.
But, Heartsong, with The Maestro,
All things are conceived.
In his wisdom and guidance
Must we place our certainty.

Roakel took over the melody.
Then our way is clear.
Let us speak to the other three.
Yet Khalen, I fear,
Will not look upon it favorably.

Saryn let out a brief chuckle.

When the affairs of governments are discussed
Or the interests of politicians are involved,
There is not much of anything
To which Khalen is quite resolved.

11

KHALEN AND THE *LIGHTBRINGER*

"**THIS REEKS WORSE** than a festering mound of frolb manure!"

Roakel and Saryn were seated at the table in the common room of their ship, the *Lightbringer*. Across from them, Khalen, paced like a caged animal as he processed what he had just been told.

"I get it that you want to help this Lah'grex leader rescue his family, but...but what about the search for the ancient instruments? We're so close! We spent nine standard months tracing one of them to Gal'grea, and another three narrowing it down to Stron'zek. Now you want to leave?"

Roakel decided to remain silent as Saryn stood and walked over to Khalen, her expression filled with sympathy. "We understand your concerns. In fact, we share them. But we also trust the Great Composer. We are his instruments, and he is the Conductor. The Sacred Songbook instructs us to continue on with our present calling until such time we are presented with a new one." Drawing near to him, she looked down at the Mih'schen and placed her hand on his shoulder. "We believe finding the instruments is of vital importance. But, for the near future, we have been given a new assignment. That means any unfinished work we leave behind is in the hands of Dominuus. Do you not trust that he knows the future? Worry only demonstrates lack of confidence in his sovereignty."

Roakel watched as Khalen's eyes turn a pale red, revealing his irritation. "Yeah, yeah. I've heard it all before. But I still don't like it," the Mih'schen said. "I thought we had an understanding not to get involved in politics."

Saryn smiled as she removed her hand from his shoulder and walked back to her seat. "Yes, we know how you feel. However, a composer uses many different types of instruments to comprise his orchestra. All callings are equal. Being involved in politics is no greater or lesser than others. Those who call themselves Symphonians must be faithful to influence culture within their vocation or sphere of influence. Remember the eloquent words of the great Solemsiel teacher, Kiyapur, 'There rests not a single strand of matter in the entirety of existence over which the Great Composer does not call his own.'"

Khalen raised an eyebrow and shot her an irked look. "You sound like a schoolteacher. I know my mere sixty-two years is nothing compared to you two ancient ones, but I wasn't born yesterday either." Grabbing the chair across from them, he sat down hard. "And what about Nara and Jov? Are you just going to drag them along with you into what could turn out to be a dangerous situation? How can you be fine with that? Or are you just going to leave them here with one of the widows and abandon them like their parents did?"

"You know we would never allow that!" Saryn stated, tears forming in her eyes.

"Nara and Jov will travel with us," Roakel said. "We made an oath to complete their transition to adulthood. We would never abandon them or abrogate our promise."

"But you're getting involved in a situation that has the potential to turn volatile. What if you're attacked? Do you really want to drag Nara and Jov into a war?"

"They will remain on the ship during the negotiations," Roakel reassured. "If the worst were to occur and we never returned, the ship is programmed to take them to the nearest Solemsiel or Faluvinal embassy, where they will be cared for."

Despite Khalen's frustration, Roakel knew the heart of this warrior was in the right place. For several moments, the Solemsiel remained quiet as his thoughts dwelled upon this Mih'schen who had become his friend since the death of Riveruun.

For a race that can live as long as two hundred and fifty years, Khalen was in his prime. His toned muscles and tanned skin reflected his disciplined character. Roakel respected the man's daily routine of physical, mental, and spiritual training. Even though they had not had the need to engage in any combat since that tragic day at the Great Star Song Cathedral, the Mih'schen still insisted on keeping his skills sharp through regular practice. Roakel often wondered if the training was a part of Khalen's war-torn past he refused to release.

Khalen leaned back in his chair and roughly unbuttoned the top of his blue jacket in irritation.

"It is always possible our calling is no longer the same as your own," Roakel said at last, breaking into the momentary silence.

"What're you saying?" Khalen asked, shifting his weight to lean his forearms on the table. "Are you wanting me to leave?"

"No! Of course not!" Saryn replied immediately. "Roakel was just stating a fact. We must never assume the will of the Creator is for us to always remain in communion. You may have a divergent part to play, perhaps in a different ensemble."

Roakel leaned across the table and placed his hand on Khalen's arm. "My friend, Saryn speaks the truth. Do not read into my words that which is not there. I only suggest you pray and seek the will of the Composer. I know you commune with him differently than we Solemsiels, and you do not typically hear his audible voice. But you must nevertheless ask for his guidance. If he confirms that you are to remain in communion with us, then accept this new calling. If not, then although it would sadden us all, we must part ways so you can fulfill the work that has been entrusted to you."

Despite the truth of his words, Roakel could tell Khalen's stubbornness refused to allow him to let go of his irritation so easily. The Mih'schen male pulled his arm away, pushed his chair back from the table and stood. "You're right. Maybe it *is* time I moved on. If you won't avenge Riveruun's death by finding the rest of the ancient instruments, then I'll do it by myself." Without giving the others a chance to reply, Khalen turned and headed for the door.

Saryn began to rise from her seat but stopped as her husband gently took hold of her hand. "*Let him go,*" Roakel sang gently, before reverting to their telepathic bond.

We must remember the teachings of our instructors:

When the Major races struggle,
When strife rises to the fore,
Emotions ignite like firelight
And consume with flames of war.

Their judgment becomes impaired,
Their vision clouded.
Restraint unbounded
And their tongues wag in the air.

Only later do they regret
Words spoken in anger
In hindsight they sorrow
Over pain caused by a flippant tongue

Saryn let out a deep sigh, releasing some of the tension that had built up.

I know what you speak is true,
But it confuses my mind and heart.
How a feeling can sharpen them so?
How passions overpower their constraint?

A symphony is made of harmony,
Not to pierce a friend in haste
With words composed of calumny
That leave a bitter taste.

Who can fathom such waste?
Who can comprehend those fallen from grace?

Roakel smiled tenderly at his wife.
Deep is the well of your compassion, Heartsong.
Your love clouds your comprehension.

The anger of the fallen ones
Their shifting emotions
Tossed by the oceans
Are but one of many stones
Through which sin has twisted Creation.

Come, let us away.
In three hours' time
The Lah'grex will expect us -
And preparations must be made.

Brin'tac stood in the hangar bay that rested above his mansion — the very same hangar where his family had been taken from him. He forced himself to push the negative thoughts from his mind. He knew he would see them again, and if all went according to plan, sooner than later. Yet it could not be soon enough. Every moment apart from them was torture as his mind wandered to fears about their treatment.

Beside him, Vel'vikis stirred. "Eth Galithar, the *Lightbringer* just signaled its final approach."

Nodding, Brin'tac acknowledged his bodyguard's update. As announced, a ship came into view a moment later.

The beautifully crafted Solemsiel ship circled around the mountain peak to the east and headed toward the open hangar door built into the side of the cliff wall. The shape of the ship resembled a majestic bird. *Probably native to the Solemsiel homeworld*, Brin'tac mused as he watched it gliding on the air currents. The wings were spread wide and a little forward of the central body of the sleek, and obviously expensive ship. The coloring of the wings was a breathtaking red along the front, then progressed outward to green, light blue, and finally dark blue on the tips and rear edges. The tail of the ship, which housed the primary engine, boasted the same color scheme. The main body, which was large enough to comfortably serve as a home for half a dozen beings for an extended period, was the same color red as the front of the wings. The cockpit was housed in the protruding section that stuck out like a head from the rest of the ship.

As the craft drew nearer, Brin'tac saw it contained two additional engines hidden under the wings that could pivot to allow the ship to land vertically. The pilot of the vehicle activated those engines as it made its final approach. To Brin'tac's surprise, the wings began folding forward as if the "bird" were covering its head with the wings and bowing.

Which is likely what the "always-humble" Solemsiel designers intended, Brin'tac thought to himself. *Especially considering how the very design is anything but humble. It seems they never miss a chance to remind the rest of us of their "superiority".*

Once the vessel had come to rest inside the hangar, Brin'tac strode forward, followed closely by Inspector Mak'sim, Vel'vikis, and five other armed Lah'grex. As they approached, a platform, which was supported at the four corners, detached from the center of the ship and lowered until it touched the floor. Standing on the platform were Roakel and Saryn, both of whom once again offered the traditional Lah'grex greeting.

"Noble Galithar, it is a pleasure to see you again," Roakel said.

"And you as well, maestros. I trust the preparations for the trip to Dhun'drok have been made."

"They have."

"Excellent," Brin'tac gave a quick wave of his hand in the direction of one of the other ships in the hangar. Immediately, the Lah'grex guards headed in that direction. "My pilot is even now preparing my personal ship for flight. We'll be ready to depart shortly."

Brin'tac's guests followed his gaze. The group watched in silence as the guards walked up a ramp and entered a diamond-shaped ship. The cockpit, which rested at the apex of the ship, was in the form of a crescent. Two of the other points of the diamond formed the side wings, and the rear portion covered the engine. The entire craft was painted in shades of purple and silver.

For a moment, the two Solemsiel stared at the configuration of the ship with curiosity. Roakel's expression suddenly brightened with recognition. "Ah! Now the truth presents itself," he said. "The ship is constructed in the same shape as the Galithar family crest. My compliments to the architect. Quite ingenious."

Brin'tac was somewhat caught off guard by the other's enthusiasm. "Yes. It is."

Saryn smiled and leaned closer to Brin'tac. "Two of Roakel's favorite interests are puzzles and art. Your ship touches on both."

Brin'tac nodded in sudden understanding before switching the subject. "Yes, well...while we have a moment, I would be honored to meet your crew and thank them personally for their aid."

Roakel smiled. "And, no doubt, to scan the interior of our ship?"

"Indeed," Brin'tac agreed after the shortest pause. He forced a smile onto his face, inwardly irritated by the fact the Solemsiel exposed his true motive for wanting to visit their ship. Solemsiel had the most uncanny way of perceiving the heart of a matter.

"Be at ease, Noble Galithar. We understand it is your standard procedure. When one considers that our ships will be connected during Stream travel, it is only natural you would want to take precautions. I assure you, we have nothing to hide and would welcome the opportunity to introduce you to our crew. Welcome to the *Lightbringer*. Please step onto the lift."

The three Lah'grex males quickly complied. A moment later, the platform retracted into the ship. Once the lift came to a halt, Brin'tac found himself standing in what appeared to be the cargo hold of the ship, which was currently stocked with only a few boxes and crates. Straight ahead was a much smaller magnetic lift that led to the floor above. Unlike many Lah'grex ships which were designed with straight corners and sharp edges, the Solemsiel shipbuilders preferred smooth edges, rounded arches, and flowing designs. The vessel was as much a work of art as it was functional.

Once they were aboard, Vel'vikis removed a small probe from a holster on his belt and began taking readings as Roakel and Saryn led the group to a magnetic lift. As it rose toward the second floor, Roakel explained the basic layout of the ship. "There are three floors. As you can see, the lowest level consists primarily of the cargo hold and various storage areas. The living quarters are in the middle, and the top-level houses non-essential rooms such as the observatory, workout room, music practice rooms, and turret controls."

"Yes, I noticed the turret when you arrived," Mak'sim said. "I must admit I was a bit surprised. I thought Solemsiel were strictly non-violent."

"That is an inaccurate assessment," Roakel countered. "As the wise Faluvinal prophet Plantell penned in his *Thirty-six Treatises,* 'Even the gentle orrin of Kaelia will bear its teeth to defend its young.'"

"Of course," Mak'sim said. Beside him, Brin'tac grinned at the Solemsiel's comment.

Once they reached the middle floor, Roakel and Saryn led the small group into the main living quarters. The comfortable room was filled with a table and chairs on one side and several couches and plush recliners on the other. Eight steps on the opposite side of the room led up to what Brin'tac assumed to be the cockpit. A lone figure appeared and descended the steps toward them.

Brin'tac knew by the Mih'schen male's posture and bearing that he was a warrior. Vel'vikis and Mak'sim tensed, their hands moving almost imperceptibly closer to their weapons. While keeping his attention fixed on the newcomer, Brin'tac gestured to his companions and commanded them to stand down.

"Noble Galithar, this is Khalen Daedark," Roakel said by way of introduction.

"It's a pleasure to meet you, Mr. Daedark," Brin'tac said politely. "Or should I say, maestro? I see you wear the traditional jacket of a Mih'schen music master."

"You're good. Nothing slips past you," Khalen stated, tilting his head sideways to accent his sarcastic remark.

Brin'tac frowned at the comment. Before he could reply, a sudden warning sound from Vel'vikis's scanner blared loudly. Brin'tac turned in alarm as Vel'vikis jumped in front of him and withdrew his laser pistol. Thrown off balance, Brin'tac stumbled backward in confusion, his eyes searching for signs of danger.

Vel'vikis was pointing his weapon toward the top of the steps behind Khalen, a wary expression on his face. Brin'tac followed his gaze and spotted the source of concern.

Perched at the top of the landing were two winged reptiles, each standing nearly four-feet high on their muscular legs.

12

TESTS

STUNNED BY the sudden threat, Brin'tac could only watch as Khalen sprang into action. His right arm chopped Vel'vikis's hand, the force of the blow knocking the weapon to the floor. Khalen followed with a quick kick toward Mak'sim's hand which had begun to draw his own weapon from its holster. Again, the Mih'schen's well-timed attack sent the pistol flying out of the inspector's grip even before he could raise it.

However, Khalen seemed to have underestimated Vel'vikis's speed. Despite the Lah'grex's large size, he moved surprisingly fast. Recovering from the initial attack, the bodyguard leapt forward and wrapped his thick arms around Khalen, pinning the Mih'schen's own arms to his side. The embrace lasted only a moment. A roar from the left casued Vel'vikis to turn his head just in time to see one of the winged, reptilian beasts lunging at him. He released his hold on Khalen and raised his hands to ward off the creature's attack. The animal's momentum knocked Vel'vikis from his feet and sent him crashing to the ground on his back.

Simultaneously, the second animal landed on the deck and roared at Mak'sim, who began backing away in terror.

Sharp, staccato notes pierced the air, snapping Brin'tac out of his stupor. The reptilian beasts responded to the whistled melody and leapt over to stand in front of Khalen protectively, their slit eyes still watching the Lah'grex warily.

"They're...they're with *you?*" Brin'tac stammered, his voice cracking from the spike in adrenaline.

Khalen nodded, and then crossed over to where Vel'vikis still lay on his back. He reached out his hand to help the other, but the bodyguard pushed it aside angrily. His pride wounded, Vel'vikis rose to his feet and scowled at Khalen and his pets.

Khalen raised his hands apologetically. "I'm sorry I attacked, but I was afraid you'd accidentally shoot them. The drallmari were only defending me. They wouldn't have seriously injured you."

"I'm not convinced of that! Drallmari have a reputation as extremely vicious and aggressive!" the inspector exclaimed, his normally gray-tinged skin turning a dark shade of purple and his eyes blazing red.

Khalen flinched at the statement. "Like most creatures, the drallmari are only aggressive if they're raised that way or forced to fight for their survival."

Roakel bowed to the three Lah'grex. "My deepest apologies! The animals normally sleep during this hour of the day. I wanted you to meet my crew before I broached the subject of their presence. If I had any inkling they were awake, I would have instructed Khalen to secure them in another room."

Now that the danger had passed, Brin'tac's curiosity of the beasts replaced his fear. He marveled at the way in which the scales on their reptilian hides shimmered in the light and seemed to shift as he examined them from different angles. Their leathery wings, which were folded against their sides, produced a similar effect. The spikes running down their backs were intimidating and made the Lah'grex thankful the beasts were no longer a threat.

"Of course. I should've guessed," Brin'tac stated. "The old saying rings true. 'Where there is a Mih'schen maestro, a beast is surely nearby.' Are they tame?"

Khalen reached out and stroked the head of the nearest one. "Tame is a relative term. I trained them to be comfortable around others, so long as the others aren't a threat," he finished with a lopsided grin.

"And, that whistle you produced—is that how you speak to them?"

Khalen nodded. "Drallmari communicate through whistles and snorts. In many ways, they have their own musical language."

Brin'tac took a step forward but was brought to a halt by Vel'vikis's hand on his shoulder. "Don't, eth Galithar."

The Lah'grex ruler brushed the hand aside and ignored the warning. Although the two drallmari were still curious of the newcomers, they showed no further signs of aggression as Brin'tac drew near. As the Lah'grex reached out a hand toward their snouts, Khalen let out another brief series of whistles. The drallmari responded by touching Brin'tac's hand lightly with their two forked tongues. Before long, the beasts seemed content he was a friend.

Brin'tac smiled broadly as the animals warmed to him. "They're magnificent!"

"How did you come to own them?" Mak'sim asked. Although he had relaxed noticeably, he still remained a safe distance from the creatures.

Khalen snickered. "I wouldn't say I 'own' them. I'm more like their adopted father."

When the inspector's expression remained full of confusion, Khalen explained further. "Like many of my people, I learned how to use music to communicate with animals. During one of my travels, I came upon a wounded drallmar fighting a pack of wild volli. Although I fought off the remaining beasts, the drallmar was too wounded to survive. As it was dying, it used its whistle," he said, stroking the single protrusion on one of the animal's snout for emphasis, "to call to its children. A moment later, these two came out of a nearby cave. They looked to be less than a year old at the time."

As if the animals knew he was talking about them, the two creatures stood tall and proud with their heads held high. Khalen smiled and stroked their beak-shaped snouts fondly. "They're extremely intelligent. In fact, I'm convinced their mother used her dying breath to tell them to stay with me."

"They are beautiful animals," Brin'tac said in admiration. "I see why you reacted the way you did. I'm sure they can be quite dangerous if provoked. As such, I trust you also understand why Vel'vikis reacted the way he did."

"Sure," Khalen replied, his voice and demeanor neutral.

"I am indeed relieved no harm was done," Roakel stated. "Come, Noble Galithar. I'd like you to meet our other crew members."

"Yes, as long as there are no more extreme surprises," Brin'tac said.

"You have my word."

Roakel and Saryn led the small group deeper into the ship. Vel'vikis walked behind Brin'tac and cast a glance over his shoulder. Brin'tac saw the tension in his bodyguard's expression ease as he confirmed that Khalen had sent the drallmari away before falling into step behind the group. Roakel brought the group to a halt outside a closed door and rapped lightly on it with his knuckles.

It opened to reveal a young Tii-Koona female. Although the top of her head did not even reach Brin'tac's shoulder, he was still surprised by her height, which was unusual for her species. She wore a two-piece matching body suit that had an opening in the back to make room for her three-foot long tail. Based on the deep-violet tones of the scales covering the skin of her bare arms and face, Brin'tac guessed her ancestors were from either Varv Major or Minor, or Rovik. Yet despite the dark color, her eyes, which seemed overly large for her face, shone with a youthful exuberance and innocence.

"Hey, Roakel. Oh! These must be the visitors you told me about. It's nice to meet you. I'm Nara!" The words tumbled out of her mouth so rapidly it took the three Lah'grex a moment to process what she had said. As she spoke, her left hand toyed with her hair, which had the texture and consistency of seaweed. After a moment, she recognized she was fidgeting with it and dropped the end of her ponytail onto her right shoulder.

Brin'tac found himself both flustered by the Tii-Koona teenager and completely shocked by her presence. *She can't be much older than Shea*, he thought. *It's one thing to involve Solemsiels, but I can't drag a teenager into this.* "I...Yes, it's... nice to meet you, too," he said, his mind still preoccupied.

"Nara, this is Brin'tac *eth* Galithar," Saryn said, placing a slight emphasis on the middle word.

Nara stared blankly for a moment, her mind clearly searching for a connection. Suddenly, her already large eyes grew even larger. "Wow! I mean...I'm honored to meet...wow... So, you're like a Harmonized One of atonalism or something, right? I've never actually met one in person!"

Saryn's teal-colored skin turned a shade darker in embarrassment. "No, Nara," she interjected. "A Harmonized One has the word 'ith' between his or her name. 'Eth' refers to a high ruler, a king, or governor of a Lah'grex province."

This time it was Nara's turn to look embarrassed. "Oh! I'm...I'm so sorry, your excellency!"

Amused, Brin'tac smiled at the girl. "No harm done. It's a common mistake. It can be quite confusing for those unfamiliar with the nuances of Lah'grex culture."

"And this is Inspector Mak'sim and Noble Galithar's bodyguard, Vel'vikis," Saryn said, hoping to complete the already awkward introductions.

Nara smiled pleasantly at each of the Lah'grex before turning her attention back to Brin'tac, who was now looking at her intently.

"I must admit I'm a bit surprised," he said at last. Turning, he addressed the two Arrangers. "Masters Roakel and Saryn, I wasn't aware you had anyone underage aboard.

Surely you can't mean to bring her along on this trip. This is very irregular."

Nara frowned. Saryn opened her mouth to say something, but the diminutive Tii-Koona beat her to it. "Thanks, but… Jov and I can take care of ourselves."

Brin'tac exchanged a puzzled and somewhat alarmed glance with Mak'sim before replying. "I must protest, Master Arrangers. You must recognize there is always the possibility, although remote, that the negotiations could end badly. I don't feel it's appropriate to take this young child along."

Nara's face darkened noticeably at Brin'tac's words. She opened her mouth to protest, but this time Saryn anticipated the response and interjected before the unfiltered words spilled forth. "We have contingency plans in place in such an event."

The angry retort froze in the girl's throat. Biting her lip, Nara remained silent.

"Nara and Jov are family," Roakel said. "Where we go, they go. They will remain on the ship during the negotiations. They should be quite safe here."

Although still not happy with the others' decision, Brin'tac did not want to press the issue and instead conceded the point. He stepped forward and forced a pleasant expression onto his face as he looked down at her. "You've mentioned Jov a couple times now, but we have yet to meet him. Is he your brother?"

"No. He's my cousin."

"Where is he?" Saryn asked. "Did I not inform you that I wanted both of you to greet our guests when they arrived?"

"Yeah, but…you know how he gets sometimes. He's busy fixing one of Scamp's loose actuators. Once he gets in 'the zone' there's no getting him out of it." Nara said with a roll of her eyes.

"No need to bother him," Brin'tac said, hiding his inner turmoil. "Perhaps I can meet him another time. We really should be getting back to our ship so we can depart. Vel'vikis, Inspector, are you satisfied with the readings?"

Vel'vikis responded with a simple nod as he and Mak'sim closed their scanners.

"Very well," Brin'tac said, his irritated expression at war with his polite words. "Nara, Khalen, thank you for agreeing to come with us. I know if my wife were here, she would offer her thanks as well. My entire family owes you a debt of gratitude."

"You're welcome," Nara said, despite her own frustration.

Khalen merely nodded.

Roakel and Saryn led the three Lah'grex back to the lift and Nara returned to her quarters. When the two Arrangers returned, Khalen was waiting for them. At the sight of the Mih'schen, Roakel frowned. Although he had grown to respect the man over the past year, it was times like this that made Roakel question his choice to invite the Mih'schen to travel with him and Saryn.

"Why did you not lock Kovitch and Shosta in their pen? I informed you we were bringing the Lah'grex on board!"

Khalen sat in one of the chairs and kicked his feet onto the table. "I did it on purpose."

"You did what?" Saryn said in surprise. "But...but why?"

The man grinned mischievously and shrugged. "I wanted to see their reactions and gauge their combat expertise."

"You were testing them," Roakel stated matter-of-factly.

"Exactly. Just like you were."

"What are you implying?"

"Oh, c'mon. Don't play so naive. I know why you didn't tell Nara he was a high-ranking government official, or why you didn't tell Galithar about Nara and Jov. You did it for the same reason: you wanted to see their reactions."

Saryn looked sideways at her husband in mild surprise. "Did you truly do such a thing?"

Roakel raised an eyebrow. "Yes, I confess I did so. You can tell a great deal about a person by how they treat others unlike themselves. I wished to see if he was prejudiced. Also, those in power are often accustomed to thinking more highly of themselves. I wanted to find out how proud our Lah'grex ruler truly is. And you saw the way Nara fawned over him the moment she learned the truth. I wanted her initial reaction to be genuine.

"However, gauging one's reaction to others is a far cry from endangering lives," Roakel continued. "That was reckless, Khalen. Weapons were drawn, and you attacked the guards of a powerful Lah'grex leader. There could have been severe repercussions."

Khalen stared back at Roakel. "Listen, I took a calculated risk. I was confident no one would get hurt. And if these Lah'grex couldn't handle my little test, then I'd take that as a sign that we shouldn't be putting our necks on the line to negotiate for them. You wanted me on this trip with you, and I almost decided against it. But I'm here now, and you just have to accept the way I do things."

Saryn sighed heavily. "Of course we want you with us, but I know I speak for my husband when I express that these kinds of decisions should be made together in advance. You should have confided in us."

"That'd be fine, if I'd thought about it far enough in advance to have asked you. But I didn't."

"Very well," Roakel interjected. "As long as you know our minds on this issue. Now then, what were the results of your test?"

Khalen shrugged. "They're trained, and Mak'sim and Vel'vikis have decent reaction times. And, of course, the fact that Galithar was willing to let the incident slide and even warmed up to Kovitch and Shosta is credit to his character. How about you? What was the result of *your* test?"

"As you observed, I was impressed by his willingness to overlook the incident. He also appeared sincerely concerned for Nara and Jov's well-being."

"Yeah," Khalen harrumphed. "Almost *too* sincere."

Saryn tilted her head in disapproval. "You need to believe the best in people, Khalen."

The Mih'schen stood abruptly. "I'm all for believing the best. But when you've been through as much as I have in this life, you learn that a healthy dose of skepticism can often keep you alive. And I've told you before, as a general rule, I don't trust politicians. Don't let your desire to see good in everyone make you naive. But for now, I'm gonna go get the engines prepped." With that, Khalen bounded up the stairs toward the cockpit, leaving the Solemsiel couple to their thoughts.

13

BRIN'TAC'S REQUEST

"WE'RE APPROACHING the Stream. I'm moving us into position under the *Eternal Harmony*. Prepare for docking."

Khalen switched off the comm and studied the readouts on the console in front of him. He grabbed the piloting stick and maneuvered the *Lightbringer* under the Lah'grex ship with practiced ease. Once in position, he flipped on the automated docking computer which finished the task with computerized precision. Outside the viewport, the magnificence of the Stream stretched into the far reaches of space.

At this proximity, the enormous flow of continuous musical energy that connected every solar system in the known universe appeared as a pulsating wall of red light. In addition, the droning pitch at which it vibrated, a low C natural, could be felt more than heard as it rumbled through the resonite walls of the *Lightbringer*. Somewhere along that flow of musical energy was their destination.

"Alright, Roa. We're locked and loaded," Khalen said into

the commlink. "We're heading in. Prepare your song, Old One."

A heavy sigh came through Khalen's earpiece followed by Roakel's reply. "I'm assuming that since you have ignored my request the first dozen times, it does no good asking you once again not to call me that."

Khalen smiled mischievously. "I don't ever remember you asking me not to call you 'Old One.'"

"That is not...My name is Roakel, not Roa."

"Right. I'll keep that in mind. Anyway, *Roakel*, we're entering the Stream. You and Saryn can take it away!"

Almost immediately, Khalen felt his chair begin to vibrate as the first waves of sound were produced. Although he had taken his fair number of trips sitting in the maestro's chair, he was thankful to not be saddled with that task this time around.

Most races required three musicians working together to play the trio of instruments in the Studio, which was located in the heart of each ship. However, due to their extra hands and extreme talent in music, a single Solemsiel could accomplish the same task. Two could do it with ease.

In essence, each ship was one large instrument made of resonite. The clarichord, Solemsiel variation of the bindara, and rikka drums in the Studio were attached by cables to the hull. The energy created by the music was transferred through the cables to the specialized metal, causing it to hum and vibrate.

It took several minutes before enough energy was created to proceed due to the sizes of the two interconnected ships. Immersed in the reddish glow of the Stream, Khalen heard the texture of the Solemsiels' song thicken and rise in volume until the vessels' vibrations matched the frequency of the nearest note in the overtone series. Once aligned, the ships rapidly increased their speed and flowed along with the Stream, guided only by the song.

During each journey, the maestro, or maestros piloting the ship, had to adjust the music at every juncture along the way. Due to the enormous distances between star systems, this afforded them several long respites typically lasting an hour or more. However, if they failed to alter their song at the right moment, they would continue along the Prime Stream indefinitely, sending them light-years off course, or even into other uncharted regions of space. Overall, it could be an exhausting venture, and one Khalen would rather not be responsible for.

Resting on the floor of the cockpit, Kovitch let out a series of staccato whistles, accompanied by a low rumble in his throat. Khalen glanced down at him in amused surprise. "Hungry already? Didn't I just feed you two hours ago?"

The reptilian creature sat up and placed one of his claws on the armrest of the piloting chair, his tongue flicking in and out of his mouth rapidly. Not to be outdone by her sibling, Shosta roused herself and crossed over to sit next to him, her own gaze expectant.

Khalen threw his head back in defeat. "Fine! You two have insatiable appetites. C'mon."

Climbing out of his chair, Khalen exited the cockpit, walked down the steps, and headed toward the kitchen with the two drallmari in hot pursuit. He withdrew two food pouches from the freezer, ripped them open, and emptied the contents into nearby feeding bowls. The reptilian beasts devoured the fish filets, the frozen consistency of the meat barely slowing them down.

"What a couple of frolbs! And you two are gonna be as fat

as those little buggers if you keep eating like that."

Khalen threw a slight smile in Nara's direction as she entered the kitchen and patted the hindquarters of each of the drallmari. Focused on their meal, the two reptiles paid her no attention.

Crossing over to where Khalen stood by the refrigerator, she used her shoulder to shove him out of the way. With a smirk, she opened the door and stared at the contents in search of a snack.

"You better watch it," Khalen said in mock anger. "Shove me again and see what happens."

Without even shifting her eyes away from their ever-important-task of locating food, she let out a chuckle. "What'ya gonna do, big shot? You couldn't take me down if I had one hand tied behind my back."

Khalen let out an obnoxious guffaw. "Ha! I think you got that scenario backward, you overconfident little kriplin. Perhaps it's time the teacher put the student in her place. You're getting good at hand-to-hand combat, but you've got a long way to go before you can beat me."

Snatching a piece of fruit from the fridge, Nara shoved it into her mouth and turned to face Khalen. "Maybe not. But I've been getting in enough hits lately to make you suffer a little, right?" she asked through a mouthful of food.

Khalen was about to respond when his comm chirped. He frowned as he glanced at the I.D. display. "What does he want?" Khalen mumbled aloud.

"Who is it?" Nara said, her interest piqued.

Instead of answering her question, he flicked on the commlink. "Yes, Galithar. What do you want?"

"Please, call me Brin'tac. It'll be a long two-day journey

indeed if we continue on with formalities."

Nara rolled her eyes at the sound of the Lah'grex's voice and shoved another piece of fruit into her mouth as she listened. Khalen smiled at the teen's response. Yet at the same time, he was surprised the rich politician had ignored his rudeness and lack of title use, especially given what Khalen had dredged up about him from the hyperlink feeds. It seemed out of character for him not to remind 'lesser-folk' of his obvious superiority. "Okay. So what can I do for you?"

"I was wondering if…well, since we have some time on our hands, I was hoping to get better acquainted. In fact, I have a request."

Khalen raised one eyebrow toward Nara, whose own expression was filled with shock. "What kind of request?"

"If you don't mind, I'd like to discuss it with you in person."

Khalen paused. *Great. The last thing I want to do is entertain a stuck-up, wealthy know-it-all.* "Actually, I was…just getting ready to teach Nara a thing or two," he said as he glanced over at her snidely.

"So you're used to being a teacher. Excellent," Brin'tac replied. "That's exactly why I was contacting you."

Khalen's expression shifted to one of confusion. "Really? What's that supposed to mean?"

"Again, I'd rather explain in person."

"Well, I have to admit you've got my attention," Khalen said as he exchanged a curious glance with Nara. "Let me know when you want to stop by."

"Please contact me when you're finished with Nara's lesson."

"Actually, I think I'll put that on hold for the moment," he said with a wink toward Nara. She replied with a sarcastic grimace. Khalen ignored her and continued. "You can come on over now if you want, as long as you don't mind Nara tagging along."

"That would be appreciated, but I don't want to impose."

Khalen muted the comm. "Too late for that," he said to Nara, causing her to snicker loudly. He turned the comm back on. "I'll head over to open the connecting hatchway. See you in a moment."

Shutting down the comm channel, he washed his hands as Nara shot him a quizzical look. "That was weird. So, what'ya think 'ol boy wants?"

Khalen shrugged. "Who knows? But we're about to find out. Are you going to stick around to help me welcome him?"

"I don't know," Nara said, her voice oozing sarcasm. "It's getting close to bedtime for this 'young child', don't ya think?"

Khalen laughed. "I do! Especially since you've been talking back to your elders and pushing them around."

"Maybe if you weren't so easy to push around, I wouldn't do it so much."

Khalen smacked her playfully on the back of her head. "C'mon, troublemaker. Let's go see what he wants." The two of them left the kitchen, leaving the drallmari to lick their bowls clean.

As they strode toward the hatch, he opened a channel to the rest of the ship. "Hey, gang. Just a heads up: 'his high-and-mightiness' is coming over. He's got some kind of request to make."

"I'm just finishing helping Roakel with the Stream juncture calculations. I can be there in about ten minutes," Saryn replied.

"I wouldn't worry about it. I don't think he was expecting to talk to everyone. And if I'm wrong, I'll contact you. Besides, I got Nara with me to keep me in line."

"Right. And who's going to keep *her* in line?"

"We'll be good, Aunt Saryn," Nara said into Khalen's comm. "We promise."

"I trust you will. Khalen, please attempt to show him grace and respect."

"Of course." Khalen shut off the comm and glanced sideways at Nara. "Don't I always?" She replied with a roll of her eyes as they drew near the hatch. Khalen paused, then took a deep breath in the hopes it would help him remain patient as he was forced to interact with one of the most despised beings in the universe: a politician.

"Eth Galithar, I must state one last time that I believe this is a mistake."

Brin'tac studied the dark patch of gray skin that covered the right eye of his chief of security as he waited for the hatch between the ships to open. He felt his irritation rise at Vel'vikis's statement. "You made that abundantly clear the first three times you said it. And if you value your job, you'd be wise to remember that *you* work for *me!*"

Vel'vikis inclined his head in deference. "Of course, eth Galithar. It's just, I don't trust Mih'schen. Most are too similar to their vile Meh'ishto kin. And, if I may be so bold, I'm also aware of the circumstances surrounding my predecessor's fate. It is my highest priority to make sure you are safe."

Brin'tac felt the corner of his lip curl in amusement. "This is nothing like what happened to that fool. Besides, I'm confident Mr. Daedark and his pets won't cause any problems for us. These Arrangers are quite reputable, and they vouch for him. Besides, it's my *job* to be able to read people. Khalen is like his beasts—dangerous, but only if provoked. Yet, he's hiding something. I want to get to know him better, just as he clearly wanted to get to know us with that little 'test' of his. Surely you didn't think it was coincidence that the drall-mari showed up?"

"No, sir. Of course not."

"Then remember your place and accept that I have my reasons for requesting this meeting. I know what I'm doing," Brin'tac stated harshly. The end of his sentence was lost in the sound of the airlock pressurizing. "Now do what you're told."

Vel'vikis opened the hatch inside the *Eternal Harmony* and extended the ladder from the opening to the deck of the *Lightbringer*. The moment the ladder was secure, the bodyguard grabbed the top rung and started down. Once he was through, Brin'tac followed. As he entered the ship, he noticed that Khalen and Nara were standing several feet to the right near a console. Reaching the bottom, Brin'tac stepped off the ladder and adjusted his fine overcoat as Vel'vikis bent over and lifted the bottom rung, causing the ladder to retract. The moment the hatch was clear, Khalen pressed a button on the nearby console, sealing the hatch.

"Welcome aboard."

"Thank you, Khalen," Brin'tac said cordially. "Hello, Nara. I hope you don't mind, but, as always, Vel'vikis insisted on coming along."

Khalen threw a quick glance in Vel'vikis's direction and shrugged. "Bodyguards tend to do that. So what's this request of yours?"

Brin'tac felt his irritation increase at the man's lack of

etiquette at not inviting him to sit, offering him refreshments, and dispensing with small talk. "Well, all my life I've focused my attention on politics, philosophy, and theology," he began, putting on a well-practiced smile, "I never had much time to learn about music. Raena, my wife, is a maestra, and my daughter, Shea, is studying to be one as well. I've always found the world of music to be…mysterious. I was wondering if—since we have some time on our hands— would you perhaps be willing to teach me some of the basics? In a way, I see it as a means of connecting with my wife and daughter. I'm also hoping it'll help to keep my mind off what lies ahead."

"What do you want to know? Are you wanting to learn to sing well, play an instrument, or something deeper?"

"I'd like to learn how to use music to do what my wife does: to create and shape rock! I want to use it to both attack and defend myself. Yes, my tutors taught me the basics of self-defense, and I was trained to use a pistol years ago, but I want to do more."

Brin'tac studied the man's expression, which seemed to reflect both disinterest and mild admiration. "You're asking the wrong maestro," Khalen replied after a moment. "You should talk to Roakel and Saryn. They'd be able to help you better than I."

"That may be true, but—if I may be blunt—I find it…a little hard to connect with them," Brin'tac stated uncomfortably. "I mean no disrespect. It's just that…Solemsiels often seem aloof. Perhaps it's because they're so ancient. Or maybe it's their extreme and rigid moral stances on issues. It's hard to relate to them, if that makes sense."

Nara snickered. "Try living with them on a regular basis."

Brin'tac relaxed at her jest. "I'm glad you understand. I also believe you'd be better suited to explaining music to me in a way I can grasp."

"Fair enough," Khalen said. "But I hope you realize it takes years of training to be able to perform the more complex songs that will allow you to manipulate the energy. There are at least five basic skills you have to master just to shape rock. You have to play or sing the right chords in the right progression, with the right rhythm, with the correct melody, sung using the right solfege syllables, all while conducting the correct pattern with your right hand and directing the energy with the left. You can't learn it overnight."

Brin'tac smiled. "Yes, I understand. I know I may look older, but I'm actually less than a century old. I hope to have at least another hundred years to learn about music. There's no time like the present to begin."

Khalen shook his head, his expression shifting. "I'm sorry, but I'm not interested."

Out of the corner of his eye, Brin'tac saw Vel'vikis frown and stiffen at the refusal. But to his credit, the bodyguard remained silent.

Brin'tac had been prepared for the possibility of such a response and feigned confusion. "You haven't even given me a chance to explain my offer. I would never expect such a service for free. I'm prepared to provide compensation, of course."

"Look, Galithar, I'd love to help you, but I've got too many other things that require my attention," Khalen said. Nara tried to cover her snicker at the comment but was unsuccessful.

Brin'tac remained silent as he considered Khalen's refusal. Lost in thought, he absentmindedly used his right hand to massage the skin on the back of his left arm. Although he had applied a thin layer of oleera cream to keep his skin moist to compensate for the lower humidity on the *Lightbringer,* he still felt his skin beginning to itch.

"While I have no doubt that is true," he stated with a knowing glance in Nara's direction, "surely you could make an exception for the right price," Brin'tac replied. "After all, it shouldn't take more than an hour for a lesson. And please, call me Brin'tac."

Khalen grimaced. The Lah'grex ruler recognized the expression of one who did not want to do something but was trapped by both responsibility and by Brin'tac's political station. After a moment, the music maestro finally spoke. "I'm not a very good teacher. Besides, with your education, I'm sure you know that Lah'grex have their own style and tonal center. You should really find a teacher from your own race."

Vel'vikis grunted softly. Brin'tac glared at him briefly before returning his gaze to Khalen. "I do understand that," he said, forcing politeness into his tone. "But since we had to leave Gal'grea so quickly, and my normal crew of maestros were unavailable on short notice, I have no other options. Khalen, I am facing a foe who knows how to manipulate music. It's time I quit putting this off. I need to understand this discipline from the perspective of one who can control it. I can't wait any longer."

"Well, you've come to the right place," Nara interjected. "Don't listen to Uncle Khalen. He's a great teacher. He not only knows about music, but also about fighting. He's teaching me a thing or two about defending myself. He complains all the time about not having anyone to spar with, so I volunteered to—wait a second! I've got an idea! What about a trade?"

Khalen, Brin'tac, and Vel'vikis all studied the teen with

confused expressions on their faces. "What are you babbling about?" Khalen asked, clearly not liking the tone in her voice.

"Well, you're always saying you miss training with someone at your level, right?" Nara asked as she pushed a loose strand of her seaweed-textured hair out of her face. "Now you've got one!" she finished, pointing at Vel'vikis enthusiastically.

For the first time in the conversation, Brin'tac was genuinely surprised. Based on the expression on Khalen's face, he was caught off guard as well. After a brief moment, the Mih'schen man looked over at Vel'vikis, a sly smile creasing his features. "I *am* a little rusty. And it would be nice to face a *real* opponent for once," he said sarcastically toward Nara.

Brin'tac felt his hopes rise as Khalen turned to face him.

"Fine. I agree. I'll give you a lesson in music in exchange for a sparring match with Vel'vikis."

14

SPARRING

KHALEN WATCHED IN AMUSEMENT as Brin'tac's expression shifted to one of agreement and excitement. "Of course! He would be glad to oblige." Based on the look on the bodyguard's face, Khalen could tell Vel'vikis did not agree with that statement. But, as expected, he bowed his head to his superior and forced a smile.

"As you wish, eth Galithar." Vel'vikis's gaze hardened as he turned to address Khalen. "When do we begin?"

Flashing the other a smug look, Khalen tilted his head to the left. "No time like the present. Follow me." Leading the way, Khalen and Nara led the two Lah'grex down the short hallway to a door located at the end. It slid open as they approached, and he strode confidently inside.

The rectangular room contained an assortment of workout equipment fastened to the walls. The floor was cushioned and open, allowing just enough space to move freely without fear of hitting the equipment.

"Brin'tac, the room wasn't designed for spectators," Khalen said as his opponent removed his jacket and began to stretch, "so it would probably be safest if you and Nara watched from one of the corners."

The Lah'grex politician agreed and moved to the one located behind Vel'vikis's left side while Nara took position behind Khalen as he began to stretch.

"So, what's the goal of this little exercise?" Vel'vikis asked with a clear edge to his voice. "And what rules are we using? I don't want to injure you, but you should know I won't hesitate to respond with the same force with which I'm met."

"I should hope so, otherwise it wouldn't be any fun," Khalen replied. He felt the blood pumping through his veins as the excitement of the coming match filled him. "I merely want to refresh my skills. We can use speed, but pull your punches and no head shots. After a few rounds, perhaps you can teach me a new trick or two."

Khalen smiled inwardly as Vel'vikis's expression relaxed from the compliment. *More than likely, I'll be the one teaching you,* Khalen thought as he moved into his fighting stance. His Lah'grex opponent did the same. A moment later, Vel'vikis launched his attack.

The Lah'grex bodyguard quickly closed the distance between them and led with a combination of kicks and punches. Khalen felt his old fighting reflexes take control, blocking each attack as he studied his opponent's moves. In a matter of seconds, he recognized the fighting style and came up with an effective counterstrike. With a flurry of movement, Khalen pushed forward and forced Vel'vikis to retreat in order to evade his attack. However, just as he was beginning to feel his confidence building, his opponent dropped to the ground and swept his leg out, tripping Khalen.

Behind him, he heard Nara let out a soft groan of sympathy as he hit the mat.

"You've got excellent form and technique, but you dropped your guard," Vel'vikis said as he stepped back to allow him time to recover.

Furious at his failure, Khalen leapt to his feet and returned to his starting position. "Yeah. Like I said, I'm a little out of practice. It won't happen again. Trust me."

This time, Khalen initiated the attack, using one of the fighting forms he had learned years earlier. His frustration grew as Vel'vikis was obviously familiar with the form and countered every kick, punch, and chop. Realizing his mistake, Khalen prepared to launch into a different style of attack but was forced to retreat as his opponent went on the offensive.

For the next thirty minutes, the two continued to spar as Brin'tac and Nara looked on, the teen offering cheers of support periodically. Although it took him longer than expected to regain his fighting edge, by the end of their time, he was winning a majority of the matches.

"Well done, Master Khalen," Brin'tac stated once they had finished. "I must tell you, I hired Vel'vikis because, in addition to his brilliant tactical mind, he was also one of the best fighters in the province. Yet you managed to hold your own against him, and even best him from time to time."

"Yes, I agree," Vel'vikis said as he bent over to retrieve his discarded jacket. "Tell me, where did you learn to fight? I'm familiar with most of the popular combat techniques used by the Major races. Yet once in a while, you surprised me with a move I haven't seen before."

Khalen shrugged as he wiped sweat from his brow with a towel extracted from a nearby drawer. "I've had numerous teachers from all over. I picked up some things from the hololink and from various opponents, like yourself."

The Lah'grex bodyguard was clearly not satisfied with his answer. "But warriors don't become this good at fighting unless they started young. Did your father train you?"

A long-buried memory rose in Khalen's mind, bringing with it a rush of emotion. "Yeah, he did," Khalen paused before continuing flatly, "until he was murdered."

Nara gasped aloud, and the two Lah'grex exchanged surprised glances at the revelation. Brin'tac was the first to respond. "What happened?"

Khalen looked at the guests for a moment, then turned away and threw his towel into a receptacle before turning back to face them. When he did, he saw Nara wiping a stray tear from her eye. "It was long ago, and...just forget I brought it up."

Brin'tac nodded in understanding. "Very well. We respect your privacy."

Khalen crossed his arms and changed the subject, annoyed at himself for dropping his guard. "What about you, Brin'tac? How much combat training do you have?"

"Some. I know how to handle a weapon, and I've learned the fundamentals of hand-to-hand combat. My lessons were primarily focused on self-defense, though." As he spoke, Khalen noticed the Lah'grex glancing toward Nara, obviously concerned about her emotional state. To her credit, she caught sight of his perusal and offered a slight smile of reassurance.

"So can you show me some basic fighting stances?" Khalen asked.

"What for?" Vel'vikis interjected, his posture suddenly wary.

"Relax," Khalen replied coolly. "I'm not planning on fighting him, if that's what you're worried about. But I want to see something."

Brin'tac held up a hand toward his bodyguard. "It's all right. I'm sure Khalen has his reasons. Very well." Standing straight, the Lah'grex noble took a deep breath to prepare himself. After a moment, he took a step back with his right leg, settled into a slight crouch, and brought his arms near his sides in a defensive posture.

"Okay. Now show me a punch."

Although his brow furrowed momentarily in confusion, Brin'tac complied and thrust his right arm forward.

"Can you do it again, but this time put more energy into it and yell as the energy is released."

Again, the Lah'grex ruler complied, much to the consternation of his bodyguard. This time, as he punched, Brin'tac accompanied it with a forceful yell.

"Good. That's what I was looking for."

"And what exactly would that be?" Vel'vikis asked as Brin'tac returned to his normal stance.

"Brin'tac, you want me to teach you music," Khalen said, taking a step closer to him. "But music requires physical energy to produce strong tones from your vocal cords. It has to come from your gut, much like that powerful yell. I need you to keep the strength you just felt in mind as you sing. Performing music requires a focus and forcefulness nearly equal to that of physical combat."

"Yes," Brin'tac nodded and smiled. "I see the connection."

Khalen chuckled. "I doubt it, but you will. Time to uphold my end of the trade. Follow me."

15

THE LESSON

NARA FELL INTO STEP next to Khalen as the small group exited the room. As they walked down the short hall to the door leading into the music practice room, Nara leaned close to him. "I had no idea your father was murdered," she whispered. "Why didn't you tell me?"

Khalen kept his gaze fixed on their destination as he responded. "Nara, you and Jov have become like family to me over the past nine months. But there's still a lot about me you don't know. And honestly, I'm not sure I ever want you to know it. I buried my past for a reason, and I'd prefer to leave it that way. Forget I mentioned it."

To emphasize his point, he turned his attention to his Lah'grex guests as they reached the door. "This is our practice room. Vel'vikis, you and Nara can sit over there," he said, indicating a small couch and a chair on the right side of the room near the old, but still functional clarichord. Khalen headed over to the instrument and stood in front of the small, padded bench. Turning around, he gestured for Brin'tac to face him.

"In order to know where to start, I need to figure out how much you already know," Khalen said.

A thoughtful expression came over Brin'tac. In the silence that followed, Khalen noticed the politician was once more using his right hand to massage the skin on the back of his left arm.

"I know that at a fundamental level, music creates colored light and energy related to the pitches and rhythms used," Brin'tac said. "The standard keyboard contains seven different white keys and five black keys for a total of twelve different pitches and their corresponding colors. The black keys are in alternating groups of twos and threes. Also, there are no black keys between the pitches B and C or between E and F. The patterns of the keys repeat several times."

"Right. Every octave has the same pattern."

"Octave? That refers to eight of the white keys, correct?"

"More or less," Khalen confirmed. "It's a bit more technical than that, but for now, that definition will work. If you start on the low C and count eight keys up to the next C, that's considered an octave. What about the colors of each?"

"Well, the seven basic pitches correspond to the seven colors of the rainbow. My tutors drilled that much into me. C is red; D is orange; E is yellow; F would be green…G blue; A indigo; and B violet. The five black keys are shades of the primary colors. And solfege is what you call the vocal syllables assigned to each note: Do, Re, Mi, Fa, So, La, Ti, and Do starts the pattern over again. That completes the octave, right?"

"Right. But head knowledge will only take you so far. I want you to sing the major scale."

Khalen felt a small dose of twisted satisfaction at the sight of the uncomfortable politician. He guessed his 'student' was feeling self-conscious, especially with Nara watching. "Now, take a deep breath. But make sure you don't raise your shoulders. Breathe from your diaphragm. If you do it right, your stomach should rise slightly. There you go. Now use the solfege syllables and sing each pitch slowly, matching the pitch I'm singing."

Together the two of them sang the notes in succession. As they did so, the air in the small room crackled with energy and the color of each pitch appeared as swirling tendrils of light.

"Not bad. At least you can match pitch. That's *slightly* important," Khalen said once they had finished. "Now, what do you know about chords?"

"That's when you sing or play three notes, using every other note. There's another name for it I can't quite remember. A tri-chord or something."

Khalen winced. "That's a bit of an oversimplification, but it's pretty close. Technically, a chord is two or more notes played at the same time. But for our purposes, we're talking about triads. Nara, play a C major chord for us."

The teen, no doubt happy to have something to do, moved over to sit at the bench of the clarichord and played the notes.

"Now, let's see how you do with splitting your vocal chords."

Breathing deeply, Khalen began to sing the note C until Brin'tac matched the pitch. As the Lah'grex continued singing, Khalen split his voice so that while the C continued, the note E was also produced. After a few off-key attempts, Brin'tac finally managed to sing both pitches. With those notes in place, Khalen split his voice again to sing the third note, G. Brin'tac struggled to get it to sound without affecting the previous two. Finally, after nearly a minute of effort, he succeeded.

"Not bad," Nara said as they finished singing. "You figured it out way faster than I did."

Brin'tac breathed deeply, somewhat drained by the effort. "Thank you, Nara. That was quite the challenge. I hope there aren't too many different chords."

Khalen let out a full-throated laugh. "Ha! That's the first and most basic chord there is! There are hundreds, maybe *thousands* of different chords. In fact, it's the changing progression of the various chords that truly forms the backbone of all musical pieces. Let's try a few more."

For the next twenty minutes, Khalen sang each of the seven basic chords in the C major scale and had Brin'tac repeat them note-by-note. Finally, the music master called a halt. "With those seven chords, you can sing a whole slew of pieces. In fact, most popular tunes that are being written and performed today use only the first, fourth, fifth, and sixth chords in various progressions."

Nara let out a chuckle. "No kidding. You could go through most of my playlists and not find any other chords but those four."

Brin'tac's expression brightened. "That sounds easy enough."

Khalen cast him a lopsided grin. "Don't get too excited. That's popular music, not the musical sciences. They're *way* more intricate. The seven chords we sang through are just the beginning. We haven't even touched on the various musical styles and scales preferred by each race."

"Yes. I've heard that before. Each uses a specific pitch center, right?"

"Tonal center," Khalen corrected. "Each style is made of specific rhythms, instrumentation, melodic patterns, etc. And, as you mentioned, every one of the two Perfect races, four Major races, and even the five Minor cultures, tend to write their music based on a specific tonal center in order to manipulate the energy properly."

Brin'tac held up a hand. "Each tonal center is based on the location of the races' territories within the Twin Galaxies, correct?"

Khalen nodded. "It all correlates together. For example, the Rey-Qani use a tonal center based on the interval of the major second, or the pitch D. Their name is derived from the solfege Re. Their skin tends to be shades of orange, and their territory lies closest to the center of the Dominuus Prime galaxy. The Mih'schen Expanse neighbors the Rey-Qani Enclave, followed in succession by the Faluvinal, the Solemsiel, the Lah'grex and the Tii-Koona, just like the white keys of the clarichord."

"While the territories of the Minor races—the Ra-Nuuk, Meh'ishto, Fiihkren/Seyvreen, Ley'cryst and Tey-Rakil—are in the position of the black keys," Brin'tac said, completing the analogy.

Khalen's expression darkened for a moment at the mention of the Meh'ishto and the color of his eyes dimmed slightly. A part of him wanted to correct the politician for using the term 'races' to refer to the Minor cultures, but he decided it was not worth the effort. Brin'tac appeared not to notice the shift in Khalen's demeanor. Instead, the Lah'grex sat in the chair Nara had vacated, his expression becoming pensive. "It makes one wonder which came first: the borkrin or the egg?"

Khalen raised an eyebrow. "Careful. Now you're wading into theological and philosophical waters."

"Come, now," Brin'tac replied with a grin. "You don't strike me as the type to shy away from a little philosophy."

"Trust me, he's not!" Nara interjected. "But if you go there with him, you might wish you hadn't!"

Brin'tac smiled. "Ah, but my father used to say the wise person recognizes that although most don't like to discuss politics and religion, they are the two most important topics in life. One gives you a foundation for how you view the world; the other helps you shape that world based on those beliefs. I know you consider yourself to be a Symphonian, but tell me, have you ever considered the beauty of the Path to Enlightenment found in the teachings contained in the Holy Score of Osmoni?"

"Uh oh. Don't say I didn't warn you," Nara said lightheartedly.

Khalen nudged her with his elbow. "Pay her no mind. Anyway, yes, I'm familiar with them. They contain many noble sentiments I agree with."

"You should meditate on them," Brin'tac stated as he closed his eyes momentarily. "They bring so much peace to one's life."

When Khalen failed to respond, Brin'tac looked over at him. "What's wrong? You seem troubled. Please, say what's on your mind, no matter what. I won't be offended."

"I've seen this type of situation play out too many times before, and it doesn't usually end well," Khalen answered. "Are you sure you want my answer? In my experience, too many are ruled by their feelings instead of logic. When someone says something they don't agree with, their feelings flare up, and they get offended. I've even seen people get so upset they either verbally or physically attack the other person."

"I can assure you, I will *not* take offense," Brin'tac replied. "In fact, you should know that I *long* for civil discourse. Most of those I converse with either don't see the value in the discussion or lack the intellectual capacity or are from a lower caste." He threw a quick glance at Vel'vikis, who remained silent and still as a statue. "It's quite nauseating. I assure you, I abhor those who 'think' with their feelings," Brin'tac finished.

"Fine," Khalen said hesitantly, troubled at the other's obvious slight against Vel'vikis. "If you want a straightforward answer, I'll give you one. Tell me: does the Path to Enlightenment bring you comfort now, with your family taken?"

A flash of pain flickered in Brin'tac's expression, but he managed to rein it in quickly. Taking a deep breath, he let it out before speaking. "I'll admit, my daily meditations are not bringing the peace they once did. Perhaps I've become too attached to the things of the universe, including my family."

"Attachment to family is a good thing," Khalen stated. "I ask because I grew up under an oppressive system of rules and laws. They're cold and impersonal and leave you empty. I've found a whole lot more comfort knowing the Composer is in control of my life, and I've learned that even much of the negative garbage in life can serve a positive purpose. I'd much rather serve a personal God than some cold, all-powerful force or mystical energy field that is neither good nor evil and doesn't care whether I live or die."

"Well, that may be true for you, but it isn't true for everyone."

"I used to say the same thing, but my mentor challenged me on that," Khalen replied.

"How so?"

"Riveruun said that if something isn't true for everyone, then it isn't really true at all, but rather an opinion. Truth, by definition, is 'that which matches reality'," Khalen said, getting drawn into the conversation despite his previous reservations. "Religion isn't just academic. Every belief system makes truth claims about the universe. They make claims about reality, about the way things really are. He often said that two beliefs that make contradictory statements can't both be true. For example, either there really is a being who created the universe, or there isn't."

"Hm...an intriguing concept. My instructors always insisted there were many paths to understanding the ultimate reality of the universe. Each religion is one path to that truth."

"But if that's the case," Khalen pressed, "then what's 'true' is that all religions are false in their primary beliefs and only contain small elements of what is ultimate reality. Any time you make a truth claim, you're being exclusive. All religions do that, not just Symphonians."

"Give me an example," Brin'tac said eagerly. Nara, on the other hand, seemed to have lost interest in the discussion. The teen had taken out her digital scroll and was staring at the screen.

Khalen remained silent for a moment as his memory searched for one of Riveruun's illustrations. "Okay, what about the meaning of life. From an evolutionary perspective, all life in the universe came about by unguided, random chance, right?"

"That's the prevailing scientific view, yes."

"I think there are strong scientific reasons why evolution doesn't work, but I'll save that discussion for another time. But assuming it's true, then life itself is an accident. There's no overarching purpose. We're just insignificant specks in a cold, meaningless universe. Life, therefore, is cheap. But if there really is an all-powerful, ever-present, intelligent, personal being who created us all, then he determines our purpose. He created each of us for a special reason.

"Do you see?" Khalen said, pressing his point. "They can't *both* be true. Either there *is* a creator, or there isn't. And if there's a creator—a Great Composer—then he gives value to *all* beings, even those from the Minor cultures like the Meh'ishto and Ley'cryst. We're his instruments. He made us for a purpose. No being is of more value than any other, no matter how frail, small, or infirm."

"I've heard this argument before, and I'll admit it's an extremely powerful sentiment. However, I can't accept that those that do such vile things—like the Ra-Nuuk that stole my family—have the same value," Brin'tac stated, his expression turning dark. "Some people are born to a higher caste because of their good deeds performed in a previous life. Others, like the Minor races, are obviously paying for their misdeeds. To use your analogy: if we're all instruments, then we damaged ourselves and as a result produce an inferior tone quality. We have to suffer in order to repair the damage. Only then can we create beautiful music."

Khalen took a deep breath in order to remain calm. "One of my favorite verses contained in the Sacred Songbook says, 'The Composer uses the weak instruments to play the solo, while the strong accompany. He confounds the wise by placing the spotlight on the innocent and humble.'"

A sudden warbling wail filled the air, halting the conversation. It was clearly the sound of someone singing, but it was so off key, Brin'tac grimaced noticably. "What...what's that?"

Nara smiled and rejoined the conversation. "That is the most beautiful sound in the universe."

Brin'tac looked at her strangely, as if trying to figure out whether or not the Tii-koona teen was making a joke at his expense. When he realized she was serious, he frowned. "I don't understand."

"C'mon," Khalen said as he stood. "I think it's time you meet our final crew member."

Nara jumped to her feet as well. "I've gotta see this."

Still confused by the previous comment, Brin'tac rose and followed Khalen and Nara down the corridor. As always, Vel'vikis fell into step behind them. As they drew closer to the source of the off-key singing, Brin'tac spoke to Nara. "So this is your cousin—Jov, if memory serves. But...help me understand. Why would you say his singing is the most beautiful sound? It's rather...unnerving to listen to."

Khalen brought the small group to a halt just outside the door to Jov's room. "Because what you hear is pure worship. He's singing praises to the Great Composer," he said, answering for Nara.

"But if there was such a supernatural being, wouldn't he expect his followers to learn to sing properly? Wouldn't he expect the best from them?"

Nara smiled again. "This *is* Jov's best."

Before she could say any more, the singing stopped. A second later, the door to the room slid open and the four of them were struck by a wave of teenage Tii-Koona body odor. Brin'tac covered his nose with his hand before quickly pulling it away. Based on the apologetic look on his face, Khalen guessed the other was concerned his actions would offend. A moment later, Jov stepped into the doorway and looked up at his visitors quizzically.

Like his "cousin", Jov was less than five feet in height and wore a two-piece jumpsuit, although the bottom section was shorts instead of pants. His seaweed-like hair was cut short but was still a tangled mess. Unlike Nara's scales, which were dark violet, Jov's were teal along the back of his arms and legs, and light green everywhere else.

But the most prominent feature was the young Tii-Koona's eyes. They continually shifted and moved, rarely settling on anyone or anything for more than a few seconds. The Lah'grex leader sucked in a breath in surprise at the teen's appearance.

"Hey, Jov!" Khalen said.

"Hey, Unca Khawen," Jov returned, his face lighting up. Throwing his arms into the air, he enveloped the Mih'schen in a big hug.

After several long seconds, he loosened his grip, allowing Khalen to breathe. As he did so, Khalen grimaced slightly at the intensity of the teen's body odor. "This is Brin'tac eth Galithar. We're traveling with him to help him rescue his family."

Turning toward the Lah'grex, Jov threw his arms out in the same fashion. "Hi, Mista' Gawifar. I'm Jov!"

Khalen watched in bemusement as Brin'tac stiffened. Completely oblivious to the other's reaction, Jov leaned in, wrapped his arms around him, and squeezed the air out of his lungs. Instead of returning the hug, Brin'tac stood awkwardly with his arms at his sides, a look of severe discomfort plastered on his face. When Jov finally released him, the Lah'grex leader took a step back, his expression shifting to one of profound relief. Out of the corner of his eye, Khalen saw Vel'vikis trying unsuccessfully to hide his own smile.

The smile vanished immediately as Khalen gestured toward him. "And this is Vel'vikis." In a near perfect repeat of the previous few seconds, Jov hugged Vel'vikis, his expression identical to Brin'tac's.

"I'm hungwy," Jov said as he released the hug. "I'm gonna go get some food. Mista' Gawifar and Mista' Vewl'vikis, do you wanna come wit' me to get a samwish?."

Brin'tac, who was staring at a wet spot on his expensive shirt where Jov had drooled a little on him, suddenly realized he was being addressed. "Oh…uh…no thank you, Jov. I…maybe next time."

"Okay. Hey Nawa, can you make a samwish for me?"

Nara glanced at Khalen and the others, then shrugged. "Sure, Jov."

"Tanks. You awe da best, cuz!" he said, wrapping his arms around her briefly. "Bye evwyone!"

Immediately, he shuffled past the three others and started heading down the hallway toward the kitchen area. "C'mon, Nawa!"

Nara turned to Brin'tac and Vel'vikis. "It was nice to see you again. Thanks for letting me tag along."

Still somewhat flustered by the encounter with Jov, Brin'tac offered a quick, "You're welcome."

The others watched in silence as Nara turned and followed Jov. Once they were out of earshot, Brin'tac turned toward Khalen. "He's an untouchable!"

"If that's what you call someone with a mental handicap, then you're right," Khalen confirmed. "I forget sometimes that Lah'grex society shuns those who are different or who lack certain 'normal' traits. As Symphonians, we refer to them as Accidentals."

Taking out a handkerchief from his pocket, Brin'tac began dabbing at the drool spot on his shirt. "Yes, they're accidents of nature. That's certain."

Khalen bit his tongue to prevent himself from verbally assaulting the politician for the insult against Jov. He forced himself to take a deep breath before replying. "That's not it at all. In music, an accidental is a note that isn't in the key signature or part of the regular scale or mode. Because of that, it adds an extra element of color and life to the music. We call Jov and those like him Accidentals because, yes, they aren't part of what most of the galaxy would call 'normal'. But that's the very thing that makes them so special. They enrich our lives. Sure, Jov drives me crazy sometimes with his quirkiness, but he's taught me so much about myself and others. He's taught me that all beings have value and worth because they're made in the image of their Creator. My life is richer because I've known him."

The wealthy Lah'grex ruler remained silent. After several awkward seconds, he glanced at Vel'vikis, then returned his gaze toward his host. Although he was smiling, it was forced and betrayed his uncomfortableness. "Thank you for your time, Master Khalen. I must be getting back to my ship. I promise to do more research on the basics of music so I'm more prepared for our next lesson. I also hope to continue our discussion on politics and religion. You've already given me much to consider and think about."

"Yeah. Sure," Khalen said curtly, still fighting his own frustration.

"Perhaps we can do another music lesson before we reach Dhundrok."

"Maybe. Look, if you're serious about learning music, you might want to watch a few tutorials on how basic triads are constructed," Khalen said. "Make sure you know the difference between major, minor, diminished, and augmented. I don't have time to teach you everything."

"Yes. I'll do that."

Khalen led Brin'tac and Vel'vikis back to the connecting tube and opened the hatch. Brin'tac said his final goodbye and climbed the ladder. As he neared the top, Vel'vikis stepped to the ladder and placed one hand on a rung. However, before ascending he paused and turned toward Khalen. The burly Lah'grex looked him in the eye for a moment, then nodded respectfully before turning and following his employer.

16

ARRIVAL AT DHUN'DROK

City: Balec's Tower
Planet: Dhun'drok
System: Thrar'sig
Region: Lah'grex Sovereignty

THE *LIGHTBRINGER* and *Eternal Harmony* arrived in the Thrar'sig System nearly two galactic-standard days later. Dhun, the fifth planet of the system, lay directly ahead. Several moons orbited the gas giant. The largest one, Dhun'drok, was their destination. Although Dhun's orbit was beyond the habitable zone, the planet itself produced enough heat to warm the moon to sustainable levels.

"Prepare for separation," Khalen said into the commlink. After receiving an acknowledgement from Captain Nahoc, he counted down and hit the release button. A moment later, he watched as the *Eternal Harmony* moved off to the right before matching the current speed of the *Lightbringer*.

Once the maneuver was completed, Brin'tac's voice came over the comm. "My sources tell me that while there are currently no forces from the Dumah Dynasty in the immediate vicinity, there is a significant fleet hiding near one of the inner planets. Several large capital ships from the Hes'groc Dynasty are in orbit on the far side of the planet and are providing security until the government of Dhun'drok can build a fleet of its own. As you can see by the size of the shipyards, they've made this one of their top priorities. They expect fifteen ships to be online by the end of this year, in addition to numerous other, smaller craft. It helps that Dhun'drok's primary export is resonite. We're approaching the side of the planet that contains the Jorlinari cruisers. You can see several of them and a couple of relief aid transports docked at the three space stations."

"But even if Hes'groc and Jorlinari work together, they'll be hard pressed to protect the planet if Dumah comes in force," Khalen replied.

"Perhaps. But right now, the Dumah fleet is recovering from their losses a year ago. The current ceasefire will likely remain in place for the foreseeable future. However, the situation on the planet is a little more strained. Pockets of Dumah forces and the indigenous loyalists are using terrorist tactics to strike at soft spots within the primary cities. The entire population is on edge. The planetary ruler, Mir'eya Reskal, has placed additional security details in every city in the hopes of deterring these attacks."

"Wow. Sounds like a fun place," Nara said sarcastically from where she sat behind Khalen.

Seated next to him in the copilot's chair, Saryn shifted in her seat. Although her current outfit was simpler than the elegant dress worn when she first met Brin'tac, it still carried the beautiful designs of Solemsiel clothing. The tan, long-sleeved jacket was buttoned down the center and had texture details of suede, and design details of lace on the cuffs and waist. A matching pair of silver gauntlets with beautiful patterns etched into their surface covered her forearms. An asymmetrical, flowing half-skirt covered her left leg, while leaving the right uncovered. However, in keeping with her conservative views on modesty, she wore a pair of blue, loose-fitting pants tucked into boots that reached to just below her knees. The clothing was both formal and functional.

"Noble Galithar, where is the meeting being held?" Saryn asked into the comm.

There was a brief pause before the Lah'grex's voice returned. "The instructions we received stated we were to meet at Balec's Tower. As you know, traditional Lah'grex cities and structures are built into mountains and hills. But in this case, the tower was built by a team of musical scientists and sculptors using the surrounding terrain. According to legend, the region south of the city of Emari was overrun by large, semi-intelligent beasts and, if the stories be true, soulless monsters."

"Dodekaphs?" Khalen guessed.

"Yes. These creatures would often attack travelers, and sometimes even convoys. The situation became so desperate the Nobles of several of the surrounding cities, led by Zabor Balec, banded together to create the tower. Using music, the maestros flattened out the surrounding area, destroying the cave system that was hidden under the hills and using the rock to construct a three-hundred-foot tower. Heavily fortified, the garrison within the tower could track the movements of any of the beasts for miles from the safety of the structure.

"However," Brin'tac continued, his voice dropping in tone, "those in the tower relied upon synths to do their work. During the Synth Uprising, large portions of the tower were destroyed. In the two thousand years since, numerous rebel groups and military organizations have taken control of the ruins."

"Pardon my interruption, eth Galithar, but who controls it now?" Nara asked politely, thoroughly engrossed in the story.

"No one. Srisu reksani Dumah's forces captured it last year but were forced to retreat when Hes'groc came to the aid of the Dhun'drok militia. The Dumah-controlled territories lie two hundred miles to the west of the tower, while the free city of Emari is one hundred and twenty miles to the northeast. The remote location and distance from the nearest support made it difficult for either side to keep personnel stationed there."

"Which makes it the ideal neutral location for a meeting," Roakel added. Although exhausted from the Stream travel, he nevertheless wanted to be present when they entered the planetary orbit. His position behind Saryn still gave him a clear view of the approaching planet.

"Exactly," Brin'tac said through the commlink.

"How do we know this isn't a trap?" Khalen asked.

Brin'tac let out a brief chuckle. "You and Vel'vikis think alike. He already discussed this with the rest of the Jorlinari soldiers we brought with us. One of the reasons for choosing this location is that since the surrounding area is so flat, there's nowhere to hide an ambush. That puts both sides at ease."

"Even still, it is our job as neutral mediators to examine the location before either party arrives." Roakel said. "We will do a thorough scan of the entire structure and surrounding area. Once we are certain the location is secure, we will contact both you and the Dumah delegation and instruct you where to land."

"Understood."

"Rest assured, Noble Galithar," Roakel continued, "I sincerely doubt they would have requested the presence of two Solemsiels as mediators if they were planning something duplicitous."

Khalen glanced at him as he finished. Although Roakel appeared at ease, Khalen was still unconvinced. *I guess we'll find out soon enough*, he thought.

With their conversation concluded, Khalen piloted the *Lightbringer* through the initial orbital checkpoint. They passed through the security easily due to Brin'tac's status. Before long, they were entering the moon's atmosphere and heading toward the surface.

Although Dhun'drok contained some smaller bodies of water, it lacked any large oceans. The general climate was warm and humid, which suited the Lah'grex inhabitants. While Khalen and the others noticed traces of vegetation, the moon's surface was mostly rocky and coarse. Mountains and hills full of resonite covered large swaths of landscape, matched only by the number of mining operations.

However, as their ship drew closer to the ground, Khalen saw that many of these facilities were currently dormant.

"Wow! Look at the damage to the equipment and buildings!" Nara stated. "This place looks like it got hit by a bomb! See the impact crater over there? And you can see how the damage lessens the further away it gets. I wonder what kind of bomb they used?"

Saryn frowned. "A more appropriate question should be: how many lives were lost?"

When Nara failed to respond, Khalen glanced back at her just in time to see her lean back in her seat and roll her eyes. He suppressed a grin at the teen's attitude and returned his focus to the viewport.

Before long, the mountainous terrain gave way to a flat plain. Off in the distance, the group could see the tower standing majestically on the horizon. After several more minutes of flight, the building grew close enough for them to make out the details.

Its general shape consisted of a large circular disc resting atop a long central pillar, almost as if it were a gigantic plate skewered by a thick pole. Adding support and beauty to the structure were numerous buttresses that arched out from the pillar and reached to the edges of the disc.

However, the damage sustained over the recent years severely hindered the tower's majesty and architectural splendor. Numerous sizeable sections of the roof were missing or had collapsed inward. A dozen of the supporting arches had broken free and either fallen to the ground or were leaning precariously against the other portions of the building. Dark splotches of discolored rock bore evidence to previous fires that had once raged in and around the building.

"Um…are we sure this place is safe?" Nara asked nervously.

To her right, Roakel studied a display. "Although there has been extensive damage, the scans from the *Lightbringer* reveal the tower is still structurally sound. Certain areas are no longer accessible, but the location Brin'tac indicated for the meeting appears undamaged."

"I am not detecting any life readings," Saryn said. "It appears to be deserted."

"So far so good," Khalen replied. "It looks like the roof is designed as a landing pad. I'm going to set us down by that lift access point."

Khalen set the *Lightbringer* down near the center of the landing site. Once they had gathered their gear, Khalen, Roakel, and Saryn exited the ship, the two drallmari flanking their master on both sides. The team surveyed the tower for the next two hours, searching for any signs of traps or other tampering. Satisfied that the meeting location was secure, they returned to the ship.

Roakel first contacted the Dumah dynasty and instructed them to begin their approach, then he opened a channel to Brin'tac. "Noble Galithar, the tower is secure. The Dumah delegation is en route. They will be using the landing platform on the roof of the tower. They are arriving in two *Lother*-class ships, which will utilize much of the area. Due to the structural status of the tower and for the sake of separating the parties, we feel it would be prudent to have the *Lightbringer* and *Eternal Harmony* land at the base of the tower."

"I agree. That seems the wisest choice," Brin'tac replied. "Are the lifts working? If not, how will we make our way to the meeting room?"

"The generators for the building are still mostly functional," Khalen said. "There are some areas that are in disrepair, but the lifts appear operational."

"Be that as it may, I suggest an alternative," Roakel stated. "I will remain in the meeting room to welcome the Dumah delegation while Saryn and Khalen transport you into the tower via portal."

"Yes, I like that idea," Brin'tac replied. "I don't want to trust my life to a lift that hasn't been maintained. But can a musical portal reach that far?"

"It'd be close," Khalen said. "A single maestro might not be able to create one that distance, but Saryn and I together should be able to make one stable enough to at least get us close to the meeting room. We might be a few floors below it though."

"I can use Roakel's windstaff to strengthen the song," Saryn added.

"Fair enough. Please," Brin'tac said softly, his voice changing to a lower pitch, "I know you're all strong believers in the Great Composer. Although I don't share your beliefs, I'd appreciate any positive energy or thoughts you could send on my family's behalf."

"Rest assured, Noble Galithar. We have already been interceding for the safe return of your wife and children," Saryn said. "We will be awaiting your arrival."

"Thank you."

Khalen closed down the commlink and engaged the engines, lifting the *Lightbringer* into the air. He piloted the ship over the edge of the tower and had begun their descent when Roakel's strong voice began to sing.

"A song to our strong Lord!
A shout to the wonderful Composer of all life.
Shield us on all sides and make our paths straight!"

As Roakel continued to sing, Khalen set the *Lightbringer* down at the base of the tower. The Solemsiel music master finished his song and he, Saryn, and Nara exited the cockpit, leaving Khalen alone to finish shutting down the

KEITH A. ROBINSON

engines. Although the echoes of Roakel's resounding worship stirred his soul, he still fought to shake off the unsettled feeling in his gut.

| 189 |

17

BALEC'S TOWER

BRIN'TAC'S TEAM, consisting of Vel'vikis, Inspector Mak'sim, three Lah'grex soldiers, and two of their virtually-piloted remotes, had already exited their ship by the time the *Lightbringer's* lift reached the surface of the moon. The instant it came to a halt, Khalen and Saryn stepped off the platform and headed toward where the others waited. Following behind them was a remote of their own followed by the two drallmari.

Brin'tac raised one eyebrow in surprise at the sight of the six-foot tall, bulky robot. "Unless there is yet another crew member you failed to introduce me to, I'm assuming this is being piloted by your young Tii-Koona friend."

Inside what appeared to be the remote's helmet, an image of Nara's head suddenly materialized, brought to life by the machine's holographic imaging. The effect made it appear as if the robot was merely a giant suit she was wearing. "Hi, eth Galithar," her cheerful voice said through the remote's speaker as the teen's image moved its lips in perfect synchronization.

"Hello, Nara. Glad you could join us."

"I figured you could use all the backup you could get. I call this remote Roadblock. He's pretty clunky, but he makes up for it in durability. Besides, he's also carrying—"

"Nara, perhaps another time," Saryn said, cutting off yet another of the teen's ramblings.

"It allows her to stay safely behind in the ship, yet still contribute to our mission. She is as adept at piloting her remotes as Jov is at fixing and modifying them."

"Jov?" Brin'tac echoed, his surprise deepening.

"Yes," Saryn affirmed with a smile. "He has a natural gift for working with machines."

Feeling that more pressing matters needed to be discussed, Khalen skipped the rest of the conversation and strode over to stand next to Vel'vikis. As he walked, he drew reassurance from the presence of Riveruun's Twin Discs of Arrguin that hung from his thigh belts. Although he had spent many hours practicing with them, he had yet to use them in combat.

Shosta and Kovitch trailed behind their master, their reptilian tongues flicking in and out of their mouths as they tasted the air. As Khalen and his pets drew closer, the Lah'grex bodyguard eyed the two reptilian beasts warily.

"Are you and your team ready?" Khalen asked.

"Yes. Are you sure the tower is secure?"

"As secure as we can make it. Our scanners didn't detect anything abnormal."

"Even still, I insist on having some of my people accompany us. They need not be involved in the meeting, but I want them nearby all the same."

"We expected that. Let's get this over with." Khalen turned and strode back over to where Saryn and Brin'tac stood. "We're ready when you are."

Letting out a deep sigh, Brin'tac nodded. "Very well. Master's Saryn and Khalen, please open the portal."

Khalen crouched and stroked the chins of Kovitch and Shosta affectionately. "You two keep an eye on things while I'm gone. I'll be back soon." Standing, he turned away from the drallmari and nodded to Saryn.

The Solemsiel activated the pump within the windstaff, sending air flowing through the numerous tubes. Once the style and chord progression were established, she began to sing. Khalen added his voice to hers to strengthen the harmonies and melodies. Bright colors filled the air, fueled by the strength of the maestros' song. After several seconds, the energy flowed from Khalen's fingertips to form the portal in front of them. Before long, the aperture was a full ten feet in diameter.

The images on the opposite side of the swirling wormhole shifted along with the melody as the two music masters sought out a safe and secure location within the tower. After numerous discarded options, a dimly-lit room came into view. Having at last located a viable option, Khalen and Saryn ceased altering the melody and continued to repeat the simple progression of four chords in a homophonic texture. Seconds later, the image of the room grew clearer as the energy stabilized.

Brin'tac's two remotes moved forward and traversed the portal followed by Vel'vikis, Mak'sim and the other three Lah'grex. Brin'tac went last, his expression stoic. With everyone safely inside the tower, Khalen and Saryn passed through, then ended their song, closing the aperture.

The room they had entered had the distinct layout of a restaurant or dining hall. Due to extensive damage, only a quarter of the lights were still functioning. Overturned tables and chairs, many of which were severely damaged, were strewn about the room. To the left rested a set of doors that led into what had once been the kitchen. Another set of doors to the right led into one of the primary corridors on this level.

Standing near a panel of windows located in the exterior wall of the tower, Mak'sim and Vel'vikis were huddled over a scroll. The tablet-sized, rectangular device displayed the floorplan of the tower on its screen. "Eth Galithar, according to this schematic, the Arrangers' portal brought us to the sixty-first floor, just two floors below where the meeting is scheduled to take place," Vel'vikis said. Grabbing the half-cylindrical handles located on the short edges of the scroll, he pushed them toward each other until the screen rolled into them, forming a full cylinder. Sliding it into its holder on his belt, the Lah'grex bodyguard headed toward the doors that led to the hallway.

Before opening them, he halted next to one of the remotes standing guard. "Has the Dumah delegation arrived at the meeting room?"

"Yes. Our thermal scans show four figures in the meeting location. Other readings indicate the presence of a remote as well," the robot's pilot said through its vocalizer. "Two other figures are currently en route from the ships on the roof. Based on the scan, it appears one of them is a female prisoner."

"Tet'rick, keep your remote here with Chovan, Dostal, and Khalen," Vel'vikis commanded. "Hujik, take point with your remote. Eth Galithar and I will come next, followed by Maestra Saryn. Tas'anee, you and the inspector come last."

"Wait a second," Khalen said, his gaze intense. "I never agreed to stay behind. I'm with the Arrangers. I go where they go."

"Not this time, *Mih'schen*," Vel'vikis said with emphasis. "This is a Lah'grex affair. The Arrangers are here to mediate. No others are allowed. Be thankful we allowed you to tag along this far."

Khalen felt his blood begin to boil, causing his eyes to take on a reddish hue. In response, several of the Lah'grex soldiers gripped their weapons tighter. Khalen opened his mouth to respond but stopped as a gentle hand came to rest on his shoulder.

He glanced up at his friend and recognized the look of caution on Saryn's face. "This is neither the time nor the place. You will not win this battle, my friend. It is common protocol for these types of negotiations for there to be an equal number of representatives in the room."

Khalen let out his breath forcefully in defeat. "Fine. But at least take Roadblock with you."

Vel'vikis narrowed his eyes. "Only to the meeting room. It waits outside until we're done."

"Thank you," Khalen said sarcastically. He glared at Vel'vikis one final time before turning away from Saryn and striding over to the window in frustration.

Tas'anee and Vel'vikis both handed their weapons to their comrades, as did Mak'sim. Before following the others toward the outer doors, the inspector approached Khalen. "Don't worry, maestro. They'll be safe with us. We'll make sure no harm comes to them."

Still fuming, Khalen merely continued staring out the window. As Mak'sim strode away to join the others near the door, Khalen turned his head enough to watch the group leave. Brin'tac stopped near the exit, cast a concerned look in

Khalen's direction, then spoke briefly to the remote remaining behind. Finally, he and Saryn followed the rest of the delegation from the room.

The group walked in silence down the abandoned hallway. Despite the new surroundings, Brin'tac kept his gaze fixed on the back of the remote in front of him, his pulse racing. *Keep your focus, Galithar*, he chided himself. *This may be the first real test of your current predicament, but you've been in situations like this before and came out on top.*

That may be true, but this time the lives of my family are on the line, he argued with himself. *If I slip up, I don't just lose money or political power.*

You know what you're supposed to do. Trust others to do their part and stick to the plan.

His mind was so wrapped in his own turbulent thoughts he barely registered the fact that Vel'vikis was receiving instructions from Roakel. After several more minutes of walking the broken corridors of the tower, they reached the meeting room.

One of the double doors in front of them slid into its recess in the wall with a grinding noise, while the other door failed to move at all. "Please, come in," a voice beckoned from within.

Brin'tac glanced at Roadblock and gave a small smile. "This is as far as you go, Nara. Keep your remote out here until we're finished."

Nara's likeness flickered to life inside the droid's "helmet". "Yes, sir. Be careful."

"Thank you. Maestra Saryn, lead the way."

Saryn nodded and strode forward, leading Brin'tac and the others into what appeared to be a former command center. The spacious room contained numerous pieces of damaged and discarded military-grade equipment. Several of the walls were covered in cracked display screens and monitors. Debris from the collapsed section of the ceiling filled the left side of the room. In the center was an enormous oval table with plush hoverchairs set around it.

Seated at the table across from Roakel was a Lah'grex female dressed in a tight-fitting blue outfit with flashy silver designs woven into the fabric. Her elaborate headcrest left no doubt she was from the upper caste of Lah'grex society. Standing behind her was a single remote and two Lah'grex males.

Roakel and the Dumah representative stood as Brin'tac and his entourage entered.

"Brin'tac eth Galithar, I would like to present Kuzelka Tharler, a private negotiator for Srisu reksani Dumah, ruler of the Dumah Dynasty. Lady Tharler, this is Brin'tac eth Galithar, governor of the Katloum Province on the planet Gal'grea."

"Private negotiator?" Brin'tac asked, his eyes narrowing. "More like paid lackey. I've had the unfortunate task of dealing with the reksani and her officials numerous times in the past. I'm well aware of her penchant for hiring private 'negotiators' in order to hide her nefarious dealings."

A tight-lipped smile forced its way across her features. "Think what you may, but the Arranger has verified my credentials. I speak for the Dumah Dynasty."

Brin'tac looked to Roakel for confirmation. "It is as she says," Roakel said. "The information she provided appears legitimate. Now, eth Galithar, if you and the others would please sit, we may begin."

Brin'tac allowed his suspicious expression to remain as he leaned forward placed his hands on the table. "Before any negotiations can begin, I demand to see my wife and family."

"But of course. We expected as much." The door behind Kuzelka suddenly opened and a bound Lah'grex female was shoved into the room.

"Raena!" Brin'tac cried out. He attempted to leap forward but was held back by Mak'sim. For at that moment another figure entered behind Brin'tac's wife. The figure wore the scarred, silvery mask that had haunted the Lah'grex ruler's dreams for much of the past week. The dark eyes gazing out through the hollow sockets seemed to smile at Brin'tac's fear.

Slag, the cruel Ra-Nuuk music master who had been responsible for causing so much anguish to his family, now stood before him.

18

NEGOTIATIONS

RAENA'S TERROR-STRICKEN eyes met Brin'tac's. In that moment, he saw a flicker of hope ignite within her and he longed to reveal to her the truth. He could tell she wanted to call out to him, but the small, electronic mute placed against her throat prevented her from doing so.

"Well," Kuzelka said with a disingenuous smile, "now that we're all here, why don't we have a seat and start the negotiations?"

"Wait! Where...where are my children?" Brin'tac asked, the sudden dryness in his throat choking his words.

"They're safe enough. Your son and daughter are each aboard one of my ships. I like to think of it as an 'insurance policy' in case you or your friends decide to try something... heroically foolish."

"This whole situation is unacceptable!" Inspector Mak'sim stated. "The Dumah Dynasty has overstepped its bounds. When the next Reverie is held, we'll make sure the rest of the council hears about—"

"Save your breath!" Kuzelka raised her voice, interrupting Mak'sim. "You're in no position to lecture me, and I don't have time to listen to your petty little diatribe. So shut up and sit down!"

"Please!" Roakel stated, raising his two left arms in a calming gesture while his other arms held onto his windstaff. "Lady Tharler, you requested the presence of my wife and I at these negotiations. As such, we insist the proceedings be civil. If not, we will be forced to withdraw."

Kuzelka appeared somewhat annoyed at first, but then a slight smirk spread its way across her sharp-boned features. "As you insist, Master Arranger. Please," she said, her voice oozing sarcasm, "won't you all sit down?"

Still bristling, Brin'tac sat across from the Dumah representative. Inspector Mak'sim followed suit and sat on Brin'tac's right. A moment later, Slag grabbed Raena by one arm and lifted her to her feet. Before he could do anything more, Saryn moved around the table and approached the dark-robed Ra-Nuuk. For a moment, it appeared to Brin'tac as if Slag was going to attack her for daring to get near him. Despite the fact the eight-foot tall Solemsiel towered over the warlord by more than three feet, he seemed unfazed by her presence. Brin'tac breathed a sigh of relief when Slag backed away from his prisoner, ending the brief confrontation.

Brin'tac watched with concern as Saryn helped Raena into the chair to the left of Kuzelka. Once her charge was seated, Saryn sat in the chair next to the Lah'grex female, her comforting hand never leaving Raena's arm. From all appearances, his wife seemed exhausted by her ordeal. Her eyes were a cool gray, her skin was dry and her expression full of weariness.

"Are you okay?" Brin'tac asked in concern once she was seated. "Are you hurt?"

Saryn reached over to remove the mute from Raena's throat. As she did so, Slag stepped forward once again, his posture threatening.

"Don't push it!" he warned, his voice sounding hollow through the mask. "The mute stays."

The Solemsiel appeared about to protest, but instead withdrew her hand.

"Don't worry, there'll be plenty of time to catch up with your darling dearest after we've completed our business," Kuzelka said curtly. "Speaking of which, let's get this over with.

"I've been authorized to return your family to you. In return, Srisu reksani Dumah demands that the Jorlinari Dynasty immediately withdraws all forces from Dhun'drok and agrees to no longer provide aid of any kind to the Hes'groc Dynasty."

"The Jorlinari Dynasty has chosen to remain neutral in this conflict!" Brin'tac stated. "Our only goal is to provide aid to the suffering citizens. And for that, we have been attacked by both Hes'groc and Dumah. If you believe we would willingly send aid to those who attacked us, you are deeply mistaken."

Kuzelka narrowed her eyes. "If the actions of your people are so virtuous, then explain the presence of such a sizable fleet?"

"Dumah has obviously not sent their brightest!" Mak'sim spat. "eth Galithar just told you the Jorlinari ships had been attacked!"

Roakel raised his hand toward the inspector. "I insist that personal insults against either party will not be tolerated in these negotiations. Inspector Mak'sim, you will refrain from such language or be removed from the room."

Mak'sim scowled but remained silent. Brin'tac glanced at him, then elaborated on his point. "Inspector Mak'sim is absolutely correct. The cruisers are in place solely to protect the aid ships."

"Regardless of their purpose, these are the demands of the Dumah Dynasty," Kuzelka stated. "In addition to the withdrawal of the fleet, your cousin, Tronsen reks Jorlinari, will turn over the entire dynasty of Jorlinari to Dumah, which will absorb it into its own territory."

Brin'tac blanched at the outrageous demand. The Tritonus had revealed to him very little of their overall plan or goals, and Brin'tac guessed the same was true for anyone involved in their plot. *How much did they tell Kuzelka? Has she even been in contact with the Tritonus themselves, or told what to do by others within the Dumah Dynasty? In fact, is she even...*

"That is a severe demand!" Brin'tac said, adding the appropriate amount of outrage to his voice. "Dumah asks too much. My cousin would never agree to such terms, even to save the life of my family! Furthermore, I was personally given assurances by eth Sho'dis himself just yesterday that the demands would be reasonable and achievable."

Kuzelka paused before responding. "Sho'dis is not the one in charge of these negotiations. These demands come straight from the reksani herself."

There it was. Brin'tac's suspicions were confirmed. He had been in disputes with the governor many times. He also knew that Sho'dis had died a week ago. Kuzelka was not even connected with the Dumah Dynasty. *But then, who is she? Do I call her out as an impostor or play along?*

As if sensing Brin'tac's conflict, Kuzelka raised the stakes even further. "Lastly, Tronsen reks Jorlinari will dress himself in spotted pajamas and parade through the streets of Dhun'drok on a slimy, striped oksapeg!"

Brin'tac's expression shifted from outrage to incredulity and finally to confusion. Even the normally calm Solemsiel could not help but gasp in surprise at the outrageous request. The stunned silence was broken a moment later by Kuzelka's wild laughter, further confusing Brin'tac's delegation.

"Lady Tharler, this is most irregular," Roakel said in bewilderment. "If you would be so kind as to—"

She held up a hand to stop him. As she did so, her laughter died out and she composed herself. "The looks on your faces were priceless. I assure you, we'd never request your mighty reks to do such things."

"Then...what *do* you want?" Brin'tac asked.

"Oh, I was just having a little fun, that's all. But, I suppose it's time to do what we came here to do. Go ahead, Slag."

"Captain! I'm getting electronic signatures popping up all over the place!"

Khalen turned his head at the Lah'grex soldier's words.

"What?" the soldier named Chovan asked in shock. "How's that possible? Our scans didn't show any other remotes in the tower—activated or otherwise."

"I don't know how they did it, but my remote's reading four new bots coming online as we speak," Tet'rick replied. "All of them between us and the meeting room. They're moving down the hallway!"

"They set us up! Find cover!" Khalen said emphatically as he ducked around the corner of a wall. Reaching down, he pulled the two resonite discs from their magnetic harnesses on his thighs and began singing. He split his voice into two pitches: one high and one low. The discs began to crackle with energy and glow green as each one responded to the different vocal registers.

The double doors suddenly exploded inward. The Lah'grex soldiers opened fire even before the smoke cleared, hoping their laser blasts would strike a target. Return fire spewed forth from the haze, narrowly missing the defenders.

Khalen risked a glance around the corner of the wall, seeking to locate the attackers. He felt his stomach drop at the sight that awaited him. Four rectangular beams of blood-red lights that served as eyes pierced the cloud of smoke.

These were not remotes. They were Synths.

The fully autonomous synthetic beings were efficient, clever, and deadly. So much so that the Major races of the Twin Galaxies had banned their production almost two thousand years ago after the Synth Uprising. The machines were imbued with artificial intelligence and came in various designs, shapes, and sizes. Some were bipedal, others rolled on treads, and still others walked on spider-like legs.

The Synths that came through the mist toward them contained a basic torso, a short, flattened head, two bulky arms, and plenty of armor. Instead of legs, the machines rolled forward on a single, textured, rubber sphere.

Changing the pitch of his song slightly, Khalen felt the hum of the discs in his hands increase. With a flick of his wrist, he launched the first one at the approaching Synths, followed an instant later by the second disc. The moment they were airborne, Khalen increased the dynamic of his singing until his voice rose above the din of the battle. Using the specific solfege syllables sung in the two distinct pitch ranges, he controlled the flight of each disc individually.

The circular weapons spun and created a rainbow of colored light from the musical energy. Despite the Synths attempts to intercept them, the discs twisted in the air and struck two of the machines in their heads. Although the resulting discharge of energy would have knocked out the average being, they only rendered the Synths momentarily immobile.

With the initial attack complete, Khalen changed his song in order to recall the discs. The spinning objects defied their original trajectories and performed one-hundred-eighty-degree turns in midair. They headed back toward the music master, where he caught them with practiced ease.

Chovan, Dostal, and Tet'rick's remote took advantage of the momentary lull in the attack and came out from hiding long enough to shoot at the disabled Synths. Several of their shots struck one in the head, causing it to spark and explode. However, the maneuver gave the remaining two attackers an opening. Khalen heard Dostal cry out in pain as a pair of blaster bolts struck his left arm and hip.

"Dostal's been hit," Chovan called out. "I've been trying to reach Vel'vikis and the others, but they're jamming our signals."

"And they've activated a portal inhibitor," Tet'rick's remote said.

"Hold on to something," Khalen called out. "I've got a plan." Singing once more, the Mih'schen music master altered his song, the resulting cymatic frequencies causing the Twin Discs of Arrguin to change their shape. The central section of each weapon shrunk two inches in diameter while the outer edges of the metal morphed into spikes. A few seconds later, the discs glowed their deep green. However, instead of launching them at the encroaching Synths, Khalen hurled them at the window. The spikes and discharging energy served to break through the reinforced glass, shattering it into pieces.

Khalen adjusted his song and brought the discs back to his hands. He returned them to their magnetic holsters, then lifted the hood of his jacket to help block out the sights of the battle and focus his mind. Taking a deep breath, he began to sing a completely different song. The new one was more complex and in a different key, style, and mode. As he sang from behind the safety of the protective wall, he started conducting a pattern of four with his right hand.

The notes of the G mixolydian mode sent streams of light blue energy swirling in front of Khalen. Although part of his mind heard the shouts of Chovan and Tet'rick, he knew he had to retain his concentration for his performance. With the basic chord progression of the song in place, he increased the dynamic and intensity of the melody until the swirling energy became a vortex. While continuing the conducting pattern, he used his left hand to direct the miniature tornado, which grew larger with each passing second. The winds from the cyclone buffeted everyone in the room. The Synths, recognizing the danger, began to roll backward rapidly. Before they could escape, the whirlwind created by Khalen's song swept them up one by one until all three remaining machines were caught in its grasp. With one final swoop, the tornado propelled the attackers through the now open window and out of the tower, where they plummeted to the ground far below.

Khalen ceased singing the instant they were gone and dropped to his knees, his body drained from the adrenaline rush and prolonged concentration. To his left, Chovan was crouching over Dostal. Knowing his friends were still in danger, he fought against the exhaustion, stood, and crossed over to them.

"Nice trick," Chovan stated, his breathing labored. "Tet'rick used his remote as a decoy to buy you time," he said, pointing toward the destroyed remote. "Dostal's hurt, but his injuries aren't life-threatening. I don't understand. Why did they bring us here to negotiate only to attack us?"

Khalen shook his head. "This was a trap. They didn't want to negotiate at all. My guess is they're after Brin'tac."

Chovan swore, pulled a small medical pack from his inside pocket, and tended to Dostal's wounds. As the soldier worked, Khalen strode over to examine the window, the evening wind whipping at his clothing.

After a few moments of perusal, Chovan's voice broke into Khalen's thoughts. Khalen turned and saw the Lah'grex gesturing to him. "I've made Dostal as comfortable as possible. As much as I hate to leave him here, we have to do what we can to stop Dumah! Let's go!"

Khalen crossed over and placed his hand on his arm just as the Lah'grex soldier was about to head toward the demolished doorway. When Chovan turned to look at him in confusion, Khalen glanced toward the window, then back at the soldier.

"I've got a better idea."

The instant the words were out of Kuzelka's mouth, the two Arrangers and three Lah'grex convulsed violently as an electric current coursed through their bodies, knocking them unconscious. Even the remote piloted by Brin'tac's soldier was taken out of commission by the unexpected shock. Only Brin'tac remained conscious.

Raena managed a muffled cry of surprise despite the mute that was restraining her vocal cords. Even though Brin'tac had expected some sort of attack, he was still genuinely startled when Slag's gloved hand gripped his left shoulder tightly from behind. He had been so caught up in his performance, he had not noticed the Ra-Nuuk cross the room to get behind him. A moment later, he felt the cold, metallic blade of one of Slag's resonite daggers pressed against his throat. "Stand."

The cold steel sent a wave of real fear through Brin'tac, and he stumbled as he attempted to comply. He knew Slag was involved in the Tritonus plot, but he had no idea how many others were privy to the overall plan.

Kuzelka motioned for the two other Lah'grex guards to grab Raena. As they did so, the Dumah representative pulled out a scroll, opened it, and stared at the readings.

"It's so rewarding when things go according to plan," Kuzelka said. Looking at Brin'tac, she smiled cruelly. "You'll be coming with us, *eth* Galithar. We've got a squad of four Synths keeping your people busy below, and your friends here are certainly in no condition to stop us. And, in case you were wondering, our little micro-remotes responsible for delivering the electric charge also took out the extra remote you had stationed outside the door, so don't expect any help from there either. Perhaps, if you cooperate, we might just let your friends live."

"You'll never get away—"

"Slag, shut him up!" Kuzelka said, cutting Brin'tac off

mid-sentence. "The last thing I want to hear right now is some stupid, heroic platitude." Before he could utter another word, Brin'tac felt a mute placed against his own throat. "There. That's much better," Kuzelka continued. "I don't know, Slag. This plan might just be going *too* smoothly."

"We'll see. Don't underestimate them."

Switching her gaze to her new captive, Kuzelka gave him one last smug smile, then turned and led the group out of the room.

"Jov!" Nara called out in surprise. "Did you see that? Something just shut down Roadblock! I think...I think they shocked everyone! What are we gonna do? They need our help!"

Although she still had her virtual piloting helmet on and could not see her Tii-Koona 'cousin', she knew he was nearby watching her remote's feed on a screen. His voice suddenly came through her helmet's speaker.

"What abou'...Scamp or Dodger?"

"Of course!" Nara said. "Since they weren't active when the electric shocky thingy hit, they may not've gotten fried. Let's try Scamp first."

For half a minute, the two teenagers were forced to wait, their anxiety building with each passing second. At last, the new connection was established.

Back in the tower, just outside the meeting room doors, a large panel on Roadblock's back slid open to reveal a smaller remote curled inside. With the connection now established, the remote pulled itself out of concealment. Nara piloted the machine into the room and had it leap onto the table.

When standing erect, Scamp was only two feet tall. The droid was modeled after a small primate, but with an extra pair of arms. Although the little bot was mostly used to climb into hard-to-reach areas to effect repairs, Nara had learned long ago it had numerous other uses as well.

In this case, she hoped to use him to rouse her friends.

Scamp scurried over to Roakel and Saryn and took a brief scan of their vitals. "Jov, they're okay! They're just unconscious. Thank the Composer!" she said through her helmet. "But what do I do now? I don't have anything I can use to wake them up!"

"Do you got a medkit?"

"No, but I betcha one of Brin'tac's soldiers has one! Good thinking, Jov!"

Nara had Scamp jump off the table, then she used the bot's four arms to sift through the items carried by Vel'vikis and the others. After another minute of searching, she found what she was looking for.

"I got it! I found some adrenaline! Let's hope this works."

Leaping back across the table, Scamp stopped in front of Roakel. Nara used Scamp to grab his arm and administer a single dose. She repeated the process with Saryn and the others. By the time she finished giving doses to each of the Lah'grex, Roakel began to stir.

"Wha...what happened?"

"Roakel! I'm so glad you're awake! You've gotta get going! They shocked all of us somehow and took Brin'tac! I think they're heading up to their ships. You've gotta stop 'em!"

The intensity of Nara's voice coming through Scamp's speaker drove all weariness from Roakel's body. He rose and crossed over to where Saryn was stirring on the other side of the table. Within a matter of seconds, he had explained the situation and helped her to her feet.

Roakel retrieved his windstaff and began using it to create a portal. However, when the musical energy failed to create the wormhole, he stopped singing, his expression dire. "Khalen was right. They do possess a portal inhibitor. We must, by necessity, use a lift to reach the roof." As the two Solemsiels headed to the door, Nara called out to them.

"Wait! What am I supposed to do now?"

Roakel paused. "Vel'vikis and his soldiers are regaining consciousness. Relate to them what you told us, then locate the portal inhibitor and disable it." With that, the pair of Arrangers sprinted out of the room, leaving Nara alone with the Lah'grex, who were just beginning to rouse.

19

CONFRONTATION

KUZELKA STEPPED OUT onto the roof of the tower, followed by her guards, the two prisoners, and Slag. Strong gusts of wind instantly buffeted the group. Brin'tac squinted both from the wind and from the last rays of the setting sun. As his vision recovered, he saw the two *Lother*-class ships that brought the delegation to the planet resting on a pair of hydraulic platforms. The entourage neared the first ship and the two guards leading Raena suddenly grabbed her by the arms and directed her toward the boarding ramp as the rest of the group continued on.

Brin'tac tried to cry out, but the mute turned his shout into a muffled whimper. He started to run after her but was stopped by the remote behind him.

"Oh, I'm sorry. I guess I forgot to tell you," Kuzelka said nonchalantly over her shoulder. She spun around to face him, her eyes flashing in triumph. "We have a different destination in store for you. Your family will be safe, as long as you play your part. Or, if you prefer to resist, we can stun you and drag you the rest of the way. What's it going to be?"

Brin'tac lowered his head in defeat. In that moment, a profound hollowness filled his soul. He felt trapped; ensnared by the schemes of the mighty Tritonus. He hated the very real anguish his wife and children were experiencing, and he was powerless to stop it. With a suddenness that surprised him, he found himself envying Khalen and the Arrangers. If only there truly was a supreme being that watched over the affairs of the universe and cared about the hurting and wounded. If only he was there to cry out to for help. If only...

The wind seemed to pick up, beating against him mercilessly as he looked toward his wife, tears streaming down his cheeks. "I'm...I'm so sorry, Raena," he whispered. Although he knew she could not hear him, he hoped she could read the message in his eyes and lips. He could see in her eyes the same sense of despair that threatened to swallow him whole.

Suddenly, as if coming from a great distance, he heard a faint song riding on the wind. Only then did he realize the increase in the gusts were not natural.

"Kuzelka," a voice from the remote said in urgency, "There are two figures coming up the *outside* of the building to the east, and a pair of flying creatures approaches from the west."

"Where?"

"There!" the remote said, pointing over her shoulder.

Brin'tac watched as Khalen and Chovan rose over the edge of the tower, carried on the wind. Khalen's song ceased the moment his feet touched the roof and the wind died almost instantly. Laser fire erupted all around him as Kuzelka and her group attacked.

In response, two wide streaks of green light cut through the orange hue of the evening sky and struck the remote and one of the guards. The electrical discharge from Khalen's discs overloaded the remote's circuits and knocked the guard next to it unconscious. Khalen's song, which was now stronger and louder, directed the discs toward the remainder of the group. Kuzelka dove toward the ground as one of the weapons flew within an inch of her head. Near the back, Slag had just enough time to block the second disc with one of his metal gauntlets. The two guards holding Raena dropped her to the ground and withdrew their blaster pistols from their holsters.

Brin'tac paused. A flicker of hope passed through his mind. *What if...what if I help Khalen rescue my family right now? We could disappear. Perhaps the Tritonus wouldn't be able to find us.* Spurred on by a desperate hope, he kicked out at Kuzelka as she attempted to activate her commlink. He managed to hit her arm with enough force to knock the device from her right hand. She cursed at him and scrambled across the ground in an effort to reclaim it.

Brin'tac was prepared to make a dash toward Raena, but a sudden blow against his back knocked him off balance and sent him sprawling to the ground. From his new vantage point on the deck, he glanced back. Slag was staring at him in warning, as if reading his intentions. Brin'tac ignored him and struggled to get to his feet. However, a sudden volley of laser blasts flew over his head, driving him back to the ground.

Searching for the source of the blasts, he saw that Khalen and Chovan had now taken cover behind a satellite dish. Chovan had a blaster in each hand and was keeping the remaining three guards pinned while Khalen was absorbed in performing a song.

"Get her out of here!"

The shout from Kuzelka drew Brin'tac's attention and sent

another jolt of fear piercing his heart. One of the guards near-est Raena grabbed her arm and started pulling her toward the first ship. Despite the firefight around him, Brin'tac fought to stand. He managed to get to his knees when, to his surprise, two dark shadows fell from the evening sky and collided with the guards, sending them skidding across the roof of the tower.

Raena's eyes grew wide in fear as her "rescuers" landed next to her. Intent on searching for other signs of danger, the two drallmari paid her no attention. Their alertness saved their lives, for at that moment, the deactivated remote came back online. Within seconds, the pilot of the machine tar-geted the drallmari and fired. The reptiles took to the air once more and circled their attacker, looking for an opening to strike.

Brin'tac's momentary excitement at his wife's rescue was dashed once again as three more guards came down the ramp of the first ship near where Raena lay and raised their weapons at Khalen and Chovan. Brin'tac knew his friends failed to see the new danger, and once again cursed the mute that prevented him from shouting a warning.

Bracing himself for the worst, Brin'tac watched helplessly as the guards opened fire. But instead of hitting his friends, the laser blasts struck an invisible energy shield that surrounded them. Brin'tac stared in surprise until he spied the small device on the ground at Khalen's feet that was producing the shield.

The minor victory was short-lived, however. From some-where behind him, Brin'tac heard another voice begin to sing. He glanced over his shoulder and stared in alarm. The Ra-Nuuk music master's hands were conducting an odd pattern of twos and threes as his voice rose in volume and pitch. Dark orange and red light began to swirl in front of him as his song crescendoed and intensified. While Khalen's song had been light and uplifting, Slag's was dissonant and ominous.

The musical energy coalesced into a glowing stream of molten lava. An intense blast of heat, accompanied by the pungent smell of brimstone, assaulted Brin'tac's senses, forcing him to stagger backward. The waves of heat stung his eyes and dropped him to his knees.

Fighting against the burning haze, Brin'tac watched as Slag gestured with his left hand, sending the lava tentacle launching toward Khalen and Chovan. The two must have realized the shield would not protect them against Slag's musical monstrosity, as they both dove out of the way.

The energy shield, which was designed to protect against laser blasts, crumbled under the onslaught of the lava. Splashes of magma flew in all directions, causing Khalen and his companion to cry out as they were struck by the superheated particles.

A barely audible scream drew Brin'tac's attention away from the plight of his friends and back toward his wife's predicament. The three guards that had appeared from the ship had recaptured Raena and were hauling her up the ramp. Kuzelka stood at the apex, a cruel smile spreading across her face as she stared back at him.

Hoping beyond hope the drallmari would once again come to his wife's aid, he searched the battlefield for signs of them. He located the two beasts, but his heart sank. One lay wounded on the pavement while the other had the remote pinned and was savagely tearing into its metal hide with its powerful jaws.

While the rational side of his brain recognized he had no chance of fighting off three armed guards with his own hands tied behind his back, Brin'tac knew he had to do something. He bent his knees and brought his bound arms around his feet so they were now in front of him. Casting aside his own sense of self-preservation, he pulled the mute off his throat and began running toward the ramp of the ship. However, before he had taken even five steps, another tentacle of lava cut across his vision. Acting on instinct, he dropped to the ground to avoid the raging basalt. Helpless once more, Brin'tac could only watch as his wife was forced into the bowels of the ship. "Raena!" he cried out in anguish as the ramp closed, his throat constricting from sorrow and lack of moisture. A moment later, the engines ignited, lifting the ship.

Lying awkwardly on the roof of the tower, Brin'tac eth Galithar, Ruler of Katloum province on the planet Gal'grea, wept uncontrollably as the ship carrying his wife and children headed toward Dhun'drok's upper atmosphere.

Khalen fought to remain conscious as the pain from the lava splashes burned through his clothing and set portions of his skin aflame. He frantically patted the flames until they went out. He knew his wounds would have been much worse had he not dove for cover the moment the lava struck his personal shield generator. Unfortunately, Chovan had not fared so well. Huddled behind a boxy cooling unit, Khalen glanced toward where he had last seen his companion. The Lah'grex lay face down and unmoving. Judging by the way his clothes were smoldering, Khalen feared he was dead.

Through the haze of disorientation created by the continuous burning sensations on his skin, he heard Slag's song shift. Fear stabbed at Khalen's heart as he remembered that Kovitch and Shosta were still somewhere nearby. He peered around the corner of the cooling unit just in time to see Brin'tac fall backward to the ground to avoid the stream of lava.

Khalen knew Slag would not injure his captive, which left the drallmari as the only target. He let out a series of high-pitched whistles, hoping to warn them. The two reptiles cocked their heads as the sounds reached them. Heeding their master's warning, the drallmari launched themselves into the air. Khalen noted with concern that Shosta was struggling to fly. Her right wing had an ugly looking splotch on the back side of it; the clear residue of a blaster strike. He pushed aside his concern to focus his attention on Kovitch, who had changed his flight path and headed straight for Brin'tac in order to fulfill his master's command.

Khalen pulled his own blaster from concealment and prepared to give the drallmari some cover fire. In the back of his mind, he heard the nagging voice of despair as he wondered about the fate of his friends. *What happened to Roakel and Saryn? Where are they?*

Images of his friends lying dead or dying back inside the tower flooded through his already pain-addled mind. Khalen pushed the negative thoughts away, took a deep breath and moved around the edge of the unit, his blaster searching for enemies. He immediately saw two guards making their way cautiously down the ramp of the second ship.

Khalen jumped out from concealment and sent a volley of laser blasts toward the two guards. One of the shots found its mark, dropping the soldier on the left. The remaining

Lah'grex dove for cover and returned fire. Khalen winced in pain as a laser blast struck his right shoulder. Gritting his teeth, he refocused his aim and, after a couple of tries, finally managed to take out the second opponent.

Throughout his brief encounter with the guards, Khalen kept part of his attention focused on Kovitch. The drallmari male descended and landed on Brin'tac, whose eyes were wide with shock and surprise. The beast grabbed Brin'tac's clothing in his claws and leapt into the air once more. However, due to the size and weight of the Lah'grex, the drallmari could not fly properly. Instead, he was forced to drag Brin'tac across the surface of the tower roof to safety.

With the guards incapacitated, Khalen spun around, searching for the final target. He cursed his own carelessness at losing track of Slag's location and scanned the area in earnest.

A black shadow suddenly leapt across his vision and slammed into him, knocking him to the ground. Pain exploded in his head once more as it struck the hard roof of the tower. A heaviness pressed him to the ground, pinning him. Dazed and helpless, he opened his eyes and struggled to focus his vision.

Slag's metal mask, which had previously been silver, was now solid black and hovered over his face. As Khalen struggled to clear his head, the mask reverted back to its original silvery shine. A burst of laughter came from its filter, knifing through Khalen's already frayed nerves. The Ra-Nuuk's laughter triggered memories deep within the recesses of the Mih'schen's mind. *I've heard that laugh before. But where?*

"You're still a fool," Slag said smugly. "Always taking your eye off your enemy and allowing him to flank you. I would've thought you'd learned that lesson by now."

Stunned both by the attack and his enemy's words, Khalen stared in confusion.

The reddish eyes that looked back at him through the eye sockets were filled with a cruel mirth. "So I see you're still hiding your heritage. When will you accept the fact that you'll *never* belong among these people? Once they find out the truth, their prejudice will cause them to throw you out with the trash."

"Who...who are you?"

Slag laughed once more, the sound grating in Khalen's ears. "Yes, of course you wouldn't recognize me with this thing on. I have your friend Belenger to thank for that. The explosion he set tore off half my face."

"Bel...Belenger?" Khalen's eyes went wide, then swiftly changed color to a deep red as an intense hatred flooded over him.

"Yeeeesss," Slag hissed. "Your dull wits finally solved the riddle."

"Skaret."

"It's good to see you again, Khalen," Slag taunted. "By the way, how did you enjoy slavery?"

Despite his injuries, a white-hot rage surged within Khalen, adding fuel to his ebbing strength. He let out a howl of fury, arched his back and attempted to throw the smaller Ra-Nuuk off his chest. However, Slag seemed to have expected the move. He lashed out with the back of his gauntlet and struck his captive in the side of the head, knocking him senseless.

Khalen felt as if the world were spinning out of control around him. Even before he could recover, he felt Slag's hand grabbing the front of his jacket and lifting his torso off the ground. Khalen fought against the throbbing ache in his head and opened his eyes. He glared at his tormentor who now stood over him. "I'd...I'd rather...die than be...a slave again."

A long blade appeared in Slag's right hand as he brought it forth from its concealed holster. "I was hoping you'd say that. Goodbye, Khalen."

With a quick motion, the Ra-Nuuk warlord thrust the blade deep into Khalen's side.

20

DEFEAT

KHALEN GASPED as the blade pierced his body. Pain overwhelmed his senses and caused his vision to blur. He tasted blood on his lips and knew he was dying.

He had failed.

He felt himself falling backward. His addled brain barely registered the collision with the hard surface of the tower roof. Desperate, Khalen covered the ugly wound with his right hand in an effort to stem the flow of blood. He gazed up at Slag and saw victory reflected in the Ra-Nuuk's eyes.

Suddenly, the bright blue flash of a laser blast split the darkening sky. Slag's eyes shifted from supreme confidence to sincere shock and anger. His left hand grabbed at his right shoulder to cover the fresh wound. Before he could react, a second blast struck his hip. His legs buckled and he fell to the ground, severely wounded.

Lying on his back, Khalen could not tell who was firing or what was happening, but through the agonizing fog that clouded his mind, he heard Slag's voice calling for backup from the Lah'grex soldiers still on the remaining ship.

A few more seconds passed before he heard additional laser fire, followed by the engines of the ship powering up. Khalen's grip on consciousness wavered, interfering with his comprehension of time. It may have been moments, or hours later, but his senses were finally aroused by the overwhelming rumble of the ship lifting off.

He began to fade once more when a shadow passed above him. In his disoriented state, all he could see was a pair of disembodied eyes staring down at him. After several attempts to make sense of the image, he finally realized the person had his or her head covered by black cloth, leaving only the eyes visible.

"The Ra-Nuuk is gone," the figure said in a deep baritone. "Your injury is very severe. I'm going to add some more pressure to the wound."

A fresh wave of pain enveloped Khalen, causing him to momentarily black out. When he regained consciousness, he heard familiar voices calling out to him.

"Your friends are coming..."

The only clue he received that his rescuer had left was the smallest rustle of fabric.

Brin'tac jolted with fear as the lift door to his right opened. His initial panic quickly morphed into relief as the two Solemsiel Arrangers stepped out onto the rooftop.

"Masters Roakel and Saryn...thanks be to the Universe."

"We are too late," Saryn said, her expression sinking at the sight of the empty landing platforms.

"Noble Galithar, what transpired here?" Roakel asked. Reaching down, he helped the still bound Lah'grex to his feet.

Brin'tac swayed unsteadily for a moment as his bruised and battered body found its equilibrium. Roakel took out a versitool from his jacket pocket and began to cut the middle section of the metal bindings from Brin'tac's wrists.

"I...I couldn't see very well," Brin'tac said. Now that his family was gone, he had no choice but to return to the plan set forth by Lady Crisenth; that meant playing the innocent victim once more. "Chovan and Khalen fought Slag. I think they're both injured or...or worse. Someone else started firing. I couldn't see who it was, but I think they wounded Slag because he had to be helped into his ship."

"Where is Khalen?" Roakel asked as his tool finished cutting the metal.

"Over there by the cooling unit," Brin'tac said as Roakel returned his tool to his pocket.

The Arrangers broke into a full run, their long strides swiftly carrying them across the surface of the roof. Brin'tac cast a quick glance at Kovitch, who was huddled near his injured sibling just a few feet away, then turned and ran after the Solemsiel couple.

The wind whipped his clothing around his legs as he ran, slowing him down. As he drew near the scene of the battle, he felt a deep sense of grief settle into his stomach. Khalen lay on the ground surrounded by a pool of blood. Saryn was kneeling next to him and examining the wound in his side. Roakel stood guard beside her, his eyes searching the area for any further signs of danger. A dozen feet away, Brin'tac caught his breath at the sight of Chovan's unmoving body. He made his way over to the fallen Lah'grex soldier and knelt on one knee to check for a pulse. When his fingers made contact with the clammy skin, he hung his head in defeat.

This is not how it was supposed to happen! They assured me they wouldn't kill my people! I knew I couldn't trust them, but I had hoped... How many more will die before this is over? Brin'tac thought in despair, his grief threatening to swallow him.

Then, from out of the darkness he heard Roakel's wind-staff begin to play. A moment later, Saryn's voice lifted in a comforting melody that sent a glimmer of hope flickering to life within Brin'tac's soul. Light from the Solemsiel's song illuminated the area in shades of soft blues, vibrant greens, and bright reds, catching Brin'tac's attention. As he listened, he felt the tension in his muscles ease and the grief in his heart lessen.

Standing, he turned and watched in wonder as Saryn's upper hands began to conduct. As she did so, her lower pair of hands came to rest on her friend's chest. Energy and light began to focus and swirl around Saryn's outstretched hands the moment they touched Khalen.

Hope filled Brin'tac as he saw the roiling streams of energy enter Khalen's body. Mesmerized, he stood rooted to the spot, a solitary tear sliding down his cheek. Saryn continued to sing for several more minutes, accompanied by her husband's skillful playing. She finally brought the song to a gentle conclusion and bowed her head. Brin'tac caught the sounds of a heartfelt prayer rising over the wind.

The three of them remained unmoving for a few moments until at long last, Khalen began to stir. Both Arrangers let out their breaths in relief and smiled. "Thank the Composer. You are alive!" Saryn exclaimed.

Brin'tac felt his guilt ease at the news. He was about to join the three of them when movement across the roof drew his attention. Vel'vikis, Inspector Mak'sim, and Tas'anee exited the lift. The sight of the group served as an additional balm to Brin'tac's grief.

As they drew closer, Vel'vikis and Tas'anee dropped to one knee and bowed. "Eth Galithar, we failed you," Vel'vikis said.

The understatement sent Brin'tac's frustration boiling over. "Yes, you did. What happened in the tower? How were you rendered unconscious so easily?"

"It appears they used miniature remotes the size of tiny insects to climb onto our legs while we were in the meeting. They delivered high-powered jolts to each of us, knocking us unconscious and disabling our remotes."

Brin'tac scowled. "Why didn't you detect these remotes? I employ you to protect me from precisely these kinds of attacks! You are obviously inept. As of now you are relieved of duty."

"Eth Galithar, please!" Vel'vikis pleaded. "Neither the Inspector nor I have ever encountered tech like this before! Remotes that small have *never* been known to carry charges strong enough to incapacitate someone and evade detection. No one can be prepared for technology that isn't supposed to exist!"

"Noble Galithar, Vel'vikis speaks the truth," Roakel interjected. "You must not hold him accountable. Even Saryn, Khalen and I did not find any evidence of a trap. The presence of the Ra-Nuuk and the usage of Synths suggests the Dumah Dynasty has chosen to align themselves with the Minor cultures."

"Synths?" Brin'tac asked in shock.

Roakel nodded. "When Khalen awoke, he informed me that he and the others were attacked by Synths."

"They must have been powered down. Otherwise our scanners would have detected them," Vel'vikis added.

Mak'sim shook his head. "That doesn't make sense. Synths *never* allow themselves to be deactivated. And surely even the Dumah Dynasty wouldn't resort to using Synths. Dumah was devastated as much as the rest of the Twin Galaxies during the Synth Uprising. Srisu reksani may be a fool, but even she isn't stupid enough to trust those glorified Autos."

"Never underestimate the lengths people will go through when pressured," Brin'tac said. "Vel'vikis, it is clear you could not have foreseen this ambush. I withdraw my previous dismissal. For now, we need to return to the ships. I must contact my cousin and the rest of the Dynasty rulers." Turning, Brin'tac addressed the Arrangers. "Masters Roakel and Saryn, are you able to open a portal?"

Roakel nodded. "Yes. I just received word from Nara's remote, Scamp. She located and deactivated the portal inhibitor."

"Excellent. Then, if you please, can you get us back inside the tower? We need to find out what happened to Dostal and retrieve our remotes as well. Vel'vikis and Tas'anee, please bring Chovan's body."

As the two Lah'grex stooped to complete their task, Khalen reached out weakly and grabbed Saryn's arm to get her attention. "Shosta...Kovitch..."

Saryn nodded and smiled back at him. "Rest assured. I would never leave them behind." Standing, Saryn raised her voice and called out to the drallmari. The two beasts responded to their names and began to make their way slowly across the roof.

Inspector Mak'sim's sudden call cut through the air, drawing everyone's attention. "Maestra Saryn. Hurry! One of the Dumah soldiers is still alive."

Brin'tac watched as Saryn sprinted over to the body. The Lah'grex guard's pulse was faint and the wound on the side of his head was covered in blood. Once again, the Arrangers repeated their Song of Healing. After several minutes, the wound had closed.

Mak'sim turned toward Brin'tac. "Eth Galithar, this could be the break we were waiting for. This soldier may have information that could lead to your family."

"That's good news, Inspector," Brin'tac said with a sigh, the evening's activities still weighing on his soul.

"Tas'anee, bind him and bring him with us," Vel'vikis commanded.

"Hurry," Brin'tac said. "Time is of the essence. Our own soldiers may still be straddling the line between life and death." Turning to Roakel, Brin'tac added. "Please, maestro. Open the portal. Maestra Saryn, we may have need of your services once again."

Roakel raised his windstaff and began the song that would produce the portal. Before long the entire group had passed through the vortex and were back inside the tower.

Vel'vikis and Tas'anee gently laid Chovan's body down while Mak'sim dropped the Dumah soldier. As he set about binding the prisoner's hands with rope, the others began searching the room for Dostal. Within seconds, Tas'anee called out to the rest of the group. "He's over here. He's barely breathing!"

Saryn and Roakel responded to the call and ran toward the injured Lah'grex to tend to him.

While they worked, Brin'tac turned to Vel'vikis, Mak'sim, and Tas'anee. "We need to retrieve Hujik's remote."

"We need to get Roadblock as well," Khalen added from where he stood leaning against a nearby table.

Vel'vikis nodded. "Yes, eth Galithar. Hopefully the damage is minimal and we'll be able to reactivate them. Khalen, keep an eye on our prisoner."

"Of course," Khalen said as he lowered himself to the ground to lean against the wall. A moment later, the three Lah'grex left the room to complete their task.

Saryn continued her song for another minute. While she sang, Brin'tac studied her movements. "I want to learn to do that," he said, sitting next to Khalen. "I wish my father would have let me study music. But he demanded I focus on politics. When I did see him, he was strict and harsh. But I didn't see him often. He was much too busy with governing the stubborn people to bother with his children. I vowed I would never be like that. Yet...," Brin'tac let out a chuckle brimming with regret, "I fell into the same trap. And now my family's gone, and they're all I can think about. It's sad that it often takes an emergency or severe trial to get us to truly recognize what we value most."

Khalen, too weak to respond, simply let the Lah'grex continue on.

"But anyway, I've always been fascinated by how musical energy can be used to speed up a body's natural healing process." He turned and looked toward Khalen's side where he had been stabbed. Through the large tear in his jacket,

Brin'tac could see the new scar on Khalen's flesh where the wound had been.

His eyes narrowed in confusion as he studied it more intently. The skin surrounding the scar had dark markings on it and did not match the rest of Khalen's skin. Taking his eyes off the man's side, Brin'tac looked closer at the rest of the now healed burn marks and injuries on his exposed face and neck. In each case, the healed area was surrounded by a flap of unnatural, loose skin. Beneath each flap was a second skin covered in the same dark markings.

Brin'tac pulled away from him in shock and horror. "Those are...those are tattoos beneath synthetic flesh!"

Although weakened by his recent injuries, Khalen swore in frustration and struggled to stand.

Brin'tac jumped to his feet and backed away, his eyes wide in alarm. "You're not a Mih'schen at all. You're a Meh'ishto!"

21

PRIDE AND PREJUDICE

BRIN'TAC CONTINUED to back away as Khalen struggled to find his balance. Further adding to his terror, the Lah'grex leader watched as Kovitch left his place next to Shosta and had begun to walk warily toward him, as if sensing the sudden spike in his master's composure.

"How...how is this possible?" Brin'tac stuttered. "You must be working with them somehow to trick me into trusting you!"

The color of Khalen's eyes began to darken as his anger mounted. "Are you serious? How could you think that? I risked my life for you and your family, and this is the thanks I get?"

"If that's what you really did. How do I know it wasn't all an elaborate ruse?"

Khalen swore again. "You're an even greater fool than I thought. You think my wounds were faked? I'm so sick of your high-and-mighty attitude. You're nothing but a—"

"Khalen!" Saryn shouted as she rushed over. Her teal cheeks were flushed with concern. "Noble Galithar, I assure you on my honor as a Solemsiel—"

"Honor?" Brin'tac spat back. "You deceived me! That isn't a trait of the Solemsiel, but of the Seyvreen! More than likely, you and your husband are both Tritonus!"

By the stunned and wounded expression on Saryn's face, Brin'tac guessed she would have been less hurt if he had slapped her. Tears welled in her eyes.

"You would never level such an accusation if you knew them," Roakel interjected. "Perhaps if you would allow us to explain—"

"I don't want your explanation!" Brin'tac shouted as he backed toward the door. "I'm going to call the Jorlinari commander on Dhun'drok and have you all arrested!"

Saryn shook her head imploringly. "Please do not do this."

"You're wasting your time, Saryn," Khalen sneered. "I told you before, the rest of the universe isn't as understanding as you and Roakel. They're blinded by hatred and prejudice."

"Noble Galithar, reflect for a moment," Roakel said firmly as he moved to stand next to his wife. "Have any of our words or actions been less than honorable? Certainly an intelligent ruler such as yourself understands that a being ought to be judged by the quality of his or her character, not on arbitrary physical characteristics. Are you going to cast aside our deeds and simply judge us because of some ink on Khalen's skin?"

Brin'tac hesitated as Roakel's words infiltrated his mind. "No. It's more than just ink. I judge him by his culture."

"Are we nothing more than this? Are we mere puppets and pawns of our culture and ethnicity? Do we not all possess the free will to select what is morally noble and just, or are some chosen to be righteous and others doomed to wickedness?"

"Yes, we all have free will. But you can't erase the past!" Brin'tac shot back. "His people are responsible for thousands of years of pain and suffering as they pillaged, kidnapped, ravaged, and…and visited numerous horrors upon the galaxies. The Meh'ishto are a blight upon the universe!"

Khalen bristled at the insult, and for a moment Brin'tac feared he would attack. However, Saryn began to sing softly. This time, however, instead of singing in solfege, she sang lyrics. As such, the still air was filled with colorful light but no energy.

"In you, and you alone do I have my being
Let me be your instrument
To bring harmony to discord
And light to the darkness
May every note I play bring honor
To your mighty name."

For a moment, Brin'tac felt he was experiencing some new aspect of the musical sciences he had never heard of before. He had always been told the solfege syllables were the key to unlocking the energy woven into the fabric of nature. There were songs that could hypnotize or calm the listener, but this ordinary song seemed to have the exact same effect on Khalen but without the use of solfege.

As Saryn finished her song, Brin'tac could see the tension in Khalen drain away and the dark red color of his eyes faded to gray. And even more, he realized his own anger had evaporated. "Maestra Saryn," Brin'tac said more calmly, his gaze still fixed upon the Meh'ishto warrior, "while I recognize the wisdom in your words, you must also understand that this is a great shock to me. We need to discuss this further, but I think it best if Khalen is not present as we do so. The others will be less...amiable than I toward him."

"Fine by me," Khalen stated. "Think what you want about me. I'm done helping ungrateful, prejudiced scumbags."

Saryn sighed, then turned and placed a hand on Khalen's shoulder. "You still need to rest so your body can recover. Let us return to the *Lightbringer*." She leaned over and whispered something to him. Although he did not appear happy with the situation, his expression showed no further signs of anger. Instead, it seemed to Brin'tac as if a sudden profound weariness of mind and soul weighed on him.

Saryn stepped back and began to sing once more, accompanied by her husband on his windstaff. As Khalen stepped over to the newly formed portal, he glanced back. Brin'tac expected to see bitterness or hostility in Khalen's eyes and was surprised to see only frustration in the man's gaze. A moment later, the three of them passed through the portal, and it closed behind them, leaving Brin'tac alone with his thoughts.

Wearied by recent events, he allowed himself to slide down the wall behind him until he was seated on the floor. Pulling his knees to his chest, he rested his arms on them and bowed his head, Saryn's song echoing in his mind.

"You have done well, Galithar."

"Thank you, Lady Crisenth," Brin'tac said. Once he was

alone in his chambers aboard the *Eternal Harmony*, he had contacted the Tritonus Overlord as commanded. The holographic image of Lady Crisenth hovered over the communications desk.

"While your 'capture' didn't go as expected, our contingency plans should work nicely with the current situation. I must say, your friends are quite resourceful."

"Yes, they are. I'm grateful to hear their interference will not disrupt your plans."

"They will not. But there are others who might. Slag has informed me there was someone else atop the tower who attacked him. The outer cameras of the ships showed only a figure in black. Do you know anything about this person?"

Brin'tac's eyes widened. *Someone else was on the tower?* he thought. *Someone even the Tritonus don't know about?* Aloud, he said, "This is the first I've heard. I was too far away to see what happened."

The Overlord's face hardened. "Indeed. Do what you can to discover the identity of this interloper and report it to me immediately."

"Yes, my lady. How shall I proceed from here?"

"I trust you discovered the wounded Dumah soldier and healed him?"

"Yes."

"Excellent. You must extract the location of the base from him. Then, you will convince the others to mount a rescue attempt."

Brin'tac nodded. "Very well. The Solemsiels will protest, but I will have Mak'sim obtain the information."

"Yes, we would not want to upset the delicate sensibilities of the Arrangers. We need them to trust your motives. Use an alternative method."

"I'm sorry, my lady. I don't follow. What other method do you suggest?"

"You are now aware of the Meh'ishto's true identity, correct? Ask him. He has ways. It was one of the reasons he and his Solemsiel friends were chosen. It will help repair the damage to your 'friendship', provide you with the information, and renew his interest in the mission. Contact me again when you are on your way to the base."

"Understood."

"This is outrageous! These…false Arrangers, or Tritonus, can no longer be trusted. We *must* contact the Jorlinari commander and have them arrested!"

Brin'tac studied each member of the group now assembled in the meeting room aboard the *Eternal Harmony*. As always, he sat at the head of the table in his plush, throne-like chair. Vel'vikis sat on his immediate right with Mak'sim pacing the floor behind him. The Solemsiel couple sat on Brin'tac's left side across from his Lah'grex advisors.

Roakel appeared unfazed by Inspector Mak'sim's rant and looked at him serenely. "Inspector, let me assure you, if my wife and I were truly covert Seyvreen, you would have been incapacitated long ago."

"Is that a threat?" Mak'sim said, spinning around to glare at the Solemsiel.

"Nothing of the sort. I was merely stating a fact."

"Master Roakel does have a point," Brin'tac interjected. "Now that I've had time to process what happened, I believe they can still be trusted. Besides the obvious fact that Khalen nearly died trying to help me and my family, they have no motive for wanting to deceive us. After all, *we* sought *their* help, not the other way around. And Khalen and our Solemsiel guests had every chance to attack me once I discovered his secret, yet they chose not to do so."

"It still doesn't alter the fact that this particular pair of Arrangers deliberately chose to hide their companion's true identity!"

"Inspector Mak'sim, with all due respect, Khalen's identity does *not* rest in his heritage," Roakel said. "His identity is found solely in his belief in the Great Composer and in the truths contained in the Sacred Songbook. As the astute Solemsiel philosopher Kalailioen once wrote, 'Only the Craftsman can determine the true purpose of the tool.' He also said, 'The virtuous places the comfort of others above his own.' In this case, it includes doing our utmost to make others feel comfortable in our presence. Would you have felt comfortable in Khalen's presence if you had observed his true appearance?"

Disarmed by the Arranger's philosophical argument, Mak'sim frowned. "No. Of course not."

"Furthermore, you would not have allowed him to accompany us had you known his heritage, and we would not have agreed to participate had you rejected him on the basis of his heritage. Yet we wished to be of service to your family. Therefore, this seemed the most logical and simplest solution."

"In addition," Saryn said, "since we first met Khalen and recognized the depth of his character, one of our goals has been to assist others to look past his outer appearance and observe the strong man of virtue that lies within."

Brin'tac leaned back in his chair and steepled his fingers together in front of him. "I'd very much like to know how you *did* meet him."

"He was introduced to us by a Faluvinal music master and prophet of the Great Composer named Riveruun," Roakel explained. "Maestro Riveruun was a beloved friend of ours before his passing last year."

"But how does a Meh'ishto become a traveling companion of a Faluvinal?" Vel'vikis asked, speaking for the first time since the meeting began.

"He was sold into slavery many years ago," Roakel explained. "He was nearly killed during that time and would have died had it not been for Riveruun's intervention. He not only preserved his life, but also introduced him to the knowledge and wisdom of the Sacred Songbook, where he learned about the love and forgiveness offered by the Creator of all life."

Although he guessed it went unnoticed by the Solemsiel, Brin'tac caught sight of Mak'sim frowning dismissively at Roakel's statements. Looking back toward the couple, Brin'tac took in a deep breath and let it out before responding. "Master Arrangers, I'm perplexed by this situation. As a believer in the Universal Rhythm, it is my understanding that all beings are caught in the cycle of life, death, and rebirth. Their status in this life is determined by the debt of karma they have built up in previous lives. So if one keeps the eightfold Precepts of Conduct, one will be born to a higher status. But if not, one is born into a lower caste. This is the origin of the Minor races and the Tritonus.

"With this understanding, it seems impossible to me that one could circumvent the law of reincarnation and change one's status within one lifetime," he continued. "Khalen was born a Meh'ishto, and nothing he does or believes can change that. Even his barely-controlled temper is evidence that, try as he might, the Meh'ishto inside of him lies just below the surface."

"But in the tower, even you agreed we all possess free will, am I right?" Saryn asked.

"Yes."

"Then everything that makes us who we are—our behaviors, thoughts, actions, words, character, passions—can be shaped and molded by our wills. You must recognize that our physical bodies are but a small part of who we are or choose to be. We are spirit beings as well as physical. And as such, we can overcome our past by allowing the Composer to change us from the inside into beings that reflect his righteous character."

"It's obvious we each view the universe very differently," Brin'tac said with a weak smile. "But I will say this: based on the time I spent with Khalen aboard your ship, I was impressed by his intelligence and respect. As such, I'm willing to trust your judgment of him for the time being."

"It brings me joy to hear that, Noble Galithar," Roakel stated with a smile of his own. "For otherwise, I am afraid we would be forced to part ways."

"Which brings up the next topic of discussion," Mak'sim said, his expression leaving no doubt in Brin'tac's mind he was unhappy about the decision regarding Khalen. "What do we do now? Although Dumah's attempt to capture you failed, they still have your family."

Brin'tac set his jaw firmly before responding. "I think it's time to take the fight to them." Everyone in the room stared back at him in surprise. Brin'tac leaned back in his chair and continued. "Dumah has proven they are beyond reason. Their demands were outlandish and were clearly a cover to get to me. My cousin will never agree to any of their requests. If I hope to ever see my family alive and safe, we will have to rescue them ourselves."

"But how do you propose to do this?" Roakel asked.

"We still have the Dumah soldier who was wounded and left behind. We could interrogate him and find out where their base is located. Then, we go there, sneak in, and rescue my family."

Saryn shook her head. "We are explicitly against any form of torture. We must never use severe pain to extract information."

"It's easy enough for you to hold such high morals. It isn't your family that's at risk," Mak'sim challenged. "You might feel differently if it were your children being held prisoner."

"In my lifetime, I have witnessed horrendous acts and heard of unspeakable suffering. My own sister was the victim of violence. I know the price of freedom," Saryn shot back. "But what must always set us apart from those who chose the path of evil is our conviction to never compromise our moral virtues. The ends do *not* justify the means. To achieve good through evil methods corrupts the soul."

Mak'sim seemed about to counter her words when Brin'tac interrupted. "Perhaps we could find another way to obtain the information. I have heard there are some songs that can be used to make other beings more agreeable. The music puts the listener at ease and causes even hostile opponents to lower their guard. Do you know of such songs, Master Roakel?"

The Solemsiel's face darkened at the suggestion. "While it is true such songs exist, we Solemsiel are opposed to using the musical sciences in such a fashion."

Brin'tac frowned. "But surely in circumstances such as these you would be willing to make an exception."

"Even if I were willing, neither my wife nor I am familiar with the chord progressions and melody of the song that must be used."

The Lah'grex leader's expression shifted. "Then perhaps there would be another willing and knowledgeable. A Meh'ishto would likely be quite adept at that skill, if I am not mistaken. Please, for the sake of my family, ask Khalen if he will help."

22

RECOVERY

KHALEN AWOKE to the sound of voices just outside his door.

"Aunt Saryn, I'm...uh...I don't want to wake him up if he's sleeping."

"Do not worry, Nara. I already spoke to him earlier. He is expecting us."

"I'm so glad to hear dat Unca Khawen is gonna be okay."

Still feeling somewhat groggy, Khalen remained prone on his bed as the door opened to his room. He had long ago developed the habit of sleeping with at least a dim source of light. It allowed him to see just enough to identify the silhouettes of Saryn, Jov, and Nara as they entered the room.

Once they were inside, Jov whispered, "Unca Khawen? Awe you seeping?"

Although Jov's quirks sometimes became a source of irritation to Khalen, the teen's innocence was just as often refreshing and uplifting to his spirit. "Yes," he replied, deciding to have a little fun with the Tii-Koona youth.

"Whu?"

Unable to contain himself, Khalen opened his eyes a little wider so he could get a better look at the confused expression on Jov's face. The movement gave him away enough for the teen to realize the truth.

"Aw, you'we such a faker. You betta watch it! I'm'a punch you'we lights out for foowen me!" Jov said playfully as he moved closer to Khalen's bed with his fist raised.

Khalen laughed at the young Tii-Koona and pushed himself into a sitting position on the bed. Saryn meanwhile raised the level of the lights, her own laughter filling the room. Nara, however, remained back by the door, her body language reserved and guarded.

Before Khalen could say anything further, Jov's eyes grew big and his demeanor shifted to one of amazement. "Wow! Unca Khawen, wha' happened to you'we face and awms?"

It was then Khalen remembered that, in his anger, he had ripped off the rest of the damaged synthetic skin, allowing his tattoos to be displayed in all their tainted glory. He now understood why Nara was so distant, and the resulting stab to his heart was as painful as the wound inflicted by Slag.

"Is dat a skull?" Jov continued. In his innocence, he was oblivious to Nara's reaction. "Dat is so awesome! An' dis pictuwe here—is dat a fwenix? Wow! It looks like he's... teawing dat guy apawrt. Amazing."

Khalen grimaced at Jov's words, yet the teen's lack of revulsion at the sight of the tattoos brought him comfort. "At least someone appreciates them," he said, his eyes coming to rest on Nara. He immediately regretted his words as he caught a glimpse of fear in her eyes. "I'm sorry, Nara. I shouldn't have said that."

Nara started to turn toward the door when Saryn laid a reassuring hand on her shoulder. "It is all right. You do not have to be frightened. Khalen has not changed. He remains the same person we all know and love."

As the Tii-Koona female turned back to face him, Khalen saw that tears had replaced her fear. "Why...why didn't you tell us?" she said, her voice cracking from emotion.

"Yeah," Jov echoed. "When did you get dese put on youw skin? Do dey rub off?"

Saryn spoke before Khalen could formulate an answer. "We did not inform either of you for the same reason we did not inform eth Galithar. Although Khalen no longer follows the ways of his people, they nevertheless have a reputation for cruelty. We wanted you to get to know him first before we divulged his secret."

Khalen could tell the explanation failed to satisfy the teen. Nara paused before speaking. "I'm...glad you're okay. I just wanted you to know that." Before Khalen or Saryn could say anything more, the teen bolted for the door and left the room.

"Wait!" Jov called after her. "Nawa, where awe you going?" When she didn't respond, Jov looked first at Saryn, then at Khalen in confusion. "Wha's her pwoblem? Does Nawa not like you'we skin-pictuwes?"

"No, she doesn't, Jov," Khalen said. He felt the all-too familiar sense of anger rising within him. He was angry at Brin'tac for his prejudice, angry at Nara for showing fear toward him, angry at himself for still allowing others to bring forth feelings of hurt and rejection within him, and most of all, angry at Dominuus for causing him to be born a Meh'ishto.

As if sensing something was wrong, Jov leaned over Khalen and wrapped him in a warm embrace. Despite the youth's body odor and dirty shirt—worn both inside out and backwards—his unconditional love for Khalen broke through the anger which had moments ago threatened to engulf him.

The Great Composer was once again using an Accidental to bring color to the music of his own life.

In typical Jov fashion, the embrace lasted far longer than most people would consider polite. Although Khalen was uncomfortable with physical affection, he could not deny the peace the innocent teen's hug brought him.

When Jov finally sat back, Khalen smiled at him and tussled his short, curly hair. "Thanks, bud. I needed that."

"Yeah. I know," Jov stated with a beaming smile. "I'm gonna go find Nawa. I tink she needs a hug too. I'm so glad you'we okay. Bye."

With that, the Tii-Koona youth waved at Khalen and Saryn as he crossed the room and exited through the door. Once he was gone, Saryn sat in a chair near the bed and wiped a tear from her eye. "I so cherish that young one."

"Yeah. He's quite a wonderful contradiction."

"I am sorry about Nara. When she heard about what happened and learned you are a Meh'ishto, she insisted on seeing you. I had my concerns about how she would react to your tattoos, but she assured me she would be respectful."

"She's young," Khalen said, reminding himself of that truth. "I can't expect more from her."

"I believe that in the course of time she will come around. How are you doing otherwise?"

"Physically, spiritually, mentally, or emotionally?"

"All of them."

Khalen sighed. "Physically I'm weak but recovering quickly. Thank you, by the way."

Saryn smiled. "It was my honor."

"Spiritually, I'm always struggling. I can't help but question the Composer's will for my life. Just when I think I know where he's leading me, he takes me in a totally different direction, just like he did when Riveruun died. Mentally, I often can't figure myself out. I know what I should do, but when the time comes, my emotions get in the way, and I wind up with an internal struggle between my will and my feelings, and my will often loses."

"This is one area that has always been a mystery for me," Saryn said. "I cannot fathom what it must be like to be at war with oneself."

"Well, I can tell you, it's no fun," Khalen said dryly. "And as for my emotions, they're a mess."

"That I can imagine. It brings grief to my soul that you had to face Brin'tac's condemnation like that."

Khalen smirked. "That's not quite what I was referring to. I'm used to having others judge me for my appearance."

"No one should ever have to get used to something like that."

"I don't blame him, I suppose. The Meh'ishto clans as a whole have earned their negative reputation. I can see why some beings don't even recognize that the Meh'ishto and Mih'schen share the same ancestry."

Saryn leaned forward and laid a hand on his shin. "You are no longer the same person who fled your homeworld all those years ago. The Composer has redeemed you. Always remember that you are made in his image and likeness. No one can take that from you. You are a new instrument in the hands of the Maestro of All Maestros. You are a child of Dominuus. Cling to the Symphonian Code. Never allow the prejudice or cruelty of anyone to cause you to doubt that truth."

Khalen stared at Saryn's compassionate countenance and drew strength from her kindness. The natural flow of her specialized Solemsiel hair follicles had a calming effect on him, as of a gentle breeze blowing on a warm summer day. The movement made the pink highlights in her hair look like waves rolling over a dark-blue sea.

"Trust me, that's one of the only things keeping me sane," Khalen said. "I don't doubt that truth, but sometimes the old me—the thoughts, the bad habits, the…the anger and rage—rises to the surface so fast it makes me feel as if I'll never truly change. Riveruun always told me I'd be able to over-come my old self, but I'm not so sure. Maybe I should just accept that this is who I am."

Saryn sat back, her expression turning playful. "I am sorry, it was not my intention to interrupt your—what do you call it?—'pity party'. Perhaps I should come back at a more convenient time."

Khalen chuckled. "Was that sarcasm? I think that's a first for you!"

"I have obviously been 'hanging around' you for too long!" She shot back as a smile spread across her face. "As even your Mih'schen philosophers recognize, 'bad company cor-rupts good character.'"

"Right. I'll keep that in mind."

After sharing a laugh, Saryn grew serious once more. "You have to be patient with yourself. While it only takes a moment to accept the Creator's love and become his child, it takes a lifetime for him to perfect us. Let me pose a question to you: how old were you when you believed?"

"Fifty-three."

"And you are sixty-one now, correct?"

Khalen nodded.

"So for fifty years of your life your brain was wired by cruelty, hatred, selfishness, and all manner of evil," Saryn said, her compassion coloring her voice. "Do you not think you should at least allow the Great Composer half that time to shape you for the better?"

Sitting up straight, Khalen turned his head toward Saryn and chuckled. "You know, you sound just like Riveruun. Do they train all of you Perfect race types at the same schools?"

Saryn chuckled. "Truth is truth. Anyway, the sooner you learn to control your flaring temper and loose tongue, the easier it will be to develop friendships."

Khalen laughed. "Yeah, I'm sure my colorful language didn't help Brin'tac look past my skin to see my finer traits."

"No, I am fairly certain it did not," Saryn said with a grimace. "The only path to gaining the respect of those who are against you is to repay their hatred with kindness. Always remember they are not the true enemy. We fight in a spiritual war against unseen forces."

Khalen growled in frustration. "Yeah, I know, I know! It's just...sometimes the anger takes over. Controlling my temper is easier said than done."

"'Narrow is the stream that leads to righteousness.'"

Khalen leaned back against the headrest once more and winced as a stab of pain lanced through his side. Letting out his breath, he began to relax again.

"It is still bothering you?"

"Yeah. Just residual pains." Khalen stared at the ceiling for a moment. When he turned his gaze back to his companion, his demeanor was serious. "Saryn, I...I know who Slag is."

Shocked by his statement, Saryn straightened. "What do you mean? Have you encountered him before?"

"More than encountered him. He was one of the mercs in Belenger's Renegades."

Stunned, Saryn looked at him intently, waiting for him to explain.

Khalen took a deep breath and plunged ahead. "His real name is Skaret. If he has a surname, he never told it to me. Like many of us Belenger took under his wing, Skaret had fled his home. He said he murdered someone and was on the run, but I found out later that was a lie.

"From what I pieced together from our conversations over the years, he was trained to be an assassin and music maestro by his father. However, he somehow dishonored his family and fled before they could kill him. He stayed with the Renegades until he found a way to regain his honor and his family's trust. Betraying Belenger and selling me into slavery was a part of that."

Saryn's eyes grew wide in shock. "He is the one? This Ra-Nuuk with the mask is the same one? Are you certain?"

Khalen nodded. "Just before he stabbed me, he told me who he was. Once he revealed himself, I recognized his voice."

Saryn shook her head in amazement. "How is it that in all the Twin Galaxies, the one person responsible for your suffering happens to be the very same one involved in the abduction of Brin'tac's family?"

"That would be a question for the Master Orchestrator," Khalen said wryly. "But for now, one thing's for sure: I have to go after him."

Saryn opened her mouth to speak but was cut off as Khalen raised his hand.

"I know what you're going to say. This isn't about revenge. As you can see, Skaret is dangerous and needs to be taken down. His cruelty knows no bounds."

Saryn was silent for several moments as she studied him, almost as if she were reading his intentions. "I am in agreement that we should do something to stop him, if we can. However, it would behoove you to pray and make certain your motives are pure. I must ask: have you forgiven him?"

This time, it was Khalen's turn to remain silent as he searched his own heart. When he answered, his voice was low and grim. "No. I haven't."

"I feared as much," Saryn replied. "Unforgiveness is like drinking rankil root juice and hoping the other person becomes ill. It leads to bitterness within your own heart. The Sacred Songbook instructs us to love those who seek us harm and pray for those who wound us. Remember what is written in the third verse of the *Song of Wisdom*?

'Seek not the discord of vengeance,
but trust the Composer.
He will remove the errant notes
And weave together a melody;
A melody of justice for the faithful.'

And the Symphonian Code states, 'A maestro uses music to promote peace, not seek revenge.' In many ways, this Skaret is not unlike how you once were. Perhaps it is the Composer's will that you pray for his conversion. Perhaps you are the instrument that will bring the knowledge of the truth to your enemies."

"That's easy enough for you to say. Have you ever had to forgive someone who had wronged you so much?"

Saryn's countenance fell. "As a matter of fact, yes, I have. One does not spend hundreds of years in the Shadow Realms and not face grief. That is what we Solemsiel call the territories ruled by the Major races and their Minor counterparts. When I was young, only 127 years of age, my sister, Elethana, enrolled to be an Arranger. She was passionate about reaching those who had never heard the truth about the love of the Great Composer. However, after three decades of service to the Tii-Koona people, she was captured and—from what we were able to discover—tortured. I never saw her again. It took me years to be able to truly forgive those who snuffed out her life."

Khalen looked at Saryn with new understanding. "I'm so sorry about your sister. I guess you know more than I thought." Not knowing what else to say, Khalen sought out a new subject. "Saryn, something's not right about all this."

"What do you mean?"

"As I've been lying here, I've been thinking about everything that's happened. Some of it doesn't make sense. For example, if Dumah's whole goal was to capture Brin'tac, then why invite a pair of Arrangers?"

Saryn shrugged. "Perhaps because it is common practice for negotiations like this to utilize a neutral party as mediators."

"Yes, but then why didn't they kill you once they had him? Why leave you as witnesses?"

Saryn remained silent. When she did not respond, he continued. "And when Skaret was fighting me, he didn't call for aid from the second ship until after..."

"Until after what?"

"I forgot. I haven't had a chance to tell you yet."

Saryn frowned with sudden concern. "Tell me what?"

"After he stabbed me, I fell to the ground and…someone else shot him!"

"Who? Who shot him?"

Khalen shook his head. "I don't know who he was. He didn't kill Skaret, but only wounded him. And it was then that Skaret called for backup. Once the Dumah ship lifted off, I saw this…face hovering over mine."

"What was his appearance like? Was he Lah'grex?"

"I don't know. His entire face and head were covered in black. Only his eyes were visible."

"Are you certain you did not imagine him? You had lost much blood and may have hallucinated."

Again, Khalen shook his head. "No. I know what I saw. And I distinctly remember the look in Skaret's eyes when he was shot. It was as if he was suddenly…afraid. It was as if the stranger's appearance was completely unexpected. And he fled just before you arrived. In fact, he told me you were coming."

Saryn was silent once more, and Khalen could tell by the look on her face she was taking his observations seriously. When she spoke, her voice was filled with concern. "I think you are correct in your assessment. There is more occurring here than what we observe on the surface. We must pray Dominuus gives us the discernment to uncover the truth. I can assure you that Roakel and I have already communed with the Great Composer, and he has confirmed that we are to continue on our current path. I will express your concerns to Roakel. Perhaps we should speak to Brin'tac about it as well."

"No. I don't think that's wise. At this point, we don't know whom we can trust. I think we should keep this between the three of us. On another note, since you mentioned talking to Brin'tac about this, does that mean he's decided to stay with us?"

"Yes, at least for the present. In fact," she said, bracing herself to deliver the news, "he requested that I come here to ask for your assistance."

Khalen laughed out loud for a moment before realizing she was not joking. "You're serious?" he asked in shock. "One minute Galithar's ready to turn me over to the authorities, the next he needs my help? If you weren't standing here, I'd probably be spouting some very unrighteous and impolite words right now. What help could he want from a filthy 'inker'?"

"The Lah'grex want to use force to obtain information from the prisoner, but Roakel and I are opposed to it. Brin'tac suggested you might know an alternate method to coerce him to speak."

"Ah, I see. I guess I shouldn't be surprised. My people have a reputation for these kinds of things. Back on Meh'ish I was quite good at it. We called it 'the art of persuasion'."

"I have heard of such things. I never knew it was something you practiced."

"There's a lot about my past you don't know, and probably don't *want* to know."

"I must also tell you Roakel and I are still opposed. We feel it is wrong to use the musical sciences to circumvent the will of someone."

"Well, there might be a way to compromise," Khalen said. "While the most direct way to get information from a prisoner is to use music forcefully, there is a way that will make the person agreeable to speaking the truth. In other words, they offer the information of their own free will."

"That sounds much more acceptable. So does this mean you agree to do it? Will you aid us?"

Khalen shook his head in resignation. "You know, Saryn, you can be both endearing and frustrating at the same time. Your compassion is one of your strengths, but for those of us who want to nurse our grudges, you can be quite irritating."

"Thank you. I will take that as a compliment."

"I'll do it, but not for Brin'tac's sake. I'm doing it because I want to find Skaret."

"I am very appreciative," she said sincerely as she rose from the chair. "I will inform the others. We can commence once you feel strong enough."

"I'm ready now. Just let me put on some fresh clothes and grab my bindara. The sooner we find out where these scum are hiding, the sooner we can finish them off."

23

PERSUASION

AS KHALEN APPROACHED the *Eternal Harmony's* boarding ramp with Roakel, he could almost feel Vel'vikis's glare boring into him. Standing behind Brin'tac's chief of security, Tas'anee and Hujik stood at attention, their expressions wary.

Where he had once seen respect and even admiration in Vel'vikis's expression, Khalen now recognized the all-too-familiar look of distrust. Of course, with his tattoos visible, he expected it.

Although he was not proud of what the images represented, in the unrepentant places in his heart, he felt a kind of perverse pleasure knowing his marked flesh would make theirs crawl.

"Follow me," Vel'vikis commanded, then turned and strode up the ramp.

Roakel looked over at Khalen, clearly concerned about how he would react.

"What?" he asked, irritated by the Solemsiel's over-protectiveness.

"Are you certain you want to proceed?" Roakel asked.

"Proceed with what: interrogating the prisoner, or dealing with suspicious glares from Brin'tac and his guards?" Khalen asked as he locked gazes with Hujik, who stared back with open contempt.

"Both."

"Yeah. I'll be fine. Right, Hujik?" Khalen said with a lopsided grin.

The Lah'grex soldier remained silent and stoic.

"See? Nothing to worry about." Khalen smiled and walked boldly up the ramp after Vel'vikis. Roakel followed behind, with Hujik and Tas'anee bringing up the rear.

Vel'vikis led the group through the ship until they arrived at a door near the end of the main hallway. He opened it and stepped aside, motioning for Khalen and Roakel to enter. Nodding his "thanks" to the burly Lah'grex, Khalen strode through the opening.

Judging by the single bed built into the wall and the presence of a table and three chairs, Khalen knew the makeshift interrogation room was nothing more than converted living quarters. The remainder of the room was devoid of items or décor.

Brin'tac was seated in one of the chairs, and, as Khalen entered, the politician struggled to hide his reaction to the tattoos. However, unlike the other Lah'grex, he managed to bury his revulsion quickly, returning his features to their typical businesslike expression. Seated across the table was a Lah'grex male who, based on his drooping eyelids and lackluster appearance, seemed mildly sedated. Mak'sim stood behind the prisoner, his hand resting on his holstered pistol.

Brin'tac rose from his chair and faced Khalen. The Lah'grex leader's body language was reserved, and he offered no greeting. "Good. You're here. Let's get this over with," he said, his eyes never once making contact.

Although he had not expected a warm welcome from any of the Lah'grex, he nevertheless felt annoyed once more by their proximity. He took a deep breath and released it to calm himself. Saryn's words echoed in his mind. *"The only path to gaining the respect of those who are against you is to repay their hatred with kindness. Always remember they are not the true enemy. We fight in a spiritual war against unseen forces."*

Setting his will against his feelings, Khalen strode over to the prisoner and examined him. "How long ago did you administer the sedative?"

"Ten minutes ago. We followed your instructions precisely."

Khalen picked up the unoccupied chair and set it next to Mak'sim. With a thinly-veiled look of distrust, the inspector took several steps to his left, yielding the spot. Ignoring Mak'sim, Khalen unslung Riveruun's bindara case from his shoulder and set it on the floor. As he opened it and gazed at the stringed instrument, his thoughts drifted back to its former owner. He paused to wonder what his mentor would think of his using the instrument for this purpose. Brushing aside his misgivings, he took hold of the instrument reverently and lifted it out of the case.

He sat in the chair and tuned each of the twelve strings. Once they were in tune, he placed his fingers on the fingerboard and strummed a few chords to warm up. He finally looked up at the others gathered in the room and noticed for the first time that Vel'vikis had now joined them.

"Roakel, dim the lights, please," Khalen said. "I need the room cleared except for Roakel and the prisoner."

"What?" Mak'sim said in surprise. "This was never part of the agreement."

"For the song to have full effect, there must be no distractions," Khalen shot back. "Only the person asking the questions can remain in the room."

"Then that person should be me!" Mak'sim retorted.

Despite the inspector's escalated tension, Khalen remained calm.

"No. I want to do it," Brin'tac interjected. "It was my idea in the first place."

"Eth Galithar, I must protest. I am an inspector!"

"And I am a politician!" Brin'tac shot back. "I know how to ask probing questions as well, if not *better*, than you. Besides, my family's lives are at stake. I will handle this myself."

Left without a choice, Mak'sim backed down.

Khalen studied Brin'tac's expression, surprised by the fire burning in his eyes. After a lengthy pause, he nodded to Khalen. "The inspector, Vel'vikis, and Master Roakel will watch from the other room. Inspector, if you have any specific questions you would like to ask, you can relay those questions to me through the commlink."

Although his expression showed his frustration at the arrangements, Mak'sim acquiesced. "As you command, eth Galithar." With one last glare at Khalen, he left the room, followed by Vel'vikis and Roakel.

As the door closed behind them, Khalen let out a slow breath and felt his tension ease. "Okay, Brin'tac. Are you ready?"

The Lah'grex leader nodded.

Khalen closed his eyes yet again and began to play. It had been years since he had performed any music based on the E-flat whole tone scale of the Meh'ishto. As the first few notes were produced by the bindara, they brought forth more than just light and energy from the instrument; they brought forth buried memories as well.

Images of previous "prisoners" flitted through his mind, reminding him of his past. Unbidden memories of his prior life on his homeworld flooded over him, causing his fingers to stumble. He ceased playing for a moment and the energy dissipated.

Opening his eyes, he saw Brin'tac looking at him with concern. "Are you well, Khalen?"

Frustrated with himself and knowing the others were watching, he strengthened his resolve. "Yeah. It's just...It's been awhile." He closed his eyes once more and offered up a silent prayer. *Composer, I've given my life to you. I'm your instrument. I've used my skill and talent too many times for evil. Now use them for your purposes.* Feeling a sense of peace wash over him, he began to play once more.

This time, the notes came forth strong and confident. Khalen's fingers moved deftly over the bindara. The hypnotic, cyclical chord progression began softly with a series of arpeggios, then changed into strummed triads. Once the meter, rhythm, and chord progression were established, he began to sing. After having sung music in other keys and scales for so long, the solfege syllables of the E-flat whole tone scale felt odd on his lips yet held a familiar comfort. His past and present collided in his mind once more, each seeking domination over his thoughts and feelings. Setting his will, he shoved the disruptive emotions to the recesses of his mind.

With his inner victory complete, Khalen opened his eyes and studied the prisoner. The pale, yellow light and energy produced by the bindara drifted toward the prisoner until it seeped into the captive's nose and mouth, as if being inhaled.

The drugged Lah'grex lifted his head and leaned back in his chair. Seconds later he sat upright and opened his eyes. Although Khalen could not see the prisoner's face, Brin'tac's shocked expression told him the eyes of the Lah'grex were now a sickly yellow. Satisfied that the song was working, Khalen nodded for Brin'tac to begin.

Khalen continued to play and sing, keeping the music going in the background as Brin'tac asked the first question in a warm and inviting voice.

"What is your name, my friend?"

"Lin'gad Yencha"

"And what planet are we on, Lin'gad?"

Khalen nodded approvingly. Brin'tac was trying to establish a baseline.

"We're on Dhun'drok."

"Good. And why are you here?"

"I'm here to help capture some wealthy Lah'grex ruler."

"And if you capture him, where will you take him?"

"Back to our base."

Khalen felt his pulse quicken.

"Where is your base located?" Brin'tac asked.

"It's on the planet Rovik."

Brin'tac glanced at Khalen, his expression full of surprise. "Rovik?" Brin'tac continued. "That's in the Tii-Koona Dominion, correct?"

"Yes."

"And where on Rovik is the base located?"

"It's forty-five miles northeast of the city of Mok Ena 2, on the island of Cita Ku."

Khalen smiled. That's it. They had it.

"Thank you, Lin'gad. We just have a few more questions to ask about the Dumah base. What kind of security...What is the matter?" Brin'tac asked. "Why are you frowning?"

"The base does not belong to Dumah."

"Then whose base is it?"

"It belongs to Shrouded Discord."

Khalen shrugged as Brin'tac glanced at him questioningly.

"Who, or what, is Shrouded Discord?"

Lin'gad paused. "We're mercenaries, of course."

"But why would the Dumah Dynasty use a base that belongs to mercenaries?"

Again, Lin'gad paused. "Dumah doesn't use it."

"But you said..." Brin'tac stopped mid-sentence.

Khalen felt his stomach drop as a disturbing thought occurred to him. He wondered if Brin'tac had come to the same conclusion. His guess was confirmed a second later with Brin'tac's next question.

"Do you work for the Dumah Dynasty?"

"No. I work for Shrouded Discord."

24

QUESTIONS

"WHAT? But that doesn't make any sense!"

Khalen did his best to ignore Nara's exclamation so he could finish sending his message. He was seated in the spacious cockpit of the *Lightbringer* and waiting for word from Captain Nahoc of the *Eternal Harmony* that they were ready to leave. In the meantime, he decided to take advantage of the peace and quiet to send an important message. He had not counted on Saryn, Nara, and Jov coming to join him in the cockpit so quickly. He finished the message and sent it as Saryn sat next to him in the copilot's chair. Nara and Jov reached down to pet Kovitch and Shosta, who were lying on the floor in the space between the four chairs. The two drallmari let out whistles of pleasure as the teens scratched their chins.

"If they aren't working for Dumah, then how'd that witch-lady get the right access codes and stuff to convince you guys she was legit?" Nara asked, her teenage enthusiasm causing the words to tumble out of her mouth. Shosta snorted as Nara stopped petting her and sat in the chair behind Khalen. He wondered if she deliberately chose that seat so she would not have to look at him. Despite the fact that he had once more covered his tattoos with synthetic skin, the tension between him and his teenage protégé still remained.

"That is a very astute question," Saryn said.

"Why did dey pretend, anyway? Seems like a lot of twouble," Jov commented as he climbed into the chair across from Nara. Khalen noted that, for once, the teen had changed out of his favorite jumpsuit and was wearing a pair of dirty blue pants and a shirt embroidered with the name of his favorite popular band. Khalen chuckled to himself: as always, the Tii-Koona was wearing his shirt backward.

Saryn swiveled her seat one hundred and eighty degrees so she was facing Jov, who was seated behind her. "From what we learned, it seems this Shrouded Discord was hoping to blame Dumah for Brin'tac's kidnapping."

"And where'd they get the tech that shocked everyone? And Synths! I can't believe they had Synths! I've never seen one in real life before. Those things looked wicked—even smashed all over the ground like they were."

"Yeah," Jov chimed in. "Dat was a cool move, by the way, Unca Khawen! Where'd you learn to cweate dose small townados? Dat was awesome!"

Khalen smiled at Nara and Jov's incessant chatter. Out of the corner of his eye, he noticed Nara had changed out of her working jumpsuit and was dressed in a shirt with colorful, diagonal patterns that matched her dark-violet scales. Hopefully, her bright choice of clothing was a sign her emotional state had improved. "Slow down, kiddo. One topic at a time. Let me answer Nara's questions first. We don't know where they got the tech or the Synths, but it seems this Shrouded

Discord has some pretty powerful allies. As for the song I used on the Synths, who do you think taught me?"

Jov thought for a moment, then his face brightened as the answer dawned on him. "Wight! Of couwse! At fiwst I tought it must've been youw teacher, Wivewuun. But den I 'membered he's a Fawuvinal. Dey're weally good at working wit' plants, wight? But Sowemsiel..." he said, switching his gaze to Saryn, "like Aunt Sarwyn and Unca Woakel...dey're weally good at working wit' wind! So dey taught you, didn't dey?"

Saryn smiled back at him in approval. "That is correct. I am very proud of both of you. It was quick thinking to use Scamp. If you had not awakened us, Khalen may have died."

"Yeah," Khalen echoed, hoping to lighten the air between him and Nara. "Thank you both. Next time we get somewhere civilized, I'm taking you out for some double-decker, triple chocolate, waffle bowls of dippy cream with extra fudge!"

Jov sat up in his chair, his eyes wide with excitement. "Really, Unca Khalen? Dat woul' be amazing!"

Khalen laughed at his response. "You betcha."

"So, where're we going now? Did we find out where they took eth Galithar's family?" Nara asked.

"Yes," Saryn replied, her expression becoming serious. "Their base is located on...Rovik."

Khalen studied Nara's reaction, wondering how she would handle the news. The instant Saryn spoke the planet's name, Nara's countenance deflated. "Rovik?" she repeated, her voice trembling slightly. "Wow. I...I haven't been back there since..."

"I know," Saryn said. "It could be difficult for you two. It may trigger some memories."

Jov simply shrugged. "I don't 'member much."

Nara glanced at her "cousin". "That's no surprise. Back then, all you cared about was eating and sleeping." Turning her attention to Saryn, she smiled. However, to Khalen, the gesture seemed forced. "I'll be fine. Like Jov, I don't remember a whole lot either. I mean, I was only six when you guys found us and took us to Hebellion. Jov and I may've been born on Rovik, but it isn't our home."

The commlink chirped, interrupting their conversation. *"Lightbringer,* this is Captain Nahoc. We're ready to depart."

"Copy that, captain. We're ready when you are," Khalen replied. "Buckle up, everyone. Here we go."

Khalen waited until Brin'tac's ship had lifted off before firing the engines. Before long they were pulling toward the sky and the space that lay beyond. Once they cleared the atmosphere and the roar of the engines died down, Nara asked another question.

"What're they gonna do with that prisoner guy?"

Saryn shrugged. "Noble Galithar's people have him detained on their ship. They would like to keep him nearby in the event they need to ask him any further questions."

"How do we know they took eth Galithar's family back to Rovik? I mean, they could've taken them almost anywhere."

"We do not know that for certain," Saryn replied. "But the prisoner stated that Shrouded Discord had plans to take the Galithars there after this meeting."

"But I don't get it. Why are a bunch of Lah'grex hiding out on a Tii-Koona world? Wouldn't it make more sense for them to have a base close by?

"We do not know. We think they may be a mixed group of Leh'cryst and Tey-Rakil spies."

"Weally?" Jov said in awe. "Dose are some bad people, huh Aunt Sarwyn?"

"Many of them do bad things, Jov. But remember: although beings may *do* bad things, they are still loved by the Composer and are made in his image," she added. Khalen noticed her eyes drifting toward Nara.

"How do you expect to get into the base to rescue them?"

Although Nara was asking good questions, Khalen felt his patience beginning to ebb. The Tii-Koona teen could be inquisitive to the point of madness. And Saryn's last comment seemed to have gone completely over her head.

Unfortunately for Khalen, Solemsiel were known for their patience.

"We will not have all the details until we reach Rovik," Saryn explained. "But eth Galithar was able to learn that the base is on an island. There are secret tunnels built under the surface that lead into it. He was also able to discover the security codes for the base from the prisoner."

"But won't they figure we'd get the prisoner to talk and expect us to attack them?"

"Not necessarily," Saryn said. "He had nearly expired—died—when I found him and healed him. They probably assumed he was dead."

Despite the assurance in her voice, Khalen had his own misgivings. If Slag was expecting them to follow, then they were all walking into a trap.

"And I suppose Jov and I will have to remain back on the ship, *again*," Nara said, putting a generous amount of frustrated emphasis on the last word.

"Yes, but we'd be happy to have Roadblock come with us. How are the repairs coming?"

"He got fwied up pretty good," Jov answered. "But I fink I can have him fixed by da time we get to Wovik."

"I sure hope so," Nara stated. "It's bad enough I gotta be left behind. I wanna at least know what's goin' on."

"And dey might need Woadblock, Scamp, or Dodger's help like last time."

"Exactly. So maybe you should get busy fixin' him!"

"I will. But Unca Khalen said I could sit in da cockpit when we go into da Stweam again. I like it. Unca Woakel says it is da song of da Gweat Composa' himsewf! Da wumble of da song tickles my belly. And when we go into it, it feews like we get swawowed by a giant wed snake!"

Khalen and Saryn's laughter was interrupted by the comm. "*Lightbringer,* we're moving into position above you. Prepare for docking."

"Roger that. I'm shutting down the engines now," Khalen replied.

"I must be going," Saryn said as she stood to leave. "Roakel will want my help. Enjoy the view."

A few minutes later, the ships were connected and were making their way toward the Stream. Behind and to his right, Khalen caught sight of Jov as he bounced in anticipation. Kovitch lifted his head from the floor and stared at the young Tii-Koona curiously, as if trying to discover the source of his joy.

"Roakel, Saryn, we're nearing the Stream. You can start playing now," Khalen said into the comm.

Over the next minute, Khalen felt Jov's joy permeate the atmosphere of the cockpit until it filled him as well. It was in moments like these he truly understood why those like Jov were called Accidentals: their innocence and sense of wonder at the little things of life helped those around them see the mundane with fresh eyes. They really did add color to life. If only the rest of the universe could see it.

25

MENDING THE FENCES

KHALEN WAITED by the connecting hatch for Brin'tac and Vel'vikis to arrive. He was struggling to keep his thoughts positive. He knew what the Sacred Songbook said about loving one's enemies, and he believed it to be true. But living it out was another matter entirely. As a Meh'ishto, he had been raised in a brutal, selfish culture where betrayal was part of life. He had to be strong if he wanted to survive. Violence and pain were part of his childhood. Yet it was difficult to erase fifty years of harsh living. He knew it took daily self-discipline and positive immersion in the Songbook to rewire his brain toward the ways of the Composer.

He concentrated on his breathing. This encounter was sure to be another test. He prayed for strength to remain composed, no matter how Vel'vikis or Brin'tac treated him.

And to make the situation more difficult and awkward, Nara had decided to tag along again. Khalen would have bet his Twin Discs of Arrguin she had been encouraged by

Saryn to be present to help Khalen retain his composure as well as hoping it might help heal the rift between master and student. And, as hard as it was to admit to himself, he knew he acted differently when the teen was around, knowing that his words and actions were an example to her.

Khalen felt the tension between them as they waited in silence. Glancing over at her, he saw that, in typical fashion, Nara had changed out of the outfit she had been wearing earlier and was now dressed in a fancy pink and white shirt paired with a knee-length white skirt. He was always amazed at how often the teen changed clothes. It was almost as if she were trying to make up for Jov's *lack* of wardrobe changes. Her long tail twitched, leaving him to wonder if it was due to anticipation of seeing the wealthy Lah'grex ruler again, or her proximity to a "vicious" Meh'ishto.

Hoping to ease the tension, Khalen tried to engage her in some light conversation. "How are the repairs coming on Roadblock?"

Nara fixed her gaze on the wall and shrugged. "Good, I guess. Jov's working on him right now."

Khalen tried to think of something else to talk about but decided it was not worth the trouble. If Nara wanted to keep her distance, then it was fine by him. He reached down and stroked Kovitch's head. Although Shosta was still resting in her bed from her recent wounds, Khalen guessed that Kovitch was sensing his master's internal struggle and wished to remain close.

Khalen was saved from further awkward silence by the arrival of the Lah'grex.

The hatch opened and Vel'vikis climbed down the ladder, his expression a blank mask. Seconds later, Brin'tac came into view. To Khalen's surprise, the Lah'grex ruler was dressed not in his typical flowing robes but in a simple yellow shirt and tan trousers. Although not as fancy or embellished as other items in his wardrobe, they were still clearly expensive and reflected his status as a wealthy governmental leader.

Vel'vikis closed the hatch as Brin'tac greeted them. "Thank you for allowing us to come aboard. I wanted to express my thanks for your help in extracting the information from the prisoner."

Still uncertain what to expect from the other, Khalen simply nodded in acknowledgment.

Brin'tac turned toward Nara. "It's good to see you again as well, Nara."

Doing her best to be respectful and polite, Nara smiled up at him. "It's good to see you too, eth Galithar."

"You don't have to call me 'eth Galithar'. It sounds too formal," Brin'tac smiled warmly as he stepped closer to her. "Please, you may call me Brin'tac."

Khalen could tell by the subtle way Nara's tail twisted that she was embarrassed and uncomfortable. "I don't know. I mean, you're a...respectable leader, and much older than me. I'm not saying your *old*," she amended. "I'm just saying... My teachers always said I should treat anyone more than twenty years older than me with extra respect, 'cause they're my elders. That means not calling 'em by their first names."

Brin'tac chuckled. "I appreciate that. You've had wise teachers. There's not enough respect in the younger generations nowadays. Okay, then how about we meet halfway? Why don't you call me, Mr. Galithar."

Nara smiled. "Okay, Mr. Galithar."

Turning his attention toward Kovitch, Brin'tac crouched so he was at eye level with the drallmar. As he scratched the creature's head, he looked at Khalen. "This one is Kovitch, correct?"

Nara happily answered for him. "Yeah. You can always tell 'em apart by the coloration along the crest. See here how Kovitch has this bluish ring around his front spikes? Shosta's are green and yellow. Although, sometimes the way their scales shimmer in the light, it's hard to make out the exact color."

Standing next to her, Khalen watched the whole exchange with growing irritation. *Is he just going to pretend nothing happened? He calls me a 'blight upon the universe' one day and then acts like we're all friends the next? Creator, help me have patience and restraint.*

As if sensing the coldness in Khalen's demeanor, Brin'tac stood and turned to face him. "Master Khalen, you're probably wondering why I asked to visit today." He paused for a moment. When Khalen failed to respond, he cleared his throat and continued. "Yes, well...I came to apologize for my previous actions. I've been under so much stress of late. And then, to be so close to rescuing my family, only to lose them again...it was just...I shouldn't have accused you. If a pair of respected Arrangers vouch for your conduct and call you 'friend', then I will do no less. I also want to thank you for everything you did to try to rescue my family."

Khalen stared back at him in surprise, a twinge of guilt twisting his gut. In the eyes of most, Brin'tac's original response was justifiable, especially given the Meh'ishto's reputation for violence. His reaction was in line with his beliefs. Yet Khalen called himself a follower of the Great Composer but responded the opposite of the beliefs he espoused. Even more, he knew from experience it is rare to find a being in a position of power who is willing to apologize for *anything*.

However, the other, more entrenched side of his character refused to let him off the hook so easily. "Apology accepted," he said. He drew a small amount of twisted pleasure at the sight of Brin'tac struggling to maintain his composure. Khalen guessed he was hoping for an apology in return and felt even more satisfaction at disappointing him.

Vel'vikis, who was standing just a little behind Brin'tac's right side, was plainly not as adept at hiding his feelings as his employer. His expression left no doubt he felt Khalen was insulting Brin'tac and would like nothing more than to force an apology from him. Brin'tac, however, appeared ready to move on. Turning, he addressed Nara once more. "Thank you for intervening back in the tower. That was quick thinking. So tell me, where did you learn to pilot remotes like that? I'm very impressed."

Nara shrugged. Although she was playing it cool, Khalen could read her well enough to know she was relishing Brin'tac's compliments. "It was nothin'. My teacher back on Hebellion—his name is Lomonaco—was big into remotes and taught me a few things. He also helped Jov learn how to repair them. I spent all my free time piloting them in games, using them to fix stuff, and do all sorts of other cool things. There was this one time…"

Khalen grimaced. He knew from experience the danger in opening this particular can of worms. If gone unchecked, Nara could go on for hours. "Save it for another time, Nara," he said, cutting her off. "We shouldn't keep eth Galithar. I'm sure he has other important things to take care of."

"Please, if we are to put our differences aside, I insist you call me Brin'tac," he said, turning back to Khalen, "And actually, I'd love to hear her story. Then, I was rather hoping that—assuming we can move beyond our recent disagreement—you'd be willing to continue our lessons."

When Brin'tac had apologized, Khalen wondered if this topic would arise. The last thing he felt like doing was spending more time with this Lah'grex. However, Skaret's reappearance changed everything. Khalen needed Brin'tac, or more to the point, he needed Brin'tac's people and resources. Pushing aside his dislike and distrust of the Lah'grex ruler, he decided to play nice. "I've gotta hand it to you, Brin'tac, you're persistent, and a bit of a contradiction. You don't quite fit the mold of the average politician."

"I believe we *both* are. You intrigue me, Khalen Daedark. Based on your heritage, your upbringing was doubtless violent and filled with instruction about evolution and survival of the strong. Yet, somehow, you defied the odds and stand before me as a self-proclaimed believer in the Great Composer who is willing to sacrifice his life for others. How is this possible?"

"It's a bit of a long story," Khalen said. "How about another trade? I'll tell you a bit about my story if you share a bit of yours."

"Agreed," Brin'tac stated. "But if we're going to do all that, might I suggest we head down to the main living area? And perhaps after that we could do another music lesson."

"Sounds fair enough. Follow me."

As they headed toward the lift which would take them down to the primary living area, Khalen picked up the conversation. "I *am* a contradiction. The Meh'ishto culture is ruled by vicious tribal leaders who bow their knee to no one but Overlord Wylock. You learn very quickly that strength leads to power and wealth. I was trained to be a music master. But like so many others, I was a tool or a pawn. My...chieftain used his maestros to hypnotize others and to create his 'pets'."

"What do you mean, 'create' pets?" Nara asked in confusion. Khalen had to remind himself that although she now knew the truth about his heritage, she was still too young to truly grasp what that meant.

"In general, each of the Major races has a musical affinity, right? Tii-Koona are adept at controlling water, Lah'grex are experts at shaping rock, and Mih'schen are proficient at speaking with animals and training them. Well, unfortunately, the Minor cultures pervert those affinities. Instead of just speaking with animals, Meh'ishto maestros use the musical sciences to reshape animals into...monsters."

"No!" Nara said, her eyes wide in shock. She glanced at Kovitch, who was walking beside them. "That's horrible! Why would anyone want to do that?"

"They do it because it grants them power," Brin'tac answered. "This is why the Minor races are almost always at war with the Major races. The culture of the Minor races fosters a desire to control, subvert, and destroy."

By this time, the group had reached the lift. Once they were inside and beginning to descend to the middle level of the ship, Nara asked a question, her voice laced with emotion. "But you...you didn't do those things, did you?"

Although Khalen knew his next statement might push Nara further away from him, he nevertheless pressed forward with the truth. "Yes, I did."

"Unfortunately, you're going to find that virtually everyone you meet, with perhaps the exception of the Faluvinal and Solemsiel, has things in their pasts they aren't proud of, Nara," Brin'tac said, his eyes turning a dull gray.

The lift came to a stop and the group entered the living area. Kovitch curled up on the ground near one of the couches as Vel'vikis resumed his silent vigil. As the others sat, Brin'tac continued, the tone of his voice subdued. "Even I have made some terrible choices in the past—choices which I profoundly regret. One of the greatest negatives about being a leader is that when you make a mistake, it is often others that suffer the consequences.

"But this is also why Khalen's story is so amazing," Brin'tac said, his voice regaining some of its previous strength. "The greater the obstacle, the greater the victory." Turning his attention back to Khalen, he inclined his head. "Please continue your story. How did you—for lack of a better term—escape from that culture?"

"I had a falling out with my chieftain. I left home and joined a group of smugglers. I traveled with them for many years but was betrayed by one of them and sold into slavery."

"You were a slave for almost ten years, right?" Nara asked.

"Twelve."

Nara lowered her head, her gaze fixed on the floor. "I can't believe someone would do that to another person. How can anyone be so cruel? Aunt Saryn didn't tell me much, but she said they almost killed you a couple of times."

Khalen nodded. "The last time was the worst. My captors dumped me into a trash heap and left me for dead. By the grace of Dominuus, Riveruun rescued me."

"Yes, Roakel mentioned him. He was a Faluvinal, right?" Brin'tac asked.

"A Faluvinal maestro and prophet of the Great Composer," Khalen added. "He healed me and showed me a different way of living. I wish I could say I accepted it all immediately, but I was stubborn and blind. Again, it's a long story. Suffice it to say, I eventually came to read the Sacred Songbook and believe in the Great Composer. Riveruun taught me what it meant to have true peace."

"That's amazing," Brin'tac said. "I'm glad you were able to find a belief system that worked for you."

Khalen raised an eyebrow. "'Worked for me?' Belief in the Master Symphony is a complete worldview. It was a huge paradigm shift. For the first time in my life, the universe made sense."

"Ah, yes. That's right. I forgot you believe truth is —how did you put it—'that which matches reality'?"

Khalen stifled a smile as Nara rolled her eyes as if to say, 'Here we go again.' Her reaction apparently did not escape Brin'tac's notice either. "I'd like to hear what our young Tii-Koona has to say about it. What do you think, Nara?"

Caught off guard, Nara blushed before responding. "I don't know. I mean, like Uncle Khalen said last time, I think truth is truth. What other kind is there?"

"Well, there are truths that are real for us individually, but not for everyone."

"Like what?"

"In Khalen's case, for example, the Master Symphony is real and true. It is so because he believes it sincerely, and it brings him peace. But I, on the other hand, believe we are all part of the Universal Rhythm. As such, all religions are but windows to the greater truth. Each religion is a different path to the same end."

Nara was silent for a moment as she tried to process his words, her right hand fell into her habit of absentmindedly playing with a loose strand of her stringy hair. "But, some-thin' isn't true just because I believe it, even if I'm sincere, right? I mean, no matter how much I might *feel* like I'm, say, a Lah'grex, that doesn't mean I *am* one. The Sacred Song-book tells the history of the universe from the beginning of creation. Either that history is real, or it isn't."

"But what if the history in the Songbook isn't intended to be taken literally?" Brin'tac countered. "In that case, it could be 'true' in the poetic sense, but not in the literal sense."

Nara narrowed her eyes and cocked her head to the side as she thought through the logic. Khalen was about to intercede but decided instead to see how she would answer.

"But…if it's only true in the poetic sense, then it doesn't match reality. That means it isn't really true at all. It's only poetic."

Brin'tac smiled and turned to Khalen. "Do you know how incredible this young lady is? Most teenagers struggle to grasp the concept of how to boil water, yet this one can hold her own in a debate on the meaning of truth! Perhaps there's hope for the universe after all!"

"She's got both brains and spunk. You'd better watch out." Khalen grinned at the teen and, for the first time since Dhun'drok, she smiled back.

Nara's commlink chirped, interrupting the moment. She checked the display, then winced and groaned. "It's Jov." Flipping it on, she said, "What is it? I'm kinda busy right now."

"Nawa, I need your hewp," Jov said, his voice tinged with distress.

"Can't you ask Saryn to help you?"

"No. I need hewp wit' Woadbwock."

"What's wrong with him?"

"Well, I…I was twying to fix da damage, but…I may have axadentawy cwossed two wires on him instead."

"What?" Nara said in alarm. "Ugh! If you messed him up, I swear I'm gonna…" As if suddenly remembering she had an audience, she stopped herself mid-sentence. "I'll be right there. Don't touch anything else!" Nara shut off the comm, offered a hasty apology, and raced out of the room.

"For Jov's sake, I hope everything's okay," Brin'tac said with amusement.

"Knowing Jov, he's probably overreacting. I'm sure it'll be fine."

"Well, since Nara had to leave so abruptly, perhaps we should take advantage of the time and practice a little."

"Fine," Khalen lied. Even though he wanted to do anything *but* practice with Brin'tac, his sense of honor forced him to fulfill his promise. "But we should head to the practice room so we can use the clarichord." Khalen repeatedly glanced over his shoulder as he led the two Lah'grex back up the lift. Although the tension between him and Brin'tac had been resolved, Khalen did not expect Vel'vikis to forgive quite as easily.

Once inside the practice room, Khalen had Brin'tac stand in front of him as he had in their previous lesson. The two practiced several vocal exercises and solfege activities for the next thirty minutes. Once they were finished, they sat on the chairs along the wall. Vel'vikis merely watched in stoic silence during the whole session.

"You've made some progress," Khalen stated. "Now, we need to get into a little more music theory. Did you get a chance to do any research about chords?"

"Yes. I studied them yesterday after we entered Stream travel. The type of chord is determined by the two intervals that exist between the three notes."

"Right. Intervals are important to understanding the relationships between notes. It helps us measure the number of half-steps between them. For example, C to D is a major second, C to E is a major third, C to F is a perfect fourth—"

"Wait a moment," Brin'tac said in confusion. "Why is the fourth interval perfect?"

"Actually, both the 4th and 5th intervals are called perfect. I think they're called that to distinguish them from the major chords and because they have a certain tonal consonance. The six intervals form pairs: M2/M7; M3/M6; P4/P5."

"I don't understand. Why are they paired like that?"

"Because of the intervals. I'll try to explain." Khalen pulled out his scroll, unrolled the screen, and turned it on. After several seconds, he found the appropriate illustration and showed it to Brin'tac. "A major third is four half-steps up from the tonic—let's use the note C—and the major sixth is four half-steps *down* from the tonic if you use the C an octave higher. The major 3rd and major 6th are collectively called Mediants. The same goes for the perfect intervals. If you start on C and go up seven half-steps to G, you get a perfect 5th. But if you go *down* from C seven half-steps, you get an F, or the perfect 4th. Collectively, they're called Dominants."

Brin'tac frowned, leaving Khalen to wonder if he had lost his student. Suddenly, his face brightened in understanding. "Wait! So that must account for why each pair of races are approximately the same height! Now that I think of it, that would also explain why the Rey-Qani and Tii-Koona both have tails, why the eyes of both the Mih'schen and Lah'grex change color according to their emotional state, and why the Faluvinal and Solemsiel both have four arms! I never made the connection to music before. It's amazingly coincidental how each pair evolved from a common ancestor in the exact combination of the musical scale.

"Come to think of it, this has to be why the Solemsiel and Faluvinal are called the 'Perfect' races! They're representative of the perfect intervals. And here I always thought it was because they considered themselves to be so flawless and above reproach."

Khalen watched in amusement as it dawned on the Lah'grex ruler that his comment might be taken as an insult. The clay-like texture of the skin on his face paled and his eyes grew wide. "I'm…I'm so sorry. I didn't mean it like that."

"Don't worry," Khalen said with a lopsided grin. "Knowing the Solemsiel, they'd take that as a compliment. You're not far from the truth. Most theologians believe the Faluvinal and Solemsiel were granted that title because, according to the Sacred Songbook, near the dawn of time, they didn't fall into sin like the rest of the races."

"Ah, yes. I'm familiar with that creation myth."

"Myth?"

"Well, of course. I mean, you don't actually believe all that nonsense about the First Dissonance, do you? Do you really believe Araklial was a real Solemsiel who led the ancient Tritonus army in a war against the Composer?"

"Yes, I do."

"Wow," Brin'tac stated in surprise. "I thought everyone understood that story to just be an allegory—something the ancient, uncivilized peoples told to explain the universe. I didn't realize there were still those in the galaxies who accepted it as real history."

"Who do you think taught Nara to think the way she does?" Khalen challenged, his irritation beginning to rise. "We were all taught by the Faluvinal and Solemsiel. And considering they don't age past adulthood, there are still many alive who were eyewitnesses to the events themselves."

Brin'tac seemed stunned by the idea, as if the thought had never occurred to him. "Was Riveruun one of those?"

"No. But Roakel's father is. Roakel even showed me a holovid of his father teaching a class where he relates his own firsthand account of the First Dissonance. He says he knew Araklial personally. You should watch it yourself."

"Perhaps I will." Standing, Brin'tac bowed slightly to Khalen. "Thank you for the lesson, you've given me much to practice, and to ponder. However, I must be going."

Khalen stood as well. "You're welcome." Although he initially said the words to be polite, he was surprised to realize he almost meant them. Exiting the room, he once more led the Lah'grex back to the hatch. When they arrived, he became abruptly serious. "Brin'tac, since you like politics and theology so much, let me give you something to chew on. We all have free will to choose to live a life of virtue or vice. We make our own decisions, for good or evil. I'm a Meh'ishto and former slave, yet you value my intellect in debating religion and politics and recognize my expertise in music. Jov has learning disabilities yet is brilliant with machines. Nara is an orphan yet is intelligent beyond her years. Let me challenge you never to look down on someone because of their appearance. You never know what that person might achieve if given the right chance."

Despite the sincerity in his statement, Brin'tac's expression remained unchanged. Khalen wondered if his words had fallen on deaf ears.

"Thank you, maestro. I'll keep that in mind." Brin'tac reached for the ladder that led back to his own ship but paused, his hand on the rung. Letting go, he turned around once more and faced Khalen. "One more question: in the creation myth found in your Sacred Songbook, Araklial's army of Tritonus was banished by Dominuus to an unknown region of space. Do you believe such an army could still be lurking out there on some distant planet or perhaps even trying to find their way back to the known universe?"

"Yes. I believe so."

A shadow seemed to pass over Brin'tac's features at Khalen's confirmation. However, just as quickly as it appeared, it was gone. "Interesting." With that, the Lah'grex leader turned and climbed the ladder back to his ship.

26

MOK ENA

City: Mok Ena
Planet: Rovik
System: Yez Vroth
Region: Tii-Koona Federation

NARA STARED OUT the cockpit window at the planet of her birth. "Wow. It looks way different than I remember." Khalen glanced over at her from where he sat in the pilot's seat. Her expression was a mixture of curiosity, sadness, and indifference. For a moment, Khalen thought about what it would be like to visit his own home planet. It had been forty years since he had left at the age of twenty-two. From time to time his thoughts returned to his childhood, and he found himself wondering what had happened to his family.

If one could call them that. They were related by blood, but that was as far as the connection went. In many ways, he had been more a slave on Meh'ish than during his captivity on Oclion. He reached up and absentmindedly scratched at the new synthetic skin covering his cheek.

"I don't 'member dis at awl," Jov said from behind Khalen. "Jus' maybe a wittle of hunger and pain."

Saryn, who was seated next to Jov, laid a comforting hand on his arm. "I am thankful Roakel and I found you in time. You were both extremely malnourished."

"So…where *did* you find us? I mean, you said it was in some sort of refugee camp, but where?"

"You observe how Rovik has one main continent? There used to be thousands of floating cities off the coast before the liberation of the planet. Now only a few hundred remain. Do you see that peninsula over there, protruding out from the southwestern edge of the continent? That is where we found you."

"What's a wefugee camp?" Jov asked.

"It is a place where people go when they lose their homes."

"How did dey lose deir homes?"

"Rovik used to belong to the Tey-Rakil Dominion," Saryn explained, her voice uncharacteristically somber. "It was utilized as an outpost and a launching point for attacks against the Tii-Koona Federation since it was adjacent—next to— their border region. The ruler of the planet, an evil Seyvreen named Lady Athaylia, made a foolish attack against the Tii-Koona. They fought back and defeated her. In addition, they attacked Rovik and took over control of the planet. Those Tey-Rakil who were unable to escape abandoned their floating cities and fled to the mainland. Although this all transpired over fifty years ago, some Tey-Rakil remain on the planet as refugees."

Nara's eyes widened with horror as the truth of what Saryn was saying pummeled her. "So Jov and I aren't really Tii-Koona at all, are we? We're...Tey-Rakil!"

Saryn reached out and stroked her hair. "Sweet child, listen to me carefully: the Great Composer created six races, not eleven. The fact that there are so many variations of skin tones, facial structure, and numerous physical characteristics within each race shows the creativity of our Creator. The only difference between the Tey-Rakil and the Tii-Koona is cultural, the same as the Meh'ishto and Mih'schen. The Tey-Rakil accent their hair and scales with dark colors and cruel imagery, while the Tii-Koona do not. The difference is only cosmetic. Every being among the Major races and Minor cultures has a choice—to follow the path of light or the path of darkness. Those that choose the light belong to the Major races, no matter their ancestry."

Despite Saryn's words, Nara still struggled to come to terms with the truth. Jov, however, seemed to grasp the concept. "I choose da light! I wanna be good. I'm a Tii-Koona fow suwe!"

Jov's words hung in the air as the *Lightbringer* entered the atmosphere. The resulting light and heat from entry caused the viewports to become completely black in order to protect the occupants. A short time later, they cleared as the ship entered the upper atmosphere. However, unlike their trip to Dhun'drok, this time the *Lightbringer* led the way while the *Eternal Harmony* trailed behind.

"Why awe dere so many big ships around?" Jov asked. "Wha's dat all about?"

"The Tii-Koona are currently at war with the Tey-Rakil," Khalen said.

"Over Wovik?"

"That is but a minor part of it," Saryn said. "Do you remember the history I taught you about the capture of Supreme Judge Sil Tala eight years ago?"

"Yeah," Jov said slowly, his eyes squinted in concentration. "Didn't da Tey-Wakil, like, tweaten to kill him if da Tii-Koona didn't do what dey wanted? And didn't dat cwazy, nasty Ove'lowd guy Shal-sometin'-or-other get all ticked off and kill da judge anyway?"

Saryn nodded. "With their leader murdered by Shal-*rahn*, the Tii-Koona retaliated, sparking the current Tey-Rakil War. The two powers have been fighting ever since. And because Rovik is the closest inhabited planet to the Dominion, it has the largest military presence."

"So where is the base where Mr. Galithar's family is being held?" Nara asked, rejoining the conversation.

"Mr. Galithar?" Saryn repeated curiously. "Since when do you address him in that manner?"

"That's what he told me to call him. He said 'eth Galithar' was too formal."

Saryn chuckled. "Well, it is still appropriate."

"The prisoner we captured said Shrouded Discord's base is located near Mok Ena 2 on the island of Cita Ku," Khalen explained. "The floating city of Mok Ena 1 is about sixty miles offshore. We're going to land there and make our way to the mainland. We don't want them to know we're coming."

"Wow! Wook at awl da water!" Jov exclaimed as they drew closer to the planet. "Aunt Sawyn, can Nawa and I go swimming while we're hewe?"

Khalen could tell by her voice that she wore a smile on her face. "Sure, Jov. Maybe we can go while Khalen meets with his contact."

"What contact?" Nara asked.

Khalen shrugged. "We need to arrange transport to the mainland. I know someone who might help."

"Is that Mok Ena? It looks nothin' like what's in the holovids! It's so...huge," Nara said in wonder.

By this time, the *Lightbringer* was close enough to the city to make out the details. The entire city was several miles in diameter and contained numerous ports and docks along the edges. Even in the fading evening light, the damage from the war became more and more apparent the closer the ship drew to the city. Where once stood magnificent skyscrapers, now only rubble remained. Several tall buildings still stood, but it was clear from burn marks and broken windows that portions of them were now unused. Below these were row upon row of dilapidated houses and shops.

But this was just the upper portion of the city. Khalen could see that, below the surface of the water, the city extended downward twice as deep as the upper section was tall. In many ways, it reminded him of a giant iceberg. The bottom levels were where the rich and powerful lived. Nearly every building located in the sealed underwater section of the city had lockout compartments, allowing the inhabitants to enter the ocean. When inside, giant windows allowed for magnificent views of the carefully selected aquatic life that was allowed to swim near the city.

Reaching high above the upper section of the city was a tarnished golden frame consisting of four massive curved beams that met in the center. Khalen knew from past experience that, in the case of severe weather or attack, the musicians of the city could create a massive energy shield over the frame that was airtight. Then, like a submarine, the entire structure could sink below the surface until the danger had passed.

The comm chirped. The voice that came through the line sounded bored and lackluster. "Approaching vessels, this is City Control. State your business."

Khalen switched on the comm. "Control, this is the *Lightbringer*, I.D. number—"

"Our scanners already picked up your registration beacons," the controller said, her voice now reflecting boredom *and* irritation. "I repeat: what's your *business* here?"

"Nice lady," Nara commented sarcastically.

"Basic stuff. We're here to meet with some friends, restock, refuel, check out a few restaurants, and perhaps enjoy the night life a little," Khalen replied nonchalantly. "My friends and I have reservations at *The Blue Rymer Lounge*. We came to hear the Arden Hydrophonic Quartet playing there tonight. We're only staying for a couple of days at most. We'd like to purchase a pair of hangar permits. Something nice would be appreciated, if available."

There was no response for several seconds. At last the voice returned. "You've been cleared for hangers K-71 and K-72. I'm sending the coordinates now. Payment must be received in advance."

"Not a problem. Sending payment now." Khalen switched channels. "Brin'tac, did you get that?"

"Yes. We just authorized the payment. We'll follow you down."

"Sounds good. Here we go."

Khalen piloted the *Lightbringer* through the sparse traffic lanes and landed without incident. Once inside the hangar, he grabbed his gear and headed for the main lift, Shosta and Kovitch on his heels. When he arrived, the others were already waiting for him.

"Are you sure this is a good idea, Khalen?" Roakel asked.

"Look, I explained it before. This whole mission depends upon intel and secrecy. Shrouded Discord no doubt has spies everywhere, especially this close to their base. If a bunch of Lah'grex show up, it'll tip them off for sure. Same with a pair of Solemsiel. I won't stand out so much and having Nara with me will help me blend in. Besides, it's not like I'm going into battle. I'm just meeting with my contact to arrange transport. We'll probably be back in just over an hour."

Nara, who was dressed once more in her one-piece jumpsuit was hesitant but appeared thankful for the opportunity to leave the ship. "Don't worry, Aunt Saryn. I'll take good care of him," she said with a wink.

"Ha! I don't doubt that."

Khalen glanced over at the teen, somewhat surprised by the change in her demeanor. Turning away, he knelt and stroked the muzzles of the two drallmari. "Stay here, you two. I'll be back soon."

The animals let out a short burst of whistles and tossed their heads in farewell. Khalen stood and hit the lift control. "Don't wait up. See you soon."

Once the lift reached the ground, the pair headed toward the hangar door. As they walked, Khalen raised the hood of his jacket. Although this particular jacket was not as nice as the one ruined by his battle with Slag, it had the added benefit of being black and worn, which was perfect for the current mission. He reached down and ran his fingers reassuringly over the Twin Discs of Arrguin that bounced lightly against his thighs as he walked.

When they reached the door, Khalen paused for a moment and turned to look at Nara. "Remember what I said. Don't gawk and look like a tourist. Blend in. And most important, let me do *all* the talking. You promised, right?"

"Yeah, yeah," she replied impatiently. "I won't gawk, and I won't say anything. I promise."

"Good. 'Cause if you do, I'll make sure you *always* stay behind on the ship. That's not a bluff."

Nara rolled her eyes. "Whatever."

Turning back to the door, Khalen hit the release. Together, he and Nara left the hangar and stepped into the streets of Mok Ena.

27

THE BLUE RYMER LOUNGE

NARA'S PROMISE lasted a grand total of three seconds. Growing up on the Solemsiel world of Hebellion, the Tii-Koona had been surrounded by a majority of Solemsiel and a mixture of the other races. Khalen doubted the teen had ever seen so many of her own people in one place.

The city of Mok Ena bustled with activity. Many shops were closing up for the day while other businesses were gearing up for their late-night activities. The hangar in which the *Lightbringer* landed was located a block from one of the main streets that crisscrossed the city. As such, vehicles of all shapes and sizes moved up and down the thoroughfare and a moderate number of pedestrians ambled to and fro.

"Nara, close your mouth. You're gawking."

She blinked rapidly as if Khalen's words had broken a magic spell she had just been under. "What? Oh, sorry. It's just...something about this place feels like home."

"Yeah, well consider this an exercise in self-control," Khalen said as the two of them began walking down the sidewalk toward the main street. "You're supposed to help me blend in."

"Sorry. I'm okay now. I got this. No big deal."

Khalen smiled despite himself. Although he had his concerns about allowing Nara to come along, Roakel and Saryn had convinced him the time together might help the teen begin to come to grips with Khalen's ancestry. *Not to mention they probably felt it would put the Lah'grex more at ease knowing the Meh'ishto wasn't running around alone*, he thought wryly. "I know how you feel," he said aloud, guiding the conversation. "The culture we grow up in may not determine our identity, but it certainly colors it. It's like the spices that bring out the flavor of the food."

"But I'm just surprised at how...comfortable it feels. I don't even know why or how to explain it."

"I do. It's the smells, the colors, the architecture, the clothing, even the atmosphere of the planet. All of it impacted your brain as a young child and those memories are being unlocked." Nara's silence informed Khalen his words were having the desired effect. He wanted to push her further but had been warned by Saryn to allow her to process things at her own pace. Although his own personality screamed at him to drive his point home, he deferred to the judgment of the Solemsiels and held his tongue. Less than a minute later, his patience was rewarded.

"Uncle Khalen," Nara began, "I...I wanted to say that...I'm sorry for how I reacted when I found out the truth. I was just confused. Your faith in the Great Composer is so strong, and you're such a good person I just…it didn't make sense. But then when Aunt Saryn told Jov and I that our parents were Tey-Rakil, I realized…if things had gone differently, *I could* have been part of that culture. *I* might have experienced so much more pain and suffering. *I* could've been…evil."

Khalen stopped walking toward the main street and turned to face his young protégé. "I appreciate your honesty. I've experienced a lot of prejudice, rejection, and hatred for my heritage over the years from beings way older than you. Yet you've shown more wisdom than most."

Nara looked at him, her eyes moist with tears. "I can't imagine what you've been through. How did you…how did you overcome so much pain?"

Her question dug down into some of the deepest places in his spirit, where his strongest emotions were buried. When he responded, he was surprised to find rare tears threatening to spill forth. "When all you've experienced in life is hatred, suffering, rejection, and pain, one act of selflessness is like a glass of cool water in the middle of a scorching desert. The day Riveruun risked his own life to save mine, I saw something I'd never seen before, and I hungered for it. The more time I spent learning from him, the more I realized that everything I'd been taught was a lie. The truth opened my eyes to a new reality—a reality where a loving Creator made me for a purpose. I'm an instrument fashioned by the Great Composer's own hand to play my part in his Master Symphony! I've never looked back since."

A tear slid down Nara's cheek. "I often get mad at Dominuus for taking my parents away from me. I always wondered what they were like. But now I realize, they were probably nothing like the perfect couple I imagined them to be. I now realize that maybe the Composer was sparing me from a life that would have been much worse. Thank you for helping me find answers. I don't ever want to doubt Him again."

Nara's words brought forth the memory of Riveruun's last words. *"Don't...doubt. He's still in control."* All at once, Khalen realized that while he was trying to help his "niece" come to terms with her doubts, he had found part of the answer to the very question he had asked when Riveruun had died. The same answer that Roakel had explained to him months later suddenly made sense. Dominuus was still in control, even in the midst of hardship and pain.

Leaning in, Nara gave Khalen a hug even as she wiped the tear from her eye.

Khalen's scroll suddenly vibrated indicating an incoming message. Nara felt the vibration and released the embrace. Khalen glanced down at the small display screen on his wrist that was tethered to the larger device on his hip and tapped it twice.

"What was that?" Nara asked.

"I hired a taxi. That was a notification letting me know it has arrived and is waiting for us just around the corner. Let's get going. I don't want to keep my contact waiting."

"Who's your contact anyway?"

Nara's question brought forth a mixture of emotions ranging from excitement to trepidation. *It's been so long. I wonder how they'll react? What'll they think of the person I've become?* he thought.

"What's goin' on? You look like you're either about to see your best friend or throw up. I'm not sure which, but your eyes changed colors about three times in the last two seconds!" Nara said with a wry grin.

A broad smile flashed across Khalen's face as he turned to look at her. "That noticeable, huh?"

"Yep. It looks like I'm not the only one who could use a little 'exercise in self-control'," she teased.

"I knew I should've left you back on the ship. Now I've gotta put up with your sassiness. To answer your question, we're meeting with some old friends of mine whom I haven't seen in twenty-four years. A lot has happened in that time. I'm not sure what to expect." Khalen paused their conversation for a moment as they reached the main street. After a quick scan of the area, he pointed. "That's it over there across the street."

"The green hovercar? I love hovercars. They feel like you're floating on a cloud. It's too bad the tech only works on the city streets. It'd be awesome if you could go driving out in the country in one of those. The sleek design is wasted in the city. You can't get any decent speed. I could just see Meznine, Sania, and me flying over the fields."

"Maybe someday they'll figure out how to make hovercars work without the magnets embedded in the roads so you and your friends can go for joyrides," Khalen said. "Maybe you and Jov should work on that."

"Maybe we *should*," Nara replied sarcastically.

"Enough chit-chat for now. Once we're in the taxi, don't say anything. All right? Now, c'mon."

Khalen and Nara reached the car a few moments later and climbed inside. After a brief exchange with the driver, they were on their way. The colorful lights of the city intensified as the sun dipped below the horizon. Nara stared out the window, soaking in the sights and sounds of the city. Before long, the street dipped down sharply as it led to the first of many sublevels.

Khalen's scroll vibrated, indicating yet another message. He felt his stomach drop as he read the simple text: [YOU'RE BEING FOLLOWED]. He felt his frustration rise. If they were being followed, it likely meant Shrouded Discord knew they were here. And if that was the case, their entire plan was shot. *I was afraid of this. But how did they know?* Khalen wondered. *They must have put a tracker on one of our ships while we were in the tower. How could they have done so without being seen by Brin'tac's people? Probably a small drone. Unless...unless there's a spy. Or maybe they have members of their organization working in Mok Ena traffic control who are on the lookout for our ships. Too many possibilities. At least we know they're there. Maybe we can turn the tables on them.*

Khalen typed a message on his scroll and sent it to his contacts. A moment later, he received a response. He read it, shut the device, and put it away. The plan was in place. All that was left to do now was wait and play the part.

The hovercar descended twice more, taking Khalen and Nara deeper into the bowels of the city. Having lived most of his life above ground, Khalen struggled with the uncomfortable sensation of being enclosed in an enormous metal bowl that could potentially spring a leak at any moment. His travels had taken him to several Lah'grex underground cities and Tii-Koona submerged cities, yet he still felt queasy each time. Hoping to take his mind off his unsettled feelings, he focused on some of the remaining beauty of the city.

With their aptitude for shaping water, the Tii-Koona musicians wove the element into much of the architecture. Numerous fountains adorned the street corners and parks. Miniature streams of vivid color flowed along the ceiling

and columns that supported the roof, held in place by automated instruments that played continually. The light from
the music also served to illuminate the streets in various
shades of violet, blues, and greens.

Through the course of the trip, Nara turned toward Khalen several times in order to point out some of these architectural wonders. However, he shook his head to remind her of
her promise. She turned away despondently causing a cyn-
ical smile to creep across Khalen's lips. In some circles it
might be considered a form of torture to require a teenage
girl to remain silent for twenty minutes.

The hovercar turned onto another street that followed a
downward spiral, bringing Khalen and Nara at last to the
fourth sublevel of the city. A minute later, they arrived at the
Blue Rymer Restaurant and Lounge. The outside, while not
overly flashy, looked inviting enough. The modern architecture of the light blue building was accented with splashes
of silver. Three large, oval-shaped panels were built into
the front wall between the windows and displayed digital
images of water flowing. The overall effect made it seem as
if the building itself were alive.

Khalen paid for the ride, then exited the hovercar while
Nara climbed out the opposite side. Although Khalen could
still see the excitement in Nara's eyes, he was thankful she
was doing a better job of keeping it under control. As the
hovercar sped away, he let his gaze sweep the area to assess
their surroundings.

While not in the best of locations, this neighborhood was
still an improvement from the surface. The three Rey-Qani
that were standing near the restaurant were dressed in mid-
dle-class attire, as were the Mih'schen couple coming out of

the shop on the right. Khalen felt the familiar sense of caution pique at the sight of the group of five Tii-Koona youth loitering further down the block. Two of the males in the group had noticed Nara and were staring openly. Khalen fought back a curse. The last thing he wanted right now was another complication.

"C'mon. Let's get inside. My friends should be here soon," Khalen said, putting a hand on Nara's shoulder and guiding her toward the entrance. As the automatic doors opened to allow them inside, he gave one last glance toward the group and saw that all but one of them were now looking in his direction. To his right, another hovercar with darkened windows had pulled over to the curb halfway down the street.

"Wow!" Nara exclaimed from just inside the restaurant.

Tearing his gaze away from the group of youth, Khalen ducked through the entrance to see what had caught her attention.

Like many buildings constructed along the outer edges of the city, the entire far wall of the restaurant was made of thick glass. Mounted outside the glass were numerous lights, which served to illuminate the water surrounding the city. Dozens of aquatic creatures swam nearby as if putting on a show for the inhabitants of the city.

To further enhance the beauty of the restaurant, a fountain stood in the center. Three Autos hung from the ceiling and used their multiple mechanical arms to play a small group of stringed instruments. In addition to the purple and violet light emanating from the instruments, the music they produced sent thin slivers of water flowing out of the fountain and snaking around the ceiling.

"It looks like some kind of living, moving web!" Nara exclaimed. "That's one of the most beautiful things I've ever seen!"

"Yeah," Khalen said casually, his focus centered on scanning the faces of those in the room. "They're not in here," he said, hoping Nara would not realize the plan had changed. "C'mon. They might be waiting in the lounge section."

Once more leading Nara forward, Khalen continued to search the room as they crossed to the hallway that led to the lounge. As they walked down the hall, the sounds of a strange, warbling music grew stronger. The moment Khalen opened the door, he understood why.

The Arden Hydrophonic Quartet consisted of four Tii-Koona musicians immersed in rectangular glass tanks of water. Specialized musical instruments rested in front of each performer, and microphones captured their aquatic singing. From time to time, each performer would pause long enough to take a breath from an air hose that floated next to him or her. Khalen had heard of such groups before, and always found their particular sound otherworldly and fascinating.

Although it was still early in the evening, dozens of beings of all the Major races were seated at small tables around the room enjoying food and drink. Once again, Khalen scanned the crowd nonchalantly for several seconds before turning toward Nara. Not wanting to alarm her, he forced himself to act casual. "Let's grab that table over there and wait. You might even talk me into buying you one of those drizzle-berry shakes you like so much."

Nara's eyes lit up. "Now you're talkin'!"

They sat at a table on the other side of the room where Khalen had a clear view of the door. He ordered them each a drink and, before long, Nara was enraptured by the musical performance.

While she was distracted, Khalen rotated his wrist and checked the new message he had just received. [2 SUSPECTS.

TII-KOONA COUPLE. BOTH IN BLACK. MALE ENTERED RESTAURANT. FEMALE DISAPPEARED. LOCATION UNKNOWN. BE CAREFUL. WE'RE IN POSITION NOW. WAITING ON YOU.]

An expletive ran through Khalen's mind before his consciousness could filter it. *What do they mean, 'disappeared',* he thought. *How could they have lost her?*

He suddenly felt an overwhelming sense he was being watched. Nara, who was thoroughly enjoying the music, remained oblivious. Khalen made another casual scan of the room and felt his pulse quicken.

A lone Tii-Koona male dressed in black was seated at a table behind where he and Nara sat. Khalen's eyes turned gray in confusion. *How did he get in the room? There are only two entrances, and I was watching them both. You must be losing your edge, Khalen.*

As if sensing the other's perusal, the Tii-Koona stood and started making his way toward the exit. The casual observer would never have noticed he was deliberately keeping to the shadows, nor would they have noticed the slight bulge inside his jacket that indicated a concealed weapon.

But Khalen was no casual observer.

"I'll be right back. Stay here."

The abruptness of his command snapped Nara out of her enjoyment. She looked at him and immediately realized something was wrong. However, knowing not to argue, she simply nodded. "Okay. Be careful."

The moment Khalen stood, the Tii-Koona observer quickened his pace and made his way to the exit. A second later, he slipped through the door leading to the restaurant. Not wanting to lose sight of his target, Khalen increased his own speed. He entered the hallway just as the other left it and entered the restaurant.

Khalen sprinted down the hall and nearly plowed into a pair of Rey-Qani females. He offered a brief apology and made his way past them. Stepping into the restaurant, his eyes scoured the room. Several precious seconds slipped away before he spotted his prey heading toward the side exit.

Dodging several servers with trays of food balanced on their hands, Khalen worked his way across the room and brought his wrist-mounted comm to his lips. "He's heading out the side door. I'm in pursuit." He sprinted the last few feet to the door and burst through it as fast as the automatic opener allowed.

By now he knew the Tii-Koona was aware he was being pursued. Khalen expected his target to either be running full speed down the side alley or waiting to ambush him the moment he came through the door. What he did not expect was for the alley to be empty. The observer had vanished.

Stunned, Khalen remained still as he searched for any sign of his target. The truth dawned on him a moment too late.

A heavy weight dropped onto him from above, driving him to the ground. A second later, he felt the unmistakable pressure of the barrel of a laser pistol pressed against his back.

28

AMBUSH

KHALEN KNEW he could easily throw the smaller Tii-Koona from his back, but the presence of the pistol made him hesitate. From somewhere nearby, he heard a whispered singing. To his utter surprise, a Tii-Koona female stepped out of a shadow that seemed far too light to have hidden her hooded form. Khalen blinked, wondering how he had missed seeing her a moment ago.

With his face near the ground, Khalen struggled to see what the female was doing. She was obviously performing a kind of music. Instead of the song creating light, however, the opposite occurred. An inky blackness spread outward from her hands and obscured a large portion of the street. Pedestrians near the main road ran for cover at the sight of the approaching cloud.

"We're not here to hurt you, at least not yet," the Tii-Koona male hissed in Khalen's ear.

"Then why are you following me?" Khalen growled.

"Merely to observe."

Out of the corner of his eye, Khalen caught sight of a thin slice of silver as it snaked out suddenly from somewhere near the roof of the restaurant. Although he could not see what was happening, he heard a sharp crackle of energy followed immediately by a cry of pain from the Tii-Koona. Feeling the pressure removed from his back, Khalen rolled into a crouch.

Perched on the edge of the roof was a Rey-Qani female dressed in a tight-fitting solid gray shirt. Her dark blue pants were tucked into black boots that reached to her mid-calf. The left sleeve of her shirt was missing, allowing the orange, cracked skin of her arm to be revealed. Between the cracks of her skin, he could see the heartvein in her arm glowing deep red as an indication of her heightened senses. Like all Rey-Qani, the heartveins traveled along her body, connecting the various limbs and extremities.

While the left side of her head was shaved, the headribbons on the top and right were a mixture of glowing reds, yellows, and oranges with flecks of blue. The rest of her ribbonmane flowed down her spine to her slender tail. In her hand she held a silvery whip with a metal appendage on the end, which was presently wrapped around the arm of the Tii-Koona male.

Before Khalen could react, his assailant shook off the whip and stumbled backward, away from his companion. The sudden attack forced the Tii-Koona maestra to stop singing and spin around to face the unexpected foe.

Locating the danger, the hooded Tii-Koona female withdrew a laser pistol from within her cloak.

She fired at Khalen's rescuer, who leapt from her perch to land on the ground, dodging the attack. Meanwhile, the male recovered and grabbed his own pistol which had been wrenched from his hand by the whip. Expecting the move, Khalen grabbed the resonite disc from its holster on his right thigh and threw it. The weapon connected with the laser pistol and knocked it several feet further down the street just before the Tii-Koona could grab it.

Weaponless, the attacker pivoted toward Khalen, closing the distance rapidly. Khalen came out of his crouch and went on the defensive, barely blocking each punch and kick. He realized quickly his opponent was a master at hand-to-hand combat. Khalen backed away, his defenses weakening as his assailant landed blow after blow.

In an attempt to dodge the latest offensive, Khalen stumbled into the cloud of darkness which had begun to dissipate. He saw through the haze the outline of the Tii-Koona preparing to strike. Another figure suddenly burst out of the darkness from next to Khalen and dove into the attacker, knocking him to the ground. Khalen struggled to his feet while the two combatants grappled. The Tii-Koona slipped away from his new foe and jumped into a defensive stance.

However, before Khalen or the other could advance, the Tii-Koonas pressed buttons on their left wristguards. Khalen and his rescuers watched in surprise at the sight before them. The left arms of the attackers faded, followed quickly by the left side of their bodies, and finally their right sides until they had disappeared. The effect left Khalen with the impression of a wave of nothingness washing over both beings and swallowing them whole.

The sound of the Rey-Qani female swearing loudly broke Khalen out of his stupor. "Where in the name of Shal-rahn did that slippery little aquatic wench go? One minute I was about to wring her scrawny little neck with my whip, the next second she was gone!"

"You said it, babe."

Now that much of the darkness had cleared, Khalen could make out the details of his other rescuer. The muscular Rey-Qani male wore a similar outfit as his companion and held the large pommel of a sword gripped in both hands. His skin was burnt orange in color, and the thick heartveins running down his face and neck glowed a deep red in response to the recent adrenaline.

"Well, Khalen, what kind of slithering grumbeck nest did you stir up this time?" the female said.

"It's good to see you, Mariska," Khalen replied with a sarcastic grin. "You too, Teg-lakis. Your timing is impeccable, as always."

"Let's save the reunion for later," Teg-lakis said, his eyes searching for signs of their vanished adversaries. "Just retrieve your Tii-Koona pet, and let's get off the street. No doubt the local law enforcement will be here any moment."

"Right," Khalen said, ignoring the offensive jibe against Nara. He brought out his comm and activated it. "Nara, meet me outside the west entrance of the building. We need to leave immediately."

Nara's reply came through the speaker a second later, her voice filled with concern. "On my way. Is...is everything okay?"

"Yes. Just hurry."

"Okay. Coming."

As he closed the connection, Khalen noticed that Mariska was finishing her own conversation on her comm. Glancing toward the main street, Khalen could see a small crowd of curious, yet cautious onlookers staring at him from the safety of shop windows and building alcoves. Turning, he walked over and retrieved his attacker's weapon which still lay in the street. He tucked it into his belt, then slid his jacket over the handle to conceal it.

The restaurant entrance opened, and Nara stepped into the street. Khalen turned toward her and gave her a reassuring smile. "Nara, this is Mariska and Teg-lakis. They're the ones we came here to meet."

"Hi," Nara said sheepishly, her eyes wide at the sight of the two warriors. The others barely acknowledged her presence with a flick of their eyes.

"Let's get out of here," Mariska called out as she began running away from the main street and down a short alley to their left. "Our rendezvous point is this way."

Khalen nodded and urged Nara to follow. Teg-lakis came last, his eyes still scanning for signs of trouble. After several twists and turns through a handful of alleys, Mariska brought the small group to a halt. Although Teg-lakis had deactivated his resonite sword, he still held the handle. Khalen knew that, should an attack arise, the moldable metal housed in the hollowed-out center of the oversized handle would leap forth to form a blade or club or a handful of other weapons. In similar fashion, Mariska's whip had shrunk to two feet long and was curled and hung on her belt. The resonite appendage on the tip had reverted to a medium-sized ball.

"Here he comes," Teg-lakis said as a nondescript, black hovervan came around the corner and headed toward them.

"Who? Who's comin'?" Nara whispered to Khalen as she struggled to catch her breath. "And why are we runnin' down a bunch of filthy alleys?"

"I'll explain once we're in the van."

A moment later, the vehicle stopped in front of them. Mariska opened the front passenger door and hopped inside while Teg-lakis continued to search for signs of danger. Off in the distance, sirens began to wail, signaling the approach of the authorities. Grabbing the handle of the side door, Khalen opened it and ushered Nara inside, then slid in beside her. Teg-lakis jumped in last and closed the door.

The driver pulled away from the curb and began heading down the street. For a minute, no one spoke as they kept their attention focused on looking for signs of pursuit.

Next to him, Khalen felt Nara's barely concealed longing to receive an explanation. Judging by the circular motions she was making with her tail, he guessed she was also fighting a swath of fear. When his eyes connected with her own, she could not contain herself any longer.

"Uncle Khalen, what's going on? Are we being followed?"

Laughter erupted from Teg-lakis, Mariska, and the driver. "'Uncle Khalen?' Wow. I never thought I'd hear those two words strung together," Teg-lakis said snidely. "Especially not from some snot-face, Tii-Koona brat."

Nara's eyes narrowed at the insult. "'Snot-face?'" she

echoed. She opened her mouth to say more, but Khalen cut her off. "Nara, these are some old friends of mine."

Khalen could tell Nara was still stinging from Teg-lakis's insult. But to her credit, she remained silent.

"Old? Hey. Speak for yourself," a voice from the driver's seat said. "Some of us are still in our prime."

The driver suddenly pulled over to the curb and put the vehicle in park. Khalen felt his excitement and trepidation return as the man's helmeted head turned toward him. It had been almost a quarter of a century since he had last seen his mentor, and the sight of the familiar helmet sent an avalanche of memories crashing down on him. Although he could not see the face behind the two-inch, red-tinted visor that encircled the entire helmet, he somehow felt the intensity of the man's gaze.

"Hello, Belenger. It's good to see you again."

The driver released the clasp holding the helmet in place. A second later, he lifted it off and turned to face his guests. Beside him, Khalen heard Nara suck in a breath in surprise. Even Khalen had to check his own reaction.

His friend's features were grizzled and weathered. The dark skin of the Mih'schen's face was covered with scars. The firm jaw sported a short, well-trimmed beard and matching mustache. The black hair on his head matched the length and style of his beard.

But the sight responsible for Nara reaction was the thick scars that ran across his eyes; the sightless orbs stared blankly.

"It's good to 'see' you too, Khalen."

29

OLD FRIENDS

"WHAT...WHAT HAPPENED to your eyes?"

Belenger offered a lopsided grin. "A former student decided he didn't like my teaching anymore."

"Skaret," Khalen said with sudden understanding. "And you retaliated by blowing a hole in the side of his face?"

"How'd you hear about that?" Belenger asked.

"It's a long story. Until a few days ago, I thought that part of my past was done with."

"Including us?" Teg-lakis interjected with resentment. "After all these years of thinking you were dead, you suddenly decide to contact us?"

"You said it, hun," Mariska chimed in. "Typical Khalen! Nice to know he hasn't changed in all this time. Still selfish, inconsiderate, and a pile of—"

"Take it easy, Mariska," Belenger cut her off. "Not in front of the kid."

The Rey-Qani female leaned back in her seat and crossed her arms in protest. "Whatever. If she's gonna be around us, she had better get used to it."

"Mariska's right about one thing, though. You do owe us some kind of explanation," Belenger said, ignoring her comment. "Why don't you fill us in, starting with Skaret and ending with why you called us now after all this time?"

With that, Belenger put his helmet back on his head and faced forward once more. As he drove away from the curb and moved into the flow of traffic, Nara leaned toward Khalen and whispered. "Oh! I get it now! He uses the helmet's brainwave interface to 'see'. The cameras built into the visor surrounding his helmet give him three-hundred-sixty-degree vision! It's just like the remote piloting helmet I use. That's so cool!"

"Yes. Belenger is an Augmented."

Nara's expression lifted in surprise. *"That's* where I've seen his helmet and armor before! I knew I recognized it from somewhere."

"Are you going to let her blabber on the whole way back to the ship?" Teg-lakis said in irritation. "We're still waiting for your pathetic excuse of a story for ignoring us for twenty-four years."

"I see you're still as friendly and tactful as ever," Khalen said, his words oozing sarcasm. The color of his eyes began to darken as he felt his temper begin to flare. "You wanna be mad at me? Fine. But don't take it out on the kid."

"Whoa. What's this? Feelings?" Teg-lakis snickered. "Since when did you start caring about others?"

"Slavery has a way of changing one's perspective."

"Slavery?" Mariska echoed, her gaze turning back to Khalen.

"Yeah. It was Skaret's doing. When he and I were paired up during that job on Oclion, his new partners got the drop on me. I got to witness the final transaction where he and Imoleth sold me to a group of vile Rey-Qani slavers."

"Imoleth, huh? I didn't realize the two of them had connected that soon," Belenger said. "Skaret told us the two of you were ambushed by the Rey-Qani and you were killed. Of course, that was just before we learned he was a traitor. When we discovered the truth, he'd already had much of his plan in place. He disabled our ship, and his new friends attacked us. We just managed to escape."

"Hey, he's telling us *his* story. We can tell him ours later," Mariska said. "So how long were you a slave, and how did you escape?"

"Twelve years. And actually, I didn't escape. My captors beat me and left me for dead. I was rescued by a Faluvinal prophet named Riveruun."

Teg-lakis snorted. "Code for plant-loving 'religious nut'."

"Well, that 'religious nut' saved my life. If it weren't for his convictions, I'd be dead by now."

"Whatever. At least it's good to know his religious zeal is good for something."

"So slavery accounts for half the time," Mariska said. "Why didn't you contact us once you were rescued?"

Khalen paused, unsure how to answer. "I ended up traveling for years with Riveruun. Believe it or not, he was a good ally and I owed him my life."

"So what? You joined his crusade to enlighten the universe or something?" Teg-lakis scorned. "Great! So you had an obligation and joined some fanatic on his holy quest, but you couldn't pick up a long range communicator before now? What? Did he have you locked up in some sort of monastery with no tech?"

"Aw, Khalen!" Mariska said, her face a grimace of disgust. "How could you fall for that stuff? You're too smart for that."

"Not exactly." Khalen was flustered and struggled to find the right words in the moment. Surrounded by these old comrades in arms, he was flooded with memories of the countless times they had saved his life. They had always had his back, as he had theirs. Suddenly, all his excuses for not contacting them sooner struck him as unacceptable.

"Believe it or not, I was too busy just surviving at first. Contrary to what you may believe, this religious fanatic, as you call him, was involved in a lot of activities that were dangerous as well and…I just…got wrapped up in a new life."

"Oh, stop it! You're gonna make me cry," Teg-lakis mocked. "So what you're saying is, he brainwashed you, sucked you into his 'following-the-musical-tone-of-the-universe' higher power nonsense. Am I right?"

"That can't be it," Mariska jumped in. "Khalen isn't that easily influenced. He may be a selfish inker, but he's not stupid. He just had new friends and didn't need his old ones any more. We get it."

"Think what you want, but belief in the Great Composer changed my life for the better. If you still call me friend, then just accept it."

Mariska shook her head in amazement. "Sure. Yeah. Good for you. So…I guess that's why you never contacted us, huh? You had new friends and didn't need your old ones."

Khalen felt his frustration rising anew. "Look, it wasn't like that. I just…my life was so different, and I was still dealing with a lot of junk from my past. I just needed time."

"Hey! It doesn't matter!" Belenger cut in sharply. "After twelve years as a slave, betrayed by one of his old comrades, maybe he just wanted to move on. I don't really care what you believe on your own time. I *do* care what you're dragging my team into now!"

"In a moment. First, I need to know what happened to the rest of you after Skaret's betrayal," Khalen said, shifting the subject back to them.

"Oh *now* he cares," Mariska chimed in.

"Stow it, Mariska," Belenger ordered. "We're never going to get anywhere with you two trying to get your pound of flesh out of the guy. I didn't come all the way to Mok Ena just to waste time on bygones. If Khalen's got a job for us, then I want to hear it."

"The job itself is pretty straightforward," Khalen said. "This Lah'grex governor's family was kidnapped. The group responsible tried to use his family as bait to get to him, but it didn't work. They've retreated to their base here on Rovik. We're hoping to catch them off guard, sneak into their base and rescue his family. There's more to it. But for now, let's just say I thought you might want a piece of the action. Oh, and did I mention this Lah'grex is rich?"

"I don't know," Teg-lakis seemed skeptical. "Risking my life to rescue some politician's brats isn't really my thing."

"Yeah, but *money's* your thing," Khalen shot back. "Besides, you may act tough, but deep down I know you've got a soft spot for kids. You used to love goofing around with Dever, Zable, and Lalonde. By the way, Belenger, what have your kids been up to lately?"

In the silence that followed, Khalen heard the man take a deep breath through his helmet filters, as if preparing to take a plunge into unpleasant memories. Mariska and Teg-lakis exchanged glances, their expressions somber. After an awkward moment of silence, Belenger spoke, his voice muffled by the helmet.

"You may remember that Jindira and I were forced to leave the Mih'schen Augmented Elite Corp because we were framed by Imoleth. What we didn't know was that Skaret had started working for that scalie trash. After your 'death', we continued to hunt Imoleth, hoping to clear our names. We eventually succeeded."

Belenger paused his tale as he negotiated the hovervan through a narrow tunnel that led them to the sea level section of the city. "Jindira and I were finally able to take our boys to their real home. We didn't have to live on the run any more. I disbanded the Renegades and took my family back home to Troth."

At the mention of the world, Khalen felt his insides twist. Nara looked concerned by his reaction. "What's wrong? What happened on Troth?"

Before Khalen could answer, Mariska continued the tale. "Troth lies on the edge of Meh'ishto space and was founded as a military outpost, kid. Most of the inhabitants on the planet are from military families. The Meh'ishto have always used hit-and-run tactics to weaken their enemies and strike fear into them. But eighteen years ago, Troth was attacked by the Meh'ishto Supremacy's primary fleet. This time, they didn't come to pillage, but to conquer." Mariska paused and glanced at Belenger as if seeking permission to continue. When she spoke again, her voice was soft and subdued. "During the early years of the war...Belenger's wife and children were killed."

Nara covered her mouth with her hand. "Oh my! That's so…that's so sad."

"Belenger, I'm so sorry to hear about your loss," Khalen said.

"Like you said, sometimes it's better to move on from the past," Belenger stated, his voice emotionless. "After their deaths, I became a spy for the AEC. I spent most of the war undercover. But during my last mission, I happened to stumble upon Skaret. He blew my cover, and I was captured. Instead of killing me, they sent me off to Mitrik B3."

Khalen's eyes grew wide. "The prison world? How'd you ever make it out of that death trap?"

"We saved him," Teg-lakis said, his expression prideful and smug.

"Now, there's a story I'd like to hear, without embellishments, please. I thought that place was escape-proof."

"Not for someone on the inside. Ya see, before I joined up with you bunch of losers, I worked for Lady Crisenth as a guard on Mitrik B3. When Mariska and I learned Belenger had been captured and sent there, I contacted some old buddies of mine and got my old job back. After that, it was pretty much just waiting for the right time to spring him."

"After we got him out," Mariska said, picking up the story, "the three of us started our own security business. It paid the bills and gave us the freedom we needed to hunt Skaret down. We finally caught up with him nine years ago on the Ra-Nuuk world of Debruin. During the fight, he…slashed Belenger across the eyes, taking his sight. But before he could escape, we were able to detonate an explosion that killed that putrid sack of gruck meat."

Khalen winced at her pronouncement. Catching sight of his expression, Mariska frowned. "What?"

"The group that abducted the Lah'grex family claimed to be connected with the Dumah Dynasty. We've since learned they are actually part of a group of pirates and mercenaries that go by the name Shrouded Discord. During the confrontation with them on Dhun'drok, I learned their leader is a Ra-Nuuk warlord who wears a damaged silver mask and goes by the name of Slag."

At his statement, both Teg-lakis and Mariska stiffened. "No. I don't believe it," Mariska said, her expression hardening.

"Khalen, so help me, if this is some kind of joke, I'm gonna kill you myself," Teg-lakis said.

Khalen's face became grim as he spoke the words his friends feared to hear. "Yeah. Skaret is alive!"

30

PLANS

AFTER A SHORT VISIT at Belenger's own ship, the *Fiery Vengeance*, Khalen and Nara returned to the docking bays and introduced Belenger, Teg-lakis, and Mariska to Brin'tac and the others. They gathered with Roakel, Saryn, Inspector Mak'sim, and Vel'vikis in the conference room aboard the *Eternal Harmony*.

"Since I thought it possible Shrouded Discord could have spies on the lookout for our ships, I asked Belenger, Teg-lakis, and Mariska to follow us," Khalen explained. As expected, the Lah'grex were none too happy to hear about the recent confrontation. "They trailed us to the Blue Rymer Restaurant and Lounge," Khalen continued. "Once Nara and I were inside, Belenger and his team identified those following us. They were a pair of Tii-Koona dressed all in black. However, something bizarre happened as they were observing them."

"Strange? Like what?" Vel'vikis asked.

"The male entered the restaurant," Belenger interjected, his helmet held under his arm. "But the female…simply disappeared."

"Disappeared?" Mak'sim echoed. "What do you mean? Did she hide in the shadows or get lost in a crowd?"

"No. We mean she disappeared," Teg-lakis said. "Listen, I've spied on and hunted hundreds of beings in my time. I've never seen anyone do what she did. One minute she was there, the next minute—poof—she vanished into thin air."

"What about a musical portal?" Saryn asked. "Perhaps she passed through one not visible to you."

"No way, sister," Mariska interjected. "We've seen beings use those plenty of times. We know what we're doing. We've never encountered anything like this."

"I saw it too," Khalen stated. "It most definitely wasn't a portal."

"Then what *do* you think it was," Mak'sim asked.

Khalen glanced at the others. His gaze halted as it came to rest on Brin'tac. The Lah'grex ruler seemed uncharacteristically silent, and he appeared disturbed.

"It has to be some kind of new tech," Belenger answered, drawing Khalen back into the conversation.

Mak'sim frowned. "You mean, like a sort of light displacement? I've heard some of the technological scientists working for the Lah'grex Augmented have been experimenting with that but have yet to perfect it."

"No," Belenger said. "We've seen that tech first hand. Although light gets displaced around an object making it nearly invisible, you can still locate it if you know what to look for. This was different."

"So were you able to catch the male?" Vel'vikis asked, returning the conversation to its original topic.

Khalen hesitated before answering. "For whatever reason, he stood and headed toward the restaurant exit while Belenger, Teg-lakis, and Mariska kept searching for the female. I followed him outside and he attacked me just before Mariska arrived. When the female showed up, she created a cloud of darkness that covered the area. Belenger was on the opposite side of the restaurant and couldn't make it in time, but Teg-lakis arrived a moment later."

"The pair of yellow-bellied borkrins must've realized they couldn't take us and split," Mariska said.

"That's when they used their tech to disappear," Khalen clarified.

"I see," Mak'sim said. "Then Slag knows we're here."

Khalen shook his head. "I'm not so sure the spies were from Shrouded Discord."

"What makes you think that?" the inspector asked.

"Several reasons. First, the female used a song of darkness. That's not a song a common criminal would use. In fact, it makes it likely they aren't Tii-Koona at all, but Tey-Rakil who didn't darken their scales but kept them their natural color. Second, before Mariska arrived, I spoke to the male. He specifically said they were there to 'observe.' I don't think he meant to observe as spies."

"That's not very convincing," Mak'sim said.

"Not by itself, no. But I recognized his voice."

"What do you mean? You recognized his voice but not his face?" Brin'tac asked, breaking into the conversation for the first time.

Khalen looked at the Lah'grex leader. "Yes. I didn't recognize his face because I'd never seen it before. The one time I met him, he was covered in black."

"The stranger who preserved your life on Balec's Tower!" Roakel said in surprise.

"I'm almost positive. He had the same tone of voice and the same slight accent."

"This mystery grows deeper," Roakel said. "First, we learn the delegation from Dumah are in reality a covert mercenary group, then we discover our actions are being observed by a third party that saves Khalen one moment and assaults him the next."

"Not to mention they have some kind of advanced tech that can turn them invisible," Teg-lakis muttered.

"So then, you still believe Shrouded Discord is unaware we're on the planet?" Brin'tac asked, his countenance lifting.

"Yes," Khalen said. "And based on the surveillance info Belenger provided, I think there's an excellent chance your family is in the base."

"What 'surveillance info'?" Vel'vikis asked.

Khalen flipped open his scroll and passed it across the table to Brin'tac. Vel'vikis and Mak'sim drew closer to Brin'tac in order to read it for themselves. As they skimmed the data, Khalen explained further. "Once we learned the location of their base, I knew we'd need the kind of expertise Belenger and his team can provide. They're experts with the inner workings of outlaws, smugglers, pirates, etc. On top of that, as providence would have it, they were currently stationed in the Tii-Koona system of Kypso, on the planet Varv Minor. They arrived here on Rovik yesterday and were able to do a casual scan of the base. As you can see on the readout, not just one, but *both* of the ships that were on Dhun'drok are docked in the hangar."

"Then there is still hope we can rescue them before time expires," Brin'tac said.

Khalen frowned. "What's that supposed to mean?"

"I was about to call off the attack and turn myself in," Brin'tac explained. "I just received new demands from the 'Dumah Dynasty' an hour ago. They stated that because of what happened on Dhun'drok, they're going to kill my son in one day unless I turn myself in. Supposedly, there's a 'Dumah patrol' on Dhun'drok waiting to take me into custody."

"That is an excellent indicator they still think we are there," Roakel added.

"It also means we've got one shot at this," Vel'vikis said, his tone serious. "If we fail, or if we're somehow mistaken that eth Galithar's family is here at the base, then it could mean the death of his firstborn."

"That is true," Saryn said. "Perhaps we should reconsider. Noble Galithar, you must make the decision."

"Eth Galithar, I encourage you to move forward with the plan," Mak'sim urged. "We have a chance to take them by surprise. And if your family *isn't* here, then we will doubtless find some kind of collateral to use to bargain for your son's life. This is their base of operations. There must be something, or some*one*, important enough to them that they'd be willing to trade."

Brin'tac remained silent as he considered the inspector's words. "I will not risk the life of my son unless there is an overwhelming possibility of our mission succeeding."

"What's your plan?" Belenger asked.

"The prisoner we interrogated informed us of a series of tunnels beneath the base itself," Mak'sim explained. "The building used to house Tey-Rakil refugees after Rovik was liberated. No doubt many of the tunnels were carved out to serve as housing as more and more refugees moved in. Since taking over, Shrouded Discord sealed off all but one of the entrances to the caves. They put a security door on the last entrance, preventing anyone from accidentally getting inside."

"How do we get through?" Teg-lakis asked. "I'm assuming they have a portal inhibitor in place."

"Yes. We will use the tunnels to reach the security door, which can be opened with a passcode," Vel'vikis answered.

"Which the prisoner gave you willingly?" Teg-lakis asked skeptically.

"I may have had something to do with that," Khalen said.

The Rey-Qani grinned in understanding. "Right. Your little song and dance trick. You always did have a way to make others more cooperative. Okay, fine. But what about security systems? Will we meet any resistance in the caves?"

"None that we know of," Mak'sim said. "The prisoner was confident there weren't any other security measures in place at the door but was vague about the caves."

Mariska frowned. "Vague? In what way? What did he say?"

"He rambled on about rumors he'd heard among the group. Something about how a new recruit wanted to prove himself by venturing into the tunnels, but he never returned," Khalen said. "But based on the scans we made, the caves appear pretty straightforward. Any side tunnels either dead end or reconnect with the main one. If the story's true, I can't imagine he got lost."

"More than likely it's just a 'ghost story' told by the leadership to keep people from going down there," the inspector said dismissively.

"Do we possess any indication of how many mercenaries currently reside in the base?" Saryn asked.

"The scan registered forty-three heat signatures," Belenger stated.

"Are you sure we can fight against that many?" Brin'tac asked in concern.

"If we can make it into the base undetected in the middle of the night, we should easily take out half of those before they know we're there," Teg-lakis said. "If your people are any good, that is."

"We can handle ourselves," Vel'vikis said, bristling at the implied insult.

"Roakel, Saryn, and I know a song of sleep. That should allow us to incapacitate most of the mercs without a fight," Khalen explained.

"What if they have more Synths?" Roakel asked.

"When we scanned the rest of the building, we were able to detect the distinct signatures of six remotes and three active Synths," Belenger said. "But my people can handle those."

"What if they have some more hidden nearby, like in the tower?" Brin'tac asked.

Khalen shook his head. "Unlikely. Those were originally inactive as part of the trap. Synths can rarely be convinced to be shut down, and even then only for short durations. That's one of the things I still can't figure out. I've worked with Synths before. Being shut down is like death for them. They hate it. I don't get how a mercenary group was able to get the Synths to do it. The only thing I can figure is because the Synths knew it was for a specific time period. There's no way they'd be shut down indefinitely."

"Well, with any luck, eth Galithar's family is being held in one of the lower levels closest to the tunnels," Vel'vikis continued. "If so, we can break in, rescue them, and get out before the mercs even know we're there. Based on an old schematic of the building we found from the city archives, we think there's a good chance. Once we're inside, Mak'sim, Tas'anee, Tet'rick, and I, as well as Hujik's remote, will locate eth Galithar's family and rescue them. Meanwhile, Khalen and his friends will provide cover and take out the mercs."

"Wait a moment," Brin'tac interrupted. "I'm not staying behind."

"I'm sorry, eth Galithar, but it's simply too dangerous."

Brin'tac narrowed his eyes and glared at Vel'vikis. "I will *not* just sit here like a coward while the rest of you risk your lives for the sake of my family. I have had numerous courses in self-defense and know how to handle a blaster when need arises. I *will* be going. That's an order."

Teg-lakis broke the awkward silence that followed with a snicker. "Are you sure, hotshot? You might get that pretty coat of yours dirty."

Brin'tac's temper flared at the insult. "Master Khalen, remind me again: who is this impudent, dry-skinned, tail-wagger?"

Teg-lakis laughed before leveling a challenge at the Lah'grex. "I may be shorter than you, mudhead, but why don't you come to this side of the table, and I'll show you how impudent I can be?"

Khalen, the two Arrangers, Vel'vikis, and Mak'sim all tensed and prepared to tackle Teg-lakis if necessary. However, Mariska's raucous laughter interrupted the tension. After a moment, she composed herself. "Take a tranq, hon," she said as she laid a hand on her mate's forearm.

Teg-lakis ignored her. "Look, we're here because Khalen offered us a job and because we have a score to settle with the Ra-Nuuk. Based on what we've seen and heard, you need our help to rescue your family. So let me offer you a bit of advice: lose your superiority complex, or we walk. We're not that desperate for your money."

"Teg-lakis, that's enough," Belenger interrupted. To Brin'tac, he added, "I apologize for the rudeness of my companion."

Brin'tac narrowed his eyes. "If Khalen had not vouched for the three of you, I would've had you arrested long ago for your insulting demeanor. However, we recognize the value of the intel you provided and will thus forgive your insolent attitude. But just know I will not tolerate further insults made against my person or the agreement is off. If you aid us in rescuing my family and learn to control your tongue, you will be compensated."

"Agreed," Belenger stated. "And if he gets out of line again, he'll be excluded from the mission and its compensation. Got it, Teg-lakis?"

"Yeah, I got it," Teg-lakis said irritably.

"Good, then can we get back to the task at hand?" Brin'tac asked. "Once *we* are inside, Mak'sim, Vel'vikis, and I will take our team to rescue my family."

"Right," Vel'vikis said, reluctantly acquiescing. "Meanwhile, Dostal will remain here with Captain Nahoc. When we're in position, they'll provide a distraction by attacking the base with the *Eternal Harmony's* weapons. Master Roakel, we were hoping you'd be willing to have your ship join that attack as well."

Roakel glanced at his wife before responding. "I am hesitant to commit my ship to such a task for two reasons: Nara and Jov are onboard, and it would require one of us to remain behind to pilot the ship."

"As to the first point, you could always break off the attack at any time if you felt it was too dangerous," Mak'sim said. "The goal is simply to make a show of force to distract our enemy."

"I understand. Yet I remain steadfast in my decision. I will not place Nara and Jov in danger."

"The danger would be minimal," Mak'sim argued. "We need another ship for the attack in order to aid in the distraction. Are you truly willing to increase the already considerable danger for eth Galithar's entire family just to keep two Tii-Koona youth from being placed in mild, controllable danger? I expected more from members of a 'Perfect' race."

Khalen spoke up before either Solemsiel could respond. "Before the inspector says anything else insulting, I'm going to interject here with another option that would solve the problem, if Belenger is willing."

Belenger frowned. "I don't think I like where this is going."

"C'mon. Saryn is a fantastic pilot. She's been flying ships for over *a thousand years!* Give her some credit. Besides, the *Vengeance* is the toughest ship we've got and has the most firepower. If Saryn used it, Nara and Jov could remain safe on the *Lightbringer.* That way, we could still have Nara pilot Roadblock to help on the mission while keeping her safe."

"Yeah, I get that. It's not that I don't trust her specifically. I just don't trust *anyone* with my ship. I was considering just using my armor's link to pilot the ship virtually when the time came for the distraction. There's no need for Saryn to do it."

Teg-lakis chuckled. "If you're not in the middle of running or fighting for your life."

"Exactly," Khalen said.

"Mr. Roth," Saryn interjected, "I make a vow to you on my honor as a Solemsiel, if you allow me to pilot your ship, I will break off from the attack long before any significant damage occurs."

"Yes, and Noble Galithar had already promised to cover the cost of any liquid resonite reserves needed to repair the damage to our own ship," Roakel added. "I am sure he would do likewise for yours."

"Of course," Brin'tac confirmed.

Belenger turned to Khalen and whispered so only he could hear. "Are you sure about this? I've not had many dealings with Solemsiels. I've heard some sketchy tales about some of them."

"The Tritonus have been trying to muddy the reputation of the Arrangers for centuries. But I've been traveling with them for a year now and I can tell you, they're the real deal. I trust them with my life."

"Fine," Belenger said, addressing the whole group. "Maestra, I'll let you use the *Vengeance* for the attack. I'm trusting you to take care of it."

"Thank you for that trust. I do not accept it lightly."

"Well, then. It seems everything is settled," Mak'sim said. "Unless anyone has anything else to add, be prepared to leave in an hour."

Roakel raised his top left hand to garner everyone's attention. "I do have one item. With your permission, Noble Galithar, I would like to offer a prayer to the Great Composer for safety and for the successful return of your family."

"Yes, you may, Master Roakel," Brin'tac said. "I will take any positive energy you can send my way."

Mariska rolled her eyes at the comment and she and Teglakis headed for the exit.

Closing his eyes, Roakel began to sing his prayer.

"Majestic Creator of life,
    we now ask for your guidance
    as we seek to set the captive free.
Order our steps and
    make straight our path.
Father, protect our lives,
    and the lives of those we love.
Keep us forever safe in your arms.
Let it be so."

31

INTO THE TUNNELS

THE LIGHTS of the large, stylish boat finally came into view as it rounded the small cliff that jutted out into the ocean. Khalen and the others had been waiting on the secluded, private dock for half an hour for the boat to appear. It had been decided that, out of everyone, Teg-lakis and Mariska were the best choices for securing transportation to the island. Shrouded Discord's spies were probably on the lookout for any Lah'grex, and Slag may have given them Khalen's description as well. Solemsiels always stood out in a crowd, and Belenger's armor drew attention to him as a member of the Mih'schen AEC. Even Vel'vikis and Mak'sim were forced to admit the Rey-Qani couple were the obvious choice. And since renting boats to foreign visitors for a quiet evening at sea was a common practice, they were not likely to raise suspicion.

Khalen grinned as the expensive yacht drew closer. *They've gotta be loving this*, Khalen thought. *With Brin'tac footing the bill, Teg-lakis and Mariska went with luxury in addition to size.* A few minutes later, the couple had the boat anchored several hundred feet from the shore.

"Master Roakel, would you please open the portal to the boat?" Brin'tac asked. The wealthy noble had shed his fine clothing and was now wearing a thick blue jacket and matching pants. A blaster pistol rested in its holster against his hip.

Roakel looked down at the Lah'grex and smiled. "A portal? Why employ the use of a portal when there are other, more enjoyable options available?" Without explaining further, the Solemsiel music master began to play a song on his windstaff.

Khalen recognized the song and let out a quiet chuckle. As the winds around them began to swirl, he kept his gaze fixed upon the faces of the Lah'grex so as not to miss their reactions.

He was not disappointed. Despite the darkness, he could still make out their expressions in the swirling light created by Roakel's song. Shock and uncertainty splashed across their faces as a wall of wind lifted the entire group off the dock, including Hujik's and Nara's remotes. Roakel, on the other hand, appeared as comfortable, if not *more* comfortable, with flying through the air as he would taking a leisurely stroll.

As they flew away from the dock, Khalen let out a quick whistle toward Shosta and Kovitch. The two drallmari leapt into the air enthusiastically, no doubt eager to spread their wings. Before long, the reptilian beasts were flying circles around the group and performing aerial maneuvers to the delight of everyone.

Once their initial panic had dissipated, the Lah'grex began to enjoy the trip. In just over a minute, Roakel brought the companions to a gentle rest aboard the deck of the yacht.

Still enjoying their freedom, the drallmari chose to remain airborne for the time being.

"I see what you mean," Brin'tac said once his feet were firmly planted on the deck. "That was magnificent."

Roakel smiled. "That song is one of the primary methods used by my people to travel between the various platforms of our floating cities."

"I've seen some holovids of the famed Solemsiel cities. Someday I'd love to see one in person."

The smile on Roakel's face wilted slightly. "Perhaps. However, the Solemsiel are a private people. We don't often allow those of the Major races to visit."

"Surely there are exceptions," Brin'tac said. "Perhaps the Solemsiel people would welcome a political dignitary, especially if you were to accompany me and my family. I'm positive after all they've been through, visiting such a peaceful realm would do them good."

"Yes. The beauty of our majestic cities have brought serenity to many. An arrangement may be possible."

"Well, then. I look forward to it."

Khalen listened to the conversation in silence, his own thoughts dwelling on what lay ahead even as his eyes stared out into the vast blackness of the ocean. Beneath him, he could feel the rumble of the engines kick in as Teg-lakis piloted the yacht toward the island. A smile creased his face as Kovitch and Shosta came in for a landing, clapping their beaks and whistling loudly in excitement as they did so.

They had been traveling for several minutes when Belenger strode over to Khalen's side, his helmet under his arm. "There's nothing like the ocean breeze to make you feel alive."

"Yeah. I miss this. It's been too long," Khalen replied. The two drallmari, who were now curled up and resting near his feet after their recent exercise, lifted their heads at Belenger's approach.

"So tell me, how much do you know about these Lah'grex."

Khalen shrugged. "Brin'tac's the cousin of their king, Tronsen Jorlinari. Vel'vikis is his bodyguard and chief of security. And Mak'sim is an inspector sent by Jorlinari to assist Brin'tac. The rest of the Lah'grex are Jorlinari soldiers."

"And you checked out their stories?"

Khalen looked offended. "What am I, some green recruit? Of course we checked them out. Like many rich rulers, Brin'tac's past is full of shady deals and moral posturing. I don't fully trust him, but he seems to legitimately care about his family. We found several documents about Mak'sim. His credentials check out, but his record seems somewhat sparse. Vel'vikis's history has mostly been intertwined with the Galithar family for the past twenty years or so. Why do you ask?"

Belenger shook his head. "I don't know. I can't put my finger on it, but something about them seems…off. Be careful. I wouldn't trust them more than I have to."

"Don't worry, I haven't, and I won't. Honestly, something about this whole *ordeal* seems off. That thing with the Tii-Koona couple back in the city has me on edge." Khalen's gaze shifted toward the lights of the city, which were being swallowed by the surrounding darkness of the night. "Yet Roakel and Saryn still believe we're on the right path."

"Just stay alert. Hopefully after today, we can rest a little easier knowing Skaret will no longer be a threat. By the way, speaking of the Solemsiels, your new faith isn't going to get in the way of you doing your job, right?"

"Don't worry about that," Khalen said. "When the time comes, I'll do what needs to be done." Khalen glanced at his friend and could tell his answer was not quite what Belenger had been looking for. Regardless, he let the topic drop. "Anyway, I'm going to go get a bite to eat. I don't want to head into a mission on an empty stomach."

"You've got a point. I think I'll join you." Together, the two of them headed into the ship to pass the time.

An hour later, at just after eleven o'clock local time, the yacht reached the island. Although the lights from the city of Mok Ena 2 were far to their right, their destination was a dark cove hidden by several large cliffs.

"The entrance to the cave system lies in there," Vel'vikis stated. "The waves look too unpredictable for us to venture in by boat. I think we should drop anchor here and have Roakel take us in."

Since no one objected, the group set about making final preparations. A short time later, they all gathered on the deck. As before, Roakel transported everyone from the ship to the mouth of the cave through his manipulation of the air currents. Once they landed, the group fanned out and scanned the area, their flashlights and lanterns chasing away the darkness.

Khalen was studying the map of the cavern system on his scroll when Roadblock came to stand next to him. "Hey, Uncle Khalen," Nara said, her voice uncharacteristically subdued. "Are you guys sure about this? I mean, that place looks creepy, and I'm not even really there. Do you think it's safe?

I watched this show one time on the hyperfeed that talked about all the bizarre and dangerous creatures that inhabit the dark places of different worlds in the galaxy."

"You're always welcome to keep Roadblock here with the boat if you want," Khalen teased, knowing full well the teen's pride would never allow it.

"What? Sheesh. I'm okay. I'm just worried about you guys."

"Right. Well, don't be concerned. We're quite capable of taking care of ourselves. Besides, I don't think the mercs would allow anything to make a home out of a cave they use as a back door. Now c'mon. We're heading out."

Per Vel'vikis's orders, the team was split into four rows of three. Hujik led the group with his remote. Tas'anee and Tet'rick followed close behind the droid. The second row was Teg-lakis, Mariska, and Belenger. Brin'tac was situated in between Roakel and Vel'vikis in the third row. Roadblock, Khalen, and Inspector Mak'sim came last. As always, the two drallmari walked next to Khalen, their tongues flicking in-and-out.

As they delved deeper into the cave, the cold, damp air seeped through their clothing, chilling them to the bone. To ward off the cold, Roakel activated his windstaff and began to sing a simple song in the key of D Aeolian. The orange-colored energy created by the song coalesced into a large flame that rested just above the top of the staff. Roakel circled his hand around the flame and drew some of the orange light down and away. In response, the heat produced from the fire began to spread out in waves. Everyone in the group felt the cold recede as the warmth permeated the air. In addition, the flickering reddish light of the fire blended with that of their lanterns and flashlights to illuminate the area. Once the entire song had been sung through, Roakel pressed a button on the side of his windstaff and ceased singing. The small, computerized component in the staff continued to play the repeating chord progression of the song and the melody that Roakel had programmed into it. The automated instrument kept the song going, sustaining the flame indefinitely.

Encouraged by the warmth and light, the group pressed on. For the most part, the cave floor was worn and smooth, making their travel easier. From time to time they were forced to climb up rocky shelves or descend down large holes. Although there were several smaller caves that branched off, the central tunnel continued on in a more-or-less straight line.

An hour into their journey, Mak'sim drew closer to Khalen to speak with him. Kovitch placed himself between them and eyed the Lah'grex warily.

Mak'sim laughed at the creature's protectiveness. "He reminds me quite a bit of the pet relkin I used to have." Reaching out a cautious hand, he let the drallmar touch his hand with its tongue. Khalen could tell that although Mak'sim was trying hard to appear relaxed around the creature, he was still on edge. After a moment, the Lah'grex felt comfortable enough to stroke the animal's scaly head.

"I would never want my relkin underfoot during battle, though. I'm surprised you're willing to bring the drallmari along. You seemed rather protective of them earlier."

"First of all, you obviously don't know much about drallmari. They're natural fighters and highly intelligent. And they are more than just my pets. They're my companions. They're quite handy in a fight."

"But aren't you afraid they'll be killed?"

"Yeah, but they aren't easy targets. The particular shimmer of their scales and their natural quickness makes them hard to hit. As a maestro, I've also been training them for protection and combat." Khalen smiled and stroked Shosta's head. "I'd even venture to say they are at least as trained as half of your Lah'grex soldiers."

Mak'sim's expression darkened briefly before a sly grin creased his lips. "Right. Well, eth Galithar certainly appreciated their help at the tower. I guess I was seeing them more like Chomper. That thing could really eat. And it had quite a bite...but unlike your companions, he was a coward. My kids loved that relkin, though."

"Your kids?"

"Yes. I have three, actually. They're all adults at this point. Raising them by myself was the hardest thing I've ever done. My wife died when they were all very young. She contracted a rare disease that took her life in a matter of months."

"I'm sorry."

Mak'sim smiled wistfully. "She was the love of my life. In some ways, the security of being surrounded by rock and stone reminds me of home. The humidity is certainly much easier on my skin than that dryness your people prefer. It must be very different for you."

"Yeah," Khalen said.

"I just wish the portal inhibitor in the base wasn't active," Mak'sim said, not taking the hint that Khalen did not feel like talking. "It would be so much faster and easier. This trudging through the cold certainly isn't fun."

When Khalen once again failed to respond, Mak'sim tried a different tactic. "Listen. I...uh...I want to say that I appreciate all you've done for the Lah'grex people. You and your friends, including your new ones, have been extremely helpful. Things would've been much worse if you hadn't come along. Thank you."

His show of respect succeeded in breaching Khalen's emotional walls, at least a little. "You're welcome."

"So...I heard you've got some connection with this Slag character. How do you know him?"

The look of indifference Khalen had previously worn morphed into one of suspicion. "Where did you hear that?"

Mak'sim hesitated before responding. "Your Solemsiel friend told eth Galithar, who mentioned it to Vel'vikis and I."

Khalen felt his annoyance flare up. *How could Roakel have told them something so personal?* he fumed inwardly. *Is he so naive he didn't realize it was something I wanted to keep private? These Lah'grex are just starting to trust me, and he has to tell them I'm connected to our enemy?* Attempting to pass it off as unimportant, Khalen shrugged. "We were part of the same group years ago. We weren't any more than acquaintances."

A look of relief crossed Mak'sim's face. "That's good to hear."

"Look, you needn't be concerned about any past loyalty. I'd like nothing more than to see him with a hole in his filthy head."

Mak'sim smiled. "I'm glad to see you don't hold the traditional Symphonian view of 'loving your enemy'."

The Lah'grex's words cut like a knife into Khalen's spirit. The simmering reddish hue that had colored his eyes moments ago shifted to a sickly green. Once again, he had let his old ways of thinking infiltrate his mind and words. And once more, it had polluted his character and dishonored the name of his Creator.

Ashamed, Khalen opened his mouth to try to undo the damage. Just as he was about to speak, Roakel stopped suddenly, surprising everyone. Kovitch and Shosta lifted their heads, their posture alert.

"Uh…Uncle Khalen? You'd better get over here," Nara said through Roadblock's vocalizer. "Something's wrong with Uncle Roakel."

The tall Solemsiel turned abruptly to the left, then spun to the right as if searching for something. In the shifting light from the windstaff's flame, Khalen could see an expression on Roakel's face that he had never seen before.

It was the closest thing an immortal being could come to fear.

Khalen stepped over to him and grabbed his arm. "What is it? What's wrong?"

Roakel shook his head, his eyes never once looking at Khalen, but instead continuing to scan the area. "We are not alone. It has been many years since I have felt the presence of this kind of evil."

A strange, whispering song suddenly fluttered through the stale air of the cave. It was unlike anything Khalen had ever heard before. He could tell it was a song of some sort, but the notes appeared random, disjointed, and dissonant.

It was then that Khalen understood their danger. At last he understood why there were not any other security systems protecting the base.

This cave was the lair of a Dodekaph!

32

DODEKAPH

KHALEN FELT the rock beneath his feet shift. He looked down and watched in horror as his feet began to sink into what was now muddy ground. Struggling against the pull of the mud, he managed to break free and tumbled to the cave floor. Before he could get back to his feet, the subterranean moss and weeds grew rapidly around him. Khalen fought against them as they wrapped around his arms and legs, pinning him down.

Two shapes suddenly appeared at his side. He turned his head as much as he was able and saw Shosta and Kovitch rip into the weeds with their sharp beak-like snouts. Within seconds he was free.

"Thanks," he said to the drallmari as he climbed to his feet. "You get extra dinner." Hoping to escape the mud and vines, Khalen jumped onto a nearby boulder. Cries from his comrades drew his attention. Brin'tac, Teg-lakis, and Tet'rick were all caught fast in the muck. Weeds had wrapped themselves around Tas'anee and rendered him immobile. The two remotes were in the process of pulling their legs free from the hardening sludge, while the others were scanning for signs of an enemy.

The drallmari let out several sharp, emphatic whistles. Khalen reacted to their warning and spun around on his perch. In the light from Roakel's staff, Khalen could just see the outline of a spinning mass of air and water. The waterspout was as tall as a Solemsiel and twice as wide. Off to his left, Mak'sim and Vel'vikis fired their laser weapons at it, but to no avail. The whirlwind responded by shooting out a host of tiny droplets at rapid speed toward the two Lah'grex. Mak'sim and Vel'vikis cried out in pain as the spray stung their faces. Ceasing their attack, they twisted around so their backs were facing the water and shielded their heads from the assault. Khalen prepared to do the same, expecting the mindless waterspout to target him next. To his surprise, the spray ceased, and the whirlwind continued to spin.

"Teg-lakis on your right!"

Khalen risked a glance toward the other and saw the source of Belenger's warning. The ground began heaving and lifting into the air. As they watched in astonishment, the churning rock became engulfed in fire and began to take shape. In a matter of seconds, Khalen could see the outline of arms, legs, a torso, and a head.

"What in the galaxies is that?" Mariska asked.

"Whatever it is, it isn't friendly," Belenger said as he fired his wrist-mounted laser at the burning rock formation. As with the whirlwind, the attack seemed to have no effect. The stone monster, now fully formed, strode toward the front of their group.

"C'mon!" Khalen shouted to the drallmari. He leapt off the rock and sprinted toward his friends as the rest of the group opened fire. Behind him, the two reptilian beasts launched into the air. As he ran, Khalen heard Teg-lakis swearing loudly at the sight of the approaching monstrosity. The Rey-Qani withdrew his resonite veristool and pressed one of the buttons on the thick handle. The cylindrical device immediately began to vibrate and hum. A second later, the liquid resonite hidden in the hollowed-out center of the handle flowed outward to form a short shaft. The head of the weapon continued to grow until the hammer took shape. Once the handle was empty of resonite, it shrank until it closed upon the solid metal core.

Khalen reached Teg-lakis's side just as he was lifting his newly formed hammer. He brought it down with a mighty swing onto the rock which had formed around his feet. After several blows, the rocky earth split, allowing him to free his right foot. He repeated the process as the flaming golem drew within two dozen feet.

Khalen grabbed the Twin Discs of Arrguin from their holsters, hoping to give his friend time to break free. He threw them at the rocky form without taking time to charge them. After several useless strikes, Khalen was forced to withdraw them.

Meanwhile, Belenger had maneuvered behind the creature. He grabbed a grenade from his belt and loaded it into the bottom section of his rifle. With one swift motion, he raised the weapon and fired the grenade at the golem. The resulting explosion blew off the right arm and created a large crater in the torso of the creature.

Following the explosion, Kovitch and Shosta flew at the rocky figure and slashed at it with their talons. The thing was unaffected by the attacks and swung its left arm at the drall-mari, the heat from its flaming hide forcing them to retreat.

Mariska's electric whip suddenly snaked out and wrapped itself around the monster's thick remaining arm. The resonite tip, which was now in the shape of a claw, was buried deeply into the rocky surface of the creature. She discharged the electricity within the whip, but like the laser blasts, it appeared to have no effect. Using a stalagmite for leverage, she wrapped her whip around it and pulled on it with all her might, hoping to at least distract the thing.

The move served to delay the monster long enough for Nara to move Roadblock into its path. Living up to its name, the remote placed its metallic hands against the torso of the flaming rock and pushed against it, preventing it from going any further. Fire enveloped the remote as Roadblock fought the lumbering rock.

And above the battle, Khalen heard the bizarre song continue to echo throughout the cave. He grabbed Teg-lakis's arm and yanked him free from the now cracked earth. As the two of them stumbled backward, they scanned the area for any other signs of attack.

The flame from Roakel's staff went out, momentarily drawing Khalen's attention to what was happening to his left. In the dim light produced by the two lanterns now discarded on the cave floor, he could see the Solemsiel preparing to use his windstaff to sing another song in order to help free Brin'tac and Tet'rick, whose feet were still trapped. Mak'sim and Vel'vikis were beginning to recover on the other side of the rocky floor.

A loud rumble echoed in the cave, and everyone struggled to maintain their balance as the earth shook violently. They were forced to lift their arms protectively over their heads to ward off the shards of stone that rained down on them.

Two screams split the air, joined by a screech coming from one of the drallmari. Fearing the worst, Khalen glanced behind him. In the shifting light, he could barely see what looked like an arm sticking out from under a large boulder. Further to the right, Kovitch lay unmoving on the ground, blood seeping from a nasty cut on his neck. Khalen feared for the life of his reptilian companion but commotion from his right drew his attention away. Peering through the darkness, he could just make out the sight of Vel'vikis and Mak'sim as they struggled to assist someone on the ground.

"Hujik! We need your remote immediately! Eth Galithar is pinned under a stalactite."

The waterspout began shifted once more as Hujik moved his remote to help Brin'tac. Khalen called out a warning just in time for Mak'sim to dive out of the way. Vel'vikis tried to move, but his right foot became entangled in weeds. The cyclone ran straight into him. It lifted him from his feet and tossed him a dozen feet across the cave until he connected with the wall and fell to the floor.

Khalen felt a hand touch his shoulder. "We have to find the Dodekaph," Roakel said. "It is the one controlling everything. Do you see the pattern? When one element is moving, the other ceases. It can only use its song to control one at a time. If we can stop it, we can stop them. I need you to sing with me."

Nodding numbly, Khalen followed the Solemsiel's lead. Using the windstaff, Roakel began to play a powerful song in C major with thick texture and homophonic rhythm. He repeated the simple progression of tonic, pre-dominant, and dominant chords. The cave grew brighter and brighter as the two maestros sang in unison. As the strength of their song grew, the Dodekaph's weakened.

While still singing, Khalen glanced over to see the whirlwind begin to dissipate. The weeds holding Tas'anee started to wither and the flames on the rocky golem began to subside. Emboldened by the power of the song, Khalen turned his gaze away from the others and focused on scanning for signs of the true enemy. After searching for several seconds, he finally discovered the shape of the monster amid the shadows.

 Hidden in an alcove straight in front of them was the Dodekaph. It was bare-chested and had the scaly skin of a Tii-Koona but heartveins like a Rey-Qani. Its features and hair were that of a Mih'schen, but it had four arms like a Faluvinal or Solemsiel. Its overly large, solid black eyes stared at Khalen with hatred, and its gaunt mouth filled with razor-sharp teeth was open wide. An ear-splitting shriek echoed in the cavern, almost breaking Khalen's concentration.

But what horrified him most was the bottom half of the monster's body. Instead of legs, it had the grotesque, bulbous body of a spider.

"There it is! Hit it with everything you've got!"

Belenger's command was unnecessary. The moment the creature was revealed, those who were still standing opened fire. Khalen was about to stop singing and join the fight, but Roakel shook his head, his own voice never faltering. Realizing their song was the only thing keeping the creature from hiding once more, Khalen continued to sing and resigned himself to watch the battle.

Nara's scream rent the air, and Khalen watched in concern as Roadblock became rigid, an indication that Nara was no longer piloting the remote.

Another grenade launched from Belenger's rifle narrowly missed the Dodekaph. However, the explosion forced it out of its alcove. Moving incredibly fast on its eight spindly legs, the creature darted toward Mariska and Teg-lakis. The nimble Rey-Qani female dove to the side, narrowly escaping its attack. Teg-lakis morphed his resonite weapon into a sword and hacked at the legs of the creature.

The Dodekaph roared in pain as one of its legs was cut off, then turned its attention toward Teg-lakis. Leaning forward, it caught his hand mid-swing with its right arms. With its prey immobilized, it used its upper left arm to grab Teg-lakis by the throat.

Shosta flew into the creature's face as it choked the Rey-Qani. The drallmar slashed at its arms with her claws while her beak pecked at its head. Still holding onto the struggling Teg-lakis, the Dodekaph flailed at Shosta. Several of the creature's sharp talons dug into the drallmar's tough hide, causing her to shriek in pain and break off her attack.

But the distraction proved sufficient. Focused on the drallmar, the Dodekaph was taken by surprise as Belenger used his suit's enhanced strength to ram into its side. The shock of the impact caused the creature to release Teg-lakis, who fell to the ground unconscious.

Belenger withdrew the vibraknife from the sheath inside his right gauntlet and leapt on top of the creature, which had been flipped onto its back. With a yell of frustration, he plunged the vibrating metal into the soft underbelly of the spider section of the monster. An unnatural, guttural howl emanated from it as it thrashed around in its death throes.

With supernatural speed, the dying creature spun itself over, throwing Belenger to the ground. Before he could regain his feet, it grabbed him with two of its arms and used the other two to pry his helmet off.

Mariska's whip snapped through the air and grabbed the monstrosity by the throat with the claw-like tip just as it was preparing to snap Belenger's neck. Still clutching him in two of its hands, it used its other two to grapple with the whip constricting its breathing.

Unable to stand by and watch any further, Khalen quit singing with Roakel. In one swift motion, he grabbed the Twin Discs of Arrguin and hurled them at the creature. He sang to them mid-flight. The cymatic frequencies worked on the resonite to form sharp spikes around the edges. With a final surge of energy, the two discs struck the Dodekaph in the chest, the force causing it to drop Belenger and topple over.

Although the creature appeared dead, Mariska and Belenger each unloaded a dozen shots into various parts of its body just to be certain.

For several seconds, no one moved. Khalen, exhausted by the battle, almost collapsed onto the ground. He reached out and leaned against a nearby boulder. A frantic call from Vel'vikis broke through the silence seconds later.

"Master Roakel, come quickly!"

"What is it?"

"It's Eth Galithar! He has stopped breathing!"

33

HISTORY LESSON

KHALEN ARRIVED at the scene a moment after Roakel to see Brin'tac, eyes wide with panic, thrashing on the cave floor, desperate to breathe. The Lah'grex clutched his chest and gasped for air, but none would come to him. His lungs had collapsed under the crushing blow of a falling boulder during the earthquake, which meant he likely had a broken rib or two as well. The situation looked grim.

"Khalen, direct the energy!" Roakel commanded.

Khalen knelt next to Brin'tac as Roakel started playing the Song of Healing on his windstaff. Closing his eyes, Khalen allowed himself to get lost in the beauty of the music. His mind drifted to a prayer hymn Riveruun taught him years ago.

"Almighty Source of Life,
Sustainer of every breath
from life even unto death,
hear this song of healing
offered to you in faith!"

Conducting with his right hand, he laid his left on Brin'tac's chest and leaned in closer as he sang the solfege syllables. Khalen felt the energy from the song flow from his own throat and fall over the panicked man before him in waves of calm even as Roakel's music flowed through his fingers and into the crushed chest cavity. The energy flowed into Brin'tac's nostrils like a visible vapor and his chest expanded.

Khalen felt the energy from the song flow through his chest, down his arm and into Brin'tac. With the connection established between them, Khalen winced as some of Brin'tac's pain flowed into his own body. He pressed in and directed the energy to begin repairing the damage to the chest. After several moments, he felt the Lah'grex relax and breathe on his own once more.

The two music masters continued the song for several more minutes, using the energy to quicken Brin'tac's natural healing process. Weak from his effort, Khalen finally ceased singing, breaking the bond of healing.

Khalen leaned back and took a deep breath, his own body aching from the shared experience. The healing tones were known to create a bond of empathy between the wounded and the intercessor that flowed from the very heart of compassion required to produce them. Everyone seemed to breathe again after the close call, but no one spoke for a few moments. A touch on his arm caused Khalen to look back at Brin'tac. The Lah'grex's eyes were filled with relief and gratefulness.

"Thank you," he whispered.

Khalen nodded. "Don't thank me. It was Roakel's quick thinking that saved you. I simply followed his lead."

Roakel smiled down at them both. "It was neither of us. The healing tones are like anything else; they are tools through which the Great Composer does his work. As are Khalen and I. We are but his vassals who are honored to be of use and greatly relieved you yet have breath in you, Noble Galithar." With that, he extended a hand to Khalen and assisted him to his feet. "Come. We need to tend to the others."

Khalen suddenly remembered Teg-lakis had been injured. The two crossed quickly over to the fallen Rey-Qani. Fortunately, after a quick examination, it became apparent his wounds were not severe. Nevertheless, Khalen and Roakel repeated their song until he regained consciousness. The two maestros moved on, leaving the rest of his recovery in the hands of Mariska.

By the time they had finished helping Teg-lakis, Hujik's remote had finished lifting the large boulder off the body of Tas'anee. However, he was already dead. The Lah'grex spent the next thirty minutes erecting a cairn over the body of their fallen comrade from the rocks and rubble that had fallen from the cave ceiling.

Meanwhile, Khalen and Roakel set about healing the rest of the groups' minor injuries and had just finished with the drallmari when Khalen's comm chimed.

"Uncle Khalen?" Based on the muted tone of Nara's voice and the edge of sadness to it, Khalen could tell she had been crying.

"Hi, Nara."

"I…I'm sorry I let you all down," she said, her voice breaking. "I…I tried to be brave. But when I saw that horrible thing, I just couldn't…"

"Don't be too hard on yourself, Nara. Your reaction is completely understandable. I've seen many brutal, frightening things in my life, yet this thing rattled me too."

"Aunt Saryn came in and told me she had spoken to Uncle Roakel through their telepathic bond. She told me what happened and that you're okay. What are you gonna do now?"

"The Lah'grex are holding a brief ceremony for Tas'anee, then we're going grab a bite to eat before continuing on. Listen, I think you should sit the rest of this out. If I had had any idea this thing was down here, I would never have let you come along."

"Yeah. I guess you were wrong about the mercs not letting something make a home down there."

Khalen chuckled mirthlessly. "I can't believe it either. When the thing moved in they must have figured it wasn't worth the effort to drive it out and just stopped using the door."

"Or maybe it moved in recently and they didn't realize it was down there 'cause they don't use that door very often."

"That could be. Either way, I don't want to risk you having to face another one again. Dodekaphs can be loners, but they have been known to travel in pairs or even groups. We'll leave Roadblock here. When you're ready, you can power him back up and take him back to the cave entrance. We'll pick him up later."

"Okay. I'm really sorry."

"We'll see you soon." Khalen shut off the comm.

"I regret she had to experience that," Roakel said. "Saryn said it took her over twenty minutes just to stop crying, even after she explained that we were safe."

"She's tough. It may take time, but she'll come around."

The Lah'grex memorialized their fallen comrade with a ceremony on the far side of the cavern away from the obscene body of the Dodekaph while the others rested and refreshed themselves with provisions.

Khalen sat nearby on a boulder staring at the Dodekaph when Teg-lakis approached.

"That is one nasty maggot-pie," he said with disgust. "Am I losing my hearing, or did your Solemsiel friend call it a Dodekaph during the fight?"

"Your hearing is just fine. Yes, that's what it's called."

"Hm. Lady Crisenth used to unleash some nasty beasts into the prison population on Mitrik B3 as part of her 'games'. The other guards called them Dodekaphs, but they didn't look much like this one."

"It all depends on what you think they are," Khalen replied. "As servants of Wylock, Lord of Beasts, the Meh'ishto were taught to believe that Dodekaphs are the evolutionary ancestors of all the races in the Twin Galaxies. Most of the creatures called by that name have at least a few physical characteristics of one race or another, but not because they are our ancestors."

"Many of my colleagues over the years believed that all the various monsters of the galaxies are related somehow," Belenger said. "Basically, they call any nasty beast with black eyes a Dodekaph. I don't know. There are too many beasties on too many worlds for me to believe that."

"Actually, that explanation is closer to the truth than you realize."

"Oh really?" Teg-lakis smirked at Khalen. "So you've got the whole truth now? Well, enlighten us then."

Khalen shook his head and smiled. "Always eager for a fight, aren't you?"

"You know it."

"Well, it makes sense that all these various creatures are indeed descendants of the first Dodekaphs for one major reason: they can alter their forms."

"Says who? And since when did you become the expert on Dodekaphs? Just a second ago you said they were our ancestors."

"If you'd actually listen for once instead of hearing what you want to hear, you'd have noticed I said I was *raised* to believe that. I don't believe it anymore."

"Then enlighten us, O Wise One," Teg-lakis joked.

"Actually, I think Roakel should be the one to answer. After all, his father was there when the Dodekaphs were created."

"What?" Mariska asked in surprise. "I mean, I've heard stories that Solemsiels and Faluvinals were really old, but c'mon. Legends of Dodekaphs go back thousands of years."

Roakel nodded. "That is correct. Creation of the Dodekaphs was 2112 years after the Exposition, or the dawn of time. It marks the end of the First Phrase of history and the beginning of the Second Phrase."

"Oh, this ought to be good," Teg-lakis said sarcastically from where he lay on the floor of the cavern, his head resting in Mariska's lap. "I just love a good myth."

Roakel ignored him. "Mariska, the stories you have heard about Solemsiels and Faluvinals is correct: we do live long lives. Once a member of the Perfect races reaches maturity, he or she no longer experiences the aging process like those of the Major races. I have been alive for over fourteen hundred years. What I tell you has been handed down to me firsthand from my father and other elders of my race who have been alive since the creation of the universe 5,641 years ago."

Teg-lakis interrupted him. "Don't you mean five *billion* years ago?"

Roakel smiled at him in response. "That is an evolutionary belief. However, I do not have time to get into that discussion right now. My point was that my father is a firsthand
witness to the history of what I am about to relay.

"Those who were there tell of how the great Solemsiel
leader Araklial became possessed by the vile daemon Vim-
oth and turned to evil to become the first of the Seyvreen.
He eventually caused other Solemsiels and Faluvinals to join
him in his rebellion. Before a quarter of a century had passed,
he succeeded in deceiving the firstborn of the Major races
and tricking them into sinning against the Great Composer."

Out of the corner of his eye, Khalen saw Mariska lightly
smack Teg-lakis for rolling his eyes.

"In an effort to increase his power, Araklial experimented
further with the forbidden musical arts until he discovered
a way to create life. However, he needed the assistance of
representatives from each of the Major races and their Minor
counterparts. He created a cult that worshiped music itself
and spread his false beliefs throughout the galaxies. Under
false pretenses, he convened a meeting of some of the most
powerful maestros. He selected those who were ambitious
and were sympathetic to his own goals.

"Until this meeting, all races were able to use music
to manipulate all forms of nature equally. There were no
modes or styles, although each race had its own musical
'dialect', if you will. With Araklial as their leader, this
assemblage of maestros joined together to create a living
being. Their goal was a direct affront to the sanctity of life,
which is the greatest gift the Composer had ever bestowed
upon his creation.

"The results of their labor was an intelligent creature with physical characteristics from each race. However, it lacked a soul or any sense of moral judgment."

"The Dodekaphs," Belenger said.

"Yes. And the music the abomination produced was a twisted mockery of all the beauty the Great Composer gave to us. The beast created sequences, or matrixes, of each of the twelve notes in the chromatic scale. It would never use the same note twice until all twelve had been sung. The results were horrifying to listen to. The 'music' lacked any tonal center, and the chord progressions failed to follow the patterns set forth since the creation of the universe. As such, this creature could manipulate all aspects of nature, but with disastrous results."

"That would explain the rock and wind monsters as well as the earthquake and its manipulation of the vegetation," Belenger said. "That's an interesting viewpoint."

"As punishment for creating the Dodekaph, Dominuus confused the musical 'languages' of the races to make it much more difficult for them to join their musical abilities together. From that point on, each race was given their own tonal center, style, rhythmic devices, and musical aptitude."

"But wait. Roakel, you used music to create fire on your windstaff," Mariska said. "But controlling fire is what the Rey-Qani maestros do. Sorry, but that doesn't mesh with your whole 'confusion of the musical languages' story."

"Yes, it does. Others can learn to perform the songs from different races through intense study and practice," Khalen explained. "Roakel has had fourteen hundred years to study the various modes and styles of each race. He's proficient in all of them."

"So you think all the tales of black-eyed monsters in dark caves all over the inhabited planets of the Twin Galaxies are descendants of that first Dodekaph?" Belenger asked. "If that's so, then why do they all look so different?"

"To answer your first point, Dodekaphs reproduce asexually. Once the first one was created, Araklial kept it locked up and studied it. Over time, the numbers of Dodekaphs grew, and he taught them how to change their shapes. Many are unaware of this fact, but we Solemsiels, and the Faluvinals as well, have been granted the capability by the Great Composer of altering our bodies through music. Yet we believe that to do so would be an affront to our Maker. The Fiihkren and Seyvreen, or the Tritonus as you called them, hold no such reservations and therefore change their shape regularly."

"Now *that* would be a cool trick!" Teg-lakis stated. "C'mon, show us! I got it! Change into Tas'anee and let's have some fun with the Lah'grex. Ha!"

Roakel frowned. "That would be highly improper. Furthermore, as I just explained, we believe it is an affront to our Maker to change our shape and only do so under special circumstances. Even if I chose to do so, it takes several hours to reconstruct one's body. The song itself is immensely complex."

"Of course it is."

"Knock it off, Teg-lakis," Khalen said irritably.

"So this Araklial taught the Dodekaphs how to change their shapes as well?" Belenger asked.

"Yes. He and his Overlords helped the Dodekaphs shape themselves into all kinds of monstrosities and abominations. Hoping to sow further discord amongst the various races, Araklial spent years having his servants transport the

Dodekaphs to the inhabited systems. Most of the creatures found holes and caves to dwell in, preferring the darkness."

"That's quite a fascinating fable," Teg-lakis said, rising to his feet with an exaggerated groan. "I bet you've given quite a few nightmares to unsuspecting children with that one. But personally, I prefer one of the other explanations. An evolutionary ancestor makes a whole lot more sense than some fallen Solemsiel possessed by an invisible evil spirit who convinces the different races to work together to create life." He let out a laugh before continuing. "I mean, all you have to do is take a look at the different leaders of the races to know this story is bunk. You can't get any of them to work together on anything. If they did miraculously get together, they probably couldn't even agree on what to have for lunch, much less create something."

Roakel seemed undaunted by the criticism. "It is not a matter of which explanation you 'prefer', Teg-lakis. But rather, it is a question of what is true. Your opinion or feelings cannot change reality."

"Well, in my belief system, my truth is that the beastie we killed is nothing more than that," Teg-lakis shot back. "It looks like the Lah'grex are done. So if the rest of you lazy moldwarps are just about finished lounging, we should get this mission over with. I've got a certain Ra-Nuuk to kill and money to collect. Besides, if I have to smell the rotting stench of that thing for much longer, I'm gonna vomit up my dinner. C'mon, babe."

With that, Teg-lakis headed further into the tunnel. When Mariska hesitated, he spun back around. "Now!" he barked. Startled, she jumped to her feet and caught up to him. As she reached his side, he put his arm around her forcefully and together, the two Rey-Qani headed into the darkness.

"I worry about those two sometimes," Belenger said to Khalen. "But he is right about one thing: we should get moving."

By this time, Brin'tac and the others had made their way across the cave and joined Khalen, Belenger and Roakel. As they drew near, Roakel stepped over to Brin'tac. "Eth Galithar, do you feel well enough to continue?"

"Yes, I'm not one-hundred percent, but I'll make it," Brin'tac replied. "Once again, thank you Masters Roakel and Khalen. I owe you my life."

"It was our duty and our pleasure," Roakel said. "Like all those with a soul, your life is precious beyond compare, which makes the loss of Tas'anee that much more tragic."

"Yes. He will be missed. He was a good soldier. I don't look forward to having to break the news to his wife and family. Although I may not agree with your worldview, I do very much appreciate your sentiments. They are comforting. Perhaps I will share them with his loved ones. But come, I long to see my own loved ones safe."

The group continued their trek through the tunnels. After traveling for another twenty minutes without incident, Hujik's remote, which had once again taken point, came to a sudden halt.

The others stopped behind him and Vel'vikis took out his scroll and examined the data on its screen. After a moment, he turned to face the others.

"This is it. We're here."

34

RECONNAISSANCE

VEL'VIKIS ADDRESSED the group as they huddled together near a slight bend in the tunnel. "The entrance to the base is a couple hundred feet ahead. However, my guess is there's a camera installed near the door. So we need to wait here until we get a better idea of what we're up against. We don't want our lights to give us away. Hujik, go ahead."

A small compartment in the shoulder of the remote opened up, revealing a bug-sized reconnaissance remote. The second the device lifted off, it became lost in the dark backdrop of the cave. Now that Hujik was piloting the miniature drone, the six-foot robot standing next to them became rigid and motionless.

"My scroll is linked to the remote's camera feed," Vel'vikis stated. As he studied the images on his screen, Brin'tac and Mak'sim moved next to him in order to see as well. Khalen and the others were forced to wait for the report.

"Yeah, as expected," Vel'vikis said. "There's a camera and

better that we can sneak in, rescue eth Galithar's family, and be out without a prolonged fight."

Roakel shook his head. "We cannot ignore the plight of these people. We must do everything in our power to rescue them as well."

"What?" Brin'tac said, momentarily forgetting about the images displayed on the scroll. His expression reflected his surprise by turning gray. "With all due respect, Master Roakel. We must remain focused on our primary objective. We came here to rescue my family, not to free a bunch of filthy Tey-Rakil slaves."

"*With all due respect*, eth Galithar," Roakel echoed, his voice rising, "I will not leave without doing all I can to help them."

Khalen could tell Brin'tac was struggling to keep his anger under control. "Your compassion is a credit to you. However, we can't save everyone. We need to focus our attention on rescuing those who matter most."

This time, it was Khalen who felt his anger rise. "Meaning the lives of your wife and children matter more than the lives of some slaves, is that it?"

Inspector Mak'sim bristled at the sudden aggression from Khalen. "As a matter of fact, yes. As royalty, the lives of the Galithar family are worth infinitely more than the lives of hundreds of mere Tey-Rakil peasants."

"In that you are mistaken," Roakel said. "In the eyes of Dominuus, all beings are created equal. Master is no greater than the slave. The rich are no greater than the poor..."

"We Lah'grex don't hold the same beliefs. Don't let your religious tropes get in our way," Mak'sim said. "We allowed you to come with us this far under the agreement you would provide assistance. Now, fulfill your promise and help us rescue his family."

Sitting on a nearby rock next to Mariska, Teg-lakis let out a chuckle. "This is so entertaining. I should be recording this."

Ignoring the rude comment, Roakel stared at Mak'sim. Despite his calm demeanor, Roakel's voice was firm and commanding. "We have every intention of aiding you in the rescue of the Galithars. However, we will also rescue these people."

"Doing so will jeopardize this mission. I can't allow that," Vel'vikis said, wading into the argument. "It's bad enough you brought in these three loose cannons," he said, nodding toward Belenger and the two Rey-Qani. "Now you're threatening the success of our operation."

"We don't answer you to," Khalen spat back, his eyes becoming a smoldering reddish color.

Seeking to prevent any further escalation, Roakel stepped between Khalen and Vel'vikis. "We will compromise. We will contact Nara and have her use Roadblock to free the slaves and escort them into the tunnels while Khalen and I assist you with rescuing Noble Galithar's family. It is possible that the freeing of the slaves will distract the mercenaries, perchance working to our advantage."

"But what will you do with the slaves once they enter the tunnels?" Brin'tac asked. "There may be more of those creatures down there."

"Khalen or I will create a portal to the other side of the cave, near the entrance," Roakel explained. "From there, they will have to fend for themselves until we can send aid."

"Assuming you can disable the portal inhibitor," Belenger chimed in.

"That is correct," Roakel stated. "With that in mind, I propose a revision to our strategy: half of us locate the portal inhibitor and deactivate it while the others rescue the Gali-thars. We bring the *Eternal Harmony* and *Fiery Vengeance* close to the base and use portals to escape to the ships."

"I don't like it, eth Galithar," Vel'vikis said. "It's more risky than fleeing back into the tunnels."

As Brin'tac was contemplating the new plan, Vel'vikis's attention was drawn to the scroll. After a moment of com-municating with Hujik, he turned his attention back to the others, his expression hopeful. "We found them, eth Gali-thar! Hujik located your family!"

"Praise to the Universal Reality," Brin'tac said in relief. "Where are they?"

"Unfortunately, they're being held two floors up. Eight of the mercs are on duty. The rest appear to be asleep."

"What about Slag?" Belenger asked. "Any sign of him?"

"None," Vel'vikis replied. "But Hujik says he couldn't access all the rooms, and he didn't check either of the ships. We'll have to move fast. Once they're alerted to our presence, they may try to flee the base in one of those."

"Where would the inhibitor likely be located?" Brin'tac asked.

"Probably on one of the two middle floors," Mak'sim said.

"Then we'll try Master Roakel's plan first. If, for some rea-son, we can't disable the inhibitor, then we make for the tun-nels. Have Hujik find the exact location for the device, along with the locations of the remaining mercenaries. Then, have him place his explosives on the cameras and return here."

"Thank you, Noble Galithar," Roakel said. He activated his comm and began explaining the plan to Nara.

"Hang on," Khalen said to Brin'tac as inspiration struck him. "We may not need him to do all the cameras. Tell him to focus only on the cameras on the second floor from the top. I've got an idea that might buy us some extra time."

35

COVER OF DARKNESS

"WHAT IN BLAZES is going on? Why did we get woke up in the middle of the night? What's so important it couldn't wait until morning?"

As the two remotes standing guard outside the slave quarters powered up, the pilot of the second remote replied. "I don't know," he said sleepily. Even the yawn came through the droid's vocalizer. "Something about the back door being accessed and the cameras going wonky. They want us to check it out."

"Man, if it turns out to be a false alarm, I'm gonna be ticked. I was in the middle of an amazing dream when the call came in. I was filthy rich, and I was flying this souped-up—"

"Hold it. What in the galaxies…"

The cloud of darkness flowed down the hallway toward the two remotes. Stunned by the sight, the pilots paused. A strand of webbing suddenly shot out from the darkness and ensnared the two robots, preventing them from firing. Two medium-sized forms launched out of the darkness and struck the remotes, knocking them to the ground.

Kovitch and Shosta kept the robots pinned down long enough for the darkness produced by Khalen's song to envelop them. Once inside the outer edges of the cloud, the smoke cleared, and the drallmari leapt off the machines. Belenger returned the rifle he used to launch the webbing to its holster and drew his vibraknife. With a quick thrust, he stabbed the foot-long dagger into the central computer core housed in the remote's torso. The second remote was taken out similarly by Teg-lakis's resonite sword.

"So far so good," Mak'sim said. "Hopefully they'll think we're a Dodekaph long enough for us to at least get to the next level."

Although part of his brain registered the whispered comment, Khalen's concentration was focused on continuing the song of darkness. He had not performed this piece for over a decade, yet the chords, solfege syllables, and melody came back to him with frightening familiarity. And with it, came the memories of the hundreds of times he had used the song; times when he had used it for terrible purposes.

"Hurry! Up the stairs!" Vel'vikis urged.

They made it to the second floor when Hujik's warning came to them. "There are four guards with laser pistols coming down the right corridor at the intersection ahead of you."

"We have a visual on them," Vel'vikis replied as he stared at the camera feed on his scroll. Although Khalen was tempted to glance over at the screen, he kept his attention fixated on continuing the song. Next to him, Roakel relayed the warning to the others and gave his personal shield generator to Brin'tac, who activated it. Fueled by some of the energy from Khalen's song, the device produced a protective wall of energy in front of the group but hidden by the cloud of darkness.

As expected, the four mercenaries leapt around the corner and fired into the murky haze. Thanks to Roakel's PSG, the shots were absorbed by the energy shield. During the entire assault, Khalen kept the blanket of darkness stationary.

"Now!" Vel'vikis whispered the moment the mercenaries ceased their attack.

Brin'tac shut off the PSG. The moment the energy shield was down, Belenger fired off another web-grenade at the guards, catching them by surprise. Khalen shifted his song and moved the cloud forward. Once the guards were inside its dark depths, Belenger and the others stunned them into unconsciousness.

"You know, that trick isn't going to work for very long," Teglakis stated. "They're eventually going to wise up. Even these stupid sacks of putrid vermin will figure it out before long."

"It served its purpose," Mak'sim said. "Now we trust in speed. At the top of this next flight, we split up. Hujik, go ahead and blow the cameras."

For a split second, the remote standing next to him went still. A moment later, Hujik's holographic image flickered to life once more. "Done. All cameras on the third floor should be inactive for at least the next twenty minutes. However, I'm detecting a new signal that's disrupting our commlinks. It isn't strong enough to effect remote signals, but we won't be able to use our comms from here on out."

"We expected as much. Let's get this finished."

The group sprinted up the next flight of stairs until they arrived at the door leading to the third floor. "This is where we split up," Vel'vikis said. "Master Roakel, please contact

Saryn and have her and Captain Nahoc commence their attack on the base."

Roakel nodded, his expression becoming blank as he focused on his telepathic connection.

Khalen stopped singing and let the darkness dissipate. The group stood two abreast in a stairwell. Standing near the door at the top of the stairs was Hujik's remote followed by the small group of Lah'grex.

Roakel glanced down at his scroll. "Nara, utilize the code we gave you to enter the base. The guards in the area have been incapacitated, so your path should be unhindered. Free the slaves and escort them back to the tunnels. Understood?"

"Yes, Uncle Roakel. Don't worry about me. I got this. I won't let you down this time," Nara said, clearly trying her best to sound brave.

As Roakel closed the scroll and put it away, Brin'tac turned around to face Khalen. "Thank you, Master Khalen. We'll see you either back at the ships or in the tunnels. May your God be with you."

"Thank you."

Khalen glanced up and saw Roakel looking at him. "Take care, old one."

The Solemsiel smiled. "And you as well. Play your part with excellence." Roakel reached down and patted the two drallmari on their heads, then turned away.

With the team ready, Hujik's remote flung open the door and stepped out into the hallway, the lasers mounted on the backs of its arms leading the way. The rest of the Lah'grex passed through the door a moment later.

"Let's get this inhibitor shut down and see if we can find

Skaret while we're at it," Belenger said. Even through the filter in his helmet, Khalen could hear his voice turn icy.

Mariska held the door wide as Belenger, Teg-lakis, Khalen, and the two drallmari passed through the opening and turned down the right hallway. Khalen glanced over his shoulder to see the others sprinting down the hallway in the opposite direction.

The sounds of booted feet running toward them turned his attention forward. He removed the Twin Discs of Arrguin from their holsters and sang softly to charge them, his eyes never straying from the half-a-dozen doors that ran along the right side of the hallway.

Mariska swore. "We've got no cover in this hallway. What now?"

Teg-lakis grabbed the handle of the door nearest them and tried to open it. "Blast it. It's locked."

"Out of the way!" Belenger commanded. Grabbing the handle, he used the enhanced strength of his augmented suit and shattered the lock.

Teg-lakis harrumphed. "I loosened it for you."

"Right," Belenger replied dryly. He opened the door just as the hallway erupted with laser fire. Several blasts struck the door, splintering it. Khalen whistled a quick command and Kovitch and Shosta dove into the large, unoccupied supply closet with the rest of them.

"That's not gonna hold 'em for long," Mariska said as she peeked around the door to gauge their opposition.

"I've got this," Khalen said. He launched his discs with a flick of his wrists, sending them hurling around the door and down the hallway, guided by his song. The discs reached the intersection and began to turn the corner. A bright flash lit the hallway as they crashed into an energy shield and discharged.

Khalen recalled the discs and saw that their flight was unstable and erratic. Once they returned to his hands, he discovered they were badly dented from the impact. He shoved them back in their holsters and withdrew his blaster.

Teg-lakis patted him on the back. "Wow. That was underwhelming," he said sarcastically.

"Shut up," Khalen growled in annoyance. "I didn't hear the singing before. It sounds too amateurish to be a maestro, but whoever it is knows enough to power a PSG."

"Now what?" Mariska asked.

"Don't you have some kind of fancy grenade you can launch at them?" Teg-lakis asked Belenger.

"Of course. But they're too close to us. The explosion would hit us more than them. We're going to have to take them out hand-to-hand," Belenger said. "Khalen can whip us up another batch of darkness to cover our approach."

Khalen nodded and started to sing once more. The hallway in front of them was soon filled with inky blackness. Belenger and Teg-lakis bolted out from behind the door and flattened themselves against the far wall. Khalen and Mariska followed with the drallmari on their heels.

Laser fire flashed past them, splitting the darkness. The four companions dropped into crouches, but the blasts ceased before they could return fire. In the stillness that followed, they heard muffled thuds and groans coming from ahead. Seconds later, the hallway was silent.

Khalen and the others exchanged confused glances. Belenger motioned them forward. They pressed ahead behind the wall of blackness until they reached the intersection.

When they arrived, they discovered the bodies of five mercenaries lying in the hallway.

"What in the 'verse happened?" Teg-lakis said.

Khalen stopped singing. In the silence that followed, he could just make out the sound of more singing coming from further down the hall. Belenger and the others opened fire blindly in that direction. As the cloud of darkness disintegrated, the group caught sight of two figures standing several feet away, protected by a PSG on the floor in front of them.

The black cloaks of the newcomers made them instantly recognizable as the Tey-Rakil couple Khalen fought outside the Blue Rymer Lounge. The maestra stopped singing and the energy shield dissolved.

"You can lower your weapons now," the female Tey-Rakil said. "We just did you a favor. The least you can do is hear what we have to say. It may just save your life."

36

WIND AND WATER

BRIN'TAC FELT his breathing become labored as his heart rate increased. *This is it! My family is so close!* Conflicting thoughts raced through his mind. Numerous possible outcomes, many too terrible to contemplate, sought to overwhelm him. If all went as planned in the next few minutes, he would be reunited with his family. If not, the outcome might be disastrous.

An explosion from somewhere on the floor above shook the entire building, sending small pieces of debris to rain down on their heads. "The ships have begun their attack. That should keep the rest of these scum busy for—"

The rest of Vel'vikis's sentence was cut off by shouts coming from further down the hallway. Looking in the direction of the voices, Brin'tac felt his stomach lurch. Standing between him and the room in which his family was being held were two remotes, three mercenaries, and a Tii-Koona maestra.

Next to him, Vel'vikis and the others threw themselves against the walls of the corridor and opened fire while Roakel began to sing. The sound of the music reminded Brin'tac that he still held the PSG. He lowered his own blaster long enough to flip the switch on the device. Vel'vikis and the others ceased firing as the shield appeared in front of the group, powered by Roakel's song.

The Solemsiel directed the blue light and energy created by his music until it became a whirlwind in front of the shield. The eyes of the three mercenaries grew wide at the sight. In a panic, one of the remotes fired a rocket toward Brin'tac's group. Roakel used the vortex to grab the projectile. Using the momentum of the swirling wind, he sent it back toward the remotes. Due to the velocity of the spinning wind, however, Roakel miscalculated its trajectory. The rocket exploded against the left wall, filling the hallway with a fireball.

Even though the shield offered some protection from the flames, the force of the explosion in the confines of the narrow corridor and the resulting heat wave knocked everyone on both sides of the conflict to the floor.

Roakel was stunned by the blast and stopped singing. The winds quickly died down and the energy shield collapsed. The mercenaries, who were further from the epicenter of the explosion, recovered quickest. A volley of laser blasts struck Hujik's remote. Another stray shot struck Tet'rick in the chest, dropping him to the ground.

"Master Roakel!" Brin'tac called out as he helped the Solemsiel to his feet. "Quickly! The song!" In front of them, Vel'vikis, Mak'sim, and Hujik's remote returned fire.

Just as Roakel prepared to sing again, the sound of another song rose above the conflict. Brin'tac watched as the Solemsiel closed his eyes and concentrated to shut out the music coming from the other end of the hallway.

The PSG raised the shield once again, giving the companions a slight reprieve from the laser blasts. However, before Roakel could establish his song to recreate the whirlwind, Vel'vikis cried out in warning.

"Look out!"

Created by the mercenary music master, hundreds of tiny droplets of water were hurled at high velocity toward them. The sheer number of globules overwhelmed the energy shield, causing it to fail. Vel'vikis and Mak'sim, who were in the front of their group, cried out in pain as they were pelted by the spray.

The wind from Roakel's song picked up just as the attack reached Brin'tac, slowing the droplets to a gentle rain. With his vortex established once more, Roakel directed it down the hallway toward the mercenaries. The whirlwind reached the two remotes, picked them up, and slammed them into the wall with enough force to knock them out of commission.

Hope surged within Brin'tac at the sight but was dashed a moment later as the Tii-Koona music master countered Roakel's song. Shifting her attack, the maestra created a wall of water between the other soldiers and the whirlwind. Pressing forward, Roakel's opponent began to wrap the watery wall around the vortex in order to snuff it out of existence.

Both sides of the conflict watched in fascination as the two musical creations fought against each other for dominance. Brilliant swirls of blue and green light filled the hallway, and the atmosphere crackled with energy. Another explosion struck the building, adding more chaos to the battle.

Mesmerized, Brin'tac felt his anxiety spike as the water completely engulfed the miniature tornado. Beside him, Roakel strengthened his song by using the windstaff to create harmony. The burst of blue and yellow energy from the instrument blended with the stream from Roakel's song.

The moment the light reached the dueling musical creations, the wall of water exploded outward, decimated by the power of the Solemsiel's song. However, the exertion required to gain the victory caused Roakel to stop singing in order to regain his strength.

This time, it was the mercenaries who were slow to respond from the sudden turn of events. Brin'tac, Mak'sim, Vel'vikis, and Hujik's damaged remote took advantage of the distraction and dropped the remaining two guards and the maestra before they could recover.

Brin'tac leaned over and did his best to help support the eight-foot tall Solemsiel as Vel'vikis and Hujik's remote ran forward to secure the area. Mak'sim, meanwhile, knelt next to Tet'rick to check for a pulse. When it became clear he was dead, the inspector moved over to help Roakel.

"I am well now, thank you," the Solemsiel said, brushing away the help from the two Lah'grex. "A moment was all that was needed."

"The area is secure. Hurry! The holding cell is just ahead."

Brin'tac and Roakel rushed forward as Mak'sim fell into step behind them to guard their backs. Elated at the prospect of seeing his family again, Brin'tac quickened his pace.

"This is it!" Vel'vikis said in excitement as he grabbed the handle of the door. Expecting it to be locked, Brin'tac was surprised when Vel'vikis was able to open the door.

Brin'tac looked into the cell and felt a torrent of emotion overwhelm him. Standing just inside the doorway was Raena, Rav'ok, and Shea, each with mutes placed against their throats. However, the terrified looks on their faces sent Brin'tac's excitement plummeting into dismay.

"Not another step, Galithar. Unless, of course, you want to bury your wife or one of your lovely children."

It was then that Brin'tac caught sight of the fourth person in the room. Standing behind Raena was Kuzelka, the barrel of her laser pistol resting against the back of his wife's head.

37

ASSAULT ON
THE BASE

"NARA, UTILIZE the code we gave you to enter the base. The guards in the area have been incapacitated, so your path should be unhindered. Free the slaves and escort them back to the tunnels. Understood?"

"Yes, Uncle Roakel. Don't worry about me. I got this. I won't let you down this time," Nara said with more confidence than she felt.

Immersed in her virtual piloting chair aboard the *Lightbringer,* Nara felt the butterflies in her stomach perform somersaults at Roakel's words. They were counting on *her* to rescue the slaves!

She switched off the comm and focused on navigating Roadblock through the dank tunnel outside the lower entrance. "Jov, are you ready to go rescue some slaves?" Nara said.

"I'm weady! We can do dis, Nara!"

Nara smiled. Jov's physical presence gave her courage and drove away the sense of loneliness she felt. Virtual piloting had its advantages, but the visuals and sounds created by the helmet made her feel like she was truly alone in a dark cave. "Let's hope Uncle Roakel is right about the mercenaries being out of commission. After all, the cameras are still functional on this level."

"Of couwse he's wight. He's always wight!"

Nara reached the door that led into the base and punched in the code. However, due to Roadblock's thick robotic fingers combined with her own shaking hands, she had to input the code twice before it worked.

Nara breathed a sigh of relief as the light on the panel turned green and the lock on the door clicked loudly, echoing in the cave. The moment Roadblock was through the doorway, Nara pushed him into a thunderous, pounding run. She reached the cells a minute later.

Roadblock moved over to the cell door. "So far so good."

"Yup. I don't see nuffin' movin' on da scweens."

"Okay. Here it goes." Nara raised the volume on Roadblock's vocalizer and called out to the slaves. "Hi, everyone. My name's Nara, and I'm here to rescue you!" She grimaced. *It sounded so much cooler when I rehearsed it in my head,* she thought. The sounds of weary but excited voices from the slaves came through the speakers of her helmet. "I'm gonna break down the door, so watch out!"

Nara backed Roadblock up a few feet, then turned its thick shoulder toward the door. "Here we go, RB. Show 'em what you're made of!" Although the comment was not intended for anyone but herself, she realized too late she had forgotten to lower the volume of the vocalizer. Wincing in embarrassment, she dialed it down, took a deep breath, and charged.

The robot crashed into the metal door with a loud boom. The force of the blow easily destroyed the lock and flung the door wide open. The droid's momentum carried it into the cell block and sent it tumbling to the floor.

"Wow!" Nara exclaimed. "That was way easier than I thought it would be!"

"Yeah! Dat was awesome!"

"Okay. Hush, Jov. I need to concentrate." Nara maneuvered the bulky remote back to its feet, then turned it to face the row of cells. As the images from Roadblock's cameras reached her, she caught her breath in shock.

While she had seen holovids and images of Tey-Rakil before, the sight of their blackened scales and shortly cropped hair, even on the females, unnerved her. The emotions were enhanced by the realization that, in another reality, she might have been one of them. In fact, for all she knew, some of these malnourished faces staring back at her through the bars might be her relatives.

Another disconcerting thought struck her as several of the males pushed forward to the entrance of their cells. *What if they really are violent? What if they attack Uncle Roakel or Uncle Khalen?* Filled with indecision, she paused. A memory of Saryn's instruction from long ago came to the forefront of her mind. *"Always remember, dear one. Trust the teachings of the Great Composer and follow the guidance of your elders. And, if you are faced with a difficult decision, err on the side of compassion."*

Taking one more look at the refugees, she knew Roakel

and Saryn understood the risks, and she trusted their judgment. In addition, the more she looked at the desperate beings in their ragged clothes and gaunt faces, the more she knew she *had* to help them.

Her mind made up, she went about opening the individual cells—each requiring only a single punch from Roadblock's powerful fist.

"Hurry!" she called out to the shocked slaves. "We're escaping through the back door! It's down the hallway to the right!"

"But that leads into the tunnels!" one of the older males said in alarm. "We...we heard rumors that there's a Dodekaph down there!"

"Don't worry. My friends and I have already killed it. We came in that way. Besides, I have another friend who's a maestro. When he returns, he's gonna create a portal that'll take you to the entrance of the tunnel. From there, you're free to go wherever you want."

Despite still appearing uncertain, the slaves ran out of the cell block and sprinted down the hall. With all the cells empty, Nara piloted Roadblock toward the exit, following on the heels of the last of the liberated people.

Laser blasts suddenly crackled through the air, striking two of the fleeing prisoners and dropping them to the ground in the hallway. "NO!" Nara yelled, urging Roadblock forward. The remote burst into the hallway just in time to take the force of the next round of laser blasts. As they struck its metal hide, Nara simultaneously felt relieved and nervous. The two mercenaries firing at her had their weapons set on stun. While she was relieved the fallen slaves were not dead, she also realized the stun blasts would short out

Roadblock's systems.

"No, no, no!" she said as the remote moved sluggishly to face the attackers. As feared, another set of blasts rendered it completely inoperable. Nara panicked and tried to move the robot, but to no avail.

"Nawa!" Jov's voice came through the comm.

"Scamp!" she shouted as Jov's voice brought back the memory of Balec's Tower. She hit the controls and waited for what seemed like an eternity as her computer switched over to the smaller remote.

As soon as Scamp was free from his housing on Roadblock's back, Nara assessed the situation. With the larger remote out of commission, the guards had once more begun opening fire on the fleeing slaves as they chased them down the hall. Nara felt her heart skip a beat. In the thirty seconds it took her to switch back to Scamp, the guards had passed Roadblock.

Leaping into action, the nimble remote leapt to the ground and bolted after the guards.

"Nawa, use Scamps welder. If you pump up da juice, it should be stwong enough to knock dose guys out. 'Member dat time I accidentawy—"

"Yeah, I remember! Good idea. Now hush!"

Catching them easily, the Tii-Koona teen activated the welder built into Scamp's lower right hand and increased the voltage. She leapt onto the first mercenary's back and buried it between his shoulder blades. The Lah'grex soldier convulsed briefly before collapsing to the ground.

As he fell, Nara propelled Scamp upward and used its upper hands to grab the water pipes located in the ceiling. The second guard, caught by surprise, spun to face his companion and searched for the source of the attack. Nara used the dim lighting and Scamp's quickness to her advantage. She dropped from the pipes and bolted under the guard's legs. Startled by the remote's nimble movements, the mercenary began shooting erratically.

Nara brought Scamp out from under the guard's legs and used the nearby wall as a springboard to jump onto his back. With another short spurt from the welder, the second guard joined his companion on the ground.

"I...I did it!" Nara shouted with glee.

"Yeah! Way to go, cuz!" Jov shouted.

Breathing heavily from the adrenaline rush, the teen once again had to force herself to relax. "Okay, okay. What now? Oh! The unconscious slaves!"

Now that the immediate danger was past, Nara returned Scamp to its compartment within Roadblock's back. She rebooted the larger remote, and after a minute, it was back online. Despite the sluggishness lingering in its movements, she was able to move it well enough to continue the escape.

Nara reached down and picked up the two fallen slaves, one under each arm. Moving as rapidly as Roadblock would allow, she managed to reach the exit by the time the first explosion rocked the building.

Saryn ignored the cold droplets that snaked past her shoulderblades as she pulled the unfamiliar trigger. The turret cannons of *Fiery Vengeance* discharged another salvo toward the weapons emplacements of the base. She felt a brief moment of satisfaction as the images sent to her virtual piloting helmet from the cameras mounted around the ship displayed a direct hit.

Like many ships she had piloted over the centuries, the cockpit of Belenger's vessel retracted into the body of the ship during battle to protect the occupants. The benefits of using the VP helmet, which was connected to her brain waves, was that it afforded her 360-degree vision.

That was, of course, until the cameras were damaged or destroyed.

Another blast of heavy laser fire struck the *Vengeance*, taking out another exterior camera. "Captain Nahoc, my field of vision is increasingly compromised and I have no maestro to repair the ship. I cannot afford to take any more damage."

"I understand, maestra. My shields are depleted as well. We've been at this for almost five minutes. Hopefully that's been long enough to give them the distraction they needed. Have you had any luck getting through their jamming?"

"No," Saryn replied as she turned the ship to avoid another round of blaster fire from the base's defensive guns. "But I have been in contact with my husband through our telepathic marriage bond. He has informed me they just arrived at the floor where Noble Galithar's family is being held."

The ship shook yet again and Saryn winced. "I can no longer remain in position. I made a promise to Belenger. I must turn back. I will meet you at the rendezvous point." Pressing the joystick hard to the side, Saryn turned the ship away from the base, sending one last shot from her turret cannons toward the building.

"I think we're going to join you," Captain Nahoc said. "We won't last long out here as the only target."

As they drew closer to the edge of the base's firing range,

Saryn frowned as several new blips appeared on her radar. *"Eternal Harmony*, my scanners indicate there are six ships approaching the base from the south."

"I see them, and I don't like the looks of this. They aren't local military or police. They're privately owned."

Saryn kept her eyes fixed on the incoming ships as her own moved further away. As they reached the base, they suddenly opened fire on it. "Did you observe that? They just destroyed several of the base's remaining weapons emplacements! They are friendly!"

When Captain Nahoc did not reply, Saryn sensed something was wrong. His voice came through her helmet a moment later and confirmed her fears. "I'm afraid you're mistaken, Master Saryn. My sensors were able to pick up some of the symbols on the ships. I cross-referenced them in the database.

"Those are most definitely not friendly ships. They are Meh'ishto heavy cruisers!"

38

OMINOUS TIDINGS

DESPITE THE TEY-RAKIL female's statement that they could lower their weapons, Khalen, Belenger, Teg-lakis, and Mariska still kept their guns pointed at the mysterious cloaked figures.

"Who are you?" Khalen asked.

"You can call me Ara, and my companion is Rakow," the female said.

Khalen switched his gaze toward the male, his brows furrowed in confusion. "What are you doing here? Why did you just help us, and why did you save me back on Dhun'drok?"

Rakow returned Khalen's stare with intensity. "As I said in Mok Ena, we're here to observe. As for why we helped you...let's just say we want to keep things balanced."

"Stop with the riddles and give us a straight answer, you weedy, soft-skinned, clotpole," Teg-lakis spat. "In case you hadn't noticed, we don't have time for chit-chat. You said you wanted to tell us something. Well, spit it out!" As if to accentuate his words, another explosion rocked the building.

"Our master has learned that the Thirteen Overlords have taken a peculiar interest in you and in this abduction," Ara explained.

"What do they care about the kidnapping of a Lah'grex family?" Belenger asked.

Ara shook her head. "We don't think they're actually interested in the family itself as much as what the family possessed. When Brin'tac's wife and children were captured, Shrouded Discord also took numerous items from the Galithar vaults. We believe one of these is of particular interest to the Overlords."

"So why tell us now?" Mariska asked.

"Because we want you to retrieve it," Rakow said. "Everything they stole from him—the artifacts, artwork, teyra chips, weapons—is being held on the floor below us. If you take the stairs just around this corner, it's the fifth door on the left."

Khalen felt his pulse quicken at his words. *Artifacts?*

Teg-lakis, however, seemed to focus on a different pair of words. "Teyra chips, huh? So why don't you get it yourself if it's so important?"

"We've done our best to help you but can't get involved any further. It's vital we aren't seen by anyone in Shrouded Discord. We can't tell you more."

Teg-lakis snorted. "Yeah, more likely there's some kind of trap on the storage area, and you don't want to get killed springing it."

The building shook once more, reminding everyone of the danger of their current situation.

"Listen," Rakow said, his tone laced with frustration. "There have been recent developments that could very well affect the lives of every living being in the universe! Other ancient artifacts have disappeared or been stolen. Shipments of weapons have disappeared. An entire fleet of strange ships have been discovered on the edge of Rey-Qani space. We believe the Overlords are gearing up for war. Whatever it is Galithar had, they *must not* get it!"

Ara grabbed his arm. "We have to go. We've spent too much time here as it is."

"Wait!" Khalen said as the two of them turned to leave. "Who is it you work for?"

Instead of answering the question, the Tey-Rakil couple pressed the buttons on their wrists. Just as they had outside the Blue Rymer Lounge, they were swallowed by a wave of nothing in a matter of seconds.

Belenger swore. "Wow. When you described it to me, I didn't imagine it like that."

Khalen felt a sense of dread settle in the pit of his stomach. *What did they mean?* he thought. *Were they telling the truth? A fleet of strange ships? War? The Overlords stealing artifacts and weapons? This can't be a coincidence. Roakel and Saryn tracked one of the ancient instruments to Gal'grea. Could it be?*

"I don't like this. Let's just get this inhibitor deactivated and get out of here," Belenger said.

"But what about Galithar's stuff?" Teg-lakis asked. "You and Khalen can shut off a little device without us. Mariska and I will raid the storage area. If that artifact is as important as they say, it could bring us a fortune."

"In addition to the pocketfuls of teyra chips, I suppose," Belenger added cynically.

"I agree with Teg-lakis," Khalen added, not wanting to divulge any more than necessary.

"Fine," Belenger said. "Just be quick about it, and be careful."

"We're always careful," Teg-lakis said with a mischievous grin. With that, he and Mariska sprinted down the hallway.

"C'mon," Belenger said to Khalen and the drallmari. "Based on the floor plan, I'd be willing to bet the inhibitor is located in the central core of the building. There's an access door on the other side of this next room."

Pushing aside his thoughts about the artifacts, Khalen focused on the mission. Reaching out, he grabbed the handle and opened the door on their right. The room he and Belenger entered appeared to have been converted into a small dining area which was now vacant. They hurried through it and entered the food preparation section. Moments later they arrived at the door Belenger had indicated.

Khalen opened it, and he and Belenger stepped into the primary maintenance area of the entire facility. Outdated furnaces were housed inside the large, circular room. Instead of concrete floors, each of the four levels in the room consisted of metal grating which gave Khalen and Belenger a view of the entire core of the building. Several large sections of the grating were open with ladders leading between them. Shelving units, mechanical equipment, major appliances, and workshops filled the various levels. Straight ahead of them in a protective metal housing was the portal inhibitor. The pulsing white light indicated it was still active.

Just as Belenger prepared to step into the room, Kovitch and Shosta hissed loudly and leaned backward as if preparing to launch into an attack. A moment later, Khalen heard a familiar laugh echoing through the chamber.

"Khalen, you're still alive. What an unfortunate surprise. And you brought our old mentor along. Belenger, how nice to *see* you again. Now, I have a chance to pay you back for the scars you gave me."

Sudden movement drew Khalen's attention to the catwalk on the floor above. There, glaring down at them was Slag, flanked on each side by four bipedal Synths.

.

39

CONSEQUENCES

BRIN'TAC'S HEART pounded in his chest at the sight of his wife and children being held at gunpoint. Waves of rage, terror, regret, and shock crashed over him.

"Slag was right. You're much more persistent than I gave you credit for," Kuzelka said with grudging admiration. "You must actually care for your family.

"Or come to think of it," she continued, her voice become icy and mocking, "maybe the real reason you came was for the money and data files that were stolen from your mansion. After all, you wouldn't want your precious wife and children to learn the truth about the source of some of your fortune, would you? My guess is you wanted to reclaim those files before we could use them to blackmail you. Isn't that right?"

Brin'tac felt his blood run cold at the look of confusion and betrayal on his wife's face. He had kept these secrets from his family for years, and now this Leh'cryst mercenary was using them as a weapon against him. His eyes blazed red as he glared at her. "You putrid piece of trash! My wife and children would never believe your lies!"

Kuzelka let out a gleeful laugh. "Oh, Brin'tac. You're so naive. Any wife will tell you she knows when her husband is lying. I'm sure Raena has suspected something for a long time. Even if she couldn't prove it, she knew deep down that something was going on."

Brin'tac wondered what Mak'sim and the others were thinking. He brushed the thought aside. He knew he could live without their approval. After all, he was a Galithar. He did not answer to them or to any Solemsiel Arrangers.

But his family was altogether different. Brin'tac glanced at Shea and Rav'ok and saw confusion on their faces. In that moment he began to comprehend the true consequence of this debacle. *What have I done? I should never have made that deal with the Tritonus. But what choice did I have? What choice do I have even now? I may save their lives only to lose their trust and love. I've failed them at every turn. We would never have been put in this predicament if I hadn't made so many mistakes. I gave Lady Crisenth all the ammunition she needed to blackmail me. Never again.*

Kuzelka's smile widened at the tormented look on Brin'tac's face. His anger boiled over and evaporated the last vestiges of self-control. "How much are they paying you? What did they promise you in exchange for your soul?"

The expression on the mercenary's face shifted from supreme confidence to shock at Brin'tac's words. She quickly regained her composure and shot him a warning look. So there it was: she *was* in league with the Tritonus.

Her warning glance brought Lady Crisenth's threat back to his mind. *"And if you deviate from that script in any way, you will come to an extremely painful death, but only after first watching your wife, son, and daughter suffer!"*

"Oh, Shrouded Discord is paying me quite well, thank you," Kuzelka said, covering for Brin'tac's slipup. "Now back away *patra* and let us through. Your family and I are going for a little walk."

Defeated, Brin'tac moved back to stand once more with Roakel and the others. Another explosion shook the building, adding to the tension of the moment.

"It is most definitely time for me to leave. Now, move slowly," Kuzelka commanded to her prisoners. "If you make any sudden movements, you'll find a hole in your back!"

Raena, Rav'ok, and Shea reluctantly began to shuffle forward out of the cell. Brin'tac watched the somber procession in silence, his anguish intensifying with each step they took. Shea's face was streaked with tears, while Rav'ok wore an expression of anger and frustration. Raena, on the other hand, had her head lifted. Her countenance was one of regal beauty and elegance. Brin'tac knew her nobility and pride would never allow her to look weak in the presence of an enemy. She was like a statue of refined beauty as sculpted as the elaborate headcrest that adorned her head.

Once they were in the hallway, Kuzelka turned her prisoners around so they were forced to walk backward, placing Brin'tac's family between her and their would-be rescuers. Unable to act for fear the mercenary would injure or kill one of them, Brin'tac was forced to watch as they edged closer and closer to the stairwell that led to the top floor.

As they reached the door leading to the stairs, Roakel started to say something. Kuzelka pointed her laser pistol at him and raised her voice. "Stop right there! If I so much as see your lips move again, I'll kill—Aaah!"

Kuzelka cried out in pain and reached toward the back of her neck with her left hand. The sudden movement caused her weapon to discharge, sending a laser bolt flying within an inch of Roakel's head.

Raena took advantage of the Lah'grex female's distraction. She spun around and knocked the weapon out of her hand. Then, with a fury born of days of captivity, Raena let out a cry of rage and kicked Kuzelka hard in the stomach. The force of the blow sent her crashing into the wall before toppling to the floor.

Hujik's remote sprang forward, running full speed toward Brin'tac's family. Vel'vikis, Brin'tac, and Roakel each broke into a full run, trailing just behind the robot. Before they could reach Raena and her children, Kuzelka came to her senses. She braced herself against the wall and leapt toward Raena, who had bent over to grab the laser pistol. Her hand had just wrapped around the handle when Kuzelka plowed into her, slamming her against the opposite wall of the hallway.

Rav'ok wrapped his arms around Kuzelka and yanked her away from his mother. As he pulled, the laser pistol in Raena's hand fired, shooting the mercenary point blank in the chest. Kuzelka's eyes went wide in horror and surprise, then her body fell limp in Rav'ok's arms. Shocked by what had just happened, Rav'ok released her and she tumbled to the ground.

Brin'tac came to a halt, stunned by the sudden turn of events. His mind struggled to accept what his eyes had just witnessed: his family was free!

At last, the moment Brin'tac had been anticipating since his meeting with the Tritonus fifteen days ago had come to pass. No enemy stood between him and his wife and children. Yet his victory was not without a price: Kuzelka's poisonous words had infected his family. Hopefully he could convince them she had been lying and undo the damage.

"Raena!" he exclaimed as he rushed toward them. "Rav'ok! Shea! Thank the Universe you're safe!"

Raena's eyes flashed toward him as she stood and removed the mute from her throat. "No thanks to you! I don't understand why all of this happened, but it's clear you had something to do with it."

Brin'tac's eyes turned gray. "Raena, Kuzelka was twisting the truth. There's so much you don't understand. I did everything I could to save you, Rav'ok and Shea."

"We'll see about that," she said emphatically. Turning, she bowed to Roakel. "Master Arranger, am I correct in assuming there's a portal inhibitor in place?"

"Yes, Lady Galithar. But it should be deactivated momentarily. For the present, I suggest we retreat to the lower levels. My wife has informed me that several Meh'ishto cruisers just attacked the base and are landing. We have to move!" The building shook as more explosions erupted above them.

"Master Arranger, would you, please, lead the way? My children and I have had enough of this place."

"Most certainly," Roakel replied as he pointed down the hallway in the direction in which they had just come. "We are all relieved to see that you and your family are unharmed."

Brin'tac watched despondently as his wife and children began heading down the hallway behind Roakel. Vel'vikis and Hujik stood nearby waiting for their leader. Pushing aside his disheartened demeanor, Brin'tac turned to follow them, his thoughts strengthening his resolve. *There'll come a time when I'll have a chance to explain to Raena why I did what I did. When that time comes, I'll make her understand and forgive. Until then, I have no choice but to continue on this current path.*

As they hurried down the hallway, Rav'ok spoke for the first time since being rescued. "I don't understand what happened to that witch back there. Why did she cry out in pain?"

Vel'vikis glanced over at Hujik's remote which was lumbering next to him. "I believe that was Hujik's doing."

The Lah'grex pilot's face appeared on the remote's head. "This remote has a small, bug-sized drone that we used to learn the layout of the building. It also has small detonators that are just strong enough to take out cameras. When I realized you were being held hostage, I hid the droid in the pipes running along the ceiling. Once she turned and began walking backward, I maneuvered it into position behind her and waited for the right opportunity. When she removed the blaster from Lady Galithar's back, I hit her with a charge."

"A wise strategy, with the exception that I was almost the target of her weapon, and Kuzelka recovered quickly enough to assault Lady Galithar," Roakel stated.

The group reached the stairway unchallenged. Hujik responded as they began their descent. "It was a calculated risk. I believed that once she was shocked, we'd have just enough time for either Vel'vikis, Inspector Mak'sim, or I to reach her or—"

"Wait!" Vel'vikis stopped suddenly, a mixed expression on his face of both confusion and concern.

"What is it? What's wrong?" Brin'tac asked.

"Where *is* Inspector Mak'sim?"

Mariska kept her blaster in her right hand and her resonite whip coiled in the other, ready to be unleashed at a moment's notice. Although she, too, was intrigued by the prospect of picking up some extra teyra chips to line her pockets, as well as perhaps a little something more, she was still very leery of the source of the information.

She had heard legends of Araklial and his Thirteen Overlords, but she had never given them much thought. Some called them "gods", others said they were Beyonders from outside the Twin Galaxies sent to rule, and still others, like Roakel, called them nothing more than daemon-possessed Fiihkren and Seyvreen.

All she knew for certain was that some of them, at least, were living, breathing beings of great power and influence. Teg-lakis had even met Lady Crisenth in his youth, or so he claimed. The other thing she knew for certain is that if they did choose to unite and wage war on the rest of the Twin Galaxies, it would not be good.

"This is it," Teg-lakis whispered, his voice a mixture of excitement tempered by caution. In his left hand he held his thick, resonite hammer poised. "This is the door they indicated." He grabbed the handle and gave it a quick test. "Locked, as expected. Your turn, darling."

Mariska reached into a compartment on her belt and withdrew a small device. She placed it on the lock and set to work. Seconds later, the lock on the door clicked and she returned the device to its pouch. "Child's play," she said with a cocky grin. She opened the door and stepped inside.

The large room obviously belonged to someone of importance as it was filled with expensive decorations, advanced technology, and plush furnishings. In the far corner of the room was a heavily-locked door.

"That's gotta be it," Teg-lakis stated as he closed the outer door behind them and locked it again. The two of them sprinted across the room to the storage door. Once again, Mariska set to work on the series of locks.

While she worked, another tremor from the attack above shook the building. "Hurry up, babe. That distraction won't last much longer," Teg-lakis said.

"Almost done. These old locks remind me of the ones I used to pick back on Ves-winda growing up. Ah. There we go. How does it look to you?"

Teg-lakis finished his examination of the door frame. "Looks clean. I don't see any wires or hidden triggers. Let's open this baby and see if those Tii-Koonas were telling the truth."

The two prepared themselves for the possibility of a trap and slowly opened the door. When it was clear there was no danger, they stepped into the storage room eagerly.

"Wow. I'm surprised," Teg-lakis said, a huge grin spreading on his face. "They were actually telling the truth! We just hit the jackpot."

Mariska felt the giddiness spread through her. Stacks of teyra chips in denominations of one hundred were wrapped neatly and placed in containers on shelves along the left wall of the rectangular room. Next to the currency were numerous jewels and small, expensive sculptures. The right wall was filled with all manner of weapons, from heavy laser rifles and grenade launchers to hand-held laser pistols. Sitting alone in an upright position against the short wall ahead of them was a long, rectangular case. On the floor next to it was a pair of exquisitely carved wooden drumsticks.

Mariska and Teg-lakis exchanged glances. "What do you think that is?" Mariska asked as she walked over to the case.

"It looks like some kind of weapon case," Teg-lakis said. "Or it could just be the protective case for the artifact the Tii-Koonas were talking about."

Mariska picked up the drumsticks and stuffed them into her belt as Teg-lakis grabbed the object by the handle and set it flat on the floor. "This is just like that one used to protect the sculpture we swiped from that collector on Prono. That case was practically indestructible. I'll bet this is the artifact they were talking about."

As Teg-lakis started to open it, Mariska frowned. "Why would they store all this stuff behind a couple of basic locks? Yeah, one of 'em was a bit tricky, but nothing an average thief with proper tools couldn't handle. It almost seems too easy."

"I don't know. They just took this stuff from Brint'ac ten days ago. They probably needed somewhere to put it temporarily and shoved it in here. Makes sense to me." Teg-lakis finally got the latches open and, eyes wide with anticipation, he lifted the lid.

Inside the case was a beautifully crafted instrument made of polished brass. The tubing and bell of the instrument was etched with swirling designs of greens, blues and purples. The mouthpiece was made of pure silver. Even the plush interior of the case spoke of care and fine craftsmanship.

Teg-lakis turned to look at Mariska, a puzzled look on his face. "This is it? This can't possibly be what the Overlords are after. They must want the money and weapons. Either that, or that whole story about the Overlords was made up. This is nice, though. I bet it'll fetch a nice price at the—"

Teg-lakis stopped mid-sentence as the sound of someone fumbling with the lock on the outer door reached his ears. Mariska stared at him in alarm. Without speaking, the two left the instrument on the floor and moved silently into the main room, their weapons drawn. Seconds later, the door opened, and a figure stepped into the room. Mariska prepared to pull the trigger on her laser pistol when she recognized the face of the intruder.

Next to her, Teg-lakis swore as he too realized who it was. "Mak'sim, you almost got yourself killed. What in the blazes are you doing here?"

Startled at the sight of the Rey-Qani couple, it took the Lah'grex a moment to respond. "I came to get eth Galithar's possessions. Hujik said he noticed the heavily bolted storage room during his reconnaissance of the base and guessed they were located here. If anything, I should be asking you what *you're* doing here," he replied, his tone becoming suddenly suspicious.

Another deep rumble passed through the building. Mariska holstered her weapon. "That story will have to wait. With your help, we'll be able to take more of it with us. Give us a hand."

Teg-lakis remained in place with his pistol trained on Mak'sim. "Actually, I think we're okay without him, hon."

Mak'sim narrowed his eyes. "Oh, I see. You want it all for yourself. I knew you couldn't be trusted."

"Actually, I think you've got that backward," Teg-lakis said as he stepped closer to the Lah'grex. "I think *you're* the one that can't be trusted. Tell me, how did you get the door to this room unlocked so fast?"

"That's right," Mariska breathed. "I didn't hear any lock-picking device."

A pair of laser blasts suddenly shot across the room, narrowly missing Teg-lakis. Mariska grabbed her weapon from its holster and started firing back at the two Leh'cryst soldiers who had suddenly appeared in the doorway. She ducked down behind a chair and watched with concern as Mak'sim grappled with Teg-lakis for control of his pistol.

Mariska reached out from behind her cover and sent several more shots in the direction of the door. She felt a moment of satisfaction as she heard one of the soldiers grunt and crash to the ground.

The sound of Mak'sim crying out drew her attention back to the center of the room. Teg-lakis had his tail wrapped around Mak'sim's legs and had used it to trip him. However, before the Rey-Qani could leap on top of his opponent, another blast from the remaining soldier at the door struck him in the shoulder. He howled in pain and leapt behind a nearby table.

Throwing caution to the wind, Mariska stood and fired back at the attacker. Her shot hit him full in the chest. But before he fell, he managed to fire off one last shot that struck her in the arm, knocking her weapon out of her hand.

It was then she heard another blast that was followed by an all too familiar groan.

Mariska spun around and saw that Teg-lakis was crouching behind the table. She watched in horror as his expression was overwhelmed by shock and pain. He turned slowly and looked at her. In his eyes she could see his love for her, and the regrets for his past mistakes, all flash by in an instant. And with it came the knowledge that this would be their last moment together.

His lifeless body crashed to the ground, taking with it her love and dreams for the future.

Before she could react, a second blast shot across the room, striking her in the chest. Crying out in pain as the energy coursed through her, she, too, fell to the floor. Unlike the shot that felled Teg-lakis, she realized her attacker had stunned her instead of killing her.

She lay on the floor still conscious but unable to move. A moment later, she saw Mak'sim's face near her own as he crouched beside her. He reached out and stroked her ribbon-mane, a cruel smile on his lips. "Don't worry. I'm not going to kill you. So sorry about your mate. He was too dangerous to allow to live."

Mariska's emotions howled within her, yet she was unable to react due to the paralysis. White hot rage and overwhelming grief clashed against each other, leaving her confused and numb. As she lay on the floor, tears spilled out from her eyelids and rolled down the side of her face.

"Ah. It sounds like the attack above has ceased. That means the rest of my friends will be arriving soon enough. Time to collect my prize. As for you, you'll soon be on your way to your new home. I expect you'll fetch a very hefty price in the slave market."

40

REVENGE

KHALEN AND BELENGER dove for cover behind a large work table to their left. As expected, the four Synths fired in unison toward the two men. Khalen whistled to the drallmari, who had leapt into the air as the attack commenced. The reptilian beasts closed their wings and dove through one of the openings leading to the floor below.

Next to him, Belenger loaded a capsule into the launcher portion of his rifle, leaned around the table and fired. A second later, the capsule exploded, releasing a cloud of smoke into the air.

"That should give us some cover," Belenger said. "I'll go high. You hold the middle. Have the beasts flank them." Without waiting for a reply, the Augmented Colonel stood and used his suit's strength to leap high into the air to land on the floor above.

The Synths on that level picked up on the sound of his landing and opened fire blindly in that direction. Still hidden behind the work table, Khalen threw his hood over his head and closed his eyes, concentrating on the song needed to create the whirlwind. His voice rose in volume and the music increased in intensity, causing the air around him to swirl with light and energy.

Just as he was about to direct his wind creation toward where he had last seen Slag, he was hit with a strange sensation. As he tried to sing, his voice echoed back to him a second later. The reflected sound of his own voice confused his brain and his song faltered. He tried to block out the echo in his head, but no matter how hard he concentrated, the audible delay of his voice shut down his ability to sing.

Glancing around frantically, he saw Slag's cloaked form appearing out of the smoke and striding purposefully toward him. In his hand was an oddly-shaped device. Its end fanned out into a bell shape filled with numerous tiny filaments.

"What's wrong, Khalen? Can't remember the solfege?" Slag gloated. "Let me introduce you to the Silencer." The Ra-Nuuk set the device on the floor and stepped behind a large cabinet for cover. "Fortunately, it is directional. So, while you may be unable to create music, I certainly can!"

Khalen's eyes burned red with anger and frustration. With his ability to sing hindered, even his Twin Discs of Arrguin were useless. He could not whistle more than a note or two to the drallmari. He yelled in frustration and withdrew the only weapon available to him: his laser pistol. Across the platform, he could hear Slag's own voice rising. Khalen immediately recognized the song the warlord had used atop Balec's Tower to create the lava tentacle.

Desperate to interrupt Slag's song, Khalen began firing toward him. The blasts were absorbed instantly by the PSG resting on the floor next to the Ra-Nuuk maestro. Trapped, Khalen prepared to rush his attacker.

One of Belenger's canisters suddenly dropped through the dissipating smoke to land behind Slag. With his song established, the warlord turned his back on Khalen and raised his newly created wall of lava in front of him to absorb any explosion. Khalen recognized his opportunity and leapt out from cover to charge his opponent.

He was within twenty feet of the Ra-Nuuk when the canister exploded. To his surprise, it was not a bomb at all. A cloud of green mist permeated the air. As it reached Slag, he gagged and choked. The lava he had controlled a moment before crashed onto the grated floor and began eating away at the metal.

As Khalen continued his charge, he watched with relief as Kovitch and Shosta flew up through the floor openings on the opposite side of the circular room and barreled into two of the Synths, knocking them to the ground just before they could fire their blasters at Belenger.

Khalen took a deep breath and plunged into the green mist. He reached the cabinet which Slag had been using for cover and tackled the Ra-Nuuk. As he hit the ground, Khalen felt the catwalk beneath him shift. He glanced to his left and realized a new danger: the fallen lava had eaten through two of the metal supports. Before he could react, the entire left side of the catwalk collapsed, sending Khalen and Slag tumbling down the long sheet of hot metal to land on the floor below.

Stunned from the fall and from the pain where the metal had burned him, Khalen struggled to focus. He looked up to see that between Belenger and the drallmari, they had managed to take out three of the Synths. However, Kovitch lay still on one of the catwalks, either unconscious or dead. Belenger's armor was blackened in numerous places from laser blasts, and his left arm hung limp at his side.

Letting out a howl of rage, Belenger leapt into the air, his vibraknife clutched in his right hand. The remaining Synth fired several shots at him as the arc of his leap brought him closer. Two of the blasts found their marks, hitting him in the leg and side. The Augmented soldier crashed into the robot and plunged the vibrating dagger into the chest of the machine.

Khalen wanted to run to the aid of his friend but forced himself to keep his mind on completing the mission. He tried several times to get his dry lips to form the whistle needed to communicate with Shosta. He finally succeeded on the third try.

The drallmar immediately followed the whistled command and flew down to the level containing the portal inhibitor. Upon landing, she began clawing at the protective case. Khalen knew it would not be long before she had it open and the device disabled.

Khalen shrugged off the remaining disorientation from the fall and scanned the area for signs of his opponent. The Ra-Nuuk had just recovered and was standing nearby, his silver mask blackened and dented. His robes had a handful of burn spots on them, and he held his resonite daggers in each hand.

"This has gone on long enough," Slag said, his voice raspy and his breathing labored.

Due to the close proximity of his opponent, Khalen knew he would never have time to use his discs. Instead, he crouched into a fighting stance. Although he was expecting the attack, the Ra-Nuuk warlord's speed still managed to surprise him. Slag launched into a series of spins and acrobatic somersaults, forcing Khalen to back away in a frantic effort to dodge and block the flurry of attacks. He quickly realized that Slag's shorter stature, tail, and lower center of gravity gave him an advantage.

Yet Khalen had worked with the Ra-Nuuk long enough to recognize his fighting style. Slag kept up the attack, continuing to force Khalen to retreat until he was nearly pressed against the outer wall. He winced from several small cuts that had made it through his guard.

As Slag launched into his next series of thrusts, Khalen anticipated the move and countered with a strike of his own. The blow sent one of Slag's dagger's flying across the room. Khalen pivoted, spun around behind his opponent, and closed the distance between them. Then, using his larger frame, he wrapped his arms around the Ra-Nuuk and drove him to the ground.

Khalen reached down and twisted Slag's wrist, causing him to cry out in pain and drop the remaining dagger. The Ra-Nuuk's tail tried to thrash out at Khalen, but he shifted his weight and pinned it to the ground with his foot. Digging his left elbow into Slag's back, Khalen used his right hand to grab the loose dagger.

A surge of adrenaline coursed through Khalen and his eyes blazed a dark red. Filled with blood lust and revenge, he struck his enemy on the back of his head, knocking him senseless. Growling in rage, Khalen flipped the stunned Ra-Nuuk over and pinned him down once more. He raised his left fist and struck Slag again, knocking the silvery mask off his face.

Khalen placed the dagger against Slag's exposed throat and studied the ruined face before him. The entire bottom left portion of his cheek and jaw was scarred from his ear to his chin. The normal cracked, Ra-Nuuk skin was now pock-marked and crisscrossed with scar tissue.

Khalen felt no pity.

Feeling the strong steel of the dagger in his hand, he removed it from Slag's throat and plunged it into his side, taking perverse pleasure in watching his opponent's face swell with pain. Khalen leaned close to his terror-stricken foe and grinned maliciously. "Now you know how it feels. I dreamt of this day during every waking hour of twelve long, miserable years in captivity. I fantasized killing you in unique and painful ways. I cursed your name with every breath, vowing to survive long enough to enact my revenge upon the one who was the source of my misery.

"Today, I fulfill that vow!"

In that moment, Slag's eyes became filled with a malice and hatred that pierced Khalen's soul. "Do it! I dare you!" Slag screamed hoarsely. "Prove your newfound 'righteousness' was a sham! I never believed the reports. I knew you were still the same, blood-thirsty Meh'ishto you always were! You can't escape your past. None of us can."

To his utter horror, Khalen suddenly felt as if he were looking in a mirror. The thirst for revenge and willful unforgiveness he had harbored all these years had now come to the surface. His own hatred had corrupted his heart and blackened his soul.

Saryn's words aboard the *Lightbringer* came back to him in a rush. *"In many ways, this Skaret is not unlike how you used to be. Perhaps it is the Composer's will that you pray for his conversion. Perhaps you are the instrument that will bring the knowledge of the truth to your enemies."*

The hatred and rage within him grappled with his will. He knew what was required of him by Dominuus, but his emotions refused to relent. He knew the right thing was to submit to the will of the Great Composer. He considered himself to be a follower of the Symphonian Code, yet he had hidden bitterness in his heart and allowed it to poison his mind.

But then his body remembered the pain, the torture, and the cruelty of his time as a slave. Images poured through his psyche, fueling his enmity. His resolution was strengthened by the memories, closing the door to his spirit. Now was his chance for revenge!

"There are some parts of a man that only time can heal," Khalen said viciously. "But unfortunately for you, those wounds are still raw, and you're out of time!"

Taking a deep breath, Khalen raised the dagger to strike.

A blaster rang out in the room and struck him in the back. As he fell off Slag, Khalen's body convulsed as the electrical shock of the stun blast coursed through him. The energy slowly subsided, leaving him paralyzed, but conscious.

Khalen stared in shock as a large contingent of soldiers poured into the room on each of the floors. But they were not Shrouded Discord mercenaries, as he expected. These were tattoo-covered men with their hair in dreadlocks and their bodies covered in animal skins.

These were his people: the Meh'ishto.

41

RESCUE ATTEMPT

ROAKEL BREATHED a sigh of relief as he and the last of the refugees passed through the portal to arrive at the cave entrance. He closed down the portal and contacted through their shared telepathic bond.

Thanks be to the Composer.
His face upon us has radiated.
He has delivered you from danger.
The portal inhibitor is deactivated.

Roakel responded, his heart becoming lighter at the news.
Praise to Him indeed.
By his name did Nara succeed.
The captives have been freed.
Now I open the portal with speed

Roakel severed the telepathic connection, activated his windstaff and began to sing. Within moments, the portal to Belenger's ship was established. He continued to sing as Brin'tac's family passed through, leaving only Brin'tac, Vel'vikis and Hujik's remote standing in the cave beneath the base. When Brin'tac began to argue with Vel'vikis, Roakel stopped singing.

"I won't leave until everyone's safe."

"But eth Galithar, we must go!"

"No! It's clear to me now I've taken the coward's road for too long," Brin'tac nearly shouted. "I won't stand by any longer while others die. I can't face my wife and children with that on my conscience."

Roakel turned to face them. "Vel'vikis, Noble Galithar's words are honorable. Let us go together to aid our comrades."

A look of resignation crossed the Lah'grex's features. "As you wish, eth Galithar."

Roakel suddenly felt Saryn contacting him once more.

I searched through the faces
Of those who passed through the veil
Yet the countenance of my dearheart
Was not to be found.
What is it that has you bound?

Roakel replied,
Alas, my love,
How could I return to you
While we yet have friends in peril
I must go back; to them be true.

Our Lah'grex Noble
Shame's student vows humble.

Refuses to leave a single soul.
His changing heart grows bold.

Saryn replied a moment later,

My heart longs to join you.
My mind holds me fast.
The call I have heeded.
Here my skills are needed.
To conduct our charges to safety at last.

To aid in your journey
Our inhibitor is in full activation
To prevent Meh'ishto music
In spiriting enemies to your location.

When our friends are rescued,
You have simply to call.
The way will be opened
To return with them all.

While Roakel continued his private conversation, Hujik led the way back into the base, followed by Vel'vikis and Brin'tac. The Solemsiel moved into position behind the Lah'grex ruler as he replied to Saryn.

My spirit within me is filled with regret
That the love of my life cannot be with me; yet
Though my soul yearns for my wife
I radiate joy that my loved ones are safe.

Concern for her husband's well-being came through their bond.

My heart is well-pleased
With the character of my mate.
His eyes fix on the conductor
To guide in this feat.

In Him is Safety.
His Glory be your Victory!

As always, Roakel replied.

I love you, Roa.
I love you too.

The small group moved through the now abandoned lowest floor of the base. As they traversed the hallways, Roakel told them about Saryn activating the portal inhibitor aboard the *Fiery Vengeance*. They climbed the stairway and were about to ascend the stairs to the third floor when they heard voices coming from the hallway on the other side of the door leading to the second floor.

"That sounds like Mak'sim," Vel'vikis whispered.

They paused behind the door and listened intently. Despite their best efforts, they could only hear snippets of the conversation.

"...heading back up...join the others," Mak'sim was saying.

"What about...?" another voice asked.

"Bring her. ...mate's body."

Roakel exchanged a concerned glance with Brin'tac. "It is as I feared. It appears the inspector has betrayed us." At his words, the eyes of both Brin'tac and Vel'vikis blazed red.

"By the blood of Ged'eroth, he will pay!" Vel'vikis exclaimed.

Recognizing the Lah'grex was about to burst through the door and attack, Roakel laid a hand on his arm. "Wait! I have a way that will prevent bloodshed."

Roakel opened the door carefully and peered down the curving hallway. A door stood open not far from where he was hidden. From inside the room came the sounds of muted conversation. Roakel crept closer until he neared the doorway. Vel'vikis was close behind, his pistol poised to attack.

Roakel began to sing so softly it was barely audible. After several seconds of singing, the song was established and a subdued light swirled near him. The Solemsiel crescendoed his song until it finally reached the ears of those within the room.

Roakel peered around the frame of the door while still singing. Two Meh'ishto stood inside and were lifting Mariska's body as the song penetrated into their ears. At first they appeared confused, then Roakel watched in satisfaction as their eyelids began to droop. Ten seconds later, they yawned and set Mariska down. Five seconds after that, they were sound asleep.

Roakel ceased his song as Vel'vikis sprinted into the room, followed a moment later by Brin'tac. Hujik, on the other hand, kept his remote at the doorway, its digital gaze fixed on the hallway.

Roakel crouched next to Mariska and felt for a pulse. "She is alive! What is the condition of her mate?"

Vel'vikis reached the Rey-Qani male and shook his head.

"That viper!" Brin'tac spat. "I swear to you, he will face justice!"

"At least Mariska's time has not yet passed," Roakel said. "I will contact Saryn and instruct her to deactivate the inhibitor long enough to transport Mariska safely back to the ship." While he did so, Vel'vikis and Brin'tac disappeared into the storage room. Roakel stood and opened a portal back to the *Vengeance*. Within moments, Saryn appeared through the opening. She embraced her husband and kissed him on the cheek. Turning, she bent down and lifted Mariska's much smaller body. With a final glance at her beloved, Saryn stepped back through the portal. The moment she was gone, he stopped singing, closing the aperture.

Vel'vikis and Brin'tac reappeared a second later. Together, the three of them rejoined Hujik's remote and exited the room. They headed back into the hallway and began checking each door, looking for a way into the central room, which they knew housed the portal inhibitor. On the third try, they found an access hatch.

Vel'vikis attempted to open the door as quietly as possible, but the rusted hinges still creaked. He winced at the sound and stopped. Then, with a quick motion, he opened the door. A brief grind of metal on metal echoed in the room.

Roakel frowned in confusion as Vel'vikis paused in the doorway. A moment later, he understood as the sound of voices coming from inside the room reached him. Vel'vikis peeked around the door frame, then turned back to face Roakel and Brin'tac. Rather than risk conversation, the bodyguard motioned for the others to look. Roakel stepped silently over to the opening and saw several Meh'ishto warriors picking Khalen's body up from the metal grating. He tensed as they began to carry him toward a door on the opposite side of the circular room. Roakel began singing the Song of Slumber once more, hoping to catch them before they reached the exit.

The song entered their ears just as they opened the far door. Within moments, their eyelids grew heavy and they set Khalen down. They were nearly asleep when a shout from above broke the stillness in the air.

"Solemsiel! Down there!"

Roakel ducked back inside the room as laser blasts struck the doorway.

"That's it! We've been seen! Eth Galithar, we must retreat now!" Vel'vikis urged.

Unfazed by the comment, Roakel altered his song and added the strength of the windstaff to the music. The wind increased around him and, once it had reached sufficient strength, he released the gust into the room.

The guards cried out in surprise as they were lifted into the air and slammed against the opposite wall. Shifting the song, Roakel directed the wind around Khalen's body and lifted it.

Shouts echoed throughout the central area as Roakel guided his friend closer to the room in which he and the others were hiding. A large Meh'ishto suddenly dropped from the floor above and landed just in front of the door, the Silencer in his hand. Roakel's swirling winds knocked the man from his feet. Yet as he fell, he managed to keep the device pointed in the direction of the Solemsiel music master. Within seconds, Roakel's song faltered and collapsed as the echo of his song confused him.

Defenseless, Roakel leapt forward into the room. He swung his windstaff and struck the Meh'ishto, knocking him unconscious. Behind him, he heard Vel'vikis and Brin'tac unleashing a spray of laser blasts in the hopes of covering his rescue efforts. Roakel sprinted over to Khalen, picked him up, and started running back toward the safety of the door.

Return fire rained down on him from the soldiers above. One struck his right leg, and another his left shoulder. Fighting against the numbness from the stun blasts, Roakel forced his body to continue by sheer will.

"Eth Galithar! They're coming down the hallway!"

Roakel glanced toward his companions and saw Vel'vikis turn toward the outer doorway in response to Hujik's cry. Brin'tac, meanwhile, was continuing to shoot wildly upward, hoping to keep the Meh'ishto at bay long enough for Roakel to reach safety.

Pushing himself onward, the Solemsiel stumbled through the door. Brin'tac slammed it behind him and reached over to assist Roakel.

"Maestro, we need that portal now!"

Still fighting off the effects of the stun blast, Roakel nodded and set Khalen down on the floor. Across the room, Vel'vikis and Hujik's remote continued to fight valiantly against the encroaching Meh'ishto.

Roakel began singing and playing his windstaff. The energy swirled about the room and lit it with colorful light. Just as the portal began to form, it collapsed suddenly. The elegant Solemsiel bowed his head, and his lips offered a silent prayer.

Beside him, Brin'tac grabbed his arm and shook him, his eyes wide with panic. "What happened? Why did you stop?"

Roakel turned and smiled weakly at him. "Saryn deactivated our inhibitor, but the Meh'ishto have now activated their own. I deeply regret to inform you that we are trapped."

An explosion erupted from the hallway outside the room, causing Roakel and Brin'tac to lose their balance. When they recovered, they could see pieces of Hujik's remote scattered everywhere. Vel'vikis lay awkwardly in the doorway, his body burned by the explosion.

Roakel had just begun to sing a song of attack when the door behind them burst open. The music master spun around and once more used his windstaff to strike the first Meh'ishto that stepped through the doorway. However, the second one sent a blaster bolt into Roakel's chest, dropping him to the floor. As the energy from the stun blast worked its way through his body, the Solemsiel caught one last glimpse of Brin'tac being shot and falling to the floor beside him. The last thing Roakel saw before losing his battle with consciousness was the sight of Mak'sim's gloating face as the Lah'grex entered the room.

Brin'tac felt his heart pounding in his chest as he waited in the communications room of one of the Meh'ishto ships. In all his years of meeting with dignitaries and other powerful people, he had never felt as nervous as he did each time he spoke with Lady Crisenth. This time, at least, he was hopeful. He had done everything according to her instructions. His family was free and he looked forward to returning home.

The Tritonus Overlord's holographic image appeared on the panel in front of him. He bowed in respect and waited for her to speak.

"Brin'tac eth Galithar. I must admit, I am very impressed. You played your role perfectly."

"Thank you, my lady."

"Due to your admirable performance, our plan is proceeding."

"It was an honor to serve."

Lady Crisenth smiled. "My, you *are* a good liar. But I believe you misunderstand."

Brin'tac felt the ship beneath him rumble as the engines ignited. Panic filled him. "My Lady, I must go. The ship is preparing to leave."

"And how do you propose to explain to the Solemsiel female how it is you escaped while her husband did not?"

"I...I will tell her—"

"You will tell her nothing for now," the Tritonus said. "The abduction of your family was but the first phase of our plan. Now we move to phase two."

Brin'tac felt the blood drain from his face. "But...that was never part of our agreement. I promised to do what you asked to ensure the safety of my family."

"That is true. But nothing has changed. They are not currently captives, but their safety is still in jeopardy. I have many agents. They are watching your family's movements even now. You see, eth Galithar, I have further need of your services."

"But...I can't! I need to...my family needs me. I have responsibilities."

The door opened behind him and two guards entered, along with Mak'sim. The Meh'ishto soldiers grabbed his arms and held him in place.

"Don't fret, Galithar," Lady Crisenth said soothingly. "I'm very happy with you. Your family is under my 'protection'. Continue to do what I ask, and soon I will release you. In fact, I plan to reward you for your service. Things are changing in the Twin Galaxies. Don't you want to be on the side that will be in power? Do well, and you may find yourself the ruler of a planet before long."

Brin'tac's eyes grew wide at the proposition. "Yes. I would find that very agreeable."

"Besides, although you are currently a prisoner, you will be treated well. Isn't that correct, Inspector?"

Mak'sim nodded. "Of course, my lady."

Lady Crisenth smiled once again. "I will contact you with further instructions once you land." The image faded, leaving Brin'tac stunned with thoughts of his possible future.

"And now, eth Galithar, it's time to rejoin your 'friends'," Mak'sim said. The pain of a needle plunging into his arm forced a cry from his lips. Seconds later, Brin'tac lost consciousness.

"He's coming around."

Roakel awakened slowly, his body aching from the stun blasts. He opened his eyes and became confused by his surroundings. He was strapped to a chair in a medium sized room. Based on the rumble beneath him, he guessed he was aboard a ship. Standing guard nearby was one of the Meh'ishto warriors.

And sitting in front of him, also bound, were Khalen and Belenger.

"Hey, Roa," Khalen teased, despite their dire situation. "I'm glad you're still with us. Sorry you had to come along for the ride, though."

Roakel's head pounded, but he managed a weak grimace. "I believe you simply fail to understand, my friend. I suppose I am forced to clarify it for you. The reason I do not wish for you to call me Roa is because it is a special name by which Saryn refers to me. And unless you wish to challenge her as my wife, I suggest you cease using it."

Khalen's eyes grew wide, and he chuckled. "Well then. I certainly don't want to do that. I had no idea. Sorry."

"Am I correct that we are aboard one of the Meh'ishto ships?"

Belenger nodded, his helmet no longer in place. "We're not sure where we're headed, though. It appears they brought us on board, gave us some basic medical treatment, and strapped us to these chairs."

Roakel's expression shifted to one of sorrow and loss. "It grieves me to share this information, but I must inform you that your friend, Teg-lakis, is deceased."

Although neither man reacted, Roakel could see the sorrow in their eyes. "He was a nasty little crark, but he saved my life more times than I can count," Belenger said. "What about Mariska?"

"She is well and safe aboard your ship," Roakel said. "When you deactivated the inhibitor, we were able to get Brin'tac's family to safety, and transport the slaves to the tunnel entrance."

"If even one person was saved from slavery, then it was worth it," Khalen said with a sigh. "I can't take credit for the inhibitor, though. Shosta disabled the device."

"And where are the drallmari?"

"I don't know. If they're still alive, they were probably brought on board. They're highly sought after in certain places in the Meh'ishto Supremacy. They're worth a lot on the black market," Khalen practically spit the words. Stifling a curse, he changed the subject. "Roakel, I can't be certain, but I think Brin'tac may have been in possession of the ancient instrument we were searching for on Gal'grea!"

Roakel's eyes widened in surprise. "What? Why do you think thus?"

Khalen and Belenger related the encounter with the Tii-Koona couple. When they had finished, Roakel shook his head in wonder. "That would explain why both Saryn and I felt strongly that the Great Composer wanted us to aid Noble Galithar. He was guiding us to this path."

"If that's true, then why did he allow us to be captured?" Khalen asked. Based on the mixed emotions evident in his expression, Roakel guessed the man was once more struggling with the questions that had plagued him since Riveruun's death. "How could our capture be part of his plan?"

"I do not know the specific answer to that question. Yet when you were sold as a slave, do you now doubt that he used that tragedy to bring about a greater good in your life? His ways are not our ways. But remember Riveruun's last charge to you: do not doubt. He is still in control."

Khalen lowered his head, clearly struggling to come to grips with the truth of Roakel's words.

"I am sorry, Khalen," Roakel stated sincerely, turning the conversation yet again. "Brin'tac and I attempted to rescue you. During the attempt, we discovered Mariska. We incapacitated the guards and Saryn took her back to our ship through a portal. Yet before she could return, the portal ceased."

"Probably another inhibitor from one of the Meh'ishto ships," Belenger commented. "At least it was shut down long enough for you to get everyone to safety."

"Not everyone. I was coming back for you both and for... Mak'sim. Alas, our current predicament appears to be his doing, for he is in collusion with the Meh'ishto! I can only guess that he betrayed Teg-lakis and murdered him."

The two men were stunned by the revelation. After a moment of silence, Khalen shook his head in sudden understanding. "I should've known you'd never tell him I knew Skaret."

"What do you mean?"

Khalen's eyes tinted red. "Back in the cave, just before we were attacked by the Dodekaph, he said *you* told him I had a connection to Skaret. I should've known that slimy crustlet was lying."

The door suddenly opened, and Mak'sim strode into the room. Behind him, two Meh'ishto guards dragged the unconscious form of Brin'tac. They deposited him into a chair and bound his hands behind his back before exiting the room.

"I hope you're enjoying your accommodations," Mak'sim said sarcastically. Grabbing one of the unoccupied chairs, the Lah'grex turned it around and sat, his arms resting on its back.

Belenger let out a curse, giving voice to Khalen's own thoughts.

"Where are you taking us?" Roakel asked.

"All in good time, Master Roakel. I see you're awake. I'm sure by now you've told them what happened to poor Teglakis. I wanted to apologize for that."

Belenger shook his head. "You made a huge mistake. *I'm sure by now* you've learned that Roakel was able to rescue Mariska. You don't know her like I do. She'll never stop hunting you. You'd better get used to looking over your shoulder."

Although Mak'sim laughed, it seemed to Roakel as if it was a bit forced. "She's welcome to try. I'm very good at blending in and hiding in plain sight, in case you hadn't noticed."

"Right. How did you fool Brin'tac into thinking you were an inspector from the Jorlinari Dynasty?" Khalen asked.

"He said your credentials checked out."

Mak'sim smiled. "Let's just say the people I work for have very good hackers."

"So Noble Galithar was unaware of your duplicitousness?" Roakel asked, glancing over at the unconscious Lah'grex. "Kuzelka seemed to indicate he received money for something and was attempting to retrieve incriminating data cards. I thought perhaps..."

"Galithar's a fool," Mak'sim spat, his own gaze drifting toward Brin'tac. "This whole thing started because he made some bad decisions that resulted in him making powerful political enemies. One of them managed to break into his files and discover the contents of his vault. When my employer realized what was in there, he sent me to retrieve it. But those Shrouded Discord idiots got there first. They not only kidnapped the Galithars but grabbed everything from their vault as well. After that, I decided to impersonate an inspector in order to find out who had taken his things and where they were now located. Thanks to you, I was successful in my mission."

"What did Brin'tac have that was so important?" Khalen asked.

Although Roakel was also eager to hear the answer, he hoped Khalen's suspicions were incorrect.

Mak'sim shrugged. "I don't care. From what I was told, it's some ancient artifact from the past. I don't even know why they want it. I highly doubt Galithar even knows what he had. To him it was just another expensive collectible."

"What's going to happen to us?" Khalen sneered. "And what did you do with Kovitch and Shosta?"

"You're going to be handed over to my employer once we arrive. He has special plans for the four of you. And don't fret, my Meh'ishto friend. You're drallmari are alive and well. I've been promised payment for them once they're sold."

"And I suppose you killed the rest of Shrouded Discord when you took over the base."

Mak'sim nodded. "You'd already taken out most of them. We just finished what you started."

Roakel watched as Khalen's expression shifted from relief to frustration. A moment later it was replaced by resignation as his eyes cooled in color. Roakel was confused by the response until he remembered Khalen's connection with Slag. It now appeared the one responsible for Khalen's slavery was dead.

Standing, the Lah'grex traitor headed toward the door. "Anyway, get comfortable. We've got a long trip ahead of us."

"Long? What is our destination?" Roakel asked.

Mak'sim paused and turned toward his prisoners once more. "Haven't you guessed? We're heading into the Meh'ishto Supremacy. More specifically, we're heading to the Meh'ishto homeworld."

Roakel saw Khalen's eyes grow wide as all color drained from his face. Mak'sim smiled at his reaction. "I couldn't believe my luck when I discovered you'd been one of those hired by Galithar. Did you even know there was a bounty on your head? We're taking you back home, Master Daedark. For you see, my employer is none other than Savatar Lexani."

Although the name meant nothing to Roakel, he could tell by Khalen's reaction he knew the man. In fact, he not only knew him, but feared and loathed him. A moment later Roakel understood why.

Mak'sim smiled wickedly at Khalen's discomfort. "Yes, Khalen. I'm taking you home to your step-father!"

EPILOGUE

SARYN STUDIED the faces of those gathered in the conference room aboard the *Eternal Harmony*. To her left was Mariska, her expression solemn. To her right sat Raena and Captain Nahoc.

"I'm going after them," Mariska stated.

"But according to what Master Roakel told Saryn through their bond, they're heading deep into Meh'ishto space! That's a suicide mission," Raena said.

"Honey, I've been there before. In fact, I've got connections that'll get me onto the planet."

The others stared at her in surprise. Saryn was the first to respond. "I am going as well. I cannot leave my husband in the clutches of those vile men."

Raena looked uncomfortable. "Master Arranger, I beg your forgiveness. After all you sacrificed to rescue me and my children, I feel I should go along as well. However, with everything that's happened these past ten days, I simply...I just can't do it right now. Please. I hope you understand."

Saryn smiled back at her in reassurance. "Pay it no mind. I can only imagine the trauma you experienced."

"Thank you. If you'd like, I will offer you whatever funds

you need to rescue my husband. And I am more than willing to open my home to Nara and Jov. It's the least we could do." Turning, she addressed Nahoc. "Captain, we'll have to hire some music masters in Mok Ena, and put together a team to assist Master Saryn."

Captain Nahoc inclined his head. "Hiring musicians shouldn't pose a problem, my lady. However, it'll take some time to pull together a strike team."

"We can't wait," Mariska stated. "I know what the Meh'ishto are like. We don't have time. With Belenger gone, I'll pilot the *Fiery Vengeance*. We're gonna need its fire-power and false IDs. If I could connect with your ship, it'd save me the trouble of hiring musicians."

"Of course," Saryn said.

A small bug-sized remote suddenly flitted over the table and flew over to Saryn, hovering before her eyes. She recognized it as Dodger, the tiny reconnaissance remote Nara kept housed in Roadblock's shoulder. "Nara, what have I instructed you regarding eavesdropping?" She took out her scroll and opened it, allowing the teen to respond through the device's speaker.

"Jov and I are coming too!" she said, half-pleading and half-demanding. "You saw how much we were able to help both on Dhun'drok and here on Rovik. C'mon, Aunt Saryn. Please? We're not kids anymore. Under some Tii-Koona laws, we're already considered adults!"

Jov's voice cut into the audio. "Yeah, Aunt Sawyn. I can even fwy da ship by myself! Nawa's been teaching me how ta use da vertuaw piwoting system."

Saryn's frown deepened. "It is going to be extremely

dangerous. I would be absolutely distraught if anything happened to either of you. I believe it would be wiser if you remained with the Galithars."

"Aunt Saryn, you need us! Uncle Roakel, Uncle Khalen, and Mr. Galithar need us!"

Saryn closed her eyes momentarily, then opened them again. "Perhaps you are correct. We *do* need your help. I...I need your help." She jumped in surprise as Nara's excited cry of victory startled her.

"You won't regret it."

"Well then, so be it," Saryn said, her heart heavy. "As soon as we resupply, we depart for Meh'ish!"

The two black clad figures stood in front of the large holographic display as they waited for their call to be answered. Finally, the three-dimensional image of their master came to life before them. He gazed at them through the cowl of his hood from his seat on the elaborately-decorated throne. At his appearance, they bowed deeply.

"What tidings do you bring?"

"We followed the Lah'grex and the Arrangers as you commanded. We successfully infiltrated the mercenary base on Rovik," Ara explained.

"Are you certain you were not seen by eye or lens?"

"We are certain, Lord," Rakow replied.

"And the artifact?"

"You were right, as always. It was a musical instrument. We couldn't get a detailed look at it, as it was enclosed in a case. As you suspected, the Lah'grex was in possession of it, but it was stolen by the mercenaries. However, we were unable to acquire it due to our limitations. We attempted to have the Solemsiel's friends steal it for us, but there was a Lah'grex traitor among them who interfered."

"What is the fate of the Lah'grex and his family?"

"The Arrangers managed to free the family, but in doing so, Galithar, the Solemsiel male, and their two friends were captured," Ara said. "No doubt the others will attempt to rescue them."

The eight-foot tall figure rose from the throne, the holographic image capturing his imposing presence perfectly. Towering over the diminutive Tey-Rakil, he smiled down at them. "Well done. However, the task is now that much harder. *HE* must not return. You must do all in your power to prevent them from succeeding," the hooded figure continued. "The instrument must not remain in the hands of the Meh'ishto. And if by some chance the Solemsiel female succeeds in rescuing her husband and the others, our options will be limited.

"You will have to kill them!"

The Tey-Rakils exchanged glances, then bowed once more. "Yes, Lord Rathvaen."

ABOUT
KEITH A. ROBINSON

**Author of *The Origins Trilogy*
and *The Tartarus Chronicles***

Keith Robinson has dedicated his life to teaching others how to defend the Christian faith. Since the release of Logic's End, his first novel, he has been a featured speaker at Christian music festivals, homeschool conventions, apologetics seminars and churches, as well as appearing as a guest on numerous radio shows.

He is currently writing the Master Symphony Trilogy, an epic space fantasy set in another galaxy where music can control and manipulate nature.

When not writing or speaking, Mr. Robinson is the full-time public school orchestra director at KTEC school, a professional freelance violist in the Milwaukee/Chicago area, a graduate of the Colson Fellows program, and a director of the Ratio Christi ministry in Kenosha. He currently resides in Kenosha, Wisconsin, with his wife, Stephanie, their five children, and a Rottweiler named Thor.

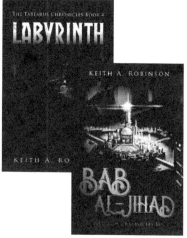

Logic's End, BOOK 1 OF THE *Origins Trilogy*

Rebecca Evans has joined a team from NASA to explore the newly discovered planet, 2021PK. Their mission is to find evidence of life in the universe. But they found more than they bargained for.

"There it is!" Ricky said triumphantly. "Do you see it? Right there in front of those mountains. And there's the lake we saw in the reports."

As promised, the probe sat near the edge of a small lake, which looked to be about four miles in diameter. Behind it stood a tall range of mountains.

"Put her down over there," Captain Coffner said, indicating a flat area near the probe about a half of a mile from the edge of the lake. Ricky nodded in acknowledgment and set the shuttle down gently onto the alien soil, the vertical thrusters kicking up clouds of chalky gray dust.

"Well, everyone, welcome to 2021 PK," Ricky said, impersonating the voice of an airline pilot. "And thank you for flying on the *Vanguard.* Enjoy your stay."

Captain Coffner looked at him wryly. "Thank you, flight attendant." Clicking his radio, he said, "NASA, we've touched down. Preparing to disembark." As he began unstrapping himself, he addressed the others who were already in the process of extricating themselves from their chairs. "Okay, everyone. Remember, although 2021 PK's atmosphere is breathable, there's still a lot of carbon dioxide in the air, so wear your protective breathing gear. Let's get the perimeter secure with our motion detection units, and then we'll unload the laser drill. Joel and I will head to the north by the lake, Jen and Scott will go west, Adam and Dave head to the east, and Lisa and Rebecca go south near the mountains. Ricky will stay with the shuttle and finish post-flight. So far, our readings show nothing moving out there, but keep your blasters ready. Report in once you have your MDUs up and functional. Let's go, people."

Rebecca checked her jumpsuit to make sure that it was properly sealed. NASA's new astronaut suits were not nearly as bulky as the older ones and looked much more like slightly oversized coveralls. Despite their appearance, they were much more reliable. However, Rebecca was not accustomed to taking chances. After double-checking all of her connections and latches, she slipped on her helmet and locked it into place. Once satisfied that all was set properly, she moved over to where Lisa and the others were waiting near the shuttle's hatch.

"Are you ready for your first step onto alien soil?" Lisa asked, her voice full of excitement.

"Ready if you are. I still can't believe I'm here."

"Well, believe it. Here we go," she said as Captain Coffner opened the hatch. Immediately, wind blew a fine white dust through the opening as the pressure from the shuttle equalized with the atmosphere of the planet. Weapons in hand, the crew walked cautiously down the shuttle's ramp in pairs. After a few minutes of making sure that the immediate area was secure, they split up and headed off toward in their designated directions. As Lisa and Rebecca walked toward the distant mountains, Rebecca stared in awe at the landscape. *There has to be life here. I can feel it. There's something special about this place.*

After a few minutes, their headsets crackled to life. Captain Coffner's voice was clear, but the atmospheric distortion was already affecting the equipment. "Be careful out here. Keep your sensors active. This wind and dust are reducing visibility, and the distortion may have an unknown effect on our equipment."

"Copy, Captain," Lisa said.

Rebecca turned to look back toward the shuttle. "No kidding. It's difficult to see the ship already. How far out are we going?"

"One mile. Don't worry. Although there's some distortion, the equipment is working perfectly." Lisa reassured her.

They kept walking for several more minutes, passing numerous mounds of dirty white earth, each reaching no more than fifteen feet tall and about fifty feet in diameter. Finally, Lisa called a halt. Taking the MDU off of her shoulder, she set it gently to the ground. "According to the gauge, this is far enough. If we go any further, we'll run into those large boulders on the skirts of the mountain. Does your motion detector show anything in the vicinity?"

Rebecca studied the screen of the instrument panel for a moment. "It's picking up the others' movement faintly, but nothing else. This atmospheric interference is really wreaking havoc on the readings."

"Well, let's get this thing unpacked. Once all four are online, they should give us a stronger reading than that thing." Lisa removed the motion detection unit from the bag and began the process of setting it up. Rebecca walked around and looked intently at her handheld unit for any sign of movement.

"These hills give me the creeps," she said. The tinny sound of her own voice inside the helmet sent an added chill up her spine. "You never know what might be hiding behind one. And these blue jumpsuits will stand out more than a pink tutu in a St. Patrick's Day parade!"

Lisa's laughter caused her to start as it crackled over the intercom. "Weren't you the one who was laughing because your sister was worried that you'd be attacked by 'monsters' or 'aliens'? Relax. If there was anything in the area, we would've picked it up by now." She flipped up the antennae with practiced ease and threw the power switch. The small dish began rotating accompanied by a flashing light at the tip of the antennae. "All right, that does it. I'm going to check in with the others."

She pressed a button on her wrist commlink. "Vanguard, this is team four checking in. Our unit is up and running. We're waiting for your signal to initiate linkup. Over."

Static spewed from the comm for a few moments, then Ricky's voice came through, broken but understandable. "Roger, Fo—" Then the com spurted out, "—aiting for oth—" silence, "teams." There was a short pause. "Uh, stand by, Four." After a few seconds, Ricky's voice once again fought its way through the static. "Four, Te—" The com again cut off and then spurted out, "One is encount—" silence, "—ome difficulty. Stay—" silence, "—sition"—silence—"until further notice. Over."

"Great," Lisa said. "Well, we might as well get comfortable. We may be here awhile." She clicked off her commlink and sat down next to the MDU, which was whirring quietly as it scanned the area. Rebecca followed suit. Taking her backpack off her shoulder, she set it down and sat next to it, facing Lisa. She reached down with her gloved hand and picked up a handful of the gray powdery dirt. "It definitely feels different than Earth soil. The drill should be able to punch through this in no time." She looked up at Lisa. "Do you really think we will find evidence of life here, Lisa?"

"I sure hope so. I didn't spend almost three months in that cramped tin can for nothing." Just then, Lisa's commlink chirped softly. "Lisa here," she responded reflexively.

"Lisa"—static—"having"—static—"problem with"— static— "one," Captain Coffner's voice said. Even through the distortion, she could read his frustration. "I need"—static—"help over here. Rebecca,"—static—"be able"—static—"handle linkup on that end?"

Lisa gave Rebecca a look as if to say, *Great, just what we needed.* "Yes, sir, Captain. I'll be over to give you poor boys a hand in just a few minutes. Over." She stood and shouldered her empty pack.

"Us 'poor boys'"—static—"try not"—static—"break"— static—"thing until you"—static—"here," the captain replied sarcastically. "Over and out."

"Sorry to leave you, but…"

"Yeah, I know. Duty calls," Rebecca said. "Don't worry. I'm a big girl. I can take care of myself."

"That's more like it. A few minutes ago, you didn't sound so sure," Lisa said lightheartedly.

"Well, your confidence is infectious," Rebecca countered.

"Besides, this will give me a minute alone to start my audio journal. I promised my sister that I would record all my thoughts and feelings so that I wouldn't forget anything."

"Just keep an eye on your motion detector. We still have no idea what's out there." Lisa turned and started walking north.

Rebecca laughed and called to her as she walked away, "Now you're the one sounding unsure." Lisa waved back at her and continued walking toward the ship.

As Lisa's figure retreated into the distance, Rebecca felt her initial fears began to creep back into her thoughts, this time accompanied by an unexplainable uneasiness. *Come on, Becky. It's just your imagination.* She took a deep breath and shook away her troublesome thoughts. *Maybe my journal will help keep my mind from wandering.* Kneeling next to her pack, she rummaged through it until she found her verbal notebook. She removed the handheld device and set it to the same frequency as her helmet radio. "Testing, testing," she said, watching the small readout screen. As expected, her words appeared in tiny letters. Satisfied that it was functioning properly, she began.

Journal Entry #1

I can't believe it! I'm actually standing on an alien planet! It's difficult to put into words the emotions that I'm feeling right now. This moment is one of the greatest of my life.

Before I go any further, let me first say that the purpose of this journal is threefold: 1) for myself—so that I may always have a record of my feelings and thoughts during this most amazing of times in my life; 2) for my sister and other family members—so that I'll be able to tell them everything that happened in detail; and 3) for others—who knows? Maybe I'll write a book someday!

Well, I don't even know where to begin. As I'm entering these notes, I'm sitting alone next to the motion detection unit about one mile from the ship. Although I understand the importance of all of the security precautions, I must admit that I'm quite anxious to begin digging. So far, the probe reports have proved to be a hundred percent accurate. And now that I'm actually here, I believe more than ever that we will indeed find life. The planet...

Sudden movement in her peripheral vision caught Rebecca's eye. She immediately stopped speaking, stood, and turned toward the mound on her left. Pulling her blaster from its holster on her right hip, she thumbed off the safety. Her hand shook from the sudden adrenaline coursing through her veins. Seeing no further movement, Rebecca quickly scanned the area, then looked down at her handheld motion detector in her other hand.

Nothing. No movement anywhere. Did I imagine it? Without putting down either the motion detector or the blaster, Rebecca used her right index finger to touch the commlink on her left wrist. *"Vanguard,* this is Rebecca. Do you copy? Over." Static. "Team One, Two or Three, this is Rebecca. Do you copy? Over." More static. *"Vanguard,* this is..."

Before she could finish her sentence, she saw it again, this time coming from the mound on her right. She whirled around so fast she nearly tripped. Her heart was beating fast and heavy in her ears. *"Vanguard,* do you copy? If this is some sort of practical joke, I think it's in really poor taste." She looked down at the motion detector. It still showed all of the other members of the crew with the exception of Ricky, who was aboard the ship.

Rebecca felt her knees weaken. *Something's not right. Why aren't they responding?* Gathering her strength, she began walking back toward the direction of the ship. Fear held her in an iron fist, attempting to suffocate her. She gripped the hilt of her blaster so tightly that her joints began to hurt.

Suddenly, there it was again—a dim but unmistakable moving light. Her will finally giving in to her fear, Rebecca bolted toward where she believed the ship to be. Panic blinded her like a shroud, causing her to stumble and fall, her blaster falling from her grip. Gasping for air, she regained her balance, retrieved her weapon, and began to run once more.

Risking a glance behind her, she noticed the light moving steadily in her direction, as if floating on air. She turned to face forward, panic building in her so much she felt her heart would explode. Coming around one of the small hills, her heart leapt into her throat as the ship suddenly came into view. But before she could take one more step, a light brighter than any she had ever seen flashed before her eyes, instantly blinding her. She felt her body falling and pain exploding in her head before darkness quickly enveloped her.

NOW ENJOY THE PROLOGUE OF *ELYSIUM*, BOOK 1 OF THE *TARTARUS CHRONICLES*

The first sign of its appearance was the slight movement of air. In the complete stillness of the cavern, even the smallest breeze was noticeable. As the first tendril of wind brushed past the face of the haggard man leaning wearily against the wall of gleaming purple-colored rock, his eyes flew open in excitement.

Leaping to his feet, he scanned the area rapidly, hope-send-ing adrenaline coursing through his veins. Movement to his left immediately captured his attention. His eyes grew wide, and his pulse quickened at the sight of the strange purple mist that had begun to swirl fifty feet away, near the far wall of the small cavern.

"It's forming! It's forming!" the man screamed at the top of his lungs, the words echoing off the glowing walls long after his voice had ceased. An expression of panicked excitement quickly replaced the hopeless, vacant look that had almost permanently creased his forty-year-old face.

The purple mist began to thicken as it swirled tighter and tighter to form a circular shape. His attention completely enraptured by the ever-expanding circle, the man was oblivious to the sounds of excited voices and trampling feet that were gradually increasing in volume.

The circular anomaly had now grown to reach twenty feet in diameter. Although the edges still retained their gaseous form, the inner disc turned black and seemed to bend as if being pulled toward the wall of the cavern by some invisible hand. As the man continued to watch, threads of color and light began working their way from the center of the disc outward toward the edges.

The lone spectator of the bizarre event moved closer and closer, his long hair and ragged clothing thrashing in the wind created by the swirling mist. With only half a dozen feet remaining between he and the anomaly, he stopped and crouched slightly, his muscles tensing like a large predatory cat preparing to pounce on its prey.

Suddenly, three mysterious figures took shape within the center of the disc and grew from mere inches in height to full size within a matter of seconds. A moment later, the human bodies tumbled out of the black disc and fell to the ground at the man's feet. Yet before they had even struck the floor of the cavern, the man let out a cry of victory and leapt over the new-comers toward the anomaly.

As that moment, a crowd of men and women burst through the cavern opening and watched as the man's body came in contact with the swirling disc. Immediately, his body was flung backward through the air to land in a heap several feet away. Despite the painful consequences that the man's actions had produced, the crowd began shouting and running toward the disturbance.

The screaming of the mob roused the three figures lying on the cold stone floor. Dazed, they stared in shock at the wild men and women rushing toward them. Terror gripping their hearts, the three huddled close together with their faces averted.

However, the mob of crazed men and women completely ignored the newcomers. Like the previous man, they threw themselves at the circle of blackness only to meet the same fate. Within moments, the cavern was filled with bodies that had been tossed aside by the swirling mist. Then as quickly as it had appeared, the mist dissipated and dissolved until not a single trace remained.

Time passed without notice as the occupants of the cavern remained motionless. Then gradually, a soft weeping could be heard. The sound increased little by little until the whole cavern reverberated with the sounds of sobbing and cries of anguish.

In horrified shock, the three newcomers, a man and two women, continued to hug one another with their eyes closed tightly in a vain effort to shut out the sights and sounds of this nightmare.

"THAT'S ENOUGH!"

The strength contained in those two simple words instantly quelled the tumult. Every eye in the room was drawn toward the speaker. He stood over six feet in height and was strongly built. However, even without his imposing physique, he had an inner strength that demanded respect and exuded authority. Unlike many of the others, his clothes were better kept and were of a higher quality.

"How long are we going to go on like this?" he asked, his voice echoing in the chamber. "Since my wife and I first arrived here four years ago, we've tried everything we could think of to get the portals to take us back. And while I understand that none of you have been here as long as we have, and I know you also want to try everything you can to escape from here, but we need to face the horrible truth: for the time being, this is now our home."

At this statement, the sounds of muffled crying began anew. The man continued speaking. As he did so, he walked around the gathering and laid a gentle touch on the heads or shoulders of the others like a shepherd comforting his flock. "Don't get me wrong, we will continue to search for ways home. We will take the wisest among us and have them study these portals to find a way to reverse them. Others will be given the task of exploring the cave system in hopes of finding a way to reach the surface."

One of the other men rose to his feet and held his hands out imploringly as he spoke, his face filled with raw emotion. "What good will that do, Mathison? From what we've seen, we're not even on Earth anymore. This hellish place is filled with strange animals that no one has ever seen before, glowing purple rock, rivers filled with fish that shine … we can't … we can't *possibly* still be on Earth. So even if we reach the surface, that won't put us any closer to home!"

"You may be right," the man called Mathison replied. "But I believe we should still explore nonetheless. If we *have* been brought here by aliens, as many of us believe, then perhaps we can find them and seek their help to return to Earth. Either way, we have to map out our surroundings to make sure that nothing—animal or alien—will catch us by surprise. Whether we like it or not, we are pioneers facing a new frontier, and we will either pull together or die."

Mathison paused, letting his words hang in the air and sink into their souls. "But do not despair! Although I too long to return home, I would disagree that this place is 'hellish.' It may be unfamiliar to us, but only a blind man would fail to see the beauty of this world! We may be underground, but we have eve-rything we need—water, plants, and numerous raw materials. Together, we can build a new world. Then when we do finally find a way to reverse the portals, we will have already built an outpost from which others can launch further explorations."

A woman leaning against the wall lifted her head and glared at him, her face wet with tears. "You and your grandiose plans! What good will they do if we all go insane? Or have you for-gotten what happened to Kaylee and Michael, the McCrary boys, or any of the other dozen friends we've known who've committed suicide or gone mad from being trapped here? And what about the new diseases we discovered? And how many more young people are we going to lose as they go exploring? This place is no wonderful 'frontier,' it is a punishment! It is hell! It is Tartarus, a prison!"

"no!" Mathison snapped, causing several of those nearest him to start in surprise. Realizing what he had just done, he took a deep breath to calm himself. Allowing a gentle smile to soften his features, he tried again, "Julie, I know you still grieve for your children, but don't you see that by focusing on building a new life, we will have purpose! We'll have a goal! This will help to prevent madness. And the more we learn about this world, the more we can prevent diseases and accidents. But in order to do that, we need the expertise of everyone, including all new arrivals."

As he spoke, he walked over toward the trio that had appeared from the mist. They were still huddled close together, the man's arms wrapped protectively around the two women, and their heads were down. Crouching down next to them, he laid his hands gently on the shoulders of the man. "Don't be afraid. I know that this is all so frightening and new, but you're among friends. My name is George." Standing up, he looked toward two women who were sitting nearby. "Alyssa, Emily, please take these three to your cave and give them something to eat." After exchanging a brief apprehensive glance with one another, the two young women did as instructed.

Once the five of them exited the cavern, Mathison con-tin-ued. "For the sake of those still coming through the portals, we have to pull ourselves together. You all remember when you first came through—the shock of the portal travel, the unfamiliar faces and surroundings, then learning the truth that you cannot return—it can be psychologically damaging, especially if we act like fools every time a portal opens. We need to learn how to soften the blow to those just arriving to minimize the effects."

Holding out his arms to encompass his people, George Mathison looked toward the glowing ceiling of the cavern. "Come, my friends. Today is a new day! Today, we take our first step toward creating a new future! We will succeed!"

ENDORSEMENTS FOR THE *ORIGINS TRILOGY* AND THE *TARTARUS CHRONICLES*

"Logic's End *is a great read, and I highly recommend it. I very much enjoyed reading* Logic's End. *It explores the question of what life would be like on a planet where evolution really did happen. The surprising result helps the reader to see why life on Earth must be the result of special creation.* For those interested in science fiction but who are tired of all the evolutionary nonsense, Logic's End *is a refreshing alternative."*

–Jason Lisle, PhD,
Astrophysicist, *Institute for Creation Research*

"In this book, Robinson has discovered a "novel" way to communicate vital information to young adults and readers of all ages. Mainstream indoctrination on the origin of species and the age of the earth are regularly encountered, and has long needed combating. Through this unique story, truth is conveyed."

–Dr. John D. Morris,
President, *Institute for Creation Research*

"Pyramid of the Ancients will challenge you to reconsider the conventional wisdom concerning the history of our world."

–Tim Chaffey
Author, *The Truth Chronicles*
Editor, *Answers in Genesis*

"A thoroughly enjoyable read with great characters and a compelling, suspenseful story propelled by lots and lots of action. For me, the icing on the cake is the enlightening apologetics information masterfully woven into the story."

–Joe Barruso
Emmy Award Winning Director/Producer